THE VILLAINS OF THE PIECE

Graham Shelby's quality as a historical novelist was instantly recognised by the wide critical acclaim for his first book, THE KNIGHTS OF DARK RENOWN. And the praise for its sequel, THE KINGS OF VAIN INTENT, confirmed that its author combined a concern for historical authenticity with the power to tell a story and to picture a scene.

In his new book Graham Shelby moves from the glittering, exotic world of the Crusades to an England racked and torn by anarchy and civil war: the era of Stephen and Matilda described by a contemporary chronicler as the nineteen long winters in which Christ and his saints slept.

The battles and sieges, the life of camp and castle, are vividly described. The barons and churchmen whose intrigues and self-seeking bedevil a situation already sufficiently disastrous are dramatically balanced by the hero and heroine who keep their troth to each other as well as to their feudal overlord. The darkness and the colour, the nobility and the squalor of the age are brought out no less strongly in the minor characters, the soldiers and servants, on whom the system rested.

In pace, in verve and in its firm, unsentimental rendering of a medieval England that was organised for war and habituated to violence, this novel shows Graham Shelby at the top of his form.

Graham Shelby

THE VILLAINS OF THE PIECE

COLLINS
ST JAMES'S PLACE, LONDON
1972

William Collins Sons & Co Ltd
London · Glasgow · Sydney · Auckland
Toronto · Johannesburg

First Published 1972
© Graham Shelby
ISBN 0 00 221881 X
Set in Monotype Garamond
Made and Printed in Great Britain by
William Collins Sons & Co Ltd Glasgow

For SALLIE
and for F.H.J.W. and JEAN

Contents

Principal Characters

BRIEN FITZ COUNT Lord of Wallingford.

ALYSE Lady of Wallingford.

VARAN Constable of Wallingford.

EDGIVA Alyse's maidservant.

MORCAR Garrison sergeant.

HENRY I King of England.

STEPHEN OF BLOIS nephew of King Henry I.

HENRY OF BLOIS Bishop of Winchester, brother of Stephen.

MATILDA Empress, daughter of King Henry I, cousin of Stephen, Countess of Anjou.

GEOFFREY OF ANJOU husband of Empress Matilda.

ROBERT OF GLOUCESTER illegitimate son of King Henry I.

MATILDA OF BOULOGNE wife of Stephen.

DAVID King of Scotland.

HENRY OF ANJOU son of Empress Matilda.

MILES OF HEREFORD.

BALDWIN DE REDVERS.

RANULF OF CHESTER.

GEOFFREY DE MANDEVILLE.

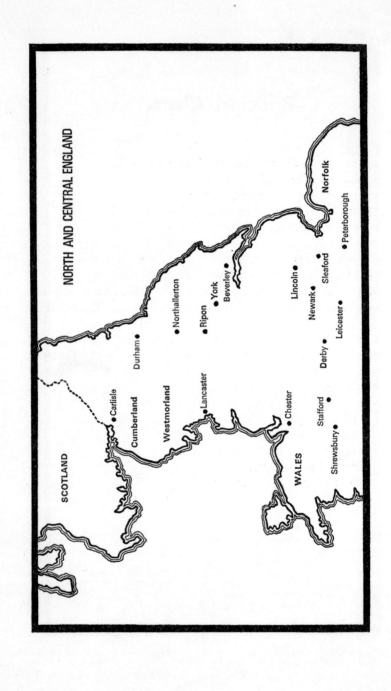

NORTH AND CENTRAL ENGLAND

SCOTLAND

Carlisle •

Cumberland

Westmorland

Lancaster •

Durham •

Northallerton •

Ripon •

York •

Beverley •

Chester •

Stafford •

WALES

Shrewsbury •

Derby •

Leicester •

Newark •

Lincoln •

Sleaford •

Peterborough •

Norfolk

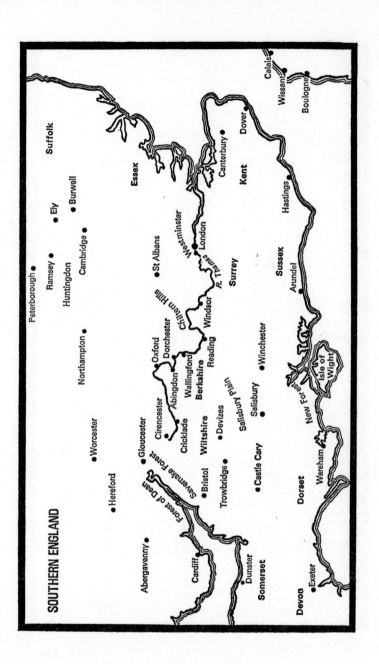

SOUTHERN ENGLAND

CHAPTER I

HOME
August 1134

THE man interrupted his slow, shuffling progress along the forest track and stood, stooped over, listening to the distant thud of hoofbeats. He had spent the morning by the river, where he had scoured the east bank in search of rushes and osiers. When he had found what he wanted he had lowered himself into the water, cut the reeds with a heavy reaping knife, then run his calloused hand along the stems, stripping them of their leaves. As the morning wore on the stretch of bank was covered with this unwoven rush mat, the first-gathered already dried by the sun.

The man was practised in his trade, and he had known to within a dozen or so stems how many he could carry. Having collected his quota, he had climbed out of the water, stacked the reeds and bound them with lengths of hemp. He had made a second stack of stripped willows, tied them, then lifted the bundles on to his back. The long stems dipped and swayed as he shuffled along the riverbank and into the forest. He grunted under his breath, a sound that only he would take for singing.

He was less than half-way through the song when he heard the hoofbeats, but he was too far into the forest to take risks. There were few laws as severe as those that governed the forests; to be caught poaching could mean a fine that would take a lifetime to pay, or the loss of a hand or an eye, or a visit to the gallows on the nearest village green. It was also against the law to cut live wood from the forest, though some more lenient barons permitted their tenants to use bill-hooks to pull down dead branches. But no one would believe that the bundle of willows had been collected in this way – by hook or crook – and if the authorities insisted that they had been taken from within the forest limits –

The basket-maker swung the bundles from his back and dragged them into the undergrowth. Then he crouched down and waited for the horsemen to pass. He growled another verse of his song before he caught himself and clamped his teeth together. The still forest air now carried the creak of leather and the chink of metal, as the horsemen approached.

They were almost opposite the man when the leading rider turned in his saddle and called back, 'In order, messires. We'll make a show of our return.' The fifteen horsemen changed position, some trotting forward, others pulling their palfreys to the edge of the forest path. When they had reformed they rode on, three by three, following their suzerain as he led them home.

The weaver stayed where he was for a while, silent and alert. But there were no laggards, so he dragged his bundles back on to the path and resumed his journey. He had recognised most of the horsemen, and he wondered if he had been over-cautious. After all, they were local men, and their leader was one of the best-respected barons in England, and one of the few who was genuinely admired by the common folk. He would probably have nodded good day and otherwise ignored the weaver. But if it had been somebody else, one of King Henry's patrols, or the verderers who were always so quick to accuse, then it would not have ended with a nod. He told himself he had been wise to get off the path. He had been doing so for forty years, and he still had all his limbs.

*

The horsemen emerged from the forest. Ahead lay the River Thames, broad and shallow at this point; hence the absence of any bridge. Fifty yards beyond the far bank lay the town of Wallingford, encircled by its distinctive Saxon earthworks and sited opposite one of the best natural crossing points on this upper stretch of the river. Twin rows of stones marked the safe limits of the ford, and the riders splashed across, aware that they made an impressive picture – King Henry's favourite baron and his retinue of knights. The high-stepping horses threw out plumes of spray, and the sun caught the droplets and added a sheen to wet leather and sand-scoured armour. A few moments ago the riders had been trading jokes and insults, disseminating gossip or, if they knew none, inventing it. But now, returning to their own lands under the eyes of their own people, they held themselves erect, their faces set, arrogant and unsmiling. For some it was made difficult by the friends who waved from the bank, or greeted them by name, but the knights remained obedient to their overlord and crossed the river in silence.

When they reached the west bank they wheeled right and reined-in in a rough circle around their master.

The strip of worn grassland – which, when occasion demanded, served as a games field, local market-place, or fairground – ran between the palisaded town and the river, and was enclosed at the southern end by a marsh, and at the northern end by the new stone walls of Wallingford Castle. The walls were the work of the man who now lifted his helmet from his head, scratched at his long grey hair and addressed the circle of riders. His name was Brien Fitz Count. He was the bastard son of Count Alan of Brittany, and his hair had turned grey ten years before, when he was twenty-four years of age.

Holding his helmet by its nasal, he told his knights, 'A constructive council, all in all. Count Stephen remarked on your bearing, and that's praise indeed coming from such an exemplary nobleman. You won't be required for another three weeks or so; time enough for you to impress your friends with stories about London.'

The remark brought a laugh from the knights. For nine of them, it had been their first visit to the capital. They had not seen the king – he was in Normandy, celebrating the birth of his grandson and namesake – but they had knelt before the king's nephew, Count Stephen of Blois, who had been delegated to conduct the Great Council in his uncle's absence. And they had seen London, so extensive a city that the nine newcomers were frightened they would lose their way and be forced to live out their days in some strange street. Eventually, Lord Brien told them to ask the way to the river, then follow it upstream, through the open fields, and they would reach their lodgings at Westminster. It was advice they could understand, and they became more adventurous in their wanderings.

Now he thanked them for their companionship, a courtesy that ended each long journey, and they replied in kind. 'It is an honour to ride with you, Lord Fitz Count. We are at your beck and call.'

He nodded, dropped the helmet over the pommel of his saddle and moved out of the circle. Behind him, wives and friends besieged the riders with questions, and the streets of London grew longer and more tortuous with every response.

Brien smiled to himself as he crossed the patchy meadow and conveniently forgot that when he had first settled at Wallingford, he had been terrified by the featureless plains and the dark, dripping forests, and the river that hissed with its quantity of water-snakes . . .

*

The castle had been founded within a few months of the Norman conquest of England. Built at the behest of King William, it had consisted of an outer ditch, the earth from which had gone to make a steep bank, topped by a wooden palisade. In the centre of the fenced-off area was another ditch, and inside that an even steeper mound, on which had been constructed a second palisade and a wooden watch-tower. But defensive techniques had advanced since then and, when Brien Fitz Count had been given the lands and honour of Wallingford, he had replaced the wood with stone, and all but gone bankrupt in the process. The castle now boasted an eighteen-foot high outer wall, complete with a wall-walk, gatehouse, interior steps and five towers, one of them still unfinished. This outer structure was enough to daunt any would-be attacker. But the centre-piece of the fortification was the keep, a square, forty-foot high building, situated on the firm foundation of the original Saxon mound. The ditches had become moats – with the Thames at one's doorstep there was no shortage of water –

and the stone shaft was reflected on all sides, a pale, un-weathered example of local workmanship.

Wallingford was not an important castle – not yet – but it was already described as impregnable, and neighbouring barons visited the place and went away, their heads reeling with stolen details.

The keep had been completed four years ago and, although the rain and flying seeds had not yet made their mark, its interior was smudged with smoke, its floors worn smooth, its doors either closing easily or warped by time. It was lived-in, this castle, and it had an air of permanence. Small wonder, for neither Brien Fitz Count nor his wife were the types to hold life in a loose grip. Brien had been given the fief by the King of England, and what the king gave, only the king could reclaim. And there was another reason. Brien was illegitimate, but he was still the son of the Count of Brittany, the man called Alan Fergant – Ironglove. And a man did not earn that nick-name by letting things slip from his grasp.

So it stood, each side of the keep measuring thirty feet at the base, almost as broad as it was high, a solid and, within reason, a comfortable home for Lord Fitz Count and his Lady Alyse.

She was in the keep now, teaching her maidservant to read. The girl, Edgiva, had spent the past hour struggling through a page of poetry – bad poetry, but in clear English – and while she mouthed the words, syllable by syllable, Alyse strolled about the second storey chamber. Known as the solar, it occupied the entire floor, and served as the living and sleeping quarters for the Lord and Lady of Wallingford. From time to time Alyse halted, corrected the girl's pronunciation, then moved on, skirting the fire, resting in one of the box chairs, prompting the uncertain Edgiva, glancing out of the single large window. The glassless aperture faced south, so she could see the town and the ford and the horsemen who were, at that moment, dispersing from the worn meadow.

Alyse would say afterwards that she had been watching for him. But in fact she hurried into the window recess, peered down until she was sure, then gave a cry of delight and spun round, her dark hair swinging around her shoulders.

Edgiva laboured, '. . . ride with you on flowing – on flowered
fields,
and seek with you sweet sol – sweet
solace . . .'

She asked, 'What does that mean, solace?'

'Comfort. Leave it now. Lord Brien is here.'

The girl rolled the sheepskin sheet. 'He's a day early.'

'A day less late,' Alyse preferred. 'Quick, you must help me
dress. The grey gown, the one with marten – '

'It's in the chest there. I'll find it.' She laid aside the poem –
with some relief, for she had found too many unreadable
words – and went over to raise the iron-bound lid. Inside,
carefully folded, lay a number of full-length gowns and a tray
of belts and tasselled girdles. She sorted through the gowns,
the red, the pale blue, the night blue, the grey, and lifted it out.
When she faced Alyse again the Lady of Wallingford had
stripped off her simple linen kirtle and stood naked, waiting
for the gown. Sunlight streamed through the single window
and through the narrow vertical slits of the arrow loops. With
no embarrassment, the Saxon maidservant carried the gown
to her Saxon lady and raised it over her head. As Alyse settled
the gown and chose an orange girdle from the tray she said,
'Give me his pendant.' Edgiva took the silver cross and chain
from its hook and hung it around her mistress's neck. Alyse
shook her hair to cover the chain, then crossed the solar to the
oval mirror, Brien's bequest from his father.

Ironglove had not left his bastard son much of material
value. His lands had gone to his legitimate children, but he
had given Brien something of greater value than any fief or
coffer. As one of King Henry's closest friends, Count Alan
had committed his son into the king's care, and Brien had
grown up in Henry's court, where, in time, he had been
knighted at the king's hand and earned a place in the king's
affections. The one saleable item Ironglove had bequeathed
had been the mirror, a sheet of hammered silver, chased at the
edges, a delicate and valuable piece which he had brought back
from Palestine after the first crusade. It could have been sold,
perhaps, for five Spanish warhorses, or ten times its weight in

silver coin, and it would certainly realise enough to finance the completion of the fifth tower. But Brien Fitz Count would not think of parting with his distorting mirror.

Alyse derived some comfort from this, for it was the only one in the castle. But whenever she used it, it was with a fleeting sense of trepidation. No nightmare was more vivid than the one in which the mirror slipped from her hands and fell into the fire, where it melted.

She stood in front of it now, knowing that Brien was spurring his horse along the narrow path between the east wall and the river. She stayed there, sweeping the comb through her hair, aware that he must have entered the main gate and was about to dismount in the outer courtyard. She delayed another instant, another comb stroke, sensing that he had handed his reins to the waiting ostler and was striding across the yard. Then she tossed the comb into the nearest chair and, followed by Edgiva, hurried down the stairs and across the first floor of the keep and down more stairs to the main hall and out into the sunlight.

The women reached the drawbridge, where the servant waited while Alyse went on alone. Solace, Edgiva thought, yes, that is what they find with each other. She retreated to the entrance and watched from the darkness as Brien came forward and embraced his wife.

The forests of England were infested with brigands, so it was advisable to travel armed and armoured. Merchants would hire mercenaries, whilst men like Fitz Count relied on their own abilities, and the added protection of their knights. For the journey to London, the young baron had worn helmet and hauberk – a knee-length link-mail tunic, with long sleeves and mittens laced at the wrists – and carried a small, circular shield, a pitted longsword and a dagger. It would be an intrepid band of brigands who dared to ambush such a spiky column, but it had been done, and every month brought news of another nobleman hacked down among the trees. The shield and hauberk afforded some protection, though they also acted as a lure to the brigands. A carefully-forged tunic would fetch a good price at market, and a well-tempered sword was prized as highly as an obedient horse. So to ride out in armour was to issue a challenge, though to travel without it was to risk easy butchery.

Brien grinned down at his wife, his arms around her waist. His metal mittens hung like empty purses. He had been away for five days, and she thought of it as five weeks, too long for him to have been gone, too long for the master of Wallingford to be away from home.

'You look tired,' she told him; then, 'You scratched your face on a branch.' She licked her finger and wiped a trace of blood from his jaw.

He said, 'We rode hard on the way back. If you had seen us cross the Chilterns you would have thought we'd started the devil from his lair.'

'And were charging in pursuit, like brave men?'

Matching her gentle mockery, he retorted, 'No, lady, and were fleeing for our lives, like sensible cowards!' He laughed with her, then glanced round the inner yard and asked, 'Have things been peaceful here?'

'Varan found some counterfeiters in town. They're locked up in the guardhouse. Otherwise, nothing of account. Did you see Count Stephen at court?'

'I did, and he sends you affectionate greetings. Do you know, he told me the population of London now exceeds ten thousand. I can understand why my knights were terrified to stray from their lodgings.'

'Does it still smell as bad? I remember my few visits there with disfavour, especially in summer.'

Brien nodded. 'If anything, it's worse. If the wind's against you, you can catch the scent before you see the first building. With all the extra people, the authorities have been forced to dig public latrines along the riverbank. There's one at Edredshithe, nicely placed between two churches, if you can believe it. God knows what they'll do; the city has already spilled out beyond its own walls. I suppose they'll have to prohibit further settlement, or build on this side of the River Fleet and lay roads across Moorfield. It's changed so much since I was there. And to think I once spoke of it as a paradise.'

'I'm not surprised,' Alyse said tartly. 'You had a room at court, and your pick of the women. It's a wonder you ever left the place.'

With a nonchalant gesture, he remarked, 'The king advanced me and offered me a holding of my own. It seemed worth a look.'

Alyse smiled, aware that he had taken the reins of mockery. 'You flatter me without restraint, my lord.'

Brien gazed at her for an instant, feigning ignorance. Then he leaned down and kissed her and murmured, 'You know the truth of it. When the king gave me Wallingford, I accepted it with misgivings. But I did not then know that the castle contained a gentle-eyed young widow, a beautiful Saxon creature who kept well away from court. That was King Henry's humour, to let me ride down here unaware and find you in residence.'

'No,' she replied quietly, 'that was his kindness. I knew he would send someone for me to marry, and that I would have no choice in the matter. It could have been a monster. Why not? The trail was well worn before you arrived.'

Remembering the hard, carbuncled faces of those who had attended the Great Council, Brien acknowledged, as he had throughout the five years of his marriage, that good fortune had brushed against them both.

Alyse was his opposite in many ways. She was a high-born Saxon, a distant descendant of the English king, Edmund, whereas he was a bastard, and a Breton. She was a country-woman, who had lived all her life within a day's ride of Wallingford. For his part, Brien had visited most of Brittany, Normandy and England, travelled twice to Germany, once to Italy and once to Flanders, where he had almost died of some damp disease.

Alyse had been married at the age of fourteen, and widowed six years later. She had expected the king to send another husband without delay, but three years had passed before Henry's favourite baron had ridden down, unsuspecting, from London. Such a delay was remarkable. Wallingford was of strategic importance for, with Oxford and Reading, it barred the eastern approaches to the capital. Yet none of the land-hungry barons who came to pay suit – and they came in droves, ten and twenty a year – were able to obtain the king's permission to marry the Lady Alyse. At no time did King Henry admit that he had earmarked the young widow for his grey-haired favourite, but when Brien asked for her hand, the king looked at him with surprise and commented, 'Well now, you can hardly take the house without its contents, can you?'

There were other differences. Until his marriage, Brien's life had been spent in the service of the king, active service for the most part, sometimes as a warrior, often as a trusted emissary. He found little time to read, though he admitted later that if he had halved the time he had spent sweet-talking women, he might have been one of the best-read men at court.

So Alyse had encouraged him to study the *chansons de geste*, the epic poems that were so much in vogue, and give food and lodging and a few coins to the troubadours and *jongleurs* who wandered the country, armed with lutes and a good voice. The young couple could not afford a resident minstrel, but scarcely a month passed without some form of musical entertainment, and the summer evenings were enhanced by strident tales of heroism and plangent, soft-sung ballads, in which love was invariably unrequited until the final verse.

On a practical level, Brien taught his wife to be more inventive in bed. He tried not to think of her first husband, but he came to the ungenerous conclusion that the prior lord of Wallingford had lacked imagination, to say the least. However, as Brien responded to the love songs of Europe, so Alyse showed an equal willingness to learn. Yet neither the six-year union with her first husband, nor the five years she had so far spent with Brien, had produced any children.

A similar thought was in her head now as she asked, 'Was Queen Adeliza at court?'

'She was about,' Brien said, 'but she kept clear of the council. She has turned more and more to religion these days – '

'So there is no change in her condition?'

'She will never bear a child, the physicians are convinced of it.'

With some hesitation, Alyse ventured, 'Perhaps it is the king, himself – '

' – who is unable? I doubt that, my love, when he's credited with nineteen bastards.' He laid his wife's arm over his own, her hand curled on his, their fingers intertwined, and they walked towards the drawbridge and the waiting Edgiva. As they reached the bridge, Alyse murmured, 'Did you see the Empress Matilda?' She had meant the question to sound casual, but the words had come out high and strained. She did not look at Brien, though she knew he had turned his head towards her.

Even before he spoke, she was nodding acceptance of his words. 'No, I heard she was with her father in Normandy.' He looked at her a moment longer, but she did not pursue the topic. One day, he knew, she would give expression to her feelings, and ask him about the rumours concerning King Henry's legitimate daughter, heiress to the throne of England, and her most loyal supporter, Brien Fitz Count. One day she would ask him and, because he loved her, he would answer her with the truth.

*

Varan, constable of the castle, shared two things in common with Brien Fitz Count; unswerving loyalty to those he had chosen to serve – in this case his king and suzerain – and parents who had forgone all ceremony. Varan knew neither his father nor his mother, though both must have been physically strong, implacable by nature and of unsurpassed ugliness. Anyway, it was a fitting description of their offspring.

He had been many things in his life, this massive, flat-nosed Saxon, and on more than one occasion he had come close to the gallows. At the age of fourteen he had taken service as a mercenary and accompanied the first crusading army across Europe to the Bosporus, then on through Asia Minor to Palestine and the bloody capture of Jerusalem. He would have stayed on in the Holy Land but for the return home of his master, Alan Ironglove, Count of Brittany. He had entered Ironglove's service because the count paid better than other leaders, but within the first six months of the campaign Varan had grown to respect the Breton above any of his peers. Before the crusaders had reached the borders of Serbia, the young mercenary was promoted to sergeant. Three weeks later he was offered a place in Ironglove's permanent contingent.

As the only Saxon among forty coarse-tongued Bretons, Varan was required to prove his worth time and again. Eventually, goaded beyond endurance, he rounded on his tormentors and strangled one of them with a spare bow-string. Such a crime was punishable by death, but Ironglove showed uncharacteristic clemency towards his ill-featured recruit and reprieved him at the foot of the gallows. Instead, he laid a red-hot bar to the soles of Varan's feet, then told him to follow the column barefoot, if he chose to. The branded man did so for a week, stumbling across the mountain wastes of Serbia. He moved with his mouth open, his breath rasping in his throat, each step driving blades of pain up through his body. The Bretons listened hard for his plea for mercy, or for the thud that would signify he had fallen. But whenever they glanced back he was there, sometimes on their heels, sometimes far behind, always hobbling forward, using his spear shaft as a crutch.

On the eighth morning when he opened his dust-swollen eyes he saw one of his companions standing over him, a hand on the bridle of a Spanish palfrey. The Breton recited, 'Count Alan says he has no further need of your horse.' It was not Varan's mount, and they both knew it, but enough had been said. His punishment was over, and he had earned his reinstatement.

So, in 1099, having survived the battles and diseases, the rigours and deprivations of the crusade, the nineteen-year-old Saxon accompanied his master to Brittany and a further decade of fighting.

In late July 1100 a woman in Rennes sent word to Count Alan that she had given birth to a son. She asked the count if he would acknowledge it, or at least contribute towards its upkeep. He immediately took the boy from her, paid her for her trouble, then told his wife he was bringing his bastard son into the castle. The boy would be called Brien, and would be accorded the same treatment as their legitimate children. Brien would, of course, inherit nothing, but if the infant grew to manhood, Ironglove would make some alternative provision for him.

On 2nd August, on the other side of the Channel, William Rufus, King of England, was killed in a hunting accident in the New Forest. Three days later his brother Henry seized the throne. When the news reached Brittany, Count Alan swore fealty to his longtime friend and set out to defend Henry's Norman dominions. Varan rode with him. The journey was to last nineteen years, until Alan's death. By then, Brien had become one of King Henry's youngest knights, and been all but adopted by the monarch.

With the death of Count Alan, Varan was forced to look elsewhere for work. He thought of approaching Alan's son. After all, Brien had spent his childhood under Varan's watchful gaze and, even after the boy had entered Henry's court, they had met from time to time. But the Saxon had been away from his own country too long. He was homesick, though he had never had a home in England, and he had almost forgotten his native tongue.

He reached Dover in the spring of 1120, a powerful, battle-scarred warrior, the veteran of a five-year crusade and the endless campaign in Normandy, a professional soldier skilled in the arts and techniques of warfare, a man who was as much at home in a conference chamber as in the fierce, horse-to-horse fighting of a Saracen ambush. He would not blame the English if they regarded him as something of a hero.

But his countrymen placed a different interpretation on Varan's attributes. They saw a monster with a spatulate nose and a seamed face and heard him mouth a scarcely intelligible mixture of English and French. His forthright manner put them on the defensive and, if they answered him at all, it was in order to be rid of him. He was finding what thousands would find in later years on their return from other, more glorious crusades. The common soldier was only to be respected whilst he plied his trade. Away from the battlefield, he was a conjurer without tricks, a fish out of water. He was a reminder to others of what they might have dared; but he had no right to shame them, for he, too, had ceased to fight.

Angry and embittered, he took what work he could find; fletcher, harness-maker, quarryman. For three years he roamed England and Wales until, in the bitter winter of 1123, he was taken on as castle steward by a certain Roger d'Oilli, an important baron with holdings in Berkshire and at Oxford. The baron's nod of approval laid the foundations for the one truly remarkable coincidence in Varan's life, for Roger d'Oilli's wife was a high-born Saxon lady named Alyse, and the castle was at Wallingford.

When Roger died three years later, Alyse looked to Varan for protection. She need not have worried, for he was devoted to her, and every would-be suitor who rapped at the gate had first to meet his critical gaze. Like his mistress, Varan found none of them worth their words; none, that is, until a young, grey-haired rider crossed the ford and announced without any trace of self-satisfaction that he had come on King Henry's orders as the newly appointed Lord of Wallingford.

When that happened, when Varan stared down from the then wooden palisade and recognised the rider, he gave a roar that must have carried clear across the county and leapt down the steps and ran out to embrace Ironglove's bastard.

It was a day neither of them would forget, least of all Brien Fitz Count, for when he had finished pounding shoulders with the old boar who had bullied him and encouraged him and been with him throughout his childhood, he went on into the castle and for the first time set eyes on the Lady Alyse . . .

*

Brien dealt with the counterfeiters that afternoon. Varan presented the evidence, all of it taken from their hideout, and arranged the exhibits on one of the long trestle tables in the ground-floor hall of the keep. Moving alongside the table, he pointed to each object in turn, explaining its function to his presiding overlord. Hemmed in by guards, the three counterfeiters – father, son and nephew – gazed impassively at the tools of their trade. Had they been brought before one of the town councillors they might have blustered, or even attempted to bribe the man. But it had been their misfortune to end up in front of Lord Fitz Count, and they awaited his verdict with dull resignation.

'Moulds and dies,' Varan indicated. 'A cauldron for melting down the coins – '

'How do you know that?' Brien inquired. 'Why not for boiling vegetables?'

'It might have been, at one time. But if you scrape here, on the inside, you will find traces of silver. And no one sells silver-lined cooking pots.' He illustrated his claim, and Brien nodded. 'What's in that sack?'

'There is more than one way to cheat,' the constable explained. 'At the end of the table are the knives they use to shave the coins. The shavings go into the pot, while the coins, a little smaller than before, are passed on again. The sack contains lead plugs. You don't shave the penny this time, but core it. You just cut a hole in the centre, replace the silver with lead, then pass it on again, like the others. I'd say five coins would make a sixth. But from the size of these plugs, our moneyers were unusually greedy. They'd probably get seven from five.'

He moved on again, held up a number of discs and explained that these were the most bald-faced forgeries of the lot. 'They're nothing more than lead coins, stamped in the usual way, HENRICUS and the king's head, and the cutting cross on the other side.' He came round the table and handed one of the pennies to Brien.

The baron said, 'We are gullible, I admit, but surely none of us are going to mistake lead for silver.'

'We would, sire, when these three have finished with it. They coat it. It looks real enough.'

Brien studied the cutting cross, the guideline along which every subject was allowed to halve or quarter the coin. The silver penny was the standard coin of the realm, but when hens cost half a penny each, and a measure of wine a quarter of a penny, it became necessary to divide the coin. So, following the line, it could be cut into half-pennies, or quarters, known as fourthings.

Brien tossed the counterfeit on to the table and turned towards the prisoners. 'Do you deny all this? I'll hear whatever you have to say.' He waited, but none of them spoke. 'Very well,' he continued, 'I assume you admit your guilt.' Singling out the father, he said, 'Do you remember what happened at Winchester about ten years ago? Some ninety or so moneyers were summoned there by the Chief Justiciar and asked to explain why they had allowed the country to become flooded with homemade coins. Whatever reasons they gave, they were not good enough, and all but three of them lost their right hands. It used to be the practice to nail the hands over the nearest smithy – sufficient warning to hopeful forgers. That's no longer done, but I see no reason to amend the punishment. You grow rich, whilst with every mutilated coin this country becomes the poorer. Give it time, and you and your kind will possess the only coinage that's worth its value. There are ways of making money, but yours is not one I accept.

'As the father, and so the leader, you will lose your right hand. Your nephew, his left hand. Your son, because he is young enough to be in your sway, will be whipped out of the county. Your property is forfeit, though you may keep whatever clothes you have. Everything else will be sold, and the proceeds, together with your hoard of silver, will be sent to the mint in London. In that way we will at least ensure a fresh issue.' He nodded at the guards, who herded the prisoners from the hall.

When they had gone, he asked Varan, 'There's no doubt, is there? They are all implicated.'

Sour with knowledge, the constable growled, 'They've been in business for years, my lord.'

'Then why was nothing done?'

'They weren't around here.' He looked across the table at his master and added, 'I'd say you were hoodwinked. You will not allow me to speak against such vermin before their trial, but if you did allow it I could have told you. The father is one of the three who kept his hands at Winchester.'

CHAPTER 2

THE HEAT OF WINTER
December 1135

WATER dripped from the trees and from helmet nasals and fingertips. Men who moved without looking winced as branches slapped them in the face. They opened their mouths to curse, then hurriedly stifled the words. No cursing today. And no shouting, or swordplay, or dice. No salacious stories. No mulled wine to keep out the chill. Just muttered exchanges and more waiting and the drip of water and the occasional surreptitious glance at the low stone building and at the priests and barons who ducked in and out.

The rain had turned the ground spongy underfoot, so the men moved awkwardly, their boots sinking into the compost of leaves and bracken. It seemed right that they should pick their way with care, heads bowed, as though with respect. And it was right that the rain coursed down their faces, for then they looked alike, the truly sorrowful and the insincere.

Many of them had been there, in the Normandy forest, for the past six days. When they had first arrived at the hunting lodge the ground had been covered with snow. But an unseasonal warm spell had dissolved the white carpet, and for the last three days it had rained without pause. The men had been patient enough until then, but most of them now shared a common, unspoken thought. They wanted the king to die, or get well, but to do so before his followers drowned on their feet.

On the sixth day of his illness, King Henry was visited by a deputation of his senior earls, among them his eldest illegitimate son, Robert of Gloucester. They had come to see for themselves if the king was as close to death as was rumoured and, if so, to hear him name his successor. Bulky as bears in their thick, fur-lined cloaks, the earls stooped as they entered the lodge, then sank to their knees around the candle-lit bed.

29

One glance was enough to reveal the hopelessness of Henry's condition. Until a week ago, when he had gorged himself on the one thing his system could not absorb – lampreys cooked in wine and goat's milk – he had been a stocky, well-fleshed man, unbowed by age. He had come to the Forest of Lyons to pursue his passion for hunting, and from the moment the hounds were let loose, he had ridden his barons to exhaustion. That night, in defiance of his physician's advice, he had eaten the lampreys and gone to bed complaining of stomach cramp. By morning he was vomiting blood, and a messenger was sent the twenty miles to Rouen, to fetch Archbishop Hugh. He arrived in time to hear the king's confession – twice, since most of what Henry said was inaudible.

Now, on this sixth day, the first day of December, all trace of the hunter monarch had wasted away. The earls gazed down at the sunken features of a sick old man, and found it hard to imagine him on horseback. The king was sixty-seven years of age. He had never been without enemies, but he had defeated all who set themselves against him. It seemed unjust that such a giant should fall prey to a plate of boiled fish.

Robert touched his father's hand. The skin was cold and damp. The king's eyelids fluttered and he stared up at the ring of faces. He did not know where he was, nor did he recognise his son. He mouthed something and the nobles leaned forward, rainwater dripping on to the sheepskin coverlet. One of them queried irritably, 'What did he say?'

Robert was not sure, and ignored the question. He put his head close to Henry's ear and murmured, 'My lord king, it is your son, Earl Robert. You will soon be well – '

Another of the barons barked, 'God, Gloucester, don't tell him that. Allow him the truth, or we will hear nothing from him. He must believe he is dying. He must know this is his last chance.'

Robert glared at the man, then turned back to his father. He broke off once as Henry coughed blood, and waited while a physician wiped the king's face. Then he moved close again and said, 'One question, my lord. In front of these witnesses, Surrey, Perche, Meulan and Leicester. Affirm your successor;

30

say finally who it is to be. Do you remain in favour of the Empress Matilda, or would you now have your nephew, Stephen of Blois? Or do I take the reins as your male child? In the name of God, sire, make your choice, or your dominions will be seized piecemeal by usurpers. We will follow whomsoever you say.'

In fact, Henry had already named his successor and, on three separate occasions, he had extracted an oath of allegiance from his barons. First at London, then five years later at Northampton, and finally at Le Mans three years ago, the king had compelled the Norman nobility to accept his daughter Matilda as heiress to the English throne. Since then father and daughter had quarrelled and parted, and there were many who believed that Henry had undergone a change of heart, and would renounce Matilda in favour of his favourite nephew, Stephen of Blois. A third faction supported Robert of Gloucester, even though his illegitimacy weakened his claim. It was essential that the situation should be resolved, if necessary with King Henry's dying breath.

Robert gently squeezed his father's hand. The old man responded slowly and bubbled what might have been '. . . terminate your misery . . . do as I have arranged . . .' then something else, so indistinct that each man heard what he wanted to hear. Then the king coughed again, and a violent shiver ran through his frame and his life force shook itself free, leaving him still and settled, diminished in death.

The men looked at each other across the body of their king. They held their gaze for a long time, until Robert murmured tonelessly, 'He said his daughter. He said the Empress Matilda.'

The earls of Surrey and Leicester shook their heads. 'We heard otherwise. He said he had renounced her. We heard him say Stephen.'

'Be warned,' Robert told them. 'Keep your imaginings to yourselves.'

'Why?' the Earl of Surrey retorted. 'You won't.'

*

Some stayed to escort the royal corpse west to Rouen, thence via Caen to England. Others set out for Lisieux, where they went into conclave to discuss the situation. And one enterprising minor baron turned his horse northward and thundered through the rain-washed forest in the direction of Boulogne. He felt sure his news would be of interest to its overlord, Stephen of Blois.

*

For three weeks the arguments raged back and forth.

From Lisieux, emissaries were sent to fetch Stephen and Matilda, but neither could be located. Stephen was no longer at Boulogne, which meant perhaps that he was already on his way to the conference. As for Matilda, she was thought to be with her husband Geoffrey in his counties of Anjou or Maine. But no one could discover their precise whereabouts, so the conference continued without them.

Robert made his position clear from the outset. He *was* King Henry's son, albeit a bastard, and he knew he could gain some support from the continental overlords. Normally they would have added their weight to any legitimate claimant, but this time they were confronted by a major obstacle, a mental barrier they were unwilling to surmount. The only legitimate claimant was the Empress Matilda, and it was not in the Norman nature to follow a woman.

Yet three times they had sworn fealty to her, and they were hesitant to break their word. King Henry was dead, so they had nothing to fear from him, though they would be happier when his body was in the ground. But even then they could not, in good conscience, sweep aside his daughter. Neither could they bring themselves to fulfil their thrice-spoken vows. It was one thing for a man to say he would obey a woman, and another to kneel and nod. If only Matilda had been of the other sex. If only Robert had been born in wedlock. If only Henry had mastered his weakness for lampreys . . .

It was Robert himself who simplified the situation. He waived all personal claim to the throne, and announced that he would champion his half-sister.

'Men have been ruled by women before. History is speckled with them; it is not such an outlandish thing.'

'That's only part of it,' the Earl of Surrey countered. 'Bad enough that she is a woman, but far worse that she is married to that primping Angevin. It's a disgusting union, and no Norman will take orders from Anjou.'

'You are very noisy on the subject, Surrey, yet you also pledged allegiance to my sister.'

'We all did. Henry was not a man to cross. But remember this; the first time we swore fealty, Matilda was not married to the Angevin. We were supposed to choose her husband; that was the condition we set. I discount the repeated oaths. They were forced from us.'

'So now where do you stand?'

The Earl of Surrey shrugged. 'That's what we're here to discuss. For myself, I favour Stephen of Blois. The king named him on his death-bed – '

'He did not. The only name that left his lips – '

'He did. We heard him.'

' – was Matilda.'

'No. Stephen.'

'You are a liar, Surrey, an easy liar and an oath-breaker!'

'And you are in your sister's pocket! And elsewhere, maybe!'

They squared-off, the tall, long-jawed Robert, and the shorter, more powerfully built William of Surrey. They went for their swords at the same instant, and other nobles shouldered between them, snarling restraint. 'The world would like to see this, how we elect our king! Bury your weapons, my lords, before we are all disgraced.' One of the barons wisely suggested they adjourn the debate and spend some time clarifying their thoughts. 'We can speak for and against every candidate; Empress Matilda, Count Stephen, Earl Robert, although he says he is no longer in contention. But those who favour one candidate will not be swayed by their opponents. Perhaps we should compromise. Anyway, let's catch our breath.' They moved away in groups, scowling and muttering. Outside, the rain had followed them from the forest.

*

They reassembled three days later to find that someone had installed a number of tables in the council chamber. The tables were arranged in a hollow square, so there was no longer any excuse for the barons to cluster together, or poke chests. They could still glare at each other, and pound the table to emphasise a point, but none of them risked ridicule by stalking an adversary around the trestle square. They sat and they talked, and a new candidate was proposed.

There was still no sign of Matilda, and, whichever direction Stephen had taken when he had left Boulogne, it had not brought him to the conference at Lisieux. But the wintry light of dawn had revealed an unexpected visitor – Stephen's elder brother, Theobald of Blois.

Throughout his life, Theobald had remained loyal to King Henry, and his presence at Lisieux was welcomed by the rival factions. Whereas Stephen was Count of Boulogne and Mortain, and master of extensive holdings in England, Theobald was Count of Blois, Champagne and Chartres, and grandson of that most famous Norman, William the Conqueror. He was also King Henry's eldest nephew and, the more the barons thought about it, the higher Theobald's star ascended. Stephen might have been Henry's favourite, but Theobald preceded him in every way. He was a true Norman, easy to get along with, and renowned for his generosity. He suffered from a bad stammer, but that was no problem. He could always find someone to read his speeches for him.

There followed two weeks of proposal and counter-proposal. Robert continued to champion Matilda, while others looked directly at Theobald and told him they still preferred Stephen.

'You are a Norman, no doubt of it. But you have never been to England, you do not speak one word of their native language, and no one here has ever heard you mention that island. Stephen, on the other hand, owns more land there than anyone, save the church. And his mother is King Henry's sister.'

'D-d-damned fool!' Theobald exploded. 'D-don't you think I know that? I'm his b-b-brother! She's m-my mother too! She was m-mine before she was his, idiot!'

34

The spokesman slumped down in confusion, buried beneath the raucous laughter of his peers.

But the succession was no laughing matter. Robert would not be swayed, though he grew increasingly anxious at the reports of violence among the small landowners. Eager to extend their borders, they were taking advantage of the situation to launch surprise attacks on their neighbours. It was time the conference delivered its verdict. But for whom? Matilda? Stephen? Theobald?

With a show of hands they chose Theobald, and he stammered his acceptance. It was by no means a popular decision – he had merely gathered more votes than the empress, or his brother – but the nobles recorded that on 19th December they had elected him King of England.

If Theobald's arrival at the conference had been thought timely, the date of his election was a supreme irony, for exactly one day later a messenger reached Lisieux to explain Stephen's disappearance from Boulogne. He had travelled north to Wissant and caught a ship for England. He had landed at Dover, where he had been refused entry by the constable of the castle. Undeterred, he had ridden on to Canterbury, and again been refused admission.

Small wonder, Robert thought, since both castles belong to me. But he allowed himself no smile of satisfaction, for the messenger had not come to tell them that. There had to be more.

Unnerved by the hard-eyed assembly, the messenger mumbled, '. . . then, when they . . . that's to say, when Count Robert's men – '

'Speak up!'

'. . . when Count Robert's men turned him away from Dover and Canterbury, he went straight to London.'

'Why not? He's no stranger to the place.'

'Let him tell it, will you? Go on, man, get it said.'

'. . . went to London, yes, and the people . . . well, they accepted him.'

'What does that mean?'

Terrified that he would be made the object of their fury, the messenger blurted, 'The people of – *They've elected him King!* They say it's their right to do so, to choose their own ruler. When I last heard, the church had also acknowledged him. He's to be crowned tomorrow, or the day after, at Westminster. He's – ' But the rest was lost in an uproar of joy and anger. It was the most audacious theft imaginable – the taking of a country. And it was *fait accompli*, a bloodless victory that left the thief in residence in a palace, his short black hair encircled with a crown. It also left the conference chamber at Lisieux well stocked with enemies.

*

Mid-December, and Wallingford lay under snow. It was a pretty enough sight to make the coldest traveller pause and slap his hands against his thighs and nod with admiration at the white-capped castle. Fox and rabbit tracks criss-crossed the surrounding fields, and a number of farmers had reported seeing wolves within half a mile of the town.

On both sides of the ford the riverbank was rutted by cart wheels, the marks of each day's traffic freezing overnight. The ice was broken anew, every morning, and the carters prayed that their wagons would not break down in mid-stream. It was unbearably cold up there on the driving seat, but if one had to climb down and stand in the river –

They made good use of their whips, and their curses carried through the still air.

Brien Fitz Count could hear them as he descended from the wall tower. The upper section of the tower had only been finished a few months ago – to be a baron did not necessarily mean to be rich – and the fortifications were now complete. Shaped like a horseshoe, with towers for nail holes, the outer wall enclosed the keep, inner and outer courtyards, a smithy, guardhouse, kitchens, stables, a storeroom and armoury, and a well that froze, like the river, every night. The inner courtyard also contained a vegetable garden, but this was hidden under several inches of snow.

Brien crossed the outer bailey, mounted the last tower and stood for a while, conversing with the guards. His regular tours of inspection were appreciated by his men. Most of them had served under other leaders and, like soldiers everywhere, they expected their suzerains to meet certain required standards. They had no time for warlords who hibernated in winter, or emerged, swaddled in sheepskin, whilst they themselves shivered in threadbare cloaks. And on that score, Lord Fitz Count came off well, dressed as they were dressed, his face and hands as blue as theirs. If they could fault him at all, it was for his insistence that every tower be manned, day and night, as though an attack was imminent. He was right to protect what was his, but they had yet to see anything more warlike than one of King Henry's patrols, *en route* to Oxford.

That, at any rate, was how they had felt until the first week of December. Then, like ripples in a pool, the news of King Henry's death spread through Normandy and across the channel and up from the English ports, and violence erupted around them.

They looked at Fitz Count with renewed respect. He could not have known that the king would die in that distant forest, but he had prepared for the eventuality. And so far the snow-covered fields around Wallingford were devoid of siege machines.

Bracing himself against the battlements, Brien leaned forward and studied the frozen moat. 'D'you think that would bear a man's weight?'

The two guards shook their heads. One of them said, 'I saw Constable Varan go out and test it this morning. He kicked a hole in the ice near the gate. He couldn't have stood on it.'

Brien grunted. 'Even so, we'll keep the moats open. Ice can double its thickness in a day. Next week it will be a carpet for uninvited guests.'

'Do you think we'll come under attack, my lord?'

'I don't know. At present we are the eye of the storm. There's fighting at Newbury, and around Abingdon, and the manor at Wycombe was set alight. But Wallingford is not a contested fief. No one has any cause to covet it.'

The second guard hazarded, 'My Lord Fitz Count, may I ask something?'

'Ask on.'

'Who is going to rule England? They say you're among those who swore loyalty to the Empress Matilda – '

'I am, and proud of it.'

'But you are also a friend of Count Stephen.'

'One of the closest. We grew up together at court.'

'Then surely you feel some conflict, now that the Londoners have accepted him.'

'It's a temporary thing,' Brien assured the man. 'Count Stephen is aware of the need for stability. He will act for his cousin until she arrives in this country. There's no question of his keeping the crown.'

The guard nodded. If Lord Fitz Count said the crown would be passed peaceably from head to head, that's how it would be. But why would Count Stephen take it, if he intended to hand it on almost immediately? It hardly seemed worth the trouble.

Turning towards the slippery steps, Brien said, 'Keep your eyes open. I'll send one of the servants up with soup before long. Shout if you see anything that arouses your suspicions, however slight. There's many a castle been taken through the shyness of watch-guards.' He went down the steps, his boiled-leather boot heels crunching on the ice.

As he made his way towards the keep, he thought of what he had just told the guards about Stephen and asked himself if he believed it.

Today was the fifteenth. If the latest news was reliable, Stephen was now at Winchester with his younger brother, Bishop Henry. They were very close, these two, and, in Henry, Stephen had a brilliant and well-respected ally. The younger man had only been in the country a few years, and in that time he had risen from comparative obscurity to become the most powerful bishop in England. In an age in which churchmen owned extensive private holdings, rode to battle in full armour, and played an influential part in the government of the country, Bishop Henry was very much a man of his time.

He was also far-sighted, for the moment King Henry left for Normandy, on the journey that would eventually take him to the forest of Lyons, the young bishop set about preparing the ground for Stephen's arrival. Like Brien Fitz Count, Bishop Henry anticipated the inevitable. But he was not content to post guards and build towers. Instead, he approached William Pont de l'Arche, Treasurer of England, and coolly suggested that, in the event of the king's death, William should make over to him the entire treasury and the massive castle at Winchester.

'Is this a joke?' William snapped. 'Is it? Is it a joke?' He favoured repetition, in the belief that it added weight to his comments.

Henry, bland and smooth-featured, said, 'No, Lord Treasurer, I am quite serious.'

'You think you are. It's a trait in madmen. Madmen always think they are serious. Well, sir bishop, we are both busy men – '

'It would be to your advantage to listen, Pont de l'Arche. Its value is not diminished by its novelty.'

'Yes,' the treasurer nodded, 'I admit, I am curious. One does not often come upon such high-placed madness. So if our king, God preserve him, should enter heaven from the mounting block of Normandy – '

'Say die, treasurer. Leave such embroidery to us. If the king should die – '

'You want me to pass over his entire fortune. You know that the coinage alone amounts to more than one hundred thousand pounds. Then there's his property, his plate, his jewellery, his horses – '

'I know.'

' – his packs of hounds, his clothes, his furniture, his personal rents, loans that have yet to be repaid – '

'I said I know.'

'And I'm to give you all this. And Winchester Castle. What supreme effrontery. It really is a joke, though I doubt if the king's daughter will be amused by it.'

'It won't matter what she thinks. My brother Stephen will inherit the throne, not Matilda.'

'He'll do nothing of the kind,' the treasurer snorted. 'The king doesn't want him, and England won't have him.

'And if you are wrong, then will you make over the treasury?'

The treasurer had heard somewhere that one should humour madness, and he treated Henry to a pitying smile. 'Let Stephen be made king,' he said, 'and I shall festoon you with royal keys. You shall have all the royal keys. I shall hang them around your neck. Though, of course, if Matilda succeeds to the throne, as she will, you may find yourself wearing a hempen rope instead. We might dress you in that, you see. A noose. Do you follow my meaning?'

'Just,' Henry murmured sarcastically. 'You have such a delicate touch with words.'

Anyway, that was how the story went. Brien accepted that it had been embellished in the re-telling, but he had no reason to doubt that Henry had asked for the treasury. It was not the sort of thing one could invent.

He reached the drawbridge, stamped the snow from his boots, then made his way carefully across the iced-over planks. He wondered what Pont de l'Arche was thinking, now that London had elected Stephen king. If Winchester also welcomed him – and with Henry as their bishop it was a foregone conclusion – Pont de l'Arche would have to swim with the tide.

The Lord of Wallingford suddenly realised that he no longer believed what he had told his guards. Give a man a crown and one hundred thousand pounds, and he is unlikely to relinquish them to a female cousin he actively dislikes. And yet, if he does not relinquish them, he risks pitching his country into civil war.

Would Stephen go that far? Would he fight to keep what he had taken?

Brien could not bring himself to answer, but for the first time that day he felt chilled to the bone. He went on into the keep and roared at Varan to organise a work-party and break the ice in the moats.

*

Four days later – while the terrified emissary was recounting the news of Stephen's election to the barons at Lisieux – Brien

heard that Pont de l'Arche had surrendered the treasury, and
that the Chief Justiciar of England and several important
churchmen had allied themselves with Stephen.

*

Next morning Brien and Alyse were woken by Varan, who
handed his master a heavy parchment scroll. It was secured
with silk ribbon, the ends of the ribbon buried in a black wax
seal. The seal measured more than three inches across, and
bore the inscription STEPHANUS DEI GRATIA REX ANGLO-
RUM – Stephen by the Grace of God King of England – and
on the reverse, STEPHANUS DEI GRATIA DUX NORMAN-
NORUM. The contents of the scroll summoned Brien Fitz
Count and his lady to the coronation of King Stephen at
Westminster Abbey on Sunday, 22nd December.

Beneath the summons Stephen had penned, 'It has been a
long while since we were together, dear friends, and never
under such happy circumstances. Come the day before, so we
may have some time to talk, and bring your finery, for I have
reserved a place close by for you.' It was signed, again somewhat prematurely, 'Stephanus Rex'.

'That,' moaned Alyse, 'is the Stephen I remember. He
invites us to come early, quite uncaring that it will take the
best part of a day to get there. You realise what it means.'

Brien nodded. He was not yet fully awake, and from time to
time he picked up the scroll, flattened it with his hand and re-
read it. He mumbled, 'It means we must make a start. How long
will it take you to prepare – '

'A week, at least.'

'Yes,' he said gently, 'I know. There's an unseemly haste
about the whole affair.' He put his arms around her, massaging
her bare shoulders. No one wore night-clothes. In winter one
piled more covers on the bed, or moved the bed closer to the
fire. Again he asked, 'How long?'

'I shall need to take Edgiva. She knows how to do my hair,
and I don't want some excitable court servant – '

'Of course. Take who you like.'

Alyse allowed herself a long sigh, to show how inconsiderate she thought the world, then turned to her husband and kissed him, and suddenly became businesslike. 'Keep clear of me until midday. I'll be ready by then, though God knows what I shall look like at the ceremony.'

He opened his mouth to tell her she would look beautiful, as always, then thought it better to match her mood. 'Very well, midday. With luck we should reach London by dark. If not, we'll stay the night at Windsor.' He lay back on the bed, the cold air brushing his chest. So Stephen was making the act official. Now what I am to do about that, Brien mused. What do I say when my old friend asks for a solemn oath of fealty? How do I tell him that I hold to the vows I made to Matilda, and regard him as nothing more than a usurper? *Christ Almighty!*

He swore aloud before he could stop himself, and Alyse mistook the reason and said, 'Don't fret, it's not your fault. We'll be there in time.'

'No,' Brien frowned, 'we won't. We're already too late.' He lay where he was for a moment, then swung himself abruptly from the bed and made a dash for his clothes.

CHAPTER 3

STEPHANUS REX
December 1135

THE coronation of King Stephen had been a bleak and ill-attended affair. Many of the senior nobles had remained at Lisieux, or raced for England in a vain attempt to reach Westminster in time. Others, who lived within riding distance of the Abbey, had pleaded indisposition and sent their sons to represent them, or simply ignored the summons. The ceremony had been conducted by the Archbishop of Canterbury, assisted by Stephen's brother Henry, and the Bishop of Salisbury. But this impressive triumvirate was unsupported by the mass of the clergy. In short, the place had been three-fourths empty, the singing cheerless, the atmosphere tense and urgent.

Brien and Alyse had been present, although they too had all but missed the service. The roads between Wallingford and London had proved impassable, and the riders were forced to follow the course of the Thames, thus doubling the length of their journey. As a result, they had not yet spoken to their old friend – their new king.

The young couple, together with Edgiva and six members of the Wallingford garrison, had been lodged in the palace precincts, and they waited there now, Brien and the women in an upper room, the guards directly below, with the horses.

Alyse gazed out of the window, watching the other guests hurry across the cobbled yard to their own quarters. She tried to gauge their movements, but it seemed that they were also awaiting instructions. Brien came to stand beside her, looked down at the snowy yard and asked, 'Anything happening?'

'Not that I can see.' She turned, appealing as much to her maidservant as to her husband. 'I do not know whether to change out of these robes, or stay in them, or what. Look how the snow has stained the hem.' She shook her head. 'Nobody

43

but Stephen could become king in such a casual way. It's a wonder he didn't keep the crown beside his bed last night, then put it on when he got up this morning. It would have saved us all – '

'Wait,' Brien said. 'There's a steward coming round.' He called down to the guards, and one of them went to the yard door to take a folded square of parchment from the official. He brought it up to Brien, who unfolded it and held it so Alyse could read it with him.

It was untitled, and read, 'Stephen by the Grace of God King of England, to our barons and faithful friends, greetings. We bid you present yourselves at the Great Hall of the Palace and eat with us and receive our love on this most joyous occasion. If you have brought members of your family with you, we extend our welcome.'

Brien gave the note to Alyse and strode back to the window. After a moment he saw what he was looking for and said quietly, 'God's pity, it's sad.'

'What is?'

'That steward. He's gone round, and he is still left with a pile of letters. That's why they carry no title. Stephen did not know how many of us would attend. And that's why he's stretched his invitation to the entire family. He's worried that his banquet will turn into a meal for ten.'

'I wish I could be so compassionate,' Alyse told him. 'Perhaps I'd see it differently if he had given sufficient warning. But what else can he expect, when half the nobility are out of England, and the rest snow-bound? The only reason *we* are here is because we rode half the night. It's not sad, husband, it's inevitable.'

'I suppose so.' He called downstairs again, then asked the sergeant of the guard if he had arranged food for the men. The sergeant, who was in the throes of a secret affair with Edgiva, tried hard to avoid her gaze. 'I have, lord,' he nodded. 'They will feed all the troops in the kitchens. Do you wish me to, uh, see that mistress Edgiva gets fed?'

'No, she can join the other maidservants. There will be a room set aside for them near the hall.'

44

The sergeant nodded again, with less enthusiasm, then bowed and went back down the stairs. Edgiva stifled a sigh of relief. She was enjoying her affair with the sergeant, though tonight she was happy to forgo his attentions. He would be there tomorrow, but she might never again get the chance to eat in the next room to the King of England, and exchange gossip with the servants of a dozen great households. Well, not *exchange* gossip. She was not given to that sort of thing. Just listen to it; listen and learn.

Brien collected the invitation, draped his cloak around his shoulders and fastened the throat clasp. Edgiva helped Alyse into an embroidered mantle – and the hem of *that* was snow-stained, Alyse noticed – then donned her own woollen cloak and followed Fitz Count and his lady to the head of the stairs.

*

The Great Hall at Westminster lived up to its name. Built by King Henry's predecessor, William Rufus, it measured two hundred and forty feet in length, and was sixty-seven feet wide. It had been constructed over and around an earlier wooden building, so that at no time was the banquet-loving king denied his comforts. When the vast, ragstone hall had been completed, the wooden structure was torn down, and clay tiles laid from wall to wall. In the forty years since then, almost every tile had been cracked or chipped.

A raised platform covered the northern end of the floor, and supported a single, fixed table. Rows of less substantial trestle tables filled the body of the hall and, because of its extreme length, the building boasted three fire-pits. The smoke rose to the vaulted ceiling and escaped through louvres – unless the rain or snow drove it back, or the wind blew it under the rafters to fall as soot on the guests. Chests and benches and dismantled tables stood against the walls, interspersed with helmeted guards from Stephen's Norman and English fiefdoms; men he could trust.

Each long wall contained twelve large windows and twenty-five smaller apertures. There had been talk of importing glass from Palestine, or commissioning inferior work from the

45

blowers at Guildford. But nothing had been done about it, and the windows remained unglazed. They were, however, covered by heavy leather curtains, and these did something to lessen the draught.

Outside, Brien directed Edgiva to the servants' chamber, then offered Alyse his right arm, his hand palm downward, his fingers extended. Alyse rested her left arm on his. As they approached the south door of the hall, she asked, 'Is there any way by which you could come to terms with him?'

'One I can think of, though I don't hold out much hope for it.'

'May I know?'

Surprised, he said, 'Of course you may know. Do you believe I would risk alienating us from Stephen without first consulting you? I'll swear fealty to him, if he will acknowledge that he is simply custodian of the crown.'

'And will pass it on to Matilda?'

'Exactly. The day she sets foot in England.'

'Then you are right.'

'Hmm?'

'There's not much hope of it. It is hardly the question to ask a king within an hour of his coronation.'

'He is not king,' Brien said firmly, 'not until we say he is king.'

Alyse glanced at her tall, grey-haired husband, then walked on with him to the door. She wanted to agree with him, but she could not. Yet neither could she tell him that his truth was distorted by reality. There *had* been a coronation, and there *was* a king. He did not accept it, but it was a fact. In a moment they would see Stephen, *King* Stephen, and they would be expected to address him according to his rank. Whatever Brien saw in the mirror, England and the world would accept the reflected image.

But it was not acceptance or rejection that concerned Alyse. It was something much less admirable, something she dare not put into words. Brien did not acknowledge Stephen as his king. Very well. But was it for the reasons he had given, or was it because not only his loyalties, but far more, belonged to

46

Stephen's rival cousin, the Empress Matilda? Was Brien enamoured of her, as the rumourmongers said? Had she once held him in thrall, and could do so again, whenever she chose? Ashamed and angry, Alyse thought, the devil snatch her, before she ruins Fitz Count!

Guards stopped them at the door. Brien thrust the invitation at them, and they stamped to attention.

'You're poorly trained,' he told them. 'Anybody could have obtained one of these. And I doubt that you can read it. As it happens, I *am* the Lord of Wallingford, and a close friend of the – of Stephen, but you will have to settle for my word. I could be an assassin. Think of that.'

He escorted Alyse between them and entered the smoky, candle-lit hall. The guards grimaced at each other. That was the third baron who'd snapped off their heads. It was going to be an eventful evening.

*

Stephen was making a fool of himself, and knew it. He could not decide whether to stay at the high table and wait for his guests to present themselves, or come down and greet them man to man, friend to friend. So far, he had mounted and descended the side steps a dozen times, like an actor who has lost his nerve. He would have to settle for being on stage or off, one or the other.

He climbed on to the platform, looked along the hall, then hurried down again. But this time his smile was sincere.

'Fitz Count! My Lady Aline – Alyse! I thought I glimpsed you in church. God, what a chilly performance that was!' Alyse, he told himself, it's Alyse. What is the matter with you, you don't even know anyone called Aline.

Alyse took her hand from Brien's arm, raised the hem of her gown and made a deep curtsey. She said nothing and thought immediately, now there is no turning back. I am as one with my husband. I did not call him king.

She raised her head, smiling, and Stephen thought the smile was for him.

Brien bowed, stood erect again, and said with complete

47

honesty, 'My Lord Stephen. I am pleased to see you again.'
He gazed directly at his thin, black-haired friend, remembering
that if all else was lost between them, they would still share the
same birth date. Stephen was three years older, although today,
weighed down by his regalia, he looked young, uncertain of
himself, a son who had stolen away to dress in his father's
clothes. He had grown a moustache, which had come out
paler than his head hair. He looked – yes, *vulnerable*. And God
knew, he was.

'And I am pleased to see you,' Stephen said. 'Both of you.
My lady, you are without doubt one of the most beautiful
women in England.'

Alyse smiled. 'And you, my lord, are one of the most per-
ceptive of men.'

*Why do they both call me lord? I thought they'd be among the first
to exercise my new title. Well, no matter. They're the truest friends
I've seen today.*

He grinned at Alyse's rejoinder and held out his arm,
inviting her to take it. Then he led her along the hall, past the
fire-pits – *to hell with you other women, you never stretched your lips
until London opened its gates to me* – and up the steps to the high
table. Brien followed, nodding politely at his peers.

Only one side of the table was furnished with chairs,
enabling the occupants to overlook the hall. The chairs were
heavy and uncomfortable, but they were the only individual
seats in the chamber and it was enough for a guest to be up
there – above the bench. Such an honour was normally
reserved for senior members of the clergy and barony, and
both Brien and Alyse felt out of place. Although they were
Stephen's friends, they were embarrassed by the casual way he
flouted tradition. He was not only making enemies for himself,
but was directing the angry glare of excluded nobles at the
Lord and Lady of Wallingford.

However, they were on the platform now, and stood facing
the table while Stephen effected the introductions. Brien had
met some of the guests before, and Alyse knew one or two by
sight, but this was the first time they had been invited to sit
with the magnates as social equals.

Stephen gripped Brien's arm above the elbow and announced, 'My lords, may we commend to you our lifelong
friend, Brien Fitz Count, Lord of Wallingford-on-the-Thames,
and his Lady Alyse, who is descended from an earlier English
king.' He then indicated the aged Archbishop of Canterbury,
William of Corbeil; the bishops of Winchester and Salisbury;
the treasurer, Pont de l'Arche; Earl Ranulf of Chester and a
smattering of local dignitaries. Stephen's brother, Henry of
Winchester, was the only one to smile, though it was hard to
assess the sincerity of his bland welcome. The others merely
nodded, or looked at Stephen, as though waiting for him to
explain his behaviour. Their expression seemed to say, who
will you next invite to sit with us, your pet monkey, another
lifelong friend?

Brien and Alyse took their places at one end of the table,
Alyse between her husband and the corpulent Bishop of
Salisbury. The churchman had discarded his robes of office
and was now dressed in an embroidered woollen tunic and
long, fur-lined mantle. His fingers were heavy with rings, two
of which were known as casket rings and could be opened to
reveal a splinter of wood, said to be from the True Cross, and
a fragment of bone from the right hand of the blessed St Joseph
of Arimathea. The rings were so large that the bishop had had
holes cut in the fingers of all his gloves.

Alyse knew little about him, save that he was one of the
most powerful men in the kingdom – Brien would not have
used that word; in the land, then – and that Stephen had done
well to win him over. Ah, yes, she remembered, and one other
thing. At a recent ecclesiastical council, Bishop Roger had
spoken out against the hundreds of parish priests who had
flouted their vows of celibacy and engaged in clandestine
marriages. Then, having decreed that these hapless wives could,
if discovered, be sold into slavery, he had returned to his
mistress, Maud of Ramsbury.

Food was brought; stews of beef and venison; spit-roasted
lamb, salted bacon, dishes of onions, and circular loaves of rye
bread. Roger poured wine for Alyse, then leaned across to
pass the jug to Brien. As he did so, he dragged the sleeve

of his mantle in her stew, then let the mixture drip across the table. Alyse sat quiet, exhaling against the odour of his breath.

His first slurred comments confirmed her suspicions; he was well and truly drunk. Nevertheless, he was one of God's senior servants, and she sat in fear of him, aware that it was within his power to have anyone who offended him struck down, burned to a cinder by a bolt from heaven. The laity, whether nobleman or commoner, were as weeds in the hands of such men. They could be stamped flat, or plucked from the earth, or, if they were fortunate, earn an episcopal blessing.

He put a hand on her shoulder and let his other arm rest on the table, unaware of the stew-stained cuff. 'Are you educated in drink, Lady Alyse? Taste what I've given you. Tell me where it comes from.'

'My lord bishop, I am not well versed – '

'That's it, swill and swallow. Did you say Poitou?'

'I could not say where – ' She felt Brien nudge her, and nodded quickly. 'Yes, at a guess, Poitou.'

'Well now,' he beamed, 'that's right.' He gave her shoulder a congratulatory pat. 'It's rare to find a lady who knows her wine. It was brought out from La Rochelle. As you probably know, I have my own fleet.'

Brien put his head back, gazed incuriously at the rafters and murmured, 'Rack or harvest?' Alyse glanced at him, then took her cue and in complete ignorance echoed, 'Rack or harvest, Lord Bishop?'

The florid churchman croaked with delight and turned away to tell his neighbour. While he did so Brien hastened, 'If the weather's right they get two shipments. In spring it's called rack wine, in September it's harvest. I can smell his breath from here.'

She nodded, then once again surrendered herself to the bishop's wine-laced attentions. There was nothing more Brien could do for her, so he let his gaze roam the hall, now and then nodding at recognised friends. Stephen edged behind the chairs and leaned on the end of the table, sharing Brien's view of the hall.

'We have a few chairs left at the other end, and the venerable William of Canterbury is beginning to bore me. Who else shall we have up here?'

'That's for you to decide, my lord.'

Stephen said, 'No, no, you're free to suggest – ' Then he broke off, cleared a space on the table and hitched himself on to it, his stockinged legs dangling over the end. 'Why do you still call me that? I know my crowning was a hurried affair, but even so, I am wearing the headpiece.'

Brien looked up to see his friend smiling apologetically. He could hear Bishop Roger droning on, but he sensed that Alyse was no longer listening. The moment they had dreaded had arrived.

'I could call you king,' Brien measured, 'but I would not mean it.'

'Oh? Why not? I *am* king. Does the word come awkwardly to you? I suppose it does seem strange after all these years. It's only when we're in public. In private I shall always be Stephen.'

'It's not that.'

'What then? You called Henry king, and I never heard you stumble over it. Why do I present such a hurdle?'

'I accepted your uncle. There's a difference.'

Stephen's frown was slow in coming. He did not understand why Greylock, his, yes, as he had said, his lifelong friend, should suddenly turn against him. 'What difference?' Somebody called to him from the body of the hall, but he waved the caller down without looking. 'Tell me, Brien. I must know why you, of all people – '

'Because we swore fealty to your cousin, Empress Matilda. We made our vows, made them – '

'You don't seriously – '

' – three times, and I see no reason – '

' – hold to them. Henry bullied them from us!'

' – to break my given word. I have never done so yet.'

'I tell you, he extracted them from us under threat! How many ways must I put it? They were empty promises! And apart from all else, we swore on condition that we could choose her husband. How were we to know she would marry

that trouble-maker Geoffrey, a proven enemy of England?'
He glanced sharply at Alyse, then said, 'You must forgive me,
my lady, but Lord Fitz Count is in need of instruction. We
both know he is inordinately fond of the empress, and is blind
to all her faults.'

'Address me directly,' Brien said. 'I'm not in the next
street.'

'Very well. I shall risk your wife's discomfort and say
straight out that from all I have seen and heard you are under
Matilda's spell.'

'Then both your senses are faulty. Matilda can be credited
with many things, but not with magic. You talk of the conditions we set, but you know as well as I that no one dared
curb King Henry with conditions. We swore fealty to Matilda
because she was, and is, the rightful heir to the throne. You
have the throne, I don't dispute it, but it remains her property
until she relinquishes it.'

'You may as well call me a thief,' Stephen said indignantly.
'You're skirting around it.'

Brien looked at him, then shook his head. 'No, I would not
call you that, for it is not yet a fact. I'd prefer to think of you
as the custodian of the crown, safe-guarding it for your
cousin.'

'And Geoffrey? Am I keeping it polished for him too?'

'He has no rights. He can be controlled.'

'Maybe, maybe not. But there's one point you omit. On his
death-bed, King Henry renounced Matilda, and made me his
heir. The messenger who came to me at Boulogne – that was
the first thing he said. Or would you call me a liar as well as a
thief?'

'I believe he told you, yes. But I don't believe Henry ever
said it. It's a game we can all play. Whisper into your cupped
hands, and we will all hear something different. Henry was
your uncle and my guardian; we have both spent the greater
part of our lives in his presence. Yet when did he ever change
his mind at the last instant, or make some momentous decision
without committing it to paper? You find the document, my
lord, the one that confirms you are his heir, and I shall be the

first to swear fealty to you. But I don't think you'll find it, because it doesn't exist.'

It was then, after a moment's pause, that Stephen made the first grave mistake of his reign. He was prompted, perhaps, by the sudden silence that blanketed the high table, or by the need to impress his authority on Fitz Count. Whatever the cause, he sprang down from the table and in an over-shrill voice shouted, 'As you say! You *shall* be the first! Get to your knees. Say you love and honour me as your king. Come on, Fitz Count, here and now, in front of your peers. I *am* king, damn you! Let me hear you say it! Come on. Come on.' His voice echoed around the hall, and then there was no other sound but the flap of the leather curtains and the crackling of the fires.

The Norman nobility awaited the outcome with interest. They had heard little of the preceding conversation, but it was clear that King Stephen and Lord Fitz Count had had a serious falling out. Eruptions of anger were commonplace among the touchy, quick-tempered nobles, and it was a rare meeting that did not contain at least one noisy altercation. A man was not worth his salt until he had learned the value of a raised voice.

By their own critical assessment the nobles were not overly impressed by their new king's show of temperament. He had a long way to go before he matched the splenetic rages of Ranulf of Chester, or the destructive precision of Robert of Gloucester. But the content of his speech made up for its hysterical delivery. He had issued his first command as king, and it was essential that he be obeyed.

The guests watched in silence, as Stephen indicated where his lifelong friend should kneel.

During her six years of marriage to Brien Fitz Count, Alyse had done many things to amuse or enrapture him. But she had never before been called upon to parade her loyalties; indeed, she abhorred public displays, preferring her emotions to be kept private. Yet now, without thinking, for that would open the doors to fears and uncertainties, she rose to her feet, to find that Brien had risen with her.

Stephen turned triumphantly towards the body of the hall.

That's better. They will do it and, when they are finished, I shall help them up and embrace them. Let everyone see that from the first day I was a magnanimous king.

He smiled down at the assembly.

Then the Lord and Lady of Wallingford bade him good night and crossed to the steps, and his smile shrank and he was forced to clamp a hand on the table to steady himself. He thought, they are walking out on me. Bones of Christ! *They are walking out on me!*

He shouted after them, and later he had to ask someone what he had said. Smoke and wine fumes blurred his gaze. The scene twisted and shivered, elongating faces, splintering the firelight. 'You leave me now,' he roared, 'and you are *branded*! Do you hear me? I *am* the king! You saw me crowned! You *saw* me!'

The Bishop of Salisbury, his eyes veined with blood, flapped a hand at the tables. 'See what you've done . . . There's quite a procession of them . . . Miles of Hereford, he's going . . . And Baldwin de Redvers . . . And two over there. Damned smoke, I can't see that one . . .' He lolled forward, fumbling with his wine glass. 'Rack or harvest, eh . . . Surprisingly knowledgeable for such a pretty creature . . . Don't know why, but one doesn't expect it, in such a pretty . . .'

Stephen stood on the platform, blinking to clear his sight, unaware that he was tearing at one side of his sparse moustache.

*

They waited for the others to come out. Then, while Brien exchanged a few words with Miles and Baldwin and the four or five more who had emerged from the hall, Alyse went to collect Edgiva from the servants' chamber. By the time the two women returned, the disaffected barons were striding away across the snow-covered yard.

Edgiva said, 'I thought you would be in there most of the night, my lady. Was the strain of the service too much for the king?'

'Rather for us,' Alyse answered. Then, looking to Brien for confirmation, she said, 'We will start for home tonight. Go on ahead and get the things packed. And Edgiva – we are pressed for time; don't be too perfect with the creases.'

The girl nodded and picked her way across the slippery cobbles. Several questions crowded her tongue, and she decided to ask her sergeant-lover if he knew the reason for their sudden departure. She was sorry they were leaving Westminster so soon. She had hoped to see the palace and the cathedral by day, and more especially to catch a glimpse of King Stephen. But the visit had not been completely wasted; she had heard more gossip in one evening here than in a year at Wallingford, and it would be exciting to match stories with the sergeant. She would have to ration them out, of course; if possible make them last the winter.

Brien took his wife's arm, then glanced back, half expecting to see guards pour out from the building. Alyse shared his thoughts and asked, 'Will he have us arrested?'

'I don't know. And I don't imagine he knows, not yet. He has been taken by surprise, and that should give us time to get clear.'

'What did you arrange with Miles and the others?'

'Nothing of substance. We'll return to our lands and sit it out. The next move is up to Stephen, though I'm anxious to hear from the barons at Lisieux. In a day or two we'll know for certain what King Henry said on his death-bed, if anything.'

'But you are already convinced he did not disown Matilda. You don't think it at all possible?'

'No, I do not.'

Alyse slipped on a patch of ice, and Brien pulled her to him. 'Take care,' he smiled. 'If anything happens to us now, Stephen will claim it is divine retribution. Still, Bishop Roger will not denounce you to God. He has quite an appetite for you, along with his wine. Rack or harvest. You set him on his ear with that one. He may very well send you samples, for your opinion.'

'You don't have to.'

'Don't have to what?'

'Make light of it, for my sake. I have no doubts. I believe what we did was right.'

As they neared their quarters Brien said, 'Do you think I am under Matilda's spell, as he claimed?'

'Let me answer you with your own words,' she told him. 'I don't know. And I don't imagine you know, not yet. We will have to wait until she comes ashore.'

'Then pray heaven it's soon.'

No, Alyse thought, I won't pray that. I'll pray it's never.

*

The riders clattered alongside the lighted cathedral. The king was expected to spend the latter part of the night in silent vigil at the foot of the altar, but he would more likely pass the time in conference with his leaders. Meanwhile, the monks chanted their prayers and shivered with cold.

Once clear of the cathedral, the columns divided. Brien decided to return the way he had come, following the Thames all the way to Wallingford. It was a longer and more hazardous route, but it was passable, or had been a few hours ago. So, if no more snow had fallen out in the country, and they were not set upon by brigands, and none of the horses slipped and sent their riders crashing through the ice, and no sleepless peasant pointed the king's guards in their direction, then they would reach the castle by dusk tomorrow. But if the wind had blown the snow from the main road, and Stephen's troops had taken the more direct route, Brien's party would find their pursuers waiting for them on the doorstep.

With this in mind, they rode for home.

CHAPTER 4

CHESSMEN
January–April 1136

THE sense of shame stayed with them for several weeks. They did not regret having spoken out against the king, but the urgency of their departure – in truth, their flight – left them feeling faint-hearted, almost cowardly. And yet, if their fears had become reality, they would have congratulated themselves on their promptitude. They knew this, and it did not help.

They had reached Wallingford two days before Christmas, to find the place exactly as they had left it. There were no armed horsemen in the bailey, or outside the gate. Nor did any arrive next day, or the day after, or ride in on the tail of the year.

They heard that Stephen had spent Christmas at Westminster, then left for Reading, where, on 4th January, he had attended King Henry's funeral. That done, he was free to wreak vengeance on those who had left his table, but still there was no sign of catapults and siege-towers. It was as though he had forgotten the incident, or been advised to dismiss it as a childish tantrum, unworthy of his attention.

At Wallingford, shame gave way to perplexity. 'I'm beginning to feel damn foolish,' Brien told his wife. 'We've sealed ourselves in against an invisible enemy. I almost wish he *would* attack, or at least pitch camp around us, so we could re-assert our views. I don't think I have an exaggerated sense of my own importance, and if I had been the only one to speak against him, I could understand why he would ignore me. In his place I would do the same. But neither Miles, nor Baldwin, nor any of the others have come under attack.'

'Perhaps he expects you to go to him. It was always King Henry's boast that he would forgive any man who faced him at court. Stephen may wish to emulate his uncle.' Quickly she added, 'Not that we seek his forgiveness.'

'Not unless he has made it clear that he holds the throne for Matilda. And we would have heard about *that*, I'm sure.' He prowled the solar, his hands clasped over the buckle of his sword-belt. Alyse sat in one of the box chairs, watching his distorted reflection as he passed in front of the hammered silver mirror.

'Please,' she said, 'don't be so restless. You agreed with the others to sit it out. Wait a few more days. Then, if we hear nothing, send Constable Varan – '

'Three days,' he told her, 'after which I'll go myself. This thing must be resolved. He either claims the throne for life, in which case I am not his man, or he guards it for Matilda. One or the other.'

'I thought he had made his position clear at Westminster. And who's that man, Hugh somebody-or-other – '

'Bigod.'

'Yes, who said he had heard King Henry name Stephen as his heir.'

'The man's a liar. Robert of Gloucester was with his father at the last, and he says Hugh Bigod was not even in the room. It's a cooked-up story, to strengthen Stephen's claim. Anyway, Stephen has had time to think since his ravings at Westminster. He might still relinquish the crown.'

Alyse stifled a sigh. There it is again, his unshakeable belief in Matilda's destiny. She said, 'I would ask you something.'

'I know,' he grinned, 'stop pacing.'

She shook her head. 'No, sweet, do as you please. But tell me this. You are prepared to see Stephen again – '

'In three days, if he does not break his silence before then.'

' – and risk his anger, even imprisonment, for the sake of the empress.'

'You just told me Stephen will emulate his uncle.'

'I said he may. It's something Varan can find out for us. But you would rather go yourself, and risk your own safety for Matilda's sake.'

'For her, and for us. I swore fealty to her – '

'Yes, I know, three times.'

'Then you know all of it. I was King Henry's man when he

was alive, and now that he is dead my loyalties devolve upon his daughter. It's very simple. I take no special pride in saying I honour my word.'

'God knows,' she said gently, 'no one would doubt it. So, very simply, you do this for her.'

'For the woman who will be queen here one day.'

'And if I asked you not to put yourself at risk; if I asked you to stay clear of Stephen, would you do it?'

'*Are* you asking?'

'I'm setting myself in the balance,' she said. 'I want to see who weighs heavier with you, she or I.'

He looked down at her for a moment. Then he smoothed the grey hair on the nape of his neck and replied, 'Very well, my lady. I will sit it out.'

Suddenly close to tears, she said, 'Thank you. It's a pity, though, that you had to hesitate so long.'

*

While the dissident barons awaited his reponse, King Stephen assembled one of the greatest armies ever seen in England. By the end of January it was ready, not to crush the rebellious few at Wallingford, or Hereford, or in Baldwin de Redvers's castle at Exeter, but to halt an invasion of the country by King David of Scotland. This powerful monarch was Empress Matilda's uncle, and he posed the first serious threat to the English king.

The armies faced each other a few miles north of Durham and, while the troops rehearsed their simple battle tactics, or took shelter from the ceaseless winter drizzle, their commanders sat down to talk.

King David held the honour of Huntingdon, and thus carried the extra title of an English earl. But from the outset he refused to pay homage to Stephen, challenging him to prove that King Henry had named him as his heir. 'By word and pen,' David growled. 'If he'd said it, he'd have made some record of it. And if he could press his seal, he could mouth the words. I want both, or I'll cut your kingdom at the throat.'

Stephen was confident that the English army, supported by several hundred Flemish mercenaries, could hold the Scots in check, but he could not afford to maintain such a large and expensive force permanently in the north. War had to be averted, particularly when a border conflict would leave the growing number of English defectors free to manœuvre behind his back.

The kings of England and Scotland haggled for a week, at the end of which King David agreed to surrender the towns he had captured, and to make over the honour of Huntingdon to his son, Prince Henry. As the new Earl of Huntingdon, the young man would pay homage to Stephen and, in return, the English king would grant the prince the additional honours of Carlisle and Doncaster, plus extensive holdings in Cumberland and Westmorland. Henry would accompany Stephen to court where he would be, at one and the same time, an honoured guest and a regal hostage.

Stephen was soon to realise that he had made the second serious mistake of his reign . . .

Not only had he allowed the Scottish king to get the better of the deal but, by giving over Carlisle, he had deprived one of his most important supporters, the fiery Ranulf of Chester of a cherished inheritance. Ranulf's father had governed Carlisle, and by rights it should have passed to his son. As soon as he heard what had happened, Ranulf stormed from the court and added his name to the lengthening list of disaffected barons.

He was soon followed by the Archbishop of Canterbury, who found his privileged place at the high table occupied by the Scottish stripling. He, too, swept from the hall, leaving Stephen with the knowledge that for every friend he was making, he was making an enemy.

His closest companion, Brien Fitz Count, was now immured in Wallingford. Miles of Hereford had deserted him, as had Baldwin de Redvers, and a dozen others. They had all been friends once, for they had served together under King Henry. Yet now, within three months of his coronation, they had turned against him.

And why, he raged; because of that accursed woman . . .
widow of the German emperor . . . King Henry's daughter . . .
King David's niece . . . my own sweet cousin . . . the arrogant,
sharp-spoken, bloodless and beautiful Matilda, may she burn.
That is why I have alienated my friends. That is why my throne
creaks beneath me. Because we swore a hollow oath, and too
many still hear it echo in the darkest recesses of their minds.
They are under her spell, as I said. She is the lodestone, and
they are drawn like metal flakes to the magnet. But for Christ's
sake! We were *terrified* of King Henry! We never *wanted* a
woman! We would never have *accepted* a woman! We were in
awe of him, and so we said what we said, to earn his smile.
And now he is dead, and I have taken his place, and I want my
friends around me, God knows how I want them. So what do
they do? They walk out on me. They tell me I am a usurper,
and they go and sit in their castles and whistle up the wind
that will bring Matilda to England and prepare themselves for
the day when they will rise against me. It is not enough that
they are flakes of iron. They want to draw the magnet to them!
Such is the power of the magic Matilda. And to think – her
childhood nickname was Mouse.

Earl Ranulf's desertion drove the king to take counsel with
his brother, Bishop Henry. They talked in the Great Hall at
Westminster, seated in the same chairs they had occupied
at the coronation feast. But this time they were alone,
and the long table bore nothing but wine stains and knife
marks.

Henry rested his feet on the scarred beam that ran beneath
the table. He was shorter than his brother, fuller in the face,
thicker around the belly. He was a man of cultivated tastes,
and spent much of his enormous income on Italian statuary
and on his bestiary, a prized collection of European and African
wildlife. His menagerie at Winchester already included a number of lions, leopards, camels, lynxes, the jumping rats known
as jerboas, bears and porcupines, and he was awaiting delivery
of a pair of ostriches, hopefully male and female.

A superior example of the warrior monk, Henry of Winchester could be by turns charming and ruthless, compassionate

and vindictive. If he envied Stephen anything, it was his physique. The king ate like a pig, yet never put on weight, while the bishop starved his body and grew fat.

Now, tapping his heels against the beam, he mused, 'You ask what you should do about your vanished friends, but you have waited three months before putting the question. My advice changes with time and circumstances. When Fitz Count and Hereford and de Redvers first set themselves against you, I'd have suggested you pursue them with all the force at your disposal. But today I'd say leave them be. You are costing them a considerable fortune, you know. For the past quarter-year they have been locked in their castles, their walls and watch-towers manned day and night. They must have laid in extensive food-stocks, hired extra bowmen, added more horses to their stables, employed spies to report any troop movements in the district, and so on and so forth. It's a costly business, waiting for war.'

'Don't use that term,' Stephen protested. 'There'll be no war. So I'm to starve them out, am I, men who control ten or twenty fiefs, men like Ranulf of Chester, who is second only to me in the extent of his lands?'

Henry wagged an admonishing finger. 'With respect, brother king; *you* are second. The church is the greatest land-lord.'

'Yes, yes, whatever you like. What I am saying is that Ranulf and his kind are too rich to starve. I shall have to wait fifty years before they run short of money.'

'Surely that is not true of Brien Fitz Count?'

With heartfelt sincerity, Stephen admitted, 'You are right. He is not wealthy by Ranulf's standards, and I cannot enjoy watching my closest friend sink into penury. But what else can I do? It's ridiculous to suppose I would attack him, yet so long as he champions Matilda he is opposed to me.'

Henry put his head back and stared up at the rafters. 'You think of them as your vanished friends,' he said. 'Good enough, so they are, most of them. But what the people see is an exodus of barons and prelates – take William of Canterbury, for one – all streaming out of your court, and arming themselves for war.

Yes, I know, you do not like the term. No more do I, but it looms on the horizon. So these are the choices. Attack their castles, an undertaking that will spread your army across most of England. Or leave them be, and wait for the less wealthy among them to empty their purses. Or, and this is what I would advise in the circumstances, show yourself to be magnanimous, as befits a monarch. Let them know you admire their loyalty to Matilda, and grant them what they want.'

'Which is?'

'Which is a firm assurance that you safeguard the throne for her, and will pass on the crown when she requests it.'

Stephen frowned and hunched forward, once more worrying the ends of his moustache. 'Is that it?'

'Not quite,' Henry said. 'You must also leave for Normandy, to defend your duchy against Matilda's repeated assaults.'

'But she isn't attacking it. Her husband eggs her on, but so far – '

'Yes, she is,' the bishop measured, 'if you say she is. In the same way that she intends to impose a crippling property tax when she becomes queen.'

'I didn't know she – Ah, I see. I'm to paint her picture in sombre colours, is that it?'

Henry clicked his tongue, a tutor with a slow-witted pupil. 'You are painting her to the life, brother, and showing her portrait to the people of this country. A property tax of, say, two hundred pounds a year for every castle, manor, hunting lodge and suchlike will be taken much amiss by Ranulf and his kind. The more they have, the more it will hurt. And as for our poorer barons, like Fitz Count, there is always the invasion of Normandy, the duchy he spent so many years securing under King Henry. You'll see, my lord king. Their views of Matilda will change markedly when they learn what an avaricious young woman she really is. And, of course, you will attain heroic proportions, by comparison.'

'Brother bishop – '

'Yes, my lord?'

'I hope you and I never fall out.'

'As do I,' Henry agreed. 'Though rather more for your sake than for mine.'

*

So it stood, while the rumours were conceived and nurtured and brought to life. They were then circulated by tongue and letter, and the first disaffected barons emerged from their strongholds. The king's Easter court at Westminster was attended by the majority of those who had deserted his coronation feast, and he welcomed the contrite warlords with open arms. His brother's scheme was working beautifully. Before long the family would be reunited, standing shoulder to shoulder against their common enemy, the avaricious Angevins.

*

At Wallingford, the news took Brien by surprise. He had adopted Alyse's suggestion and sent Constable Varan to test the wind at Westminster. But he had not expected it to blow so warm for his penitent friends, or so cold for those who still held to their vows.

When the massive, flat-nosed Saxon had growled out his report, delivered on the battlements of the keep, Brien said, 'You are quite sure about this? They have all been pardoned, all those who went back to the king?'

Varan was no politician, and he did not enjoy playing a role for which he was unsuited. He remained steadfast in his loyalty to Brien and Alyse, and that, for him, was where it began and ended. All this talk of broken vows and reversed decisions was for creatures of the court. But he had been asked a direct question, so he said, 'Yes, my lord, I'm sure. They have all been confirmed in their lands. Whatever they held under King Henry, they now hold under Stephen. And in some cases they've had their grants increased. Miles of Hereford – '

Brien brought his fist crashing down on the crenellated wall. 'That's what carries it beyond belief! A man like him! He was the first to follow me from the hall and, in the short time we were together, he made it clear he would *never* acknowledge Stephen. God see us, we are a sorry bunch!'

He stood in silence for a moment, his hands pressed flat on the sloping merlons. The castle was laid out beneath him, the horseshoe-shaped walls curving towards the river. He looked down into the outer bailey, where Edgiva's sergeant-lover was putting his sweating, cursing men through their paces. They stood in two lines, each man facing an opponent, the ground between them littered with quarter-staves, horse-collars, lengths of timber, branding-irons, anything that a man might use to defend himself in the event of a surprise attack. And that was the object of the exercise, to snatch and strike when the enemy had invaded the castle and the arrows were expended and the daggers snapped.

On his command, the twin rows hurled themselves forward, reared back, armed with whatever they could find, then set to as they'd been taught; swing and parry, jab and block, go down moaning, then rise up and strike when the adversary relaxes. It was a bloody and brutal game, but it was necessary if the castle was to be defended foot by foot, and the invader made to pay for his aggression.

Brien grunted, satisfied with their efforts. His gaze shifted briefly to the river wall and the gate-tower. Then he raised his eyes until he could see beyond the Thames, beyond the forest, in his imagination beyond the Chiltern Hills to Westminster and through one of the arched windows and along the high table to where Stephen sat, smiling at his prodigal barons.

Behind him, Varan growled, 'Some of them are still with you, Lord Fitz Count. Robert of Gloucester hasn't attended court since he came over from Lisieux. And Baldwin de Redvers keeps away.' In a clumsy effort to cheer his master, he added, 'That's just two I know of. Likely there's more.'

Brien turned from the parapet. He gave a sigh and, without a trace of mockery, echoed, 'Yes, my well-meant liar, likely there's more.'

'There is a final thing,' Varan said. 'I have no proof of it, but I heard talk of the court moving to Oxford. That would bring Stephen within a few miles of us. And we know the country.'

'Christ,' Brien exclaimed, 'I hope I'm not reading your

thoughts. We will offer him no violence. I want him off the throne, yes, but it must be a voluntary descent. We'll defend what is our own, but we won't kill kings, however they get their crown.'

Varan gazed impassively at him. There might have been the hint of a shrug. 'If there's any truth in the rumours, he'll reach Oxford within the week.'

Brien nodded. 'Not before time. It would be shaming to run short of money even before the enemy arrives.' He turned away again and let his gaze roam over the ploughed fields and the stretches of grazing land and the twists and turns of the river as it meandered down from Oxford. The spring sunshine warmed his back, and had already darkened his wrists and forearms. It was a fine place to be, Wallingford-on-the-Thames, and he had no wish to be driven from it, or have it confiscated by royal decree. Nor did he wish to prolong his quarrel with Stephen, or inflict upon Alyse the disciplines and restrictions of their present way of life. It would be good to push open the gates and let fresh air blow through the barred and shuttered castle. And it would be good to ride out and assure the towns-folk of Wallingford that the quarrel was over; Stephen loved his friend again, and Fitz Count acknowledged his king. It would be good, but it would not be the truth, not yet. In a week, perhaps, with the help of commonsense and angels.

*

It was said that one would know him anywhere by his pro-minent jaw, and that, if he turned too abruptly, he risked flooring the man at his side. It was a humorous exaggeration, but no more than that, for the traveller had just completed a one-hundred mile journey through southern England without once being recognised. True, he had travelled *incognito*, dressed in a hooded cloak and plain tunic, and had driven a light, wicker-sided wagon, for all the world like a common merchant returning from market. But he had done nothing to disguise his face. He was who he was and, if he had passed unnoticed, it was by taking such an unlikely part, not by wrapping his jaw in a scarf.

66

Even so, he was pleased to have reached the river and the castle without incident. He reined-in beneath the gate, then dismounted, massaging his thighs and buttocks. The wall-guards had watched him from the moment he had turned out of town, and they had alerted the men on the gate. Now one of the garrison called down, 'What's your business here?' and the visitor took two folded letters from his purse, chose one and held it up, as though the guard could reach the fifteen feet between them.

'I have a message for Lord Fitz Count. He'll want it.' With a brief, tired smile he added, 'It's safe to open the gates. The cart's empty, as you can see, and there's no army crouched beneath.' He had said much the same thing a dozen times before and knew it would arouse no response.

The guard said, 'Wait there,' and after a moment another man emerged through a small Judas gate. He took the pro-ferred letter, unimaginatively echoed, 'Wait there,' and went back inside, closing the gate behind him. The visitor yawned and stretched, then gazed at the broad, slow-moving river. Well, he thought, of all of them, Fitz Count has the prettiest place.

*

Brien opened the letter, read it, then frowned at the guard. 'A merchant, did he say?'

'He didn't say, my lord, but he's dressed like one, and he drives a *bronette*. What else would he be?'

'Nothing,' Brien lied. 'Very well. Bring him in, and find a place for his cart. And treat him well – you'll know why soon enough.'

The guard nodded, wishing he could know now, then went to fetch the drover. He felt foolish, ushering the man into the castle, and he knew by the expressions on the faces of the other guards that he looked damn foolish. One of them called down from the wall, 'What is he, Ernard, made of glass, or are you after a job in his business?'

'Shut your mouth,' Ernard snarled, torn between giving the merchant a shove and gesturing towards the inner bailey. His charge murmured, 'Don't let them annoy you, soldier. Behave with me, and you'll have them babbling apologies.' It was a strange thing for a one-horse traveller to say, but it matched Lord Brien's warning, and Ernard decided to play it out. 'This way,' he muttered, and then, too quietly for his comrades to hear, 'master.'

They went into the inner courtyard and found Fitz Count there, waiting for them. The merchant looked at him, saw what he was about to do and said, 'No, Wallingford, it will keep. This man of yours has been the model of hospitality. Now dismiss him.'

Ernard blinked as Brien said, 'Of course. Go back to your post.' The soldier retreated, astonished that Lord Fitz Count could allow himself to be cowed by a common merchant. It had looked for an instant as though he was going to *kneel* to the caller. Hell's smoke, who *was* this man?

He saw Brien watching him, and hurried back to the gate. His companions asked, 'Did he break on the way? You should have cradled him in your arms, if he was so fragile. Aah, don't fret, Ernard, he'll take you into the business. It must be thriving, one spavined horse and an empty *bronette*!'

Ernard swung his head left and right and swore vilely into the cloud of laughter.

*

In the inner bailey, the long-jawed visitor motioned Brien ahead, then followed him across the drawbridge and into the keep. Sunlight gave way to the flare of torches, and both men paused, waiting for their eyes to become accustomed to the gloom. The single shaft of light from the entranceway bisected the ground-floor chamber, and after a while the traveller saw his surroundings. As with most of the dozen places he had visited, he was in the main hall.

Brien took the letter from his belt, glanced at it as though for confirmation, then asked, 'Shall I make us private in here?'

'It would be better, though I hope to meet Lady Alyse before I go.'

'You shall, sire, whenever you wish.' He closed the outer

door, slid the bar in place, then repeated the procedure with the single inner door. That done, he shouted down to the cellar, heard nothing, but lowered the trap-door for good measure. Everyone who was now in the keep would have to remain there, imprisoned on one of the upper floors, or shut in with the siege stores. He came back to the centre of the hall, knelt quickly and said, 'My Lord of Gloucester, I heard you were in the country, but I was unable to find you.'

'Well, I'm found now,' Robert said. 'Are you still my man, Brien Fitz Count?'

'I am, sire, as ever. I belong to you and your sister. Whatever has changed here, in this country, nothing has changed in my heart.'

'Nor had my expectations,' Robert smiled. 'Get to your feet, Greylock. Matilda has instructed me to embrace you for her, and I share her sentiments.' The two men wrapped their arms around each other and kissed and stood away, their eyes wet with tears. Men who could not weep for rage or joy were to be pitied, as were those who had been denied the gift of laughter. Occasionally, one came across a knight or nobleman who consciously withheld his tears, and such a man was viewed with suspicion. What other natural outlets might he have dammed? Might he not, for instance, still his tongue when it should be moving, or keep his purse closed when it should be stretched wide through generosity? And in battle, might he not sit tight instead of striking out at his enemies? No, there was not much to be said in favour of walled-up tears and a sawn-off laugh.

Matilda's brother untied the leather thong that fastened his merchant's cloak and tossed the garment on a chair. Brien brought a flask of wine and two stone mugs from an alcove in the wall, then manhandled another of the heavy box chairs so that they could sit facing each other, with a corner of the table between them. Robert did not wait to be served, but poured the wine, passed a mug to Brien, then raised his own in salute. 'I'd have come to you before this,' he said, 'but the geography of the country is against you.'

'Where *have* you been, Lord Robert?'

'Where have I not? Your friends, or should I say Matilda's

supporters, are widely-spaced throughout England. I've been calling on them, one by one.'

'Then you've heard of the defections back to Stephen.'

'I should hope so,' Robert smiled wearily. 'I contrived them.'

Brien lowered his mug, then brushed a dribble of wine from his chin. 'You? *You* sent them back?'

'Don't look so grim. I may be dressed to mislead, but as you said, nothing has changed in my heart. Sit back awhile and listen. You would probably obey me without question, but I have a greater regard for your mind. Also, Matilda would make my life a misery if she thought I'd bullied you into it.'

'She is well, I hope.'

'Well enough, for someone who has been robbed of their throne. By the way, I have a reward for you, if you'll hear me out.' He took the second letter from his purse, allowed Brien to see that it was from the empress, then put it away again. 'As I told you, the geography prevented my bringing it to you sooner. Anyway, let me say my piece.'

Robert of Gloucester gave some thought to what he would tell Fitz Count. Taking his own advice, he sat back in his chair and said, 'You and I have been close for many years, Greylock, but I wonder if you have ever assessed the extent of my holdings.' He held up a hand. 'It's not a guessing game; I'll answer my own question. I am, as you know, Earl of Gloucester, a position I've held for fifteen years or more. I also hold the honour of Torigny in Normandy, the lordship of Glamorgan in Wales – and so Cardiff Castle – and, in this country, Dover, Canterbury and Bristol, among others. Put another way, I am an extremely rich and powerful man, on a level with the king and his brother Henry. I have earned what I own, and I have no wish to lose it. Nor, I imagine, are you anxious to lose Wallingford.'

'If I were,' Brien said, 'I would not have spent every penny I possess on its defence.'

Robert came forward in his chair, his feet slamming the floor. 'Don't grow impatient with me,' he snapped. 'I am not listing my properties for fun. I am telling you that I have much to lose, and that you risk losing everything.' He glared at

Brien for a moment, then cradled his long jaw and sighed, 'Forgive me. I know the straits you're in. Time will take care of that. All I am saying is – may I help myself to some wine?'

The change of direction caught Brien by surprise. He reached forward and filled Robert's mug, then said, 'Please continue, my lord. I'm more receptive than I seem.'

Robert nodded. 'I want you to go back,' he said. 'I want you to make your peace with Stephen, and to accept what he tells you as the truth. Well, no, not quite that. Rather, to convince him that you accept it.'

'What does he say?'

'Oh, that he guards the throne for Matilda, but that she is planning to invade Normandy and squeeze us dry with some ownership tax or other. I don't know the details; that's the beauty of rumours, they are so imprecise. Anyway, it's all a product of Bishop Henry's fertile mind. It is supposed to incense us against her, and draw us closer to our king.'

'Yes,' Brien murmured, 'I have heard the talk.'

'And dismissed it, no doubt. Well, don't. At least, not at court. Pretend to accept it. Stephen is so eager to reclaim you, he will not question your authority. In fact, tell him you have grown to distrust my sister, and me too, for all I care.'

'And if I do not?'

Robert had just put the mug to his lips, and his laugh sprayed wine across the floor. 'Word for word,' he spluttered. 'You all ask the same question.'

'It seems reasonable to ask it, when we are in a state of undeclared war with Stephen.'

'Yes,' Robert allowed, 'it is reasonable. And so is my answer. If you do not go back to him, he will starve you into submission. If I come out against him, he will lay siege to my castles, garrison them with his own men, confiscate what remains of my lands, reduce me to nothing. You see, Greylock, your actions are beyond reproach; they are gallant, loyal to Matilda, immediate and whole-hearted. Quite a mouthful. But they are also dangerously premature. With the greatest respect, you are not in a position to upset the throne. Not yet. Not when you have so few on your side. But – and this is important

– you *are* in a position to jeopardise any future landings, and to rob your leader of his strongholds. I mean, of course, myself.' He drank again, this time taking the wine to his stomach.

When his mouth was empty, he continued, 'Stephen's seizure of the throne took us unawares, I admit it. I was in the Forest of Lyons, holding my father's hand. I had no inkling that Stephen would do what he did, nor that he would meet with a favourable response in London. Consequently, we need time to adjust.'

'How much time?'

'A little. A few months. Enough, anyway, to land in force and achieve our aims. I want you ready to greet us and declare for us. I certainly do not want you chained up in some dank prison, a convicted traitor without a charcoal-burner's hut to your name. That is not what your former – what Matilda expects of you.' He studied his cheap, mud-caked boots, then looked directly at Brien. 'Have I said enough?'

'You want me to kiss Stephen's hand,' Brien said bitterly. 'You have said enough, yes, Lord Robert, but you have asked a great deal more.'

'Have I?' Robert queried. 'Is it more than what you do now? You sit here, your last penny spent, waiting for an attack that will never come. He won't fight you, don't you see that? He'll starve you out, and Wallingford, a very pretty place, may I say, will fall without your ever having seen the enemy. Kiss his hand? Kiss his foot, what does it matter, when it is a strategy of war?' He finished his wine, stood the mug on the table and passed over the letter. 'This may give you heart,' he murmured. 'But if you can leave it unread for a while, perhaps I could meet your lady.'

Brien took the letter, turned it over in his hands, then glanced up and asked, 'Something you said just now. Something you didn't finish. You said of Matilda that she was my former – what?'

'The only one of you I haven't visited,' Robert said. 'Baldwin de Redvers. Still ensconsed at Exeter. I really am pressed for time.'

Brien felt the breath shudder into his body as he slid the

letter inside his tunic and pushed himself from the chair. 'I'll fetch Lady Alyse. She'll be glad to see you.'

'And I her,' Robert enthused. 'It's been a long time.'

*

It was more of a note than a letter.

'To Brien Fitz Count, Lord of Wallingford, the most affectionate greetings and the most gentle embrace, from Matilda, his friend.

'I have sent my other champion, Robert of Gloucester, to encourage you and prepare you for my arrival. He has carried letters to one or two of my loyal supporters, but none so warm as this. My cousin's theft has angered and surprised me, but whatever his tricks, I know you remain constant, as do I.

'You are well matched with your young wife Alyse, of whom I have heard the kindest reports. But in your happiness, I know you will not forget Matilda, who was once Empress of Germany, who should now be Queen of England, and who is forever your close companion.

'Keep watch for us, Greylock. The sails are already run up, and we wait only for the tide.

'I shall not end this greeting, but sign as I started.'

It was a sure way to get him to re-read it.

Unwilling to destroy the missive – she might one day ask him if it was still in his possession – Brien hid it among his administrative papers.

Two days later, in all innocence, whilst checking to see how much milled flour they had ordered, and therefore to assess how much they were consuming by the week, Alyse sorted through the records and found the letter. Less innocently she allowed the letter to unfold, allowed herself to walk around the table until the words faced her, then allowed herself to read it.

Brien interpreted her silent anguish and loss of appetite as symptoms of her long-term restriction in the castle. It helped convince him to put Robert's advice into practice.

*

In the second week of April, Brien Fitz Count attended King Stephen's court at Oxford. Stephen found his lifelong companion somewhat withdrawn, and he did not risk further outbursts by demanding a public display of homage. He told Brien what Henry had primed him to say, and Brien followed Robert's suggestions and pretended to accept the king's word.

The wounds closed amid sounds of merriment, but the scars remained.

CHAPTER 5

AFTER HE SPEAKS...
March 1137 – June 1138

HENRY, Bishop of Winchester, was in love, no question of it. The relationship did not merit congratulations, and the object of his affections remained sublimely indifferent to his feelings. But there he was, every day, wrapped in his robes of office, balanced on a rickety platform and coo-cooing at his *inamorata* as she strutted about beneath his adoring gaze.

The platform was necessary, for the ostrich hen stood seven feet high and was contained within a fenced field.

On each visit Henry was accompanied by a thin, dark-skinned man named Zengi, and the bishop's servants were further intrigued by the way Henry deferred to his companion. Whatever the man said was agreed with and acted upon, no matter what cost or effort was involved.

An Egyptian by birth, Zengi had spent most of his life in Nubia, in the desert lands between the Nile and the eastern shore of the Red Sea. He was an accomplished linguist, a master boat-builder, and a respected authority on the wildlife of Arabia. It was in this last capacity, and because of the princely fee he had been offered, that he had accompanied his latest acquisitions to England and Henry's menagerie at Winchester. His charges had been caught to order; four caracal lynxes, a nest of beautifully-marked, yet deadly-poisonous snakes, and a pair of Arabian ostriches, Henry's pride and joy.

However, the huge, scarlet-skinned male ostrich had not yet paid much attention to its mate. Give them time, Zengi had said. They do not come together until the spring, and they might not yet realise that it *is* spring in this damp country. Be patient and, if Allah wills it, you will get your egg.

The Egyptian had already corrected a number of widely-held misconceptions concerning the clumsy, flightless birds.

They are not helpless, he said. They can out-run a hound over a short distance and, although they would rather flee than fight, they will strike out with their feet if they are cornered. And they do not hide their heads in the sand, imagining that because they cannot see, they are invisible. Their plumage is conceal-ment enough, so they merely crouch down and lay their long necks on the ground, and thus change their shape.

Henry sponged-up these lectures, nodding, remembering what he could, dictating the more difficult lessons to his clerks. He intended to write a book on the subject, a Bestiary, for the enlightenment of the world. He would, of course, make some mention of Zengi, probably at the end.

In the field the ostriches preened and strutted. Henry gazed benignly at them, then asked, 'In your country, do you still use them to find precious gems?'

Zengi laughed quietly. He did not wish to seem impolite, but was there no end to the fables that surrounded these un-graceful birds? What had Bishop *Enefri* in mind this time? Did he imagine they had the sense to pick emeralds from the earth, or sort rubies by size and colour?

'You have been misled, I think. These birds, and many others, are attracted to anything bright or colourful. They swallow stones, crystal, they would swallow one of your rings if you threw it to them.'

'Then there is no truth – '

'I fear not. If it were true, we would be foolish to part with such prized diviners.'

Make a note, Henry thought. The Arabian ostrich is not the jewel-mine ignorant people suppose.

He would have been content to stand all day in the spring sunshine, watching the black-and-white male, and the grey-brown hen, studying his birds and learning from his expensive expert. But duty called, and he turned reluctantly from the fence. Under his breath he murmured, 'Tomorrow. I'll visit you tomorrow.' Then he clambered down the uneven steps and became once again a power in the land.

*

So far, March had been a good month for Bishop Henry. His menagerie was thriving, and the Angevins had turned one of his political rumours into reality. One year ago, he remembered, he had sat with brother Stephen in the Great Hall at Westminster, and dreamed up ways of reclaiming the king's disaffected barons. They had decided – well, Henry had decided, while Stephen agreed – to put it about that Matilda planned to invade Normandy. Now, it seemed, truth was about to overtake invention, for they had recently heard that Matilda and her despicable husband were inciting unrest within the duchy. Good. The rebellion could not have been better timed. Stephen would raise an army and go there and crush the Angevin menace once and for all. Matilda and Geoffrey were both traitors now, for they had taken up arms against their duly-elected sovereign. They were fast losing the sympathy of the barons and, when the common people heard what they were about, they would clamour for a place in Stephen's army. Yes, Henry acknowledged, one way and another it promised to be a fruitful spring.

*

In the years before he became king, Stephen of Blois had earned himself a reputation for generosity, gallantry and easy good humour. He had been a ladies' man, charming and attentive, though not exclusively an indoor creature. He had proved himself in battle, and had been thought of as a convivial young baron, liked by men and loved by women.

He should, perhaps, have settled for that, for neither his virtues, nor his vices, had helped lighten the weight of the crown.

He was still casual in his manner, but it was now called indolence, and judged unbecoming. He was still charming to his friends, but the barons interpreted it as favouritism, and used that most damning word – soft. He was a soft king, a contradiction in terms, a soft stone on which England rocked precariously. His generosity was valueless, for he was not uniformly benevolent. He gave to one and withheld from another, and promptly lost the respect of both.

He had been king for two years and three months now, and in that time his greatest flaw showed up clearly. Had he been a building, someone remarked, he would have collapsed before now, for there was a weakness in the structure, and it became more apparent every day.

Definitions varied, for viewpoints varied, but they were brought together by a wisely anonymous poet who wrote:

> Before the sword is drawn, he cuts;
> Before the wine is poured, he drinks;
> Before the food is served, he eats;
> – After he speaks, he thinks.
> Did he shout, within the womb,
> 'I'm born! I'm born! I must have room'?
> Before the girth is tied, he mounts;
> Before the ship leaves port, he sails;
> Before the jest is made, he laughs;
> – After he acts, he wails.
> Will he cry within the tomb,
> 'I am not dead! *You* are too soon'?

This simple and widely-quoted view of King Stephen contained one line with which the barons were in whole-hearted agreement. Their monarch *did* speak first, then ruminate afterwards, and often with regrettable results. His insistence that Fitz Count and the others pay homage to him, his over-generous settlement on King David of Scotland, these and similar pronouncements all went to illustrate Stephen's impulsive behaviour. Give or take, bestow or deny, threaten or ignore, he cast aside tradition and precedence, in favour of spontaneous action. In short, in favour of favour.

It was a dangerous policy, for those he advanced were envied by their friends, whilst those he rejected plunged into the muttering undercurrent of disaffection.

He had brother Henry to advise him and, so long as he followed the advice, he came to no real harm. But when the muzzle was off, when he was allowed to act on his own initiative, there was no telling what he would do. His visit to Normandy was a perfect example of his impetuousness, and it

marked the third serious error of his reign. But he did not see
it at the time, and why would he, when, as the insolent poet
might have written, he ran with his eyes closed, then opened
them to see where he was?

He was accompanied by Matilda's brother, Robert of
Gloucester, who had feigned loyalty and was awaiting his
opportunity to strike. Stephen, true to his nature, furnished
that opportunity.

*

They crouched in the undergrowth most of the morning,
glancing at the lookouts, then turning away to fish dice from
their purses and roll the ivory cubes on the nearest clear patch
of ground. They had been told what to do, and were prepared
to go through with it, but for Christ's sake, how much longer?

They slapped at mosquitoes, crushed flies, pounded insects
into the soil. They lost or won money, cursed each other,
shielded their heads from the sun, drank wine and water,
yawned with boredom. It wouldn't happen; he wouldn't come.
Another day spent earning a pittance and gambling away a
fortune. Aah, get on with it. Come if you're coming. Let's get
to the killing, or go home. They threw the dice again, argued
about the way it fell, squeezed the last of their wine from the
skins, slapped angrily at the buzzing insects, stabbed the ground
with their daggers. Men stood up to urinate, then got to their
knees as their sergeants shouted them down. Christ! What a
day! What an endless, shaft-rotting –

The horsemen came along the road at full gallop. The lookouts were taken by surprise, rose up in their excitement, saw
that they had been spotted, and roared the alarm. 'They're
here! Block their way! Bar the way! Jesus, get to your feet
before they go through!'

The long-jawed Robert of Gloucester slammed his visor in
place, couched his lance in the crook of his left arm – no mean
feat – and drew his sword with his right. He did not yet know
the identity of the ambushers, nor did he care. When you are
attacked, don't ask names. Just take it for what it is, an
attempt on your life, and fight like Satan's maddest dog.

The ambushers scrambled to their feet, stumbled forward, loosed off arrows, hurled their spears. The members of the mounted column thundered along the narrow road, their shields raised, their lances held tip down, so they could take a man through the throat, or through the chest. There was a brief moment of chaos, in which ambushers and horsemen died, and then the bulk of the riders had charged through the unready trap and were riding on, their minds piecing together the identity of their assailants. Behind them, men staggered into the bushes, or flopped down in bloody despair. As though it would help, some screamed at the vanishing horsemen, whilst others went through their friends' possessions, hoping to regain what they'd lost at dice. The ambush had been a complete failure, but one did not necessarily have to come out of it without profit.

Robert had lost his lance in the engagement and was surprised to see that his left arm was still crooked. He straightened it, took a count of the dead and wounded, then snarled, 'Whose idea was that?'

A number of his fellow knights told him what they had seen, and he sent his visor crashing back against the crest of his helmet. 'Right. As I thought. And in keeping.' He rode on in silence, then suddenly lifted his head and roared at the summer sky. 'That has never been tried on me before! And by God, it will never be tried again! He has given me what I need . . .' He shook so violently that two of his retinue urged their horses close and held him by the arms. They did not know what frightened them more, the unexpectedness of the ambush or Robert's quivering fury. They heard him say, 'Best count yourselves with me, messires, for if you are not with me I shall surely see you buried . . .' They nodded to show they were very definitely with him.

*

Had Henry been there to guide him, Stephen might have denied all knowledge of the ambush. But Henry was with his ostriches, on the other side of the channel.

Even so, there was no proof that the incompetent assassins

were in the king's pay. Robert's knights had told him they *thought* they had recognised a face here and there, and they *thought* they had heard someone shout 'Kill the Angevin-lover!' But it was not conclusive, not until Robert strode into the court at Lisieux and shouldered his way across the crowded chamber. The mass of barons, there to discuss an imminent advance against the Angevins, sensed trouble and moved back. A few of them thought of disarming Robert before he came within swordswing of King Stephen, but no one cared to try. If he went for his sword, well, then, maybe.

The Earl of Gloucester did not trouble to bow – how do you salute your would-be murderer? – but launched into a brief account of the ambush, then demanded, 'Was it done on your say-so, or will you pretend it's fresh news?'

In fact, Stephen had received a private report of the incident a few hours earlier, but without Henry to shore up his defences, he had not prepared a riposte. So, to the astonishment of the assembly, he fidgeted under Robert's murderous gaze and confessed to his part in it.

'I heard such things about you, Gloucester. I was told you were only keeping me company in the hopes of making contact with Matilda, and that you would then go over to her.'

'So you thought you would lay for me, is that it, King?'

'It was a passing remark. I did not know it would be enacted.'

'You just said, "I wish somebody would rid me of my cousin's brother, the Angevin lover," something like that?'

'I forget. I swear to you, it was spoken and forgotten.' In an attempt to justify himself, he hurried, 'You worry me, Gloucester. You prowl at my side, saying nothing, refusing to take the field against Matilda and Geoffrey, and all the while I know you are her brother, her greatest champion!'

'I see. So, if I say nothing, you mark it as treason, whereas, when you announce that you wish me dead, it is not to be taken seriously. Well, well, it bodes ill for all the others who do *not* speak against you. Silence presages treason, does it? And a threat is not a threat. Look about you, King. Study these silent nobles. Commit their names and faces to your memory, for surely they are all traitors, condemned out of their own un-moving mouths.'

Stephen glanced round, treated his barons to a faltering smile of reassurance, then said, 'I am not suspicious of *them*. It's *you* I mistrust.'

'Ah. Then my life is still in danger. It would be prudent to withdraw from the court – '

'I did not say – '

' – and take my troops with me. Thank God I command such a large force. It seems I shall need them.'

'There is no call for that. I regret what happened. It was an unfortunate mistake.'

'The two knights who died in the ambush would agree with you, I'm sure.' Timing his appeal well, Robert turned his back on the king and paced around the perimeter of a small, imaginary circle. In this way, he faced his peers and belittled Stephen's sideways glance.

'It is a dangerous world we are in, messires. If our king mistrusts us, he will mouth his fears, and we will be struck down on some quiet country road. Of course, that would not be his intention, and he would mourn the tragedy. An unfortunate mistake. A passing remark. I regret it happened.

'Well, *I* regret it, as much as he, for I am no wooden head, to be tilted at whenever he chooses. I advise you to learn from this *unfortunate* incident. Tell him you love him every hour of the day, lest your silence be construed as treason. Or do what I shall do and retire to the safety of your own lands. Being around our king is altogether too chancy a pastime.' He nodded once, then strode out, careful to let no one see his smile, compounded of contempt and satisfaction. As he had roared after the ambush, Stephen had given him what he needed. The king had confessed to the crime of attempted murder. It would frighten some of the barons into making protestations of loyalty, but it would drive others from the court. And it gave Robert the perfect excuse to renounce his allegiance and side openly with his sister. She would be delighted, for Robert would bring half the nobility of England under her banner. Among them, Brien Fitz Count.

*

The campaign in Normandy dragged on until November. Stephen met and made his peace with his elder brother Theobald, the man who had been king-for-a-day at Lisieux. Geoffrey of Anjou continued to harrass the southern borders of the duchy, but before Stephen could draw him into battle, internal strife erupted within the English ranks. The king's regular Norman contingents came to blows with a large force of Flemish mercenaries, hired for the campaign, while the Norman barons complained that Stephen was showing excessive favouritism towards the mercenary leader, William of Ypres. These squabbles, so incessant among the Normans, mired down the entire army, and the advance never materialised.

Eventually, the king met his Angevin adversary, and they agreed on a three-year truce. But again, as with King David of Scotland, Stephen allowed himself to be out-manœuvred. Instead of threatening Geoffrey with a massive invasion of Anjou, should the truce be broken, the king came away from the conference chamber poorer by two thousand silver marks, payable annually, in advance.

He turned snarling on the baron who suggested that he was financing the enemy.

*

In England, the news of Earl Robert's imminent defection sent the barons to re-stocking their cellars and checking their defences. They had done this before, some of them, and it was Robert himself who had counselled patience. But now it was different. Now, they knew, they were nearing the brink of war. When Robert made public his renunciation – his *diffidatio* – they would be expected to declare, either for Matilda or Stephen. Whichever, the country would be torn apart.

*

None were more alert to the dangers than the occupants of Wallingford, yet few were so ill-prepared. It was a question of money, or rather the lack of it, for Brien and Alyse had, to use their own term, air in their purses.

Last year they had maintained the castle in a state of readiness for four months, awaiting the attack that never came. In that time they had emptied their coffers, and proved the accuracy of Bishop Henry's forecast. It *was* an expensive business, waiting for war.

And now they were expected to do it again, to replenish the larders, lay in stocks of arrows, javelins, crossbow quarrels, bow-strings, coarse woollen blankets, vinegar to douse any fires that might be started, wood to shore up weakened sections of the wall, horses that could be ridden in a counter-attack, then eaten when the salted meat was finished. There were a hundred other things to be bought and paid for, all essential ingredients of the life and death stew.

There were men to be hired.

As one of King Stephen's tenants-in-chief, Brien was required to furnish his sovereign with fourteen knights for a set period each year. In time of peace they would garrison one of the royal castles, or escort senior court officials about the country. In time of war they would fight.

But these self-same knights were also loyal to their suzerain, Lord Fitz Count. Last year the majority of them had sided with Brien. But last year he had been able to pay them. He wondered how many of the fourteen would again risk their lives and lands, and this time spend their own money doing it.

There were also archers and foot-soldiers to be enlisted, and such men were untroubled by divided loyalties. They fought for money, coin on the barrelhead, not for the love of a lord and his lady.

But there was no money, and unless some was found there would be no fight.

*

Lady Alyse set about the problem in her own way . . .

Several times she had suggested to Brien that he write to

Empress Matilda and explain the situation. 'Tell her how it is with us. Let her know what you're doing for her. If she thinks so highly of you, she's bound to send help. If it were not for her – '

'She is not bound to do anything,' Brien said. 'She did not ask me to show defiance last year. That was my decision. Besides, she is embroiled in Normandy. She's probably as much in need of money as we are. We're defending one castle, whilst she is financing an entire campaign.'

'Well, it won't do her much good,' Alyse responded sharply, 'not if her supporters in England are under lock and key. She needs Wallingford, and she needs you, and she should pay for it.'

Brien shook his head. 'We'll find other ways. Robert of Gloucester might help us, or Miles of Hereford, they're both rich enough. But not Matilda. I will not ask her for money.'

Why not, Alyse thought; are you too proud, or do you fear rejection? I wonder if that woman loves you as much as you think. And you must also wonder it, or you would put it to the test. Embroiled in Normandy? No, dearest, I believe the real conflict is in your heart.

She tried again next day, and a few days later, and a week after that. Each time, Brien's refusal came more quickly, more irritably. He sensed that his wife's repeated suggestion was not merely a request for help. She was growing openly jealous of the unseen Matilda. It had become a trial of strength between them. Having at one time tried to dismiss Matilda from her thoughts, Alyse was now seeking a direct confrontation. Well, he would not encourage it. And he would not write any begging letters.

His assessment was only partially correct. Alyse had repeated her request because she did, indeed, seek a confrontation with Matilda. But it was not as Brien imagined. It was simply that the young chatelaine had already decided on a course of action, and wished to learn as much as possible about the empress. It was necessary, she believed, since she, herself, would write the begging letter.

It was composed in private. The maidservant, Edgiva, was

dismissed from the solar and, when Alyse had finished with the writing materials, she replaced them exactly as before. If the letter went unanswered, Brien need never know it had been written. If there was a reply – She shrugged. She would face the consequences of that when it came.

It was the most difficult letter she had ever written. Matilda was clearly an extraordinary woman, gifted with beauty, presence, and an astonishing power over men. Over Brien, yes, but not only him. Over most men of consequence. The air was full of stories of Matilda-and-this-one, Matilda-and-that-one. They were not always stories of love, but they invariably told of her power, of the spell with which she bound her admirers.

So jealousy combined with awe, and possessiveness with an appeal for help. Alyse dared not make demands of Matilda, yet neither could she bring herself to plead. If the empress loved Brien as much as he believed, she would surely send men and money and materials. If not, it would confirm Alyse's suspicions; there was no tide of affection, merely a one-way current, flowing from Wallingford-on-the-Thames to Anjou.

She smoothed the dark hair from her face, dipped the quill pen in the small pot of squids' ink, and wrote:

'To the Empress Matilda, Countess of Anjou, from Alyse, Lady of Wallingford, greetings.

'You will have heard from your brother, Earl Robert of Gloucester, how, last year, Brien Fitz Count and several others loyal to your cause, armed their castles against King Stephen. At Earl Robert's command, these nobles feigned a reconciliation with the king, and thus avoided a too-early conflict. Now, however, with the approach of winter, we hear of the ambush that was laid for your brother in Normandy, and once more take up arms on your behalf.'

Alyse was about to start the next line with the words 'Lord Brien', but changed her mind at the last instant and, with a slight smile of satisfaction, penned,

'My husband spent all he possessed on the last long defence, yet is now required to repeat his former actions. He will not approach you for help, claiming that you are as short of money as we. I cannot believe this is so, but rather that his pride will not allow him to seek help from the woman he so much admires.'

That last phrase made her tremble, and it was a while before she could continue. It was true, of course – he did so much admire her – but it was not an easy thing for a wife to admit. However, it had to be said. The natural jealousy had to be smothered, at least until the letter was sent. Dipping the quill each time she completed a word, she continued,

'You are, Empress, well aware of the strategic importance of Wallingford, and of the necessity of its survival. If it falls, King Stephen will dominate much of the Thames and control the eastern gateway to London. It would be a sad loss for both you and me if Brien Fitz Count was forced to abdicate from his position as your foremost supporter. Whatever help you can send will double in value under his leadership.'

With cold fabrication, Alyse ended,

'I pray that you and your husband, Count Geoffrey of Anjou, may meet with success in Normandy, as I am convinced you pray for your champion, Lord Fitz Count, and his lady.'

She sat back, and let the letter dry before reading it. She thought it at the same time too formal and too flowery, but she accepted that she would never be satisfied. She was Brien's wife, and she loved him, and for his sake she had communicated with the creature who haunted them both. She could do no more.

Alone in the solar, she put her hands to her face and wept quietly, so terrified was she of the soon-to-be-seen Matilda.

*

Constable Varan set about the problem in his own way . . .

The gentleman rider sat well back in his saddle, one arm dangling at his side, the other resting nonchalantly over the red leather pommel. He hummed as he rode, while his eyes darted eagerly from side to side, watching for peasants. He was an innocent young man, one of many who now inhabited King Stephen's court, and he was anxious to test his appearance on anyone he passed. He hoped he exuded the correct air of gentility; God knew, he had worked hard enough to perfect it. He reminded himself to smile in the abstracted manner of poets, and to practise the toss of the head that would set the peacock feather rippling along his birdsbill hat. From time to time he turned his head sharply to the side, and his long, Saxon-style hair swung around his shoulders.

... And remember to slap the gauntlets against your thigh ... lift the head ... twitch ... turn ... keep the back erect ... hum as you smile ... that's it, that's the way ... you are the noble son of a noble family ... you bear fashion on your back ...

Since King Stephen had come to the throne, court fashions had undergone a dramatic change. The young Normans no longer shaved their hair from the nape of the neck to the crown, but let it grow to their shoulders, then curled it with heated tongs. Shoes were drawn to a point, the toes stuffed with wool, then turned back into a scorpion's tail. Robes had been lengthened until they dragged on the ground, while some of the more modish courtiers effected a pigeon-toed walk, or mimicked the mincing carriage of their high-born ladies. It was the thing to seem effeminate and wear a slightly dazed expression.

Such excesses appalled the clergy, and they demanded to know where it would end. A few amused observers told them it would end when the young people became bored with it. Then it would probably be hair cropped to the skull, and lasciviously short tunics, and wooden shoes painted scarlet, and a revival of dice games that went on for a week. And when those fashions were exhausted, it would be something else, equally scandalous, equally harmless. But the clergy were not convinced, and continued to speak out against the degenerate nobles. Sodom and Gomorrah, they rumbled; plagues and pillars of salt.

Meanwhile, the young rider ran a hand along the bill of his pointed hat, and prepared for his entry into Dorchester. He had seen no one in the past hour, and he rather regretted having taken this quiet back road. On the other hand, it had allowed him to practise his twitch and turn.

His eyes ached from the constant sideways movement, so

he gazed directly ahead, anticipating the gasps of wonderment that would greet his appearance in town. In this way, he did not see the figure rise from the roadside ditch and pad along behind him.

But he heard the dried-out voice growl, 'Far enough for today, master,' and turned to see a massive, black-cloaked apparition, its face concealed by a crude black hood. The hood contained eye-holes fringed with frayed straw, and a third hole, midway between the nose and mouth. The man, if it was a man, for it could well have been a demon, held a coil of rope in one hand and a butcher's knife in the other. The young rider gaped at the monster, then gulped unfashionably.

'Down you get.'

Of course it wasn't a demon. Could demons speak? Yes. Yes, they could. They knew all the languages of the world. It was a demon. Oh, dear God, it's punishment for my vanity. God forgive me, I was only following the fashions.

'I'll sell them,' he blurted. 'I'll sell everything.'

'No. *I'll* sell them. Get down.'

He dismounted, nodded as the monster motioned with its knife, then unbuckled his sword-belt. The monster growled, 'What's your name, master?' and was told, 'Gilbert de Renton. I never killed a man in all my life. I've cheated at chess, I admit it, the other player was too wined to know what was happening, but I'm not – Why do you ask my name? Don't you know it?'

'I do now.'

Gilbert de Renton realised he had been had for a fool. Whatever the hood concealed, it was not the pig's snout and bat's ears of a demon, for demons knew everybody. They did not have to ask.

He drew himself erect, straightened his birdsbill and treated the monster to a toss of the head. The feathers rippled and the long hair swung. 'You no longer terrify me,' he said. 'You are nothing more than a brigand. What do you want, brigand, my horse, my clothes? Take them. I'll buy more.'

The monster nodded. 'No doubt. But first, your father will have to buy you. By the way, are you loyal to King Stephen?'

'I shall not deign to answer that. Even through your badly made eyelets you can see I bear the imprint of the court.'

'So I can, so I can. Right, place your hands behind you. And don't thwart me, beauty, or I'll cut you like pork.' He uncoiled the rope, waited for Gilbert to fold his gauntlets and tuck them neatly in his saddlebag, then tied his hands and directed them towards a narrow forest path. 'You should have had an escort,' he said, 'a beauty like you.'

Silently, Gilbert agreed with him. But how could a gentleman make the best impression, when he was hemmed in by a dozen sweaty riders?

They went on into the forest, Gilbert leading the way, the monster following with the caparisoned palfrey. The monster thought, £25 for the horse . . . £10 for the clothes and trappings . . . check the sword for a jewelled hilt . . . and for young Gilbert, £300? No, the de Rentons are a wealthy lot, we'll make it £400, and forget the belongings . . . Christ, Edgiva will murder me if she discovers I've cut up one of her market bags . . .

*

The maidservant set about the problem in her own way . . .

She arrived late for her regular riverside assignation with her sergeant-lover, allowed him to fondle her for a while, then twisted from his grasp and told him, 'No, it's my turn to ask a favour.'

'Anything,' he grunted, 'you know I'd do anything for you. Come here now, you wouldn't want to exhaust me before – ' He lunged at her, his expression playful, his hands in earnest. Edgiva side-stepped, then repeated, 'No. First the favour. Then we'll see who tires.' She walked to the riverbank and stood beneath one of the alder trees that screened their activities from the castle. The sergeant ducked under the low branches, sure that she was only enticing him into a more secluded spot. He moved beside her under the canopy, then grinned wolfishly as she picked up a heavy branch stump. So that was it; disarm me; the game of rape. Very well, anything to excite her, though it was not often she sought such stimulus.

He stepped forward, the would-be ravisher, and she said, 'I warned you,' and clouted him with the branch. A trickle of blood appeared below his ear. He gaped at her, felt shock give way to anger, then heard her snap, 'Don't press me. I'm not in the mood.' She hefted the branch in one hand, and with the other pointed at the ground. 'Sit down, Morcar. I'll stay on top for once. Here, hold this to your head.' She produced a clean rag from her sleeve, and the sergeant dabbed irritably at the wound, then threw aside the rag. All he could think of to say was, 'No girl ever beat me off before. Or wanted to.'

'I'm sure,' Edgiva said gently, 'but how else could I make you listen?' She needed him, not only in the grass, but in an official capacity, and decided to pour balm on his wounded pride. 'I know you,' she went on. 'When you are fired with passion nothing can stop you.'

'Short of being bludgeoned.'

'Quite.'

Her awareness of his irresistible ardour mollified him enough to ask, 'Well, what is this favour, for which I have to be knocked flat?'

She studied him for a moment, satisfied herself that he was not badly hurt, then answered his question with one of her own.

'Have you heard of Hercules?'

'No, what is it?'

'He was a warrior. Lady Alyse made me read a poem about him. My reading is coming on – well, never mind. He lived in Greece.'

'Where's that?'

'Somewhere between Italy and the Holy Land, I think; it doesn't matter. But reading about him gave me an idea.'

'To club me with a tree branch?'

'No, to discover the depth of your love for me.'

'What!'

'Why such surprise? That's not very gallant. You do love me, don't you, Morcar?'

'I hadn't given it – Yes, of course. Why else would I be here?'

'Not just because you lust for me?'

'Lust, love – Nonsense.' Love, he thought? What next? Marriage? He wiped sweat from his face and smiled wanly at the maidservant. 'Hercules,' he mouthed, 'what of him?'

Edgiva looked down at him and shook her head. She told herself, his thoughts are like a fish in a pool, there for all the world to see. He has no more love for me than for any girl he can straddle. But at least he has been faithful in his mounting. Perhaps they are the same; perhaps I should have said I'll test the keenness of his lust.

'Hercules,' she explained, 'he was set twelve labours, by some king or other. I don't know what his reward was, but each time you fulfil a task we'll be able to come here and, well, enjoy each other.'

'You mean, before we tumble any more, I have to – '

'Yes, sweet.'

'And what am I supposed to do, climb the wall of the keep, wrestle a bear, learn the lute, what?'

'Nothing so difficult,' she encouraged. 'Just visit each of Lord Fitz Count's vassal knights, or anyway their sergeants, and convince them to support Wallingford when the time comes.'

'All fourteen of them?'

'There are fourteen knights, yes, but we must also have their men and weapons. All the sergeants know you, Morcar. They respect you. They'll listen.' She sent the branch spinning into the river and sank down beside him. 'It's a quest,' she murmured, one hand climbing his thigh. 'And remember, the Greek gave up after twelve.'

*

The de Rentons had no choice but to pay. Young Gilbert was an idiot. He looked idiotic in his fashionable garb, and he sounded idiotic when he spoke with his affected lisp, or his high-pitched chirrup, or whatever was the week's favourite. But he was still Gilbert de Renton and, although the family could scarcely afford to keep him, they could not afford to lose him. People would talk. They would think it odd

that the wealthy de Rentons had refused to ransom their only
son.

So they delivered the sacks of coin to the appointed place,
and in time the hooded Varan collected them, then released
the young noble from his forest hideout.

'Go on, beauty, back to court. And next time, spend less
on feathered hats and more on guards.'

'If you were a man,' Gilbert reared, 'you'd remove that hood
and show yourself.'

'Be glad I don't,' Varan growled, 'or I'd have to poke out
your bright blue eyes.'

After that, Gilbert issued no more challenges, but worked
on the story he would tell his family. By the time he had reached
Westminster, he had been set upon by a twenty-strong band
of brigands, and the remarkable thing was that, although he
had killed three of them in the ensuing fight, none of his
captors had managed to inflict a single scratch.

His family listened to the fable and chewed their tongues, or
coughed, or gazed out of the window. There was so much they
wanted to tell pretty Gilbert, even through clenched teeth.

*

The weeks passed, and the year drained away. In November,
five knights pledged themselves to Brien Fitz Count, and
Edgiva and Morcar paid the same number of visits to the river.
In December, Constable Varan told his master that someone,
some unseen well-wisher, had left a sack of money at the gate.
He'd had it counted, and it came to exactly £400, enough to
finance a lengthy siege. With it was an unsigned note that read,
'For the future of Wallingford, and the safety of England.' In
that same month, six more knights promised themselves and
their men, and Alyse warned her maidservant that she'd catch
her death of cold if she haunted the damp riverbank.

There was no word from Matilda, although the messenger
had delivered the letter into the hands of one of the senior
Angevin captains.

The dawn of 1138, and Stephen had been king for three
years . . .

In early February he hurried north at the head of a large army to forestall another Scottish invasion. Speed was essential, for there was talk of union between the Scots and the disaffected magnate, Ranulf of Chester. But the punitive expedition was bogged down, its ranks riddled with turncoats. By April, the Scots were established south of the border, and England was swept by the long-awaited rumour – Robert of Gloucester was about to declare for Matilda.

In Wallingford and fifty similar strongholds, final preparations were made. It was learned who would stay with Stephen, who would side with Matilda. Heads swung between the Scottish border and Anjou. Ears were stretched in anticipation of the news. When, Robert, when?

The answer came in May. The Earl of Gloucester gave over his continental territories of Caen and Bayeux to his sister, and announced his formal *diffidatio*. He would no longer serve King Stephen, but would lead Matilda's forces across the Channel, invade England and reclaim the throne for his sister. Those who supported her should now declare themselves.

It was as though a tarred rope had been thrown across England, and one end set alight. Bristol, Canterbury and Dover declared for the Angevins. Then Shrewsbury and Hereford, Dorchester and Wallingford, Wareham and Dunster, Corfe and Castle Cary, these and a dozen more. Salisbury wavered, as did Cirencester and Trowbridge. Abergavenny and Cardiff went over, along with Gloucester, Stafford and Worcester. A pattern emerged. Cut the country down the middle, and the majority of castles and townships to the east proclaimed for Stephen, those to the west for Matilda. England had her civil war.

CHAPTER 6

A WRATH OF BISHOPS
August 1138 – September 1139

FOR some weeks now the king had suffered recurrent night-mares and had woken, flailing the bedclothes. His wife did what she could do to calm him, and tried to discover the nature of his dreams. But the terror that had stalked his sleep, and the shock of waking, had rendered Stephen inarticulate, and by the morning they had both forgotten his garbled explanations.

The royal pair took to sleeping within a square of angled torches, and this lessened the shock sufficiently for him to bring his nightmares into the light.

'It's a conspiracy,' he mumbled. 'Those who are closest to me are those who will strike me down.'

His queen, who bore the same name and year of birth as the empress, was a pale, delicate-looking woman, whose appear-ance totally belied her character. She lacked Stephen's spon-taneity and casual manner, and substituted a clear, logical mind and a remarkable firmness of purpose. Her husband was as fine a lover as any decent woman should want, but his excesses had to be curbed, in bed and out. He was not given to introspection, nor to questioning the motives that drove him to do this and that, and so he remained unaware that it was he who cried start and his queen who counselled stop.

The flaring torches had been her idea. She wanted to expunge his nightmares, but also to reveal their contents. Why should the king scream and thresh? Who were these deadly intimates with whom he struggled? He would never know, for he would never trouble to have the torches lit at bedtime.

He came awake on that warm, mid-summer night, his face bathed in sweat, his thin arms weaving across his face. He saw the lights, and his arms dropped heavy as lead on the thin coverlet.

The queen laid her hands over his and asked, 'Who is it? Who are you fighting?'

'Must be mistaken,' he droned. 'My brother broke a bauble from the crown . . .' Then, more awake, 'My brother? Henry? But I am not suspicious of him . . . He doesn't need to pick the jewels . . .'

'Sit up. Can you feel my hands? That's better. Now, tell me again, how did Henry attack you?'

Stephen yawned and rested his head against the plaster wall. 'I don't know . . . I dreamt that they were . . .'

'What?'

'I'm sorry . . . It's gone . . . We were in a church, a cathedral, I'm not sure . . .'

'Did he go for your person? Did he bear a weapon?'

'God, no! He loomed over me, they all did, clawing at my crown. They were trying to wrench the rubies from it . . . He broke one of the points, Henry . . .'

'Yes,' she soothed, 'yes. Now, tell me, who were the others?'

'Others?'

'You said, they all did. All of whom?'

'The bishops . . . the clergy . . . Aah, let's go back to sleep, it was just a dream . . .' He slid down in the bed, rolled on his side and mouthed his good nights into the swansdown pillow. Her mind on other things, Queen Matilda murmured, 'God bless you, husband,' then lay, staring at the torches.

While Stephen slept, his wife composed a list of the senior prelates of England. So, she mused, the church are against us, are they? His own brother. And no doubt the wine-supping Roger of Salisbury and his brood; his son, Chancellor of England; his nephews, Alexander and Nigel, bishops of Lincoln and Ely. Yes, it's plausible. I've suspected that family for some time. They're more barons than bishops, the lot of them. So now they invade his sleep, and dare to mutilate the crown . . .

She was a sensible woman, Stephen's queen, but even the most clear-minded grow tired and allow themselves to be misled by the flickering of pitch-flame.

*

The weather was not so warm at Northallerton in Yorkshire. Here, towards the end of August, the royal army, strengthened by local contingents, faced a Scottish force under the command of the hard-spoken King David. The Scots were supported by a large detachment of near-barbarian Picts from the fastnesses of Galloway, mountainous eyrie of the golden eagle. These savage men boasted that no English spear could pierce them, nor arrow find its mark, and they claimed the right to lead the attack. Impressed only with results, King David waved them forward into the misty dawn.

With King Stephen otherwise occupied in the south, the English army was led by the frail Thurstan, Archbishop of York, though the mass of knights and infantry were under the individual command of the northern magnates – with the conspicuous exception of Ranulf of Chester. More than three years had elapsed since Stephen had denied Ranulf the inheritance of Carlisle, but the earl had neither forgiven nor forgotten. He remained in his castle, and offered prayers for a Scottish victory. King David was more his type than the hither-and-thither King of England. He could talk to David, and he would, when the Scots took possession of the north.

The rallying-point of the English army was a tall tree-trunk, from which flew the triple banners of York, Ripon and Beverley. The stripped tree was mounted on a specially-constructed cart, drawn by fourteen dray-horses, and was known as The Standard, from which the battle would take its name.

After a heated discussion, in which Archbishop Thurstan convinced his commanders that the Scottish battlecries would stampede their horses, the English knights abandoned their destriers and prepared to fight on foot. As they moved into line, the sky lightened over the moor. The knights felt awkward, almost embarrassed, as though they had been caught naked on the field. Damn the priest, why had they listened to him? What did he know about the battle tactics of the Picts? And what good were English knights, weighed down with armour, playing at foot-soldiers? What was a knight, for God's sake, if not armed and mounted?

But early reports on the condition of the field soon stilled their anger. Where there was no marsh, there were stumbling-blocks of rock, and whatever firm ground there was, petered out and became deadly quagmire.

Daylight seeped over the moor. In the distance they heard a moan, a blood-curdling chant, a rise and fall of unnumbered voices, shrieking like the newest inmates of hell. Then the massive Galwegians charged out of the mist, their mouths stretched wide, as though to swallow or spit out the puny sticks the English called arrows.

Thurstan's archers let fly, while the knights raised their two-handed swords . . .

Within the first hour of the battle, the half-naked barbarians learned that their pagan gods were powerless. They were not invulnerable, and their long-learned battlecries meant nothing to those who did not understand their tongue. Arrows and crossbow quarrels ripped through their unprotected bodies, and the most terrifying curse they could devise did nothing to deflect them. They came on in waves, each man believing he was safe, until the instant he was hit. Then they fell, some killed outright, others floundering in the marshes, where they drowned in disbelief.

King David's regular troops fared little better, for they stumbled upon the Galwegians before they ever saw the enemy. Arrows hissed without warning from the mist banks, and the Scots hesitated, then fell back, pursued by the iron flails of the English knights.

By full light it was over. As the sun burned the mist from the ground the Scots broke and ran, leaving eleven thousand of their people on the field. Thurstan's foot-soldiers went among them, enjoying their work, while the archbishop knelt beside the horse-drawn Standard, his face wet with piety.

One of the great myths of the time had been exposed. The men of Scotland *could* be defeated, *had* been defeated. The lion had reached up and caught the golden eagle. The border-line had held.

*

The English victory at the Battle of the Standard sent a *frisson* of fear through all those who had declared for Matilda. Her uncle, King David, had been vanquished. But more than that, his army had been utterly routed, and he had suffered as grave a reversal as any since the Norman conquest of England. Never again would he attempt an all-out invasion of England. Next time, Stephen's supporters said, the eagle would learn to fly higher, to avoid the lion's claws.

The tide turned. Stephen captured Shrewsbury, whilst his wife, who had placed herself in command of a second royal army, unhinged the gates of Dover Castle, one of Robert of Gloucester's southernmost strongholds.

At Wallingford, Brien Fitz Count waited for the first arrow, the first catapulted missile. Lady Alyse awaited an answer to her letter.

*

Stephen's queen had not forgotten the nightmares. Dipping into her private purse, she bribed a number of household servants to spy on their masters – Bishop Henry, Bishop Roger, Bishop Alexander, Bishop Nigel. She thus learned that Henry was about to sail for Normandy, ostensibly on the first leg of a journey that would take him to Rome. According to the spy, Stephen's brother sought an audience with Pope Innocent II, at which he would try to obtain the Pope's consent to his election as Archbishop of Canterbury. The aged William of Corbeil had died two years earlier, and since then the see of Canterbury had remained vacant. With good reason, Henry expected to get the job, but as Stephen had done nothing about it, his brother had decided to take the matter into his own hands. He would go to Rome, win the Pope's support, then ask Stephen to append the royal seal. He would be back in England by December.

That, anyway, was the story the spy told. The queen nodded and dismissed him, and did not believe a word of it. She preferred to see the bland, thick-girthed bishop as a potential traitor, detouring through Normandy to plot and scheme with the Angevins. It had a much more realistic ring to it, for why else would Bishop Henry choose this time to leave the country?

He'd had two years in which to make his trip, but he'd left it until now, when England was coming to the boil. An audience with the Pope? No, not unless grass turned blue. But a war council with the Angevins; ah, yes, that she could believe.

She shared her suspicions with Stephen, and received the answer she expected.

'If you're right, we must stop him. I, too, have noticed a cooling of affection on his part, though I must say I never saw him as a traitor.'

'I think you did, husband, though you refused to recognise it. Do you recollect your dreams? Who was it who broke your crown? Whose face loomed largest in your nightmares? You were seeing the truth with your eyes closed. The future was being paraded before you, but you chose to ignore it.'

'Yes, it could be. Shall I arrest him then? I'll pen him up with his damned ostriches and peacocks. Let him plot with them for a while.'

'No,' she said. 'Leave him be. Pretend ignorance. He can do little outside the country. Oh, he can scrawl victories on paper, and huddle together with Matilda and Geoffrey, but he can *achieve* nothing. We're better off without him at present. But there is one thing you can do.'

More comfortable with practice than theory, Stephen nodded. 'What is it?'

'Fill the gap at Canterbury.'

'I don't know,' he demurred. 'I've all but promised it to him. I suppose I could delay things, but – '

'But nothing,' the queen snapped. 'If you make him arch-bishop, why not throw the crown in with it! He'll be the most influential churchman outside Rome. You might as well take off your shoes and stand on a snake. Why not? You'll have built its nest.'

'Don't say that. You know I hate serpents. You know I've never visited that part of his menagerie.' He shuddered, then fiddled with his moustache and said, 'Very well. I'll find another candidate. Who do you suggest?'

*

Far removed from palace politics, the Saxon maidservant had problems of her own. Her affair with Sergeant Morcar had blossomed. She thought of him as a latter-day Hercules, and throughout the changing seasons of 1138 she had come to know every leaf on the alder trees beside the Thames, whilst he became a breathless authority on grasses and insects.

Now, when the castle had been in a state of preparedness for almost a year, they continued their outings, braving the early winter snows. The visits to the riverbank failed to produce a death chill, but instead put new life into her. Exactly that, for by the end of October Edgiva realised she was pregnant.

It came as no surprise. Indeed, she had begun to wonder if her sergeant-lover deserved his heroic nickname, though she could not remember whether or not Hercules had fathered any children. No matter, Morcar would, and had to be told.

She chose her moment wisely, a prelude to love-making in the snow, and, in the circumstances, he took it well. His breath hissed out as steam, and it was the coldness of the day that made his smile seem forced – or so she chose to believe. His voice was thick with emotion – pride, she decided – as he gasped, 'A child? You're having a child?'

'Not that,' she smiled upward. 'Our child.' Then in an innocent voice that hinted at barrel-hoops and leg-irons, '*Your* child, Morcar. Tell me you're pleased.'

'Mine? You're sure it's – '

'So jealousy does suit you. I never knew you were jealous. Yes, of course it's – '

'Who spoke of jealousy?'

' – yours, how can you think otherwise? I have been faithful – '

'No one said I was jealous.'

' – to you from the first. That is – well, you must know what I mean.'

'When did this happen?'

Edgiva rolled on her side and drew patterns in the snow. 'Not even the future mother can give the future father so precise a date. But it was here, a few weeks ago. *With you.*'

His mouth smoked in the cold air. He plucked at a corner of the cowhide and managed, 'I suppose we will – ' Then, with desperate nonchalance, 'Have you mentioned this, uh, blessing to anyone?'

'No,' she smiled, 'no one save Lady Alyse and Constable Varan.'

Morcar's skull rang with the slamming of gates. He wondered how long one would survive beneath the thin ice of the Thames. Woman, or man.

Edgiva murmured, 'You supposed what, sweet? You said, I suppose, and then I didn't hear the rest.'

'I-suppose-we-should-marry.'

'Aah, love.' She lay back again and smiled up at him. She saw his head framed, some would think pinioned, by the branches. 'Love, I did not think you would find me worthy—yes, we should. I am at a loss for words—yes, since it is what you want. You are the strongest and most handsome creature, Morcar—yes, as you say.'

He searched the snow, but there was not a single insect, not one he could pound to powder on the stone-hard ground. Instead, a voice borrowed his tongue to croak, 'I'll speak to Lord Fitz Count. I'll ask for your hand. We'll marry when he says we may.'

'Yes,' she said obediently, having never before realised the full power of the word.

*

Alyse shared Edgiva's pleasure. It was all she could share, for she was resigned to the fact that she and Brien would not have children. It was God's will, she accepted, though she could never quite see why.

*

The undeclared war continued. The royal troops re-took a number of minor castles, whilst the rival faction sent a constant stream of messages to Matilda, Geoffrey and Earl Robert, asking them when they would invade. The messages went unanswered, as did Alyse's letter to the empress. The year dragged its feet through the snow, and paused for breath on Christmas Eve.

By then, Bishop Henry was back in place. He had ridden straight through Normandy, then south to the coast and along it to Italy. He had obtained his audience with Pope Innocent and come away with papal consent for his election to Canterbury. He thought Stephen and the queen rather chilly in their reception, but so was the weather. One was rarely ebullient in December.

On the 24th of the month, Bishop Henry was at St Paul's Cathedral in London, ordaining a young deacon.

A few miles away, at Westminster, the king and queen attended a secret council of churchmen and barons, and witnessed the election to the see of Canterbury of the partially-deaf Theobald, Abbot of Bec. When the service was over, and the king addressed him by his new title, the archbishop looked round, then cupped a hand to his ear. 'Hmm? Eh? Is your majesty speaking to me?'

When one of Henry's servants brought him the news, he abandoned the ordination, snarled for his horse and rode to his fortified palace at Winchester. There, another servant told him his prized peacock had died. He had been well enough that morning. It must have been the cold. The distraught peahen was running about in the snow, beside herself with sorrow.

'What should we do, Lord Bishop?' the servant inquired anxiously. 'She runs blindly into the fence. The keepers fear she will injure herself.'

'Bring her into the palace,' Henry said. 'Into my bedchamber. We'll comfort one another.' He glanced at the astonished servant. 'It's all right, man. I plan nothing unnatural. She has lost her mate, and I have lost a brother. We'll have much in common.' He crossed the room and leaned down to study a time candle, a thick column of wax, ringed with lines to mark the hour. 'If the table's level,' he murmured, 'it's Christmas Day, God forgive us.'

*

The new year brought more skirmishes, more minor victories

for both sides. Edgiva and Morcar were married in February, and in June the maidservant gave birth to a son. She named him Alder, which drew a few smirks from Morcar's soldiers, though they made sure their faces were straight when the sergeant was present. They had heard that Lord Fitz Count was grooming him to take over the constableship from Varan; not yet, for at sixty, the flat-nosed Saxon was still the most formidable man in the castle, but at some future date, when Varan told his master he was tired.

So the men-at-arms studied their sergeant with renewed respect and marvelled at the change that was overtaking him. At first they had put it down to the fact that he was a married man, but that only explained a part of it. He had been thinner before, certainly, and more inclined to shout than growl. But he was not merely putting on weight, or growing mellow with marriage; he was changing, both in shape and manner, *changing into a facsimile of Constable Varan.*

Morcar spent much of his time with the constable, grunting where formerly he would have made some comment, standing still and flat-footed, where he would once have scratched and shifted. His nose remained unbroken, but in other things, in the muscled thickness of his body and the stoop of his shoulders, Edgiva's husband became indistinguishable from Brien's watchdog. Even his voice deepened, so that, if he was heard before he was seen, the garrison troops whirled round, thinking they had been surprised by old Stonehead. When they saw who it was, they grinned and relaxed a little – until they recognised the same chipped-out expression, the same un-wavering gaze. Satan's sting, they moaned, one was bad enough. And we've been cursed with two.

In her years at Wallingford, Edgiva had never before been treated to so many polite nods and murmured greetings. She was enchanted. Coarse soldiers though they were, they were obviously gratified to see a young bride about the place.

*

Already knowing the answer, Ernard debated whether to go or stay. Stay, he decided, just long enough to enjoy a mug of

mead, and eye the serving-girls, and overhear a few conver-
sations. Then he'd collect the cart and be on his way, a success-
ful day's work completed.

He headed east through the narrow streets, emerged beside
the Thames and glanced at the row of waterfront taverns. His
horse and cart were where he'd left them, and the boy was still
seated against one of the wheels. Ernard changed direction and
walked over to the horse-rail. The boy scrambled to his feet,
gabbling the usual mixture of justification and sales-talk. 'I
never left 'ere, master, not since you went off. I got 'ungry,
and one of my friends brought me some bread, but I never
left off watchin'. Everythin's safe, I swear to God.'

'So I see. We agreed on one penny, right?'

'That's what you said, one 'ole penny.'

Ernard nodded, took two coins from his purse, then drew
his knife and halved one. He handed the boy one and a
half coins, and dropped the remaining half into the leather
pouch. 'The extra half's for your honesty, and to pay for the
bread.'

The boy grinned and snatched the money. 'If you're in
Oxford again, master, you'll find me 'ere. I'll look after things
for you, you can trust me.' He trotted away, then turned as
Ernard called after him. 'Anyone of interest in the taverns
tonight?'

The boy came back, making a show of sucking his lip.
'Well, depends what you mean by interestin'. There's some
what'll buy and sell things, or if it's a woman you want – '

Ernard fished out the cut coin and tossed it in his hand.
'Anyone from the court, for example?'

The boy pointed at one of the larger taverns. 'There's the
bishops,' he said. 'They've prob'ly been at court today.'

'Which bishops?'

' 'ow do I know? I was watchin' your property.'

Ernard gave him the half-penny. The boy flapped a hand in
salute and hurried off, sneering to himself. Some trader, givin'
out money like it was old pebbles; 'e wouldn't get far in
business.

The boy might have been right, had Ernard been what he

appeared. But he was, in fact, a member of the garrison of Wallingford Castle, the same young soldier who, three years ago, had met the disguised Robert of Gloucester and conducted him to Lord Fitz Count. He had not forgotten the incident and, when his overlord had ordered him to travel the twenty miles to Oxford and learn what he could about the Great Council that had been convened there by King Stephen, Ernard had decided to copy Earl Robert's disguise.

He had spent the day near the palace, where he had chatted with the guards, and sweet-talked one of the kitchen maids. The Council had met in the morning so, by late afternoon, Ernard had collected a valuable amount of information. Enough, he believed, to merit a mug of mead.

So it was that, on the evening of 24th June, the young soldier-cum-merchant witnessed one of the most extraordinary incidents of Stephen's reign. He did not know that the action had been carefully planned, nor that it had been master-minded by Stephen's queen. Nor could he do more than guess at the results. But he saw what happened, and was profoundly shocked by it.

He patted his horse, crossed the riverside path and entered the tavern. It was dark in there, and for a moment he thought the boy had misled him. Then, as he made his way towards the back, he heard raucous laughter and saw that the rearmost tables were occupied by the bishops and armed escorts of Salisbury, Lincoln and Ely, and by Roger of Salisbury's son, Roger the Poor, Chancellor of England.

Ernard hesitated, moved backward, then settled himself in an alcove near the door. He had never seen such an assembly of clerical power, and he shifted with discomfort.

He came to his feet again, and collided with a serving-girl who snapped, 'If you lack the leg room, go and sit at one of the tables. Or have you mastered your thirst?'

'No, I – I'm content enough here.' She was a very pretty girl, but she spoiled herself when she scowled. He lowered himself on to the seat, and said, 'You have some distinguished guests tonight, mistress, uh – '

'So we do. What do you want?'

'Oh, just a mug of mead, and the chance to talk with a beautiful woman.'

'Then you're only half-way home,' she told him unkindly, 'unless you're waiting for her.' She left him crouched in the alcove, eyeing the air above the far tables.

The mead came, and again he tried to discover the girl's name, and again he failed. He peered along the candle-lit room, watching the corpulent Roger of Salisbury, hearing him describe the faults in the tavern wine. Alexander of Lincoln nodded at everything his uncle said, whilst Nigel of Ely sipped the wine, then spat it over the floor.

'That's the way,' Roger boomed, waving his hands so that his bejewelled fingers sparkled in the light. 'Sip and spit, or sip and swallow; the first for a dip, the last for a wallow. Any man who knows his wine will tell you that. Fill my glass. This tavern stuff is only fit for drinking.'

The girl came by, and Ernard held out his mug. 'When you are free, mistress, uh – '

Since she had first served him, she had taken time to think. He was a handsome enough young man, though his rough merchant's garb did nothing to enhance him. But with the bishops and their knights dominating the far end of the room, the mead-drinker was the only one worth talking to. The others in the front part of the tavern were all old, or ugly, or infirm. So why not give him her name? It would pass the time.

She stopped and said, 'Your speech is very halting, master, uh – '

'Ernard,' he volunteered. 'It's because you leave me hanging from the rim of the world. If I knew your name I could use it as a thread, and climb back on to level ground.'

'Well, it's Eadgyth, so you're saved. You want more mead?' She pronounced her name Edith, and her yellow hair proclaimed her a Saxon.

'Yes,' he said, 'and the pleasure of your company. Come on, there's no one else to serve. Bring something for yourself, and I'll tell you my true identity.'

She raised her eyes to the roof. 'You are really a prince, is that it? Your true place is along there, with the bishops. You dress this way because some evil enemy has stolen your inheritance, and you drink mead – '

'Because I like it. You fetch the mugs, mistress Eadgyth, and *then* you can judge my story.' He grinned at her, and watched her walk over to the barrels. He was still grinning when the armed men entered the tavern, shouldered her against the wall and strode towards the rear tables. Ernard's head swung as though jerked by the ears. He came to his feet, intent on helping the fallen girl. One of the intruders said, 'Keep out of it,' and he felt a massive blow on the chest. He sprawled back, slamming his head against the upright of the alcove. Eadgyth crawled along the wall and they crouched together, blinking at the ill-lit scene.

At the far end of the tavern, members of the bishops' households clambered to their feet. Somebody shouted, 'How dare you profane the peace?' and then there was the recognisable clash of weapons, the unmistakable howl of the wounded. Christ on earth, Ernard gaped, they're murdering the church!

The fight spilled past them and the tavern doors were wrenched open, splitting at the hinges. Men rolled on the ground, or stabbed wildly, whilst those who had the breath roared threat and defiance. A knight staggered sideways before the crouched pair, his throat open to the world. He blundered into the rack of barrels, grabbed at them and went down, bringing the casks on top of him. Eadgyth screamed into Ernard's chest, and he held her tight, if only for something to hold.

Inside the tavern and beyond the battle raged. Roger of Salisbury was pinioned by the arms and hustled out, as though he weighed no more than a child. Alexander of Lincoln was thrown down and a foot pressed against his neck. Somebody hurled a bench and it splintered against the alcove and fell, catching Ernard on the forehead. In total disbelief he sat, couching Eadgyth, blood running into his eye. It was time to leave.

He hissed, 'Can we get out by the back?' Then, when he received no answer, he grabbed the girl by the hair and pulled her face level with his. '*Can we leave by the back?*'

She mouthed a yes, and they swayed to their feet and ran

past the tables. Men lay beneath upturned benches, and there was blood on the walls. Somebody roared, 'Those two! Get after them!' and Ernard pushed the girl through the rear door and out into an alley. He followed her out, dragging a bench with him. Then he slammed the door, jammed one end of the bench against the heavy wooden latch, and gasped, 'There! That way! Get going!'

They ran along the alley, turned right, away from the river, and zig-zagged through the darkened streets. They reached a deserted market-place, lit by a waxing moon, and sank down in the deep shadow of a horse-trough. The mead fomented in Ernard's stomach, and he turned aside, retching over the cobbles. When he had finished he raised a cautious hand, scooped water from the trough and splashed it on his face. The girl shuddered with fear: 'What was it about?', but Ernard could do no more than roll his head from side to side. Where were the angels, he wondered, the hosts of seraphim? How could they, who were all-powerful, have allowed God's senior servants to be so abused? He sighed, smothering the noise with his hand, then peered round the end of the trough. The market-place was still deserted, save for a dog that trotted across the cobblestones.

He asked Eadgyth, 'Have you caught your breath?'

'Enough for walking.'

'Good. Where do you live?'

'Above the tavern. The owner and his wife, and two of us, two girls.'

'Well, you can't go back there. Those men were also after *us*, remember. I suppose because we saw what happened.' He told her who he was, and where he came from. He did not reveal why he had spent the day in Oxford, but asked her if she wanted to travel back with him. She nodded quickly. 'I've only been in this town a month or so. I was in another tavern before, but the owner there – well, it doesn't matter. But there's no one I could go to here. Are you really one of Lord Fitz Count's men? I saw him once. He has grey hair, doesn't he? He was with his lady. Alyse, is it? If I was wealthy, I'd dress like that. She's a beautiful woman, Lady Alyse.'

Ernard snorted. 'Is that what you think?'

'That she is beautiful?'

'No. That their coffers bulge with coins?'

'Of course.'

'Of course,' he echoed bitterly, 'the way all knights are honourable, and all priests pious. Come on, let's find the cart.'

*

Whatever personal satisfaction the soldier and serving-girl might have derived from their meeting, the seizure of the bishops was to have the gravest repercussions within the kingdom. Stephen's party regarded it as a signal victory, for in Roger of Salisbury they had captured the most powerful churchman in England. His lands were even more extensive than those of Bishop Henry, and he was responsible for the construction of castles at Salisbury, Malmesbury, Sherbourne and Devizes. His nephew, Alexander, who had had his neck trodden on in the tavern, had commissioned similar strongholds at Lincoln, Newark and Sleaford, whilst Roger the Poor – so-called because he, alone among the family, possessed no bishopric – held the influential post of Chancellor. *Had* held, for with his arrest he was dishonoured.

The results of the swoop had been less than perfect, for Nigel, Bishop of Ely, had escaped across the river and was now besieged in his uncle's fortress at Devizes. Nevertheless, king and queen were delighted. The cause of Stephen's nightmares had been removed. His brother had been denied the see of Canterbury, and they had netted three of the Salisbury fish. Within the space of six months, the monarchs had crushed all clerical opposition to the crown, and done so before the Church had had the chance to strike. Now, with the capture of Devizes a foregone conclusion, the victory was complete.

The rival faction saw it differently. They regarded the arrest of the bishops as an act of sacrilege and the final release from fealty to the crown. Bishop Henry's visit to the Pope had been grossly misinterpreted, and the bishops of Salisbury, Lincoln and Ely had neither spoken nor behaved in a treasonable manner. The disaffected barons remembered the lines of the poem: 'Before the sword is drawn, he cuts . . . After he speaks, he thinks . . .' How well they applied to the impetuous Stephen. How easily they could be adapted to suit Queen Matilda, architect of the tavern brawl.

They sent news of the arrests to the Angevins. Make your move, they pleaded, for never was the iron so hot. Strike now, while half the doors of England are bolted against the king. For the love of God and England, mount your invasion!

*

On 18th September, Brien Fitz Count received a letter from the Empress Matilda. It was no longer than the one the disguised Robert of Gloucester had delivered in the spring of 1136. But it did not need to be, for it said,

'Everything is now ready. As I told you long ago, the sails are run up, and we wait only for the tide. Well, Greylock, the tide is with us at last, and we are on our way. I am advised that we shall arrive in England near the end of the month. If you choose to meet us, we shall be heartened beyond measure. I know this letter will reach you safely, for I know you have not allowed my accursed cousin to come within arrow-shot of your walls. Until soon, dearest Greylock.'

He showed the letter to Alyse, then embraced her and swung her off her feet. He was surprised when she snapped, 'Let me down! Why should you be the only one? Has it always been her policy to ask, but never answer?'

He deposited her gently, then moved back to inquire, 'What is this? Why can't you share the pleasure of half England? And what do you mean, me, the only one? She will have written to fifty others.'

'Maybe,' Alyse grated, 'but she's a poor respondant. I wrote to her a year and a half ago.'

'*You* did? For what purpose?'

'To ask for help,' Alyse said coldly. 'And to learn which of you was the giver and which the taker.' She held up Matilda's letter, then let it twist and tumble to the floor. 'She sent no answer, until now. But by this I know which is which.'

Brien put out a hand, but his wife brushed it away and hurried from the solar. He stared after her, puzzled by her attitude. Then he picked up the letter and re-read it, and his frown cleared and became a smile of remembrance. Alyse was being too silly for reason. Matilda was coming!

*

On 30th September, 1139, Empress Matilda, accompanied by Earl Robert of Gloucester and one hundred and forty knights, landed at the Sussex port of Arundel, which in those days was open to sea-going ships. Legitimate sister and bastard brother knelt together on the bank of the estuary and kissed the mud. Then they rose, hand in hand, and smiled at each other.

'Well,' Robert said, 'you have embraced your kingdom.'

Their knights milled around them, calming their horses or vomiting with sea-sickness. It was difficult to envisage the landing for what it was – the first invasion of England since the Norman Conquest.

CHAPTER 7

COUSIN MATILDA
September–December 1139

SHE looked along the estuary, then shielded her eyes and gazed up at the castle. 'They are not flying the flag,' she said. 'Why is that?'

Her brother studied the towers and ramparts of Arundel. There was no sign of the Angevin banner, and he searched hastily for an explanation. 'It would have been too risky,' he told her. 'They did not know on what day we would arrive, and it would have been foolhardy to announce our landing. If one of Stephen's men had seen it – '

He heard the well-known tetch of irritation.

She said, 'They could have waited until we entered the river. It would have been safe to hoist it then.' She moved to the sun-baked ground above the waterline. Robert shrugged and started after her, noting that most of the mounted knights were already in position at the foot of the cliff path. If Stephen *had* learned the time and place of Matilda's arrival, the horse-men would fight a rearguard action, whilst Robert hurried her back aboard ship. But no archers appeared on the cliff-top, and there were no sudden shouts of alarm. The water lapped peacefully against the mud-banks, and the warm air was filled with the drone of insects. The only jarring sound had been the click of Matilda's tongue.

They walked up the path, the long-jawed Earl of Gloucester following in his sister's footsteps. She held herself erect, her arms at her sides, her elbows pressed tight against her waist. In height, Robert dominated most of the Norman aristocracy, yet he had out-grown his sister by less than a handsbreadth. She was not the tallest woman in England, for there were always freaks and the monstrous, nine-foot-high creatures of the Scottish islands, but there was no ennobled lady who could look her levelly in the eye. Throughout her life, she had made the most of this natural advantage, marrying it to a caustic wit and a viperous temper. Both issued from a wide mouth, a mouth, one might think, that was better made for love.

It would have been enough for her Creator to mould the tall, elegant body and generous lips, and judge her well-endowed. But He had further fashioned dark, deep-set eyes, a straight nose and a pale skin that remained immune to all sores and blemishes. By then He may have accepted His own challenge and worked to perfect His creation. Whatever His reasons, He had allowed her russet hair, long, slender fingers and a faultless grace of carriage. In appearance, she was in-comparable, a constant rule against which other women measured themselves, and fell short.

Why, then, Robert wondered, had her maker equipped her with the mind of a wildcat, and the tongue of a snake?

They reached the cliff-top, where they were welcomed and received into the castle by its chatelaine, the dowager Queen Adeliza, widow of King Henry, and now Countess of Sussex. Adeliza had been Henry's second wife, but had failed to bear him any children. As a result, she had lavished her affections upon Matilda, demanding nothing in return. It was as well that she was selfless, for the empress thought her stepmother fussy and sentimental. Adeliza had allowed Henry to treat her as little more than a furrow for his seed and, when it became clear that she would never conceive, he dismissed her from his mind. He had been a hard man, Henry the fish eater, but equally, Adeliza had been weak and malleable.

She had loved him, that was her undoing, for he had not loved her, and had never been heard to speak the word. Love, she seemed to think, was like the sewn bladder of a pig, which could be tossed from hand to hand, or thrown against a wall, from which it would rebound, bringing with it shards of stone and mortar. But Henry had been reluctant to part with even these fragments of affection. She was his wife for a purpose and, since she had failed to give him a son, she had failed to earn her title. Pronounced barren, she became an embarrassment to the man who had sired nineteen bastards . . .

But Henry was long-since dead, the victim of fish stew, and Adeliza had married again and was overjoyed to stand beside her husband and greet the fair Matilda.

'Well, well, so you are here at last. It's hard to believe. Life has favoured you, daughter, I can see that. As each year passes, it leaves you more beautiful, I know you will not mind my remarking on it. And now you are at home with us. Come, I urge you to greet my husband, William d'Aubigny, Lord of Arundel. Earl Robert we know from previous visits. Ah, yes, yes, it is a blessed day for England.'

She went on in that vein until Matilda said, 'Whatever pride you feel should be declared, Lady Adeliza. Or shall I send to the ship for one of my banners?'

William and Robert exchanged a glance. They had respected each other from the first, and Robert did not challenge the Lord of Arundel's curt, 'It is in hand, Empress. Flags of residence speak for themselves. We'll fly your banner when you are installed. If you'll come this way – '

Matilda gazed at him, smiling. 'How my father would have marvelled,' she said pleasantly. 'My stepmother outlives one despot, only to be drawn to another. Which way? Not that I shall get lost in such a – compact castle.'

The Lord of Arundel glanced at Robert again, then bowed the invaders into the castle. He remembered what Robert had told him during one of his earlier visits – 'Do not be deceived by her appearance, yet neither be ruffled by her manner. She *is* the rightful heir to the throne, and God will most certainly bless our enterprise. Of course, if we were able to forge swords one half as cutting as her tongue, we could go on and secure the world. If you want the best from my sister, friend William – I shall call you friend – then you must first engage her at her worst. If she bids you good morning, then grimaces at the sky, understand that she is searching for the rain. And will blame you when it arrives. God never made such an attractive creature, nor gave one such wounding ways. But don't let me mislead you; she is no simple marriage of good and evil. She's a, what, a maze, if you like, in which men tend to lose

their way. Just watch your step, friend William, and you won't
be stranded.'

The Lord of Arundel had relayed none of this to Adeliza.
But now, after his first exchange with the empress, he acknowledged Robert's warning. He *would* watch his step, by God, for
there were obviously more twists and turns in Matilda than in
his – compact castle.

*

Earl Robert did not stay long at Arundel. He was anxious to
raise his own standard at Bristol, one of his foremost strongholds, and to test the wind of insurrection in the west country.
He left Matilda in the care of William and Adeliza and, on 5th
October, set out with half his invasion force.

Early winter rains lashed the riders, and they took it in turns
to scout the road, exposing their eyes to the whip of water.
There was nothing to be heard above the hiss of the downpour,
and whatever could be seen was already within reach. The
riders cursed and spat, and shared the same common thoughts:

Was England really worth saving?

How was it that *they* had been sentenced to be drowned,
whilst the other seventy squatted at Arundel, warming their
buttocks?

It was ideal weather for an ambush.

This last thought preoccupied Robert, and he wiped the rain
from his sword-grip. Matilda's banner had flown from the
battlements of Arundel for the better part of a week; time
enough for Stephen to block the surrounding roads and order
up his siege machines. On the other hand, the rain afforded
some cover, and the ambushers might be taken by surprise.

Soaked and sullen, the knights crossed the Sussex Hamp-
shire border. If they stayed on this tree-lined road they would
reach Winchester, then continue on across the bleak expanse
of Salisbury Plain. Robert spurred ahead to join his scouts and
tell them to watch for a side track, by which they could by-pass
the town. It would not do to run foul of Stephen's brother.

A mile or so farther on, they did exactly that.

The king *had* heard of the landing and had summoned his

leaders to Arundel. He had received the news with a smile, for the castle on the estuary presented no special problems, and one hundred and forty knights scarcely constituted an invasion force. Better yet, he would catch Matilda and Robert in the same net, and defeat his rivals before the salt-water had dried on their shoes. So the call-to-arms was sounded, and Bishop Henry was among those who responded.

Escorted by some eighty knights and two hundred foot soldiers, he took the most direct route, shivering beneath the water that fell from the sky and dripped from the trees. He was still debating whether to ride under the trees and risk the more solid accumulation of water, or brave the drizzle in the centre of the road, when Robert and his scouts loomed out of the darkness.

The two columns collided, then reined· in, unable to part the curtain. The rain washed over them, guided by an erratic wind. The narrow road was choked with soldiers, while the leaders sat horse-to-horse, peering at each other. Their conversation was as extraordinary as the circumstances of their meeting.

'I know you,' Henry said. 'I was told you were at Arundel.'

'I was, Bishop. But now I am *en route* elsewhere. I heard how you were robbed of the Canterbury see. In Normandy, we all expected you to – '

'So did I, Gloucester, so did I. Is your sister still with d'Aubigny?'

'She is.'

'Yes . . . Well then . . .'

Though Robert could give no single reason for it, he knew Henry would let him pass. It seemed fitting, for the encounter had all the elements of a dream. It was dark enough for dreaming, God knew, and too miserable a day on which to die. But now that he thought about it, he wondered if Henry had been provoked by the mention of Canterbury, if it had offered him the chance to strike back at his brother. He decided to test it out.

'Can you see me?' he asked, 'or are you as blind as I in the rain?'

'If I could see you, I would have to arrest you, isn't that so?'

'In which case, I and my knights would be bound to resist.'

'Yes.' Henry nodded slowly. 'So they would. Another time then. Take your men to the left.'

'And you likewise. Oh, by the way, how do your peacocks fare in the wet?'

'They don't,' Henry said. 'They both died.'

Robert opened his hands in a gesture of sympathy. 'I'm sorry. You have some reputation abroad. Perhaps next year, in the warmer weather.'

'Perhaps,' the bishop echoed. Then he turned in his saddle and told his men to keep to the left. They were going on. The columns passed each other in silence, and the curtains closed behind them.

In later years, chroniclers saw fit to record the incident. It seemed strange, even to them, though it was simply one among many in those strange times.

Robert also thought it strange, but he did not stay to query it. He seized the advantage and took his men through the heart of Winchester and across the great plain of Salisbury and on through Wiltshire to his county of Gloucester and the impregnable castle at Bristol. Once there, he towelled himself dry and changed his clothes and hoisted the banner of rebellion. As William d'Aubigny had said, the flag of residence spoke for itself.

*

'I don't understand it,' Stephen raged. 'We had every road barred, a man at every rabbit-warren. He couldn't have escaped! So far as I know, he can't fly, so he couldn't have eluded us. Scour Sussex again. He's crouched under a hedge-row somewhere, or playing the peasant in a field. Look for him, damn you! You can't miss him, he has a jaw like a plough-blade!'

The king was at Arundel, almost within arrow-shot of the castle walls. His army was with him, a piecemeal force of regular troops, vassal knights, Welsh and Flemish mercenaries.

But there were enough for the task in hand. Arundel was, indeed, a compact castle, and it was expected to fall within the month.

Henry of Winchester had arrived, to be reunited with his brother. But the bishop had embarked on a dangerous double game, in which the bloodless exchange with Earl Robert had been but the first move. Henry was a man who believed in friendship, true and total, and so applied the same weight to enmity. He had loved his brother once, and had shown his love by securing for him the throne of England. But of late their relationship had turned sour. Stephen had misinterpreted Henry's visit to the Pope, and deprived him of the Canterbury see. Worse, he had then countenanced the clumsy arrest of bishops Roger and Alexander, and turned Bishop Nigel into a fugitive. Sparked by his queen, he had destroyed the very force that had furnished him with the throne. He had crushed the Church, stabbed deep at his friends, denied his brother, acted without restraint or reason. Small wonder that Bishop Henry played a double game and treated Stephen to a Judas kiss.

The chroniclers were soon presented with another test of credulity, for Henry made a single-handed attempt to terminate the siege of Arundel. He chose his moment carefully, when Queen Matilda was away from her husband's side, then presented Stephen with an essay in fraternal concern.

'The world is watching us,' he said. 'Every moment we spend here, beneath this paper castle, word goes out that in England cousin is ranged against cousin, that a beautiful woman is besieged by a brilliant king. Let her go, Stephen. Let her scurry away to Bristol. Or wherever Robert has gone.'

'Who said he's at Bristol? I say he's still hereabouts. He *couldn't* have got past us!'

'He could,' Henry murmured. 'I did not have the heart to tell you, but I heard recently that he and, what was it, seventy men, had been spotted crossing the Salisbury Plain. Of course, the report could be an invention, but – '

'Seventy? That's half the invading force. And they did say seventy had left Arundel. Damn the bastards!' He irritated his moustache, then accepted, 'It sounds as if he's through the net. And you want me to let Matilda swim after him?'

'From one net to another,' Henry said blandly. 'Keep them together, that's my advice.'

'But we'll soon have her. Look at the place. It's small. It's badly sited. We'll have no trouble taking it. As soon as the heavy catapults have arrived – '

'Maybe, brother. But all the while we're here, throwing rocks, Robert of Gloucester is arming in the west country. With respect, I say this. Your force here, today, does not match the great army you took north to defeat the Scots at North-allerton. I mean, the one you *sent* north, under Archbishop Thurstan.'

'I would have been there – '

'Yes, of course.'

' – if I had not had other duties down here.'

'Yes, of course.'

Stephen retreated to his final line of defence. 'Are you mocking me, Henry?'

'God forbid, brother king. I'm saying I understand. But I am also suggesting that you let this Angevin mare run to Bristol, rather than wait for Robert to descend on you with his west country minions. Be the chivalric monarch we know you are. Give her leave to pass. Follow her, that's essential, but treat her as though she is not worth the bother. Let her trot to Bristol, so far from London, then seal them in, the two of them. With the sea at their backs, they'll probably set sail for Ireland, and we'll never hear from them again.'

'You really think so? You think I should let them be to-gether? Surely that's the most dangerous thing I could do?'

'Very well,' Henry snapped. 'Look at me. Look me in the eye and tell me I deceive you.'

Stephen fidgeted. 'There's no need to get angry. I trust you, you know that.'

'As with the Canterbury see.'

'That wasn't altogether my doing. Anyway, let's discuss that some other time.'

Henry kept the anger in his face for a while, then let it drain away. Pressing his advantage, he said, 'Isn't it better to know where the rats hide in the house?'

'You mean Matilda and – Yes, I suppose it is. But would it really smack of chivalry? Do you think the people would understand why it was done?'

Henry put a hand on Stephen's arm. The king was trembling, or had just then begun to tremble. 'They'll understand, brother. They'll see a monarch who offers his poor, misguided cousin the opportunity to fly from justice. I tell you, Stephen, the world will never forget such an act. Never.'

The king teetered a moment longer, then nodded, chivalric and magnanimous. Henry's advice made sense, and if it bolstered him in the eyes of the people . . .

He commanded his army to withdraw half a mile from the walls, then sent a deputation to William d'Aubigny, offering him a royal pardon if he allowed Matilda to leave. For the first time in months, he felt he was behaving like a king.

When his cousin understood the nature of the offer, she emerged at the head of her seventy riders and trotted across the wet grass to where Stephen waited, fiddling with his moustache. Matilda could not believe her good fortune, but even as a child she had learned to snatch the apple and swallow it, then discuss the conditions. If Stephen allowed her to join Robert at Bristol, well and good. She'd do so, then look down from the impregnable walls and ask him why he had been so foolish.

Thinking this, she looked down at him now, and murmured her greetings.

'You've grown a moustache, cousin. Don't tear it off, I've hardly seen it yet.'

He let his hands hang at his sides. 'You keep your looks, Matilda, by God you do. Will you dismount and talk with me? We have much – '

'No. Not this time. Later, perhaps, when you have stopped wearing my crown. I only came over to thank you for your generosity and to see if monarchy has changed you. It hasn't really. You're just the same; thinner in the face, but that's just robber's guilt. Shed the crown and you'll fill out again. So you are pardoning d'Aubigny and my stepmother, is that right?'

'I am. It's within my power to do so, and I exercise it gladly.'

'Good,' she smiled. 'Then go the whole way, will you, and settle with them for the food my knights consumed. They're not a rich pair. You would know that if you saw the way they ration their logs. Give them something from your coffers. Forgiveness comes better in a warm room.'

She nodded to him, then to Henry, then turned her horse and cantered away towards the bridge at the head of the estuary. Stephen's queen had been there throughout the exchange, but the empress had affected not to see her.

Now, watching the seventy horsemen follow the empress, the queen ran her tongue around her mouth, chewed on some invisible morsel, then leaned forward and spat on to the grass. 'You,' she told her husband, 'you are better suited to a fairground. And *you*!' to Henry. 'There is nowhere outside hell that could so fully appreciate *your* gifts!' She strode away, the wet grass turning her doeskin shoes black to the ankle.

*

A triumvirate emerged to lead the rival party. Of these, the most important was still Robert of Gloucester, but he was now supported by his close friends and Matilda's admirers, Miles of Hereford and Brien Fitz Count. They produced more tangible assets than mere affection, for Miles had taken command of Gloucester Castle, while Wallingford was already proving an irritant to the royalists. It severed the main road from London to the west, overshadowed the most important ford on the Thames, and threatened the security of Oxford and Reading. It was clear that the lion would have to shake out the thorn . . .

*

Constable Varan swung his head in the direction of the shout. By the time he had identified the caller – a guard on the flat roof of the keep – other shouts emanated from the two southernmost wall-towers. They all said much the same thing; there were troops in the marshes on the far side of town; a column of horsemen had appeared at the eastern end of the ford; two catapults mounted on rafts were being hauled up-stream; the royal banner, along with those of Surrey, Leicester and Ypres, were in evidence.

The burly Saxon strode to the gateway in the dividing wall, squinted across the outer courtyard and satisfied himself that the main gates were shut and barred. Such obvious mistakes had been made before, and no proper defence could ever be undertaken on the basis of presumption. He saw Sergeant Morcar, waved him over, then turned back towards the keep. Morcar raced after him and the two men crossed the draw-bridge and entered the gloomy shaft.

In the top-floor chamber Brien Fitz Count had heard the shouts, interrupted his letter to Robert of Gloucester, and smiled at Alyse. 'It sounds as though the king's come to call. You'll be safe here, but stay away from the window.'

She had been helping him compose the letter – a reaffir-mation of loyalty to the empress – and it took her a moment to rid her mind of Matilda's image. When she had done so, she said, 'May I come up on top with you? They can't yet be within arrow-range.'

For answer, he nodded towards a corner of the solar, and she hurried over to collect her armour. It had not been specially forged for her, but had been chosen from the main armoury; a helmet with nasal and neck-guard, and a small link-mail tunic that covered her from neck to knee.

She said, 'Go on, I'll follow,' then called to Edgiva to help her into the flexible hauberk. Brien took his helmet from the back of his chair, threaded his left arm through the straps of his broad, leaf-shaped shield, and ran up the interior steps. As he left the solar, Edgiva entered, followed by her husband and the constable.

Alyse asked, '*Is* it the king?' and the soldiers nodded to-gether.

'He's brought his machines,' Varan told her. 'You'd best stay off the roof, my lady.'

'Don't worry,' she grinned. 'I can always stand you in the way.' She raised her arms, as though in surrender, and the maidservant lowered the metal tunic over her ankle-length gown. Varan hesitated, then followed Morcar on to the roof.

The wind caught them as they emerged on the ramparts, and they braced themselves against the crenellated wall. Brien was standing against the south battlements, nodding at something the watch-guards told him. He looked where they pointed, at the marsh, the forest, the rafts on the river, then crossed to the north side to see if the castle had been surrounded. Varan joined him, while Morcar told the guards to repeat their indications.

Scouring the fields and fallow land to the north, Brien said, 'He must have come straight up from Arundel. I'd like to know what really happened there.'

'Ask him,' Varan grunted. 'He'll want to meet with you, before he attacks. He'll come off better, if he talks us out of a fight.'

They returned to the south battlements and discussed the disposition of the army. 'We must destroy those machines,' Brien said. 'We can hold out here for months, so long as the walls are intact. Do you have any ideas?'

The guards said nothing. It was not their place to make suggestions. They were the eyes and ears and sinews of the castle; only sergeants and up could offer advice to their lord.

Alyse arrived, her slender shoulders bowed beneath the weight of the metal hauberk. Strangely, the armour made her seem more vulnerable, and the men instinctively formed a protective circle.

Several of Fitz Count's loyal knights emerged on the roof, and he realised that if a well-aimed missile hit the top of the keep, Wallingford would lose most of its leaders. Also, the weight of men made the wooden roof creak underfoot. He said, 'Stay away from the centre,' then told Morcar to check that the vinegar barrels were in place.

Alyse asked, 'What will you do about the catapults?'

Brien studied the double row of dray-horses that were dragging the rafts upstream. He said, 'If anyone has an immediate idea, let me hear it. Anyone. If not, get about your duties. You all have enough to do, God knows.' He glanced from face to face, shaking his head when one of the knights suggested a sortie, its object being to kill the drays and set the rafts adrift. Another knight agreed with the sortie, but said they should drag the horses forward and beach the rafts in the shallow water around the ford.

'No,' Brien repeated. 'It would be too costly. They may have archers hidden along the east bank. They'd kill us as we went out of the gate.'

There were other suggestions, some impracticable, others merely heroic. Morcar, who had not yet gone below to organise the fire-fighters, said, 'Perhaps we could float men downstream, disguised as driftwood.' He glanced at his mentor, and was encouraged when Varan said, 'Not that, but something similar. There's plenty of hay put by for the horses. Bundle it, soak it in pitch, then set it alight and send it down river.'

'It would sink before it got there,' somebody told him, and Morcar blurted, 'Not if we used the cork. We keep it to pad the soldiers' tunics. It gives them some protection against arrows. . . .'

'Why not?' Varan agreed. 'Our own rafts. The cork would keep the bundles afloat, and carry them over the ford.'

Brien nodded. 'Get it ready. We won't launch until they reach the ford.' He turned to Morcar. 'You help him with it. We'll find someone else to check the vinegar.'

The sergeant's lips twitched in an involuntary smile. He ignored the hard-eyed knights and shouldered his way around the roof. Wait till Edgiva heard about it, how he and Varan had out-thought the nobility.

As they reached the solar level, Varan told him, 'You're coming on.' It was the closest he would ever get to praise, but it was enough for Morcar that his wife was standing within ear-shot.

*

King Stephen splashed across the ford, then waved the emissary forward. The rider wore a plain white tunic and, as he trotted towards the castle, he raised a white linen banner. He had done this before – thus the extra two pence a day he was paid – but each time he grew more nervous. He was completely unarmed, and worse, unarmoured. He saw himself as an earthly interpretation of an angel, but without an angel's immortality. One arrow, one sling-shot, and he would be sent crashing from the saddle. As he neared the eighteen-foot-high walls, he mumbled ungrammatical prayers under his breath . . .

Strict formality was observed. The king summoned Brien into his presence. Brien accepted, on condition that the royal army stopped in its tracks, with the catapults down-river of the ford.

Stephen advocated an exchange of observers, but this was rejected on the grounds that the king had more to learn about the fortifications of Wallingford than Brien needed to know about his attackers. One army, he claimed, was much like another, but every castle was unique.

However, he would come out to talk, and bring two men with him. As a token of respect he invited the king to bring three. This allowed Stephen the last word, and the opportunity to display largesse towards his once lifelong friend. He replied that he would not, of course, bring three companions to the conference table; he would bring two, tit-for-tat.

They met in the meadow between Wallingford town and the castle. The king loaned a canopy, whilst Brien supplied the table and chairs. Wine was provided free by the trembling townsfolk. Nobody ate, for it would give the impression that one side or the other was short of food.

So in all things they were equal, save in the status of their attendants. Stephen was accompanied by the earls of Surrey and Leicester, the two men who, long ago, had crouched beside the dying King Henry in the hunting lodge in the Forest of Lyons and snarled contradictions at Matilda's bastard brother.

Brien was flanked by his senior knight, a man with the un-likely name of Ferrers de Ferrers, and by Constable Varan. It was mid-October, and tempers were kept cool by a bitter south-east wind.

The protagonists had not met since Stephen's Easter court

at Oxford, two and a half years ago. They had both changed in appearance, though the king's moustache was as sparse as ever. He blinked at the recognisable Greylock, and found it hard to accept that his friend-turned-enemy was two years his junior. Neither of them was young any more, yet dignity still eluded the forty-two-year-old king, whereas Fitz Count was every inch the suzerain, striding confidently into middle age. His overwhelming air of authority balanced nicely with the royal preponderance of earls.

Brien halted beside the table, bowed to Stephen, and identified his companions. The sinewy Ferrers de Ferrers nodded curtly at the king, then at Surrey and Leicester. Varan stood his ground, his eyes on Stephen.

The courtesies were returned, and the men took their places at the table, Surrey opposite Varan, Stephen and Brien in the centre, the Earl of Leicester doing his best to ignore de Ferrers. A volunteer from the town poured wine into silver goblets provided by the local monastery, then withdrew. He stood, a lone figure in the meadow, waiting to hurry forward at the first thirsty signal.

Stephen put a hand to his moustache, restrained himself in time, and let his forearms rest on the table. 'The life of treason seems to suit you, Greylock, though you're going white around the temples.'

'It's fear,' Surrey interposed. 'He knows he'll be performing a gallows dance before Christmas.' He gave a sudden start as Varan slammed a fist on the trestle table. Surrey's goblet jumped and fell on its side, and rivulets of wine ran to the table edge and dripped on his gown. 'A cockroach,' Varan explained equably. 'It looked ready to bite you, my lord. Must have fallen from your sleeve.'

The earl recovered quickly and amended his forecast. 'Two dancers,' he snarled. 'And I'll play the tune.'

'We've exchanged enough pleasantries,' Brien warned. 'Tell us why we're summoned, Lord Stephen, or we'll go back into the warmth.'

Anxious to avoid further unnerving interruptions, Stephen nodded at the castle. 'You know why you're here. Surrender

Wallingford, and there will be no bloodshed. Nor will there be any hangings. What I see as treason, you regard as loyalty, and, because we were once special friends, I shall not take revenge on you.' He smiled, and for an instant there was a trace of the earlier, happy-go-lucky Count of Blois. 'I'll even give you a manor house, until the war is won, then put you back in Wallingford again. I pardoned d'Aubigny at Arundel, and he and I were never so close as – '

'Why did you let Matilda go?'

With a quick sideways glance he said, 'Because I am no Surrey, that's why. He would have hanged the entire garrison – isn't that so?'

'I would,' the earl agreed. 'And your cousin would now be in the Tower of London, making her final confession.' He brushed irritably at his wine-stained gown, then addressed the assembled company. 'You go your own way to damnation, Fitz Count, you and your gristle-faced constable. But you, King – You have no right to sit here parleying with these vermin. Wounds of Christ, it's not a meal-table! You allowed Bishop Henry to convince you, and you set the empress at liberty, and that was the worst thing you could have done – '

Stephen turned sharply, his squirrel's fur collar rippling in the wind. 'Are you lecturing me, Warenne of Surrey?'

'Maybe; who cares? But whether I am or not, I'm telling you to behave like a king at war, not a quiescent rabbit! Your throne is being threatened, you may have noticed, not only by the bastard and his sister at Bristol, but by these creatures here! You smile and tell us how you pardoned d'Aubigny at Arundel. But what happens the next time Matilda calls? He'll let her in again, that's what, and they'll congratulate themselves at your credulity. Don't offer this traitor a pardon. Let him wait here to be hanged, or burn his nest to the ground! Let's see some fire!' He leaned forward, his hand wet with wine. 'Hey, Leicester! Your tongue still moves, doesn't it?'

His compeer nodded. 'If I may voice an opinion, Lord King, you do seem too tolerant with sworn enemies.'

'Oh, well put,' Surrey sneered. 'How forceful!'

There was a malevolent silence for a moment, and then

Stephen asked, '*Will* you come out, Greylock? You'll not be hanged, you have my word – '

'No. Not until you give Matilda her crown.'

'I cannot promise that, but you shall have your manor – '

'No.'

He questioned the scrawny Ferrers de Ferrers. 'Are you and your brother knights willing to lose all in the service of Fitz Count? How many of you must we ruin?'

'The answer to the first question is yes,' de Ferrers replied, 'though, if we retain our honour, we have not lost much. As for the second question, it probes our secrets.'

Stephen sighed. 'Then what choice have I, Greylock? I must attack you.'

'Or keep to the vows you thrice made to King Henry.'

'Hang in flames!' Surrey shouted. 'Let's see how you are when your women are alight!'

Brien rose to his feet and said he would send men to collect the table and chairs. The conference was over.

*

There were flames, but they did not scorch the buildings or occupants of Wallingford Castle. They arose instead from the pitch-soaked bundles that were sent drifting downstream to the ford. The cork blocks carried them over the bubbling shallows and, even though four in every five were doused, or hooked ashore by Stephen's men, enough reached the raft-borne catapults. By dusk they were both burning on the water.

Since the night of Stephen's coronation, four long years ago, the master and men of Wallingford had anticipated such an attack. They had rehearsed their counter-moves a hundred times, fired a thousand practice arrows, set alight their own outbuildings, then stifled the flames with vinegar. There was little an outsider could teach them, for they were already self-taught.

The offensive lasted five days, at the end of which Stephen withdrew his forces and set them to building two wooden watch-towers, one south of the Wallingford marsh, the other on the open ground to the west of the castle. They were each designed to hold fifty or sixty men, whose sole duty was to keep the world away from Wallingford. All carts and riders were to be intercepted, all river craft stopped and searched. The castle would be starved of food, materials, news – even of rumours. It would be a place alone; the Leper of the Thames.

On 27th October, King Stephen led his army west towards Trowbridge and Cerney, two more rebellious outposts. The leaders of Wallingford watched him go. Brien and Alyse climbed to the roof of the keep and were soon joined there by Varan, Morcar and Edgiva, and a handful of knights. Other knights watched from the walls, as did Ernard and the girl he had rescued from the tavern at Oxford, Eadgyth called Edith. One of the fourteen knights had been killed by a crossbow quarrel, and Ferrers de Ferrers nursed a shattered wrist. But the number of fatalities was remarkably low. Six men and a woman had died within the confines of the castle, and perhaps twice that number had been wounded. A section of the stable roof had collapsed – though this had had nothing to do with the siege – and three horses had been crushed beneath the broken timbers. Somebody had stabbed a dog to stop it barking, and a pig had broken loose from its sty and been shot by an archer, testing his skill. But these deaths and injuries were as nothing compared with the losses among the king's ranks. Surrey and Leicester had emerged unscathed, but the defenders' arrows had accounted for five knights, several dozen foot-soldiers, and God alone knew how many common labourers, hired to assist the dray-horses.

Brien Fitz Count could not claim a victory, for the country-side was now cluttered with two tall watch-towers. But the king had been forced to withdraw, and thus admit that he found Wallingford too tough for his teeth.

*

Three weeks later there were more flames, this time curling against the hastily-built watch-towers. Brien scrambled on to the battlements, turned to help Alyse up the unlit steps, then stared incredulously at Stephen's briskly burning fortresses.

Alyse asked, 'That's not your doing, is it? You didn't send out men – '

'No. We're nowhere near strong enough to sortie. There's an army out there somewhere, but – ' He shook his head in the darkness.

His wife peered at the twin flowers of flame, then ventured, 'Robert of Gloucester, perhaps? Or – or am I about to meet the fair Matilda?' She felt him tighten his grip, and complained, 'Don't break me!' Frowning, she withdrew her hand and massaged the knuckles. God in Heaven, did Brien have to react with such – fervour?

The fires crawled higher, and they heard shouts and screams, and then the towers began to fall apart. Single candles of flame toppled over, turning the ground red where they fell. The town of Wallingford was silhouetted against the blaze of the southern outpost, while the western tower sent deep shadows vaulting across the open fields. Figures were discernible, but it was impossible to tell who had fired the forts.

'I'm going out,' Brien said. 'Whoever did that, did it for us.' He hurried down the inside of the shaft and out into the bailey. Varan and Morcar were there. The horses were saddled, the knights mounted. They followed their leader and for the first time in a month the defenders rode to the attack.

It took them until dawn to find their saviour – the grinning, smoke-smeared Miles of Hereford, the first man to follow Brien and Alyse from the Great Hall at Westminster on the night of Stephen's coronation, and the first to obey Robert of Gloucester and feign a reconciliation with the king. Miles of Hereford, known as Sharpscent, because it was said he could sniff a wild boar's lair at a distance of a hundred feet, in thick undergrowth.

They met near the western tower, swung down from their horses and strode towards each other through the smoke. Their followers glanced around, to make sure none of the watch-tower archers were in a condition to let fly. Then they mopped their faces and exchanged stories of siege and sack.

Miles and Brien flung off their helmets and embraced each other. They clung together wordlessly for a moment, then stood back, arm on arm. Brien remembered the sense of shock with which he had received the news of Sharpscent's alleged reconciliation with Stephen, and even now, more than three years after, he felt a pang of shame. God, had he really doubted one of his truest friends?

'Hey, now!' Miles exclaimed. 'We've won, not lost, you know. Show some teeth, Greylock, or I'll think you're sorry I broke down the fence.'

'I'm not,' Brien assured him, 'and there's no one on earth I'm happier to see.'

With a wry grin, his rescuer said, 'Not quite true, though it's unlikely she'll visit you before Christmas.'

'The empress? Is she well?'

'She is, and asks when you will go to Bristol. But I must tell you, Earl Robert advises otherwise. He prefers you to stay on here – '

'I intend to,' Brien nodded. 'When Stephen learns of the fate of his towers – for which, by the way, I'll get some undeserved credit – he will make an all-out effort to destroy us here. It's no place for Matilda.'

Nor for Lady Alyse, Miles thought, but said nothing.

There were wounded to be cared for, dead to be buried, prisoners to be guarded. The two nobles remounted their horses, agreed to meet later in the keep, then wheeled apart. Behind them, the western tower lay like a giant cooking-pit, complete with charred twigs and bones . . .

*

On 11th December the wine-loving Roger, Bishop of Salisbury, died. King Stephen's chroniclers said it was of shame, for his having behaved in such a treasonable manner towards his monarch. Those who were opposed to the king maintained that the prelate had succumbed to a broken heart, brought about by Stephen's unjustified persecution of God's senior servants. Whatever the true cause, it gave Stephen the opportunity to secure the see of Salisbury and appropriate Roger's personal fortune. This was considerable, and helped pay for the royal Christmas at Westminster.

CHAPTER 8

ON THE FIELD
January 1140 – February 1141

ONE might have lifted a brazier of burning coals and thrown them on to a patch of grassy ground. That was how England looked, in the fifth year of King Stephen's reign. Magnified, the coals became castles, villages, even towns, for there were several towns razed by those who loved their country.

Much to Brien's surprise, Wallingford did not come under attack. Throughout that year, Stephen was kept busy elsewhere, and was unable to find time to lead an army against his lifelong friend. In mid-summer, Henry of Winchester arranged a peace conference between Queen Matilda and the Earl of Gloucester – the bishop was not so optimistic as to imagine he could bring the women together, queen to empress, Matilda to Matilda – but nothing came of the meeting, and the war continued.

In June the king summoned the Great Council to Westminster to discuss a successor to Roger of Salisbury. Bishop Henry put forward two candidates, both of whom were opposed by Stephen. Once again the king found himself at odds with his brother, who stormed from the chamber, as Brien Fitz Count and Miles of Hereford had stormed from the coronation feast, as others had later quit council and conference. As Queen Matilda sourly observed, her husband's guests seemed incapable of finishing a meal.

But if there were vacant chairs at Westminster, there was a shortage of seats at Wallingford. The Earl of Gloucester thrust his long jaw into the castle in February, and again in April. Miles of Hereford called by twice in three months, and scarcely a week passed without the warning shout of 'Riders on the river path!' and the subsequent identification of a noble visitor. They came to pay their respects to Lord Fitz Count, and to study this most easterly outpost of rebellion. They were charmed by Alyse, impressed by Brien, and subjected to the unsmiling scrutiny of Varan and his protégé, Sergeant Morcar. If Matilda and her bastard brother gave the barons spiritual encouragement, Brien and Alyse and the others taught them the stern practicalities of defence. They came and they went, these callers, and, when they returned home, they put into practice what they had learned at Wallingford-on-the-Thames.

Then, in early July, the most important visitor of all sent word that she was on her way . . .

Alyse felt greater foreboding at that time than she had ever felt before. From the day she had married Brien she had lived with the knowledge of Matilda. Throughout the years she had heard him speak well of the empress and, because she loved her husband, she had used smiles like brushwood to conceal her jealousy. There were long periods when the feeling lay dormant, and she accepted that whatever had been between them was over and done with. Then somebody, not always Brien, would mention Matilda, and Alyse would remember the letter she had discovered and allowed to unfold and allowed herself to read – 'To Brien Fitz Count, Lord of Wallingford, the most affectionate greetings and the most gentle embrace, from Matilda, his friend.' Then the pain would return, and the fears would mount.

It did not help Alyse to watch Brien prepare for the visit. He had never been innately vain, yet now he crouched in front of his precious hammered silver mirror, grooming his hair and brushing soot around the temples. He trained himself to walk with a spring, and for the first time cursed the natural wear and weather of his clothes. And as she watched him, Alyse realised that he, too, was living in fear. He might have presented himself as the firm and tolerant man he was. But instead he chose to play the youth, anxious to appear unchanged by time or travail. Did he really believe the empress had not aged, or would fail to recognise him if he was white around the ears? Did he think a dab of soot would make the world spin backwards?

Yes, she sighed, for everything must fit with his dream.

They had been given a week's warning, and the slender, dark-haired chatelaine woke every night and stared at the flickering candles in the bed-chamber, and listened for the shout and the hoofbeats. But Matilda did not arrive until the last day, and that seemed true to her nature.

She came in the afternoon, escorted by one of the largest columns Brien and Alyse had ever seen. They knew it must be her, and scarcely heard the alarm. They were dressed, as they had been dressed throughout the week, in their finest clothes, their newest shoes, their most valuable jewellery. High on their lookout tower, they watched the armoured column wind its way along the river path. 'It is she,' Brien announced. 'Come on down. Let's be at the gate to greet her.'

Alyse put a hand on his arm, frowned with concern, and said, 'You're trembling like a man with palsy. Wait on awhile, until – '

'Don't worry!' he joked. 'I'm thinking of all those mouths we have to feed! Men *and* horses!'

She looked at him, saw the tremor reach his lips, and murmured, 'Yes, of course. It's as well we have the food.' *Oh, my sweet Brien . . . What is she to you? How can she make you gibber, when the threat of fire and sword leaves you unmoved? You have had your women, more than most, and you are happy with me, and yet this single creature drives you to distraction. Why? For God's sake, why?*

He moved to the top of the steps, and beckoned to her, and held out his hand to guide her down. She snatched a last glance at the column, but she could not yet see Matilda. The guards continued shouting and, as she caught Brien's hand, she could hear the drum of hoofbeats and the clink of metal. She said, 'Go gentle, husband,' and he said, 'If I know anything, I know these steps.'

*

'Well, well,' she thought, 'my brother's not far off the truth. It *is* a pretty place.'

She raised a hand and stared with shadowed eyes at the battlements. The southern wall-walks were crowded with soldiers and servants, and the shouts of alarm had changed to a welcoming chorus. Only Brien and Varan and a handful of long-service troops had ever set eyes on the empress, but the banners of Anjou that fluttered above the column were enough to identify the caller. The garrison cheered as she approached, and then she removed her helmet and turned to look back at the column. The movement sent her long russet hair swinging around her shoulders, and the watchers roared with delight. *'There, d'you see? There she is, Henry's daughter!'* And then the chant – *'Mat-ilda . . . Mat-ilda . . . Mat-ilda!'*

The gates were open and she rode through, accompanied by her cavalry captain and a dozen knights. The body of the column halted on the river path, where they were kept in line by travel-weary sergeants.

Matilda entered the outer bailey, saw Brien – *He's darkened his hair; Gloucester said it was ashy* – and beside him, Alyse. *So . . . My brother was right about you, lady; you are the beauty. But let's see a smile, if only in pretence. Look, I'll show you how.*

She raised a hand to the watchers on the wall, and they took up the chant again. Ostlers hurried forward with mounting steps, covered for the occasion with orange silk, but the empress ignored them and sent her horse trotting around the yard. Brien and Alyse waited for her to come across to them, or stop and dismount. Standing at Brien's shoulder, Varan said, 'She's playing hard to catch,' and with an embarrassed scowl Brien told him, 'She has the right to be seen. The people welcome the tour, if you'll listen.'

The constable's expression had the permanence of granite, but his eyes were bleak with disapproval. *He* was one of the people, far more than Fitz Count, and he knew that when the cheering stopped they would wonder why Matilda had preferred them to their liege-lord. One did not visit a friend's house and first parade for the kitchen staff.

She came around the yard, swelling the cheers as she saluted the guards who manned the northern towers. Then, her popularity assured, she reined-in before her hosts. The ostlers positioned the steps and she climbed down. Behind her, the captain and knights stayed in their saddles, dominating Fitz

Count. Brien stepped forward and knelt on the hard-packed ground.

'The Lord of Heaven bless your arrival, Highness. This day is one for which we –'

'Too soon, Brien Fitz Count. Call me Empress, which I once was, or Countess, which I am now, but not yet Highness. That's to come, with your help.'

Varan gazed at her, his fists clenched against his thighs. Christ on the Cross, could she not allow her most loyal disciple to complete his first sentence? What did the title matter when he had crowned her with a word?

Alyse was also taken aback by the interruption, though her feelings were already confused. In appearance, Matilda surpassed Brien's most glowing descriptions and the chatelaine's worst fears. Her skin was flawless, her figure perfectly created, her voice low and strong. She was a creature of legend, the incarnation of an artist's dream. Angels were painted so, and the heroines of fable. She was Woman for all the Christian World, and an object of worship in the minds of men. One could come no closer to the ideal than to fill the reservoirs of one's gaze with the image of Empress Matilda.

Alyse distrusted her on sight. She acknowledged that part of this had to do with Brien, and it had, for how else could she feel about the woman who so completely haunted her husband? But her confusion did not arise from these expected feelings. She had made room in her mind for them, and Matilda's arrival merely gave them substance. Her confusion arose from another, more sinister fear – a premonition that could not yet be identified. Again it concerned Brien, or rather involved him, for at present his only concern was to placate his visitor.

He apologised for his anticipation, welcomed the empress to his castle – no, he smiled, to *her* castle – and presented his wife, the Lady Alyse, descendant of Saxon kings.

'We have met before,' Matilda said, 'in ink. When you were suffering your first reversals, three years ago or more, your lady wrote to me, pleading impoverishment. She said you were about to lose Wallingford.' She nodded at Alyse. 'We must all exaggerate our problems in time of need, eh, my lady?'

Alyse stared at her, then shook her head. 'It was the truth,' she said. 'It needed no embellishment. We *were* spent out on that first, hollow alert.' She thought of other things to say in defence of her plea, but Matilda's gaze had already wandered.

Incensed by such calculated discourtesy, and by the wounding misinterpretation of her letter, Alyse struck back. 'My husband can fully explain how things were when I appealed to you, *Highness*, but he will do so more easily on his feet. And your riders intimidate me. Set them down, if you will, before they're mistaken for invaders.' Ignoring Brien, a thing she had never done before, she nodded at Constable Varan. He moved forward immediately and said, 'We always separate the man from his horse, messires. Or, if you prefer to sit, shed your weapons.'

A dozen mouths sagged open, then snapped shut. Two dozen eyes scorched Matilda's russet hair, but she dared not turn to face them. To do so would be to admit that she had placed them there, aware that they posed a threat. Instead, she looked at Alyse – *how quickly you learn, for a Saxon offspring* – then at Varan – *yes, we have all heard about you, monster* – then at Brien, who was once again on his feet.

She said, 'We have set no limit on our call here,' and Alyse touched Varan on the arm, and he growled, 'It's in hand, my lady,' and told the empress, 'Correct. It's Lord Fitz Count who sets the limits. If your men have come to stay, they'll join us on foot. You see the value of it. We may be short of money, but we still control our house.'

Matilda said, 'I thought Fitz Count called it mine – ' then realised that she, once wife of the Emperor of Germany, now wife of the Count of Anjou, and future Queen of England, was being held to account by this hideous, blunt-nosed Saxon. Christ and His angels! They laid some pretty traps along the Thames!

As she sealed her lips, Varan continued, this time addressing the mounted line. 'Now you know our ways, messires, dismount, or sit outside; whichever you will. But *nobody* looks down on the Fitz Counts, Lord or Lady, *and least of all in their own home*!' His seamed and chiselled face was purpled with anger. *This* was why they kept him at Wallingford. Why else would they pay high for a bare-fanged dog, unless it could strike terror into an intruder? And there was something personal in it, for he was sixty-two years of age, and he was being challenged by a dozen disdainful knights and a grizzled captain of cavalry who should have known better. Well, messires, the dog snarls, and is anxious to bite.

'Down or out. Make your choice.'

They dismounted without a word, and the ostlers and off-duty soldiers and farm-bred servants came forward to collect the horses. As they did so, Alyse moved over and linked her arm in Brien's. He looked at her, and there was pain in his eyes, for he, too, was being forced to choose.

'Well,' Matilda said, 'now that you have confiscated our transport, you are stuck with us. Are we allowed into the keep, or would that also contravene the rules of the house?'

Brien shook his head, unwilling to hold her responsible for her words. She was tired, that was it, fatigued by the journey from Bristol, exhausted by the ebb and flow of recent events. They had demanded too much of her; no wonder she was snappish.

He slipped his arm free from Alyse and held it out parallel to the ground, his fingers extended. 'You know you are welcome, Empress. If your senior knight will escort my lady – '

'Otto de Rochese.'

Brien acknowledged the man who bowed in line, then continued, ' – we will go inside. My own knights will entertain yours in the inner yard. The tables should be set up there by now.' He moved beside Matilda, then felt his body stir with excitement as she laid her hand over his. Her skin was cool, and she curled her thumb around the edge of his hand. He told Varan to find Sergeant Morcar and see that the waiting column were fed, both men and horses. Alyse glanced sharply at him, but what was said was said, and she could not make him reverse the command. There were few warlords as well versed in administration as Brien Fitz Count, so he must be aware that his generosity would halve the food-stocks of Wallingford.

Matilda did not trouble to thank him. Why should she?

Greylock had known she would visit him, and had therefore known she would travel with a large protective force. He must have made provision, else he would not have said eat. Gratitude was unnecessary.

They went through the inner gate, Matilda with Brien, Alyse with the bulky Otto de Rochese. The knight said, 'I'm as hungry as a brachet hound,' then coughed when Alyse ignored the remark.

Varan watched them go, and let his shoulders sag to release the tension. Then he turned to the south wall and called up to the garrison knights to come and take charge of their visitors.

Sergeant Morcar also responded to the call, first helping Edgiva down the steps, then nodding as she said, 'Lady Alyse may need me in there.'

'Go along then.' He smiled at his wife. 'You want to rub shoulders with the empress, is that it?'

'Why not? I sat in the next room to her cousin, the king, you remember?'

'I remember. The night of his coronation, when you could have spent the time with me.'

Pleased that he still felt greedy for her, she repaid his smile and hurried away towards the inner gate. Morcar caught Varan's impatient gaze and went over to join him. Matilda's knights were no longer in line, but bunched together, discussing painful ways of dispatching the watchdog of Wallingford. They were astonished when Morcar arrived. Fitz Count must have a mould, from which he turned out these gravelled brutes . . .

*

Matilda stayed with them until the evening. They discussed the progress of the war, and Alyse nursed her premonition, waiting for it to die, or blossom like some colourful, poisonous weed. In the heart of her heart she knew what it was, but it was too cruel a thing to set in the light.

She believed that Empress Matilda would someday destroy Brien Fitz Count.

There it was, unsupported by evidence, an intuition that could not be communicated. There were no witnesses she could call, no example she could cite, nothing to bolster the indefensible conviction that Matilda would ruin Brien. And worse – something the chatelaine could scarcely accommodate, even within the most private recess of her mind – the more ominous conviction that it would be done without regret, since the empress felt not the slightest dusting of genuine affection for Greylock of Wallingford.

He believed he loved Matilda, and she him, and Alyse had yet to discover what, in his past, had fostered such ardent worship. She, too, had believed it, and lived with the fear of it – until now. But to-day, seeing the elegant, peerlessly beautiful Matilda for the first time, Alyse abandoned her own defences and moved to safeguard her husband.

She knew she could be accused of jealousy, possessiveness, meanness of spirit. Look at Matilda, the world would say. She is unsurpassed. Listen to her when she is not under such present strain. Hear how she can charm and hearten. Admire her for her courage, this woman who dares to out-stare men. She is faultless, can you not see it, a perfect creation.

And what are you, but a Saxon lady in a small, well-sited castle, the wife of a minor baron, a beautiful creature made plain alongside the empress, the countess, the soon-to-be-queen? Your skin is as green as emerald, Lady Alyse, as green as the stone of envy. Oh, yes, the world would say all that, and it would be impossible to deny.

But the world could go hang. Dogs scent cats, don't they? Scouts scent an ambush. Criminals scent arrest. Why, then, should a woman not sniff the perfumed air and know her husband was entranced?

Throughout that warm July afternoon, Alyse watched Brien become more deeply enmeshed in the web. Every phrase he used, every movement he made, every expression he adopted, all were arranged to please the empress. This man, who was known across the disc of the world for his courage and loyalty, and respected, even by his enemies, for his unswerving moderation – often more severe than extremism – this man who should have been the first to recognise falsity of emotion was stuck like a fly on the sticky strands of flattery.

Alyse sat in her high-backed chair and watched Matilda go to work. The last time Brien had met the empress was in the summer of 1132. Alyse had been his wife for three years then, and it was the only occasion on which he had left her and travelled abroad. And now, eight years later, he was as enamoured as ever. He laughed where, at other times, he would have smiled, and yessed in place of a nod.

Matilda drummed her long fingers on the table and said, 'I heard you were a father, Greylock. Where's the boy?'

'No,' Brien told her. 'We have no children. Who told you – '

'I forget. Someone. No matter, you'll be pleased to learn that my sons thrive. In particular, the young Henry. But you would know that.'

Alyse eased forward in her chair and watched Brien suck at the wine he had served. She heard Matilda continue, 'He's a strapping lad, though I suspect he will also discolour.'

'How so?' she asked, as Brien frowned into his glass.

'Oh, it's an unfounded suspicion,' Matilda dismissed. 'It's just that I remember, when Greylock and I were children together, he had the same pallor to his skin. Henry's healthy, as I say, but – '

'Then he is already discoloured.'

'In the face, yes. I meant, his hair might go grey.'

Alyse opened her mouth, then closed it. Her question was not yet well enough rehearsed, nor had she dredged up sufficient courage to ask it. In the silence that followed, Edgiva poured wine for the guests, then retired to her place by the door. Alyse drank, replaced the glass and murmured, 'How old is he now, your son?'

'Seven years and a few months.' She waited, perhaps in innocence, perhaps with the blade poised to strike. Then she said, 'He's a March child. It's said the happiest ones are born in the spring.' She held her glass, and smiled over the rim.

Seven years and a few months . . . A March child . . . So, in March of 1133 . . . And Brien had last seen her in the summer of the previous year . . . But not in June, surely not in –

Yes, in May and June. He had been with her then, in May and June, and the child's hair might turn prematurely grey, and she could sit there like one of Bishop Henry's diamond-headed snakes, her lips stretched above the cut-glass goblet, oh, my God, my dear merciful God . . .

'I am ill,' she said, 'forgive me. Go on with your – Edgiva, see me upstairs. I think I shall – ' She came out of the box chair, lurched against the table, then spun round, snatching at the high, carved chair rim. Brien and Otto came to their feet, and Edgiva ran forward to catch her mistress.

Matilda said, 'I always travel with a physician. He is at your disposal. Get him, de Rochese.' All the time she spoke, her eyes were on Brien.

*

In the following month, King Stephen came into open conflict with one of his most powerful magnates, the embittered Ranulf of Chester. Ranulf, known as *de Gernons*, the Moustache, was still incensed with the king over the matter of the Carlisle inheritance. More than four years had passed since Stephen had bestowed Ranulf's patrimony on King David of Scotland, but if Stephen had long forgotten the incident, the fiery Earl of Chester had not. Four years, or fourteen, or forty; they were but a click of the fingers to the indignant northern baron. No matter that he ruled the vast county of Chester, nor that he possessed fiefdoms in more than twenty English shires. Carlisle had belonged to his father, and by rights it should now belong to him, and he intended to get it back.

He laid his plans with care, and then, in the third week of August rode eastward across the waist of England. He was accompanied by his wife, his half-brother, William of Roumare, William's wife and a strong contingent of knights. The group travelled to within half a mile of the royal castle at Lincoln, then turned aside into a deserted stone quarry. While the knights relaxed and ate a cold meat and bread meal – smoke from a cooking-pit might disclose their hideout – Ranulf conferred with his local spies. They told him what he wanted to know; the castellan of Lincoln and his senior knights had left the castle an hour earlier, bent on their usual Thursday boar hunt. They would be away until dusk, perhaps until full dark.

Ranulf leaned on the hilt of his sword, watched their eyes to see if they were lying, then asked, 'How many are left inside?'

'We cannot be sure,' they told him, 'but our estimate lies between thirty and forty.'

'And the gates are shut tight?'

'As ever, sire. There is even a password, though it changes from day to day, and we've been unable to – '

'That's of no concern; we won't need it.' Careful to the last, he paid the men, then told his knights to bind them hand and foot. The spies submitted quietly, aware that they would be held in the quarry until the job was finished. They thought it an unnecessary precaution, for they would rather have crossed the devil himself than Ranulf the Moustache, but they admired his thoroughness.

That done, he discussed the situation with brother William, and they went over to apprise their wives. Two fresh palfreys were made ready, and the women mounted and rode out of the quarry and back on to the Lincoln road.

The chatelaine was more than usually pleased to see them, for Thursdays were always empty, with the men away. They had met before, on occasion, and they spent the afternoon in gossip-fed conversation. The visitors explained that their husbands would be along later to collect them.

An hour before dusk, Ranulf and three of his knights unbuckled their sword belts, withdrew their boot knives and *main-gauche* daggers, and handed them to William. Then they, too, mounted up and followed the road to Lincoln.

The gate-guards watched the four men approach, recognised the red moustache and assumed that one of the other three was William of Roumare. They were relieved to see that the riders were unarmed, for it would save embarrassment. The Lord of Lincoln had insisted that no armed stranger be allowed into the castle, but *he* had never had to voice such a command to Ranulf of Chester. The drawbridge was lowered and the gates swung inward, and the guards were in the act of saluting their noble visitors when Ranulf snarled, 'Now! Get to it!' and the riders hurled themselves from the saddle.

Before shock had turned to reason, the skirmish was over. The guards were slammed back against the gatehouse walls, their throats pricked with their own weapons. A spear shaft was jammed into the winding mechanism of the drawbridge. The gates were bolted in the open position. One of Ranulf's knights dashed out into the entranceway, waved his arms in silent exhortation, then ran back into the bailey, followed by William and the invading force. They spread out across the yard, swarmed up the watchtower steps, infiltrated the chambers and passageways. Within moments they had achieved the most audacious victory of the war. The bridge was raised, the gates shut and barred, the arrow-loops manned. The banner of Lincoln was hauled down and that of Chester run up in its place. The castle was taken and, in the solar, the unwitting chatelaine laughed at an item of scandal, amusingly presented by the Lady of Roumare . . .

*

It was not only the matter, but the manner of it, that enraged the king. It was bad enough that Earl Ranulf and his scabrous brother had turned against their monarch and seized a reputedly impregnable fortress, but to have done it in so brazen a manner reduced the Lord of Lincoln and, by association, Stephen, to a laughing-stock. With members of the nobility changing sides every day, it was becoming impossible to keep the lists up to date. Tomorrow, some other ambitious baron might knock at a royalist door and, if admitted, expel the occupants. God's teeth, it might be London itself next time!

Stephen determined to recapture the castle and make an example of the traitors. If he hanged them high and left them long, their rotting bodies might act as a deterrent to other would-be turncoats. There was something innately sobering in the sight of a hanged man, turning in the wind.

He brought his army north through the first snows of winter, and the white fields around Lincoln were soon churned into a morass by men and mounts and a bewildering variety of siege machines. There had always been an element of the experimental in siege warfare, and the terrain afforded the king the opportunity to try out some of the latest weapons. Along with the trebuchet – a massive sling, capable of launching a half-hundredweight rock – and the similar petrary and French-developed *perrier*, there were the rams and assault towers, the ballistas and springals – both forms of giant crossbow – and the straightforward mangonels and catapults. The missiles ranged from polished rocks that splintered on impact, to bales of burning, pitch-soaked straw, and the carcases of germ-ridden cattle. Metal bolts were loosed, and stone chips, and barrels of quicklime. If a man could not be transfixed, he could be torn by the shards of granite, or burned by the caustic powder.

And there were the new inventions; clay tubes that fragmented when they hit, releasing a cloud of iron darts; grappling hooks that, in flight, towed long leather ladders; four-pointed spikes, so designed that, wherever they landed, they formed a tripod, with the remaining spike erect.

This, at any rate, was the theory. In practice, the clay tubes often broke the instant they were launched, spraying the darts over the engineers. The ladders tended to twist in the air, while, nine times out of ten, the hooks failed to grapple the battlements. The spikes, called caltraps, were more effective, but if they fell short, they littered the ground beneath the walls, or whirled back at the attackers.

Apart from the freedom to manœuvre, an advantage denied to Ranulf and William, one other important factor favoured the king. The citizens of Lincoln had remained loyal, and welcomed the advent of the royal army. Ranulf had expected otherwise, and soon realised that, without outside help, he would lose his latest acquisition. No castle was impregnable; it merely resisted certain methods for a certain time.

He turned his eyes towards Bristol, towards Earl Robert of Gloucester. The long-jawed Robert was the man to ask, for although the earls of Gloucester and Chester shared a mutual antipathy, they had one thing in common. Ranulf's wife was Robert's daughter, and he would come, if only for her.

He timed his exit with the care he had given to his entrance, and used the distractions of Christmas Eve to cover his escape. He did not take his wife with him, telling her she would be safer in the castle than on the road. He did not tell her that, if she came with him, there would be no reason for Robert to play the saviour.

*

The half-year at Wallingford had brought Alyse the first real unhappiness since her marriage to Brien Fitz Count. Matilda's visit, and the inferences she had made, had thrown Alyse into the depths of despair. Time and again she went over Matilda's words, and time and again recoiled from her understanding of them. The empress had not *said* that Brien was the father of her elder son, but she had voiced her suspicions about the boy's hair, and made quite sure they acknowledged the year and month of his birth. Everything she *had* said had indicated Brien's paternity, and there was no doubt that he had been with Matilda at the time of her conception. Indeed, he admitted it, though he swore he had never lain with her and claimed ignorance of Henry's birth-date.

When she had recovered sufficiently to broach the subject, she asked, 'Why, then, did Matilda mention her son, and say you would know about it?'

Brien shrugged. 'God alone can tell. She must have meant that I'd have heard about the boy, that's all. Alyse – '

'Yes,' she said, 'that's the name to use now. But when was it Matilda? You know you are enamoured of her. You have always been. And you *were* there when she – when you – Oh, God, must I say it out?'

He so much wanted to comfort her, to roar defiance at the empress, to somehow prove to his wife that what had been almost said was not almost true. But he could not, for he *had* been with Matilda during those early summer months, eight years ago.

And he *had* lain with her.

And he believed what she had almost said.

And, if it was true, if Stephen was deposed, and Matilda

took her place on the throne of England, then her elder son would become prince of the realm, and Brien Fitz Count might well be the father of a future king.

Yes, he had lain with Matilda. He was guilty of everything Alyse suspected, and he felt laughter rise like gall in his throat. Just once, that was all. That one time, one single act of un-faithfulness in all the years of marriage, and from his seed there might spring the second King Henry of England. One brief intercourse of passion – oh, yes, brief, for Count Geoffrey had been due to arrive – and it had haunted Fitz Count and he had ever since been enmeshed in Matilda's web.

He thought of others he knew, Miles of Hereford, Baldwin de Redvers, dozens more, all of whom lived lives of easy debauchery. They were still good men, caring for their wives and those in their charge, but they were consummate – the ideal word – consummate lovers of women. House servants and pig girls tumbled beneath them; countesses and chatelaines preceded them into the bed-chamber. They sired bastards with casual indulgence, regarding fidelity as something to be offered to liege-lords and monarchs.

The laugh became more bitter with the realisation that he might have chosen any other woman than Matilda, and gone unpunished. However, he had not chosen Matilda. She had chosen him.

For Alyse, the pain cut deeper. If Brien had sewn his seed within Matilda's body, and become the father of her child, then it meant that the Lady of Wallingford was barren. It was something she had always feared, though not a thing she had ever dared discuss. There were many who were barren in those times. It was called the Eastern Disease, for the early settlers in the Holy Land were often made arid, as though by the nature of the country. It was common, too, in the West, but there was no more hurtful a question spouse could ask of spouse than, 'Are you unable?'

Until Matilda's visit, Brien had believed that it was he who was unable.

Until she heard the empress hint and insinuate, and saw

Brien's reaction, Alyse had believed that it was she who had failed.

But now, despite the denials, they both flinched from the mirror, for Brien saw himself as nothing more than a progenitor, robed in deceit, whilst Alyse turned away from her hollow, tear-stained reflection.

It was with something akin to relief that she heard Brien say he'd received a call to arms from Robert of Gloucester and was required to join the rebel army at Lincoln. 'I must go. You understand – '

'Yes. Go. I shall pray for you. Come back when you will. I'll hold Wallingford till then.'

'It's Robert's daughter. That damned madman Ranulf of Chester . . . She's ringed in by Stephen's army. We must do what we can – '

'I said yes, husband. There are no barriers in your way. Leave what men you can spare, and go along.'

'I'll leave you Morcar, he's well enough trained by now. He'll sense what Varan would do.'

Alyse nodded, then ran forward and clung to him, her body wracked with weeping. They both knew why, but they pretended it was because they would be apart. There was no time left for truth.

*

'Before the sword is drawn, he cuts . . .'

They were conversant with the poem, and knew, as soon as they reached Lincoln, that Stephen was living the part. He had come north with his army, but for every foot-soldier there was an engineer, for every archer a cooper, assembling the barrels that would hold the quicklime. Equipped for a siege, Stephen had discounted all thoughts of pitched battle and was totally unprepared for the arrival of the opposing force, under the joint command of Earl Robert, Ranulf the Moustache, Miles of Hereford, and Brien Fitz Count.

In London, and later on the windswept fields of Lincoln, the peacock-loving Bishop of Winchester had advised his brother to supplement his ranks. 'You could not even deal with a counter-attack from the castle. This collection of catapults and paraphernalia, what good is it against a hundred charging knights? You've turned the field into a forest of balanced timbers, and you risk losing the lot. What if Matilda or Robert ride to the rescue? You'll spend all your time dodging behind these constructed trees. Get more men up here, brother, before you're made to look bad.'

But the advice had gone unheeded, and the flat grey light of 2nd February, 1141, revealed two armies, only one of which was ready to fight on the flat.

That day was both a Sunday and Candlemas. On the rebel side, mass was celebrated early, and in haste, but the royal army was still on its knees when the perimeter guards raised the alarm. The enemy were advancing, and would soon be within arrow-range. Bishop Henry abandoned the service and the soldiers fled to their positions – and in many cases continued their flight.

As the sky paled, promising further falls of snow, Stephen stared aghast at his depleted ranks. As many as one-fourth of his troops had deserted the field, whilst the rest were assembled in two wavering lines.

To the west were ranged three distinct enemy divisions. The one nearest the castle was commanded by Ranulf the Moustache. In the centre was the main force, under Earl Robert. On the right flank, a contingent of Welsh mercenaries and a number of minor barons, with their sergeants and men, all under the dual command of Miles and Brien. Ranulf intended to strike the first blow, and was busy rehearsing his battlecry – 'Remember Carlisle!'

Between the armies stood the siege machines, as though arranged to form an obstacle course in the snow. Riderless horses cantered among the slings and catapults, and the cold air rang with the dissonance of menace and indecision.

Then, in keeping with the formalities of war, the rebels halted to hear the pre-battle speeches.

Ranulf claimed their attention, pointed to the castle and thanked those who had come to save his wife. She was courage itself, this daughter of Gloucester, and had proved once again that even a delicate and determined woman could outwit an imitation king.

'He's been here a month or more, and he's yet to make the slightest impression on the castle. Or on my lady. When this is over, and we have rescued her, she will probably tell us we were not needed. "But, my Lord Ranulf," she'll say, "why bring these fine men on such a cold journey? I was about to go out with a broom and sweep Stephen off the step!" '

The army roared its delight, and Ranulf bowed in the saddle. Then, no longer needing the height, he dismounted and had his horse led to the rear. The field was slippery underfoot, but it would be worse if the destrier lost its balance and threw him on to the iron-hard ground. Looking around, he saw that several of his compeers and their knights had reached the same decision.

Now Robert of Gloucester took over, listing the king's nobles and finding something scathing to say about each of them. This one was a foul excrement, that one a coward, whose feet worked in reverse. Another was undoubtedly gifted – a gifted liar and oath-breaker, while a fourth sought satisfaction with animals and dead women. They were facing, he said, the cesspool of England, and the sooner it was scoured clean, the better for everyone . . .

The insults were hurled back by Stephen's leaders. The king himself was no shouter, so he delegated his speech to one of his more resonant barons.

The Earl of Gloucester was a unique creature, for where else would one find an animal with the jaw of a lion and the heart of a rabbit? He was abnormal, and would remain so, until he rid himself of the Idiot of Chester and the embarrassing Miles of Hereford, who stained every bench and saddle. And it would not do to forget Matilda's grey squirrel, Brien Fitz Count, whose only ambition was to scurry inside her gown. What a sad collection to bring against the lawful King of England; they must be defeated, but it would be done more in sorrow than in wrath. They were the dregs of the barrel, which no one cared to drink . . .

The first snow fell and was blown across the field. The

troops settled their equipment, notched arrows into bow-strings, murmured a final prayer, snarled a late-thought curse. Then they moved forward among the war machines.

Stephen had also chosen to fight nearer the ground, and had taken up his position opposite Ranulf of Chester. He would have been more properly placed in the centre, face to face with Matilda's champion, Earl Robert, but this present confrontation would not have occurred had it not been for Ranulf's personal enmity towards his monarch. The capture of Lincoln had been Ranulf's answer to the loss of Carlisle, and it seemed right that they should seek each other out, both crying thief.

There had been no specific order to dismount, so, although most of the rebels had discarded their horses, more than half the king's knights and nobles were still in the saddle. This enabled them to move faster about the field, or smash a path through the enemy lines. But it also made escape more certain and, within the first half-hour of the battle, all but a dozen of the riders had turned and fled.

They had their reasons.

They had not come north to engage in pitched battle, but to lay siege to Lincoln Castle. As a result, they were under-manned, and had chorused Bishop Henry's advice concerning the need for more foot-soldiers. Nor had they chosen this un-likely meeting-place, but had been taken by surprise – as had their king.

All in all, he had dug a trap for himself and now invited his supporters to tumble in with him. They had stayed thus far, partly out of loyalty, partly out of curiosity, to see if the rebels posed a real threat. That confirmed, they saw no value in being massacred in the cold. They would ride back to Westminster, and take their men with them, and prosper from the experi-ence. If the king had any sense he'd keep them company, and admit his mistakes later, in the warm.

But Stephen had no intention of quitting the field. He had Ranulf in his sight, and he welcomed the chance to kill him. He had always thought the Earl of Chester a potential traitor. If it had not been Lincoln, it would have been somewhere else.

There was, too, an unspoken reason for his wanting Ranulf dead. For some time now he had been made the butt of comparisons between Ranulf's florid moustache and his own sparse growth. From all over the country – and on two occasions from Normandy, and one from Flanders – came vials and pots containing the essences and secretions that would, if rubbed on or swallowed, inhaled or sprinkled, stimulate the growth. He had tried some of them, though he had stopped short of the draughts for fear they had been poisoned. But they had only succeeded in stinging his skin, or creating a foul stench in his nostrils and making his eyes water. Some of the potions came from priests and other literate subjects and were accompanied by a letter, in which the king was promised as remarkable a moustache as that of – yes, invariably, Ranulf de Gernons.

Well, to hell with Ranulf *and* his deep-rooted hedge. He was about to enjoy his first shave in years. With a sharp, four-foot sword.

The snow fell more thickly, concealing the horrors of battle. Men staggered through the white curtain, sudden bloody apparitions that were immediately covered by the drifting lace. Friend struck blindly at friend, or mistook the enemy and was cut down. Horses ran loose, until they collided with the mangonels, or with each other, or were hit by stray arrows. Then they, too, went down, or plunged on, maddened with pain.

The rebel right, under Miles and Brien, inflicted heavy casualties on the royalist lines. The earls of Surrey and Leicester joined the mass desertions, and their leaderless troops found themselves being herded towards the centre. The two lines merged and contracted, and the rebels closed round them, like a hand around a chess-piece.

Robert of Gloucester pushed forward, and his division emerged from the forest of catapults. Stephen's depleted force wheeled within the circle, for although the lines to his left had been broken, he had forced Ranulf to give ground.

So far, he had only glimpsed the earl, and both men had been too hard pressed to seek out their adversary. But as a sudden wind gusted across the field, tearing holes in the white curtain,

Stephen and Ranulf stumbled against each other, then drew back, swords whirling.

Already, the most outstanding feature of the battle was the courage shown by the king. No one had ever added cowardice to the list of his failings, but from the outset he had fought with grim determination, endangering any who came within sword-swing. He had been cut twice on the arm and had had one of his link-mail mittens wrenched from his hand. His helmet had been dented by a sling-shot, and the side of his face was smeared with the blood of a recent victim. The snow had been stamped to water underfoot and had soaked through his leather boots. He was cold, exhausted by killing, deserted by all but a handful of his barons. He had every excuse to abandon the fight, snatch at one of the free-roaming horses, and follow his courtiers to London.

But that did not take into account his personal enmity towards Ranulf. When he had shaved The Moustache, then, perhaps, but not before.

They squared-off, the King of England, and one of his most powerful magnates, and their breath leaked like smoke in the wind. They said nothing, for they had not come there to talk, but each filled his chest with air and moved forward again, flat-footed, the swordblades shining with watered blood.

They struck at the same instant, sword on sword, and were sent reeling by the impact of the blow. Men fought around them, but no rebel thought to attack the king, nor royalist to edge crabwise at Ranulf. This was single combat, and it would be a most shameful crime to interfere.

They struck again, staggered and caught their balance. Ranulf used his powerful wrists to hold his sword horizontal, and stabbed forward with it, aiming at Stephen's groin. The king recoiled, but was unable to avoid the bruising ram of the sword-point. He hunched forward, gasping, then brought his own sword over in a desperate downward arc. It drove Ranulf's blade into the ground, but the king's sword snapped off a foot from the hilt.

He saw Ranulf lean back, dragging on his embedded weapon. In the moment it took the earl to release the blade,

Stephen glanced left and right, saw what he wanted, and mouthed, 'You? Are you with me?' As he addressed the nearby soldier he hefted the broken sword, ready to use it as a dagger if need be. But the man nodded, sensed what his king was after, and thrust a Danish axe at him, handle foremost. Stephen snatched it, glimpsed Ranulf's blade rise up from the ground, and blundered forward, wielding the axe.

It was a lucky, unmeasured swing, that might as easily have missed as hit. But it did hit, catching Ranulf a solid blow on the helmet. His sword fell from his grasp and he reeled sideways, his mailed hands flailing the air. He went down heavily, and his metal tunic seemed to ripple as he landed. He made an effort to rise, crashed over on his back and lay, staring dazedly at the three-inch spike that tipped the axe. *The devil foul him,* he thought. *He's going to spit me.*

Stephen intended just that, or at least the semblance of it. But before he could know his own mind – skewer the bastard, or keep him to be hanged – a sling-shot flew from the rebel lines and caught him square in the throat. The blow crushed his windpipe, and fresh blood dripped from where the rock had skinned the underside of his jaw. He sank to his knees, one hand covering his battered throat, the other grasping but failing to hold the axe. It twisted over, and the spike went into the ground a hand's width from Ranulf's face.

The pain in Stephen's groin was still intense, and vied for attention with his new injuries. He sank lower, his body stooped forward, his neck exposed. Never before in battle had he been so vulnerable to sword or axe blade. He awaited execution.

But his enemies had other plans for him. He felt fingers on his neck, felt someone drag off his helmet, felt his unseen assailant jerk back his head and yell, 'To me, everyone, to me! I have the king! Over here! I have the king! I have the king!'

Ranulf climbed to his feet, stared down at king and captor, then lashed out viciously with his boot. Stephen vomited over his captor's forearm, and the snowflakes spun and expanded and blew against his face like jagged white sea-birds. The sky grew dark, and there was red in it, then black, only black. . .

*

Among the prisoners was young Gilbert de Renton, the fashion-conscious courtier who had been kidnapped and held to ransom by the hooded monster outside Dorchester. As he was being led away he caught sight of Brien Fitz Count, his head and left leg bandaged, in conversation with a stocky, bleak-eyed companion. There was something familiar about the second man, something in his stance and the slope of his shoulders. Gilbert was sure they'd met before, and not at court, or on the field. He frowned, then stumbled forward as one of the rebel guards gave him a shove.

'Still your hands, oaf! I'm a de Renton, and – '

'We know,' the guard grunted. 'We watched most of your family skitter off.'

Four hundred pounds, Gilbert thought. That's what it cost them last time, when I was taken by – Then he turned and squawked, 'I knew I had – It's *him*! Hey, you, guard! What's he called, that squat creature standing with Lord Fitz Count?'

'Turn on me again like that, and I'll give you a knife to chew on. Now get moving!'

Gilbert scowled irritably and followed the line of prisoners. He could imagine how his family would react when they were presented with their second ransom demand in four years. They'd think their fashionable offspring was out to finance the entire rebel cause, single-handed.

But at least he had not run. His family would have to admire him for that. Wouldn't they? No, they wouldn't. They'd think him untimely, and expensive, and wonder why it had not occurred to them to creep up behind him in the mêlée of battle and resolve the problem of ransoms and clothes bills.

The guard pushed him again and he stumbled on, an unsung hero.

*

Ranulf did not stay to crow. He accompanied Robert of

Gloucester into the castle, embraced his wife and half-brother, then collected a large force of mercenaries and paid a visit to Lincoln town. By the time the visitors had finished, the town was in flames, the churches desecrated, the wells and sewers choked with corpses. The earl's companions specialised in rape and strangulation. It was their way of showing the inhabitants that loyalty to the crown, like treason, could be misplaced.

CHAPTER 9

THE LADY OF ENGLAND
March–June 1141

THEY had met that one brief time at Arundel, and she had told him to stop fiddling with his moustache, and to reimburse the pardoned William d'Aubigny. Then she had ridden away, astonished by her cousin's foolish gallantry.

And now they met again, one week after the battle at Lincoln, and she had more things to tell him.

She sat in a cushioned, high-backed chair in the vaulted conference chamber in Gloucester Castle. Her bastard brother was seated at her right hand, Miles of Hereford at her left. Brien Fitz Count was due some time that day, having detoured by way of Wallingford, but she was not inclined to wait for him. She would thank him later, in private, after she had disposed of the prisoner.

She made a sign, and he was brought in. His head was held high, not with pride, but because his throat had been bandaged, and the bandage enclosed within an iron collar. He moved slowly, taking short steps, as befitted a man who had been chained and manacled. Robert of Gloucester glanced sharply at his sister, then said, 'What is this? Release him, for God's sake! He is no common felon.'

Matilda snapped at the heels of his words. 'Leave him be! No, brother, he's a very uncommon felon, and he'll stay anchored down. What's that stuff around his throat? It's too bad if the collar chafes.'

Robert looked past her at Miles. 'Who commanded this?'

For answer, Miles let his gaze flicker to the empress, then away again. She repeated her question, and Robert said, 'He was wounded, can't you tell? Matilda, please, this is grotesque. At least take off the collar. Look at him, he's an ill man!'

She smiled with the thoroughness of insincerity. She had

made her point – *she* had shackled the king – and now she could emphasise it with mercy. 'Very well, unlock him. Yes, yes, and the legs. Find him a seat. Give him something to drink, whatever he wants, wine or water. Make him comfortable, by all means, make him comfortable.'

Stephen stared at her. His dry tongue scraped the roof of his mouth and butted against his clenched teeth. She looked so beautiful sitting there, robed and jewelled, her russet hair brushed until it shone, her elegant fingers curled over the carved pommels of the chair.

He thought, if only I had the juice, I would spit in her face.

Somebody brought him a stone mug of water – no goblet for the prisoner-king – and he lifted it to his lips. The water tasted stale, and he tried not to swallow. He said, 'You should change the casks here,' but the words emerged broken from his damaged throat.

Matilda frowned, seemed ready to ask him to repeat them, then said, 'You've fallen badly cousin. You've come to a messy end, wouldn't you say?' She sighed, for all the world steeped in sorrow, then again reverted to compassion, an artist changing her colours. 'I'm sorry you were damaged in the fight. But I am more sorry you were in it at all. Give it up now, Stephen. Return the crown you stole, and I'll let you rejoin your wife and take her to – where shall we say – the island of Cyprus? It's sunny there, all the year. Or join your friend, the King of France. Or settle in Ireland, we could allow that, why do you shake your head?'

Is it not evident? I am refusing you.

'Do you understand what I say?'

I'm nodding. Yes, I understand.

'Can't he speak at all?'

'Not for the present,' Robert told her. 'The physicians say his throat will heal, but slowly.'

'Well, I say this. He is finished as king. You. Stephen. Your reign is ended. If you are prepared to sign the necessary papers and surrender the accoutrements of monarchy, we will let you go. There are enough witnesses here. All you need do is nod. Do you declare that you gained the throne of England by false means, and are now willing to admit your errors, sins, failings, shortcomings and the like? In short, cousin, are you ready to step down? A nod will suffice. Just nod.'

She leaned forward slightly and watched him move his head – from side to side.

Hurry on to hell, Matilda. You are not what you seem. You have come a long way on your looks and spirit, but if you were ugly, or docile, we would not even know your name.

She sat back, stared at him for a moment, then murmured, 'Dress him again. Take him down to Bristol. Find him somewhere dark and deep. I want no more of him, until he's ready to sign. *I said dress him!*'

Guards hurried forward to clamp the irons around his neck and ankles. Robert of Gloucester came out of his chair, pushed back against the upper rim and strode from the chamber. The chair crashed to the tiled floor and the back board splintered. Miles of Hereford stood up, risked one appealing glance at Matilda, then followed Robert from the room. The empress sat impassive, watching the guards manacle her cousin. She thought it as well that Ranulf of Chester was not present, for then things would have gone badly for Stephen.

*

Success, when it comes, brings attendant dangers.

There are those who parade it, like some proud leopard on a leash, never aware that the beast must be respected and nurtured. They make no attempt to understand the nature of their prize, and are amazed when it escapes, or turns to savage them.

And there are those who track the animal to its lair, then retreat, their courage evaporated. They realise that it is the search, and not the capture that excites them, and that they are not equipped to possess the beast. They are the unhappy ones, for they know they brought the net, but must ever afterward explain why they did not throw it.

And there are those who have learned how to ensnare the animal, and contain it, and they bring back a perfect specimen, and fondle its ears. Their friends come forward to admire it, whilst their enemies steer clear.

And then, in wilful disobedience of all they have learned, they destroy that which is most precious to them. Thus do husbands alienate their wives, and liege-lords lay waste their fiefdoms, and queens despoil their thrones.

Thus did the Empress Matilda mutilate the leopard of England.

*

She watched the convoy take Stephen down to Bristol. Brien had not yet arrived from Wallingford, though he had sent word to say his wife was ill with fever. Alyse was indeed ill, but he was unwilling to give the true cause. The empress sent her well-wishes, ending her note with the cryptic suggestion, 'Join me as soon as possible. Preferences and promotions become tasteless if they are boiled too long.' Then, accompanied by Robert and Miles, she set out for London. En route, she visited Cirencester, Oxford and Winchester, where she accepted the submission of Bishop Henry. He had been one of the last to flee from the field at Lincoln, but he *had* fled – 'So that I may continue to safeguard Holy Church, for which reason I was appointed papal legate by our father in Rome.' In the face of such a selfless claim, it was difficult to accuse him of cowardice.

The activities of winter had done nothing to reduce Henry's girth, nor had defeat and flight sharpened his bland expression. He realised that he would make little headway with the empress if he defended his brother, but that even Matilda would be unlikely to attack the Pope's representative in England. His loyalties had always lain first and foremost with the Church; he simply had to make more noise about it now, that was all.

Beaming a welcome, the bishop-cum-baron escorted the empress and her party on a tour of his menagerie. He showed them the wolves and lynxes, poked about in the snake pit until a cobra emerged to bite the stick, then invited Matilda to ride a tame, Bactrian camel.

'If you sit between the humps – '

'Don't be a fool.'

'I assure you, my lady, it's almost impossible to fall off. Now that one over there, that single-hump dromedary, he's a different proposition.'

'No,' she contradicted, 'he's exactly the same, for he'll also go unridden.' She shrugged deeper inside her hooded cloak and said, 'Well, it's all very interesting, Bishop, but the cold is thinning my blood.'

'One moment more,' he hastened. 'You must see the peacocks. I took receipt of a new pair just before Christmas, and they thrive! They've survived the winter, and now – '

'Another time.'

'We can return to the palace through the trees there, it goes past their run.' He indicated the path, but she had already started back on the shorter route. He gazed after her, demolished by her refusal, and for an instant his eyes were bleak, his chubby face tightened with anger. With some people it was a horse, or a dog, or fish in a pond; one was expected to admire them, and volunteer some courteous remark. With Henry it was his peacocks. They were his pride and joy, and to ignore them was to insult his pets.

He followed his visitors along the path and round to the front of the palace. As he walked, he forced himself to forget his favourite birds, and to concentrate on the details of submission. By the time he had entered the small dining chamber, chosen because it was one of the few warm rooms in the building, the metamorphosis was complete. He was once again the politician, ready to balance Church and State, for the greater glory of God, and the advancement of His senior spokesman. He patted his belly, and heard the reassuring crackle of parchment.

Robert and Miles had both been impressed by the menagerie, and for a while they ignored the purpose of their mission. They stood together in a corner of the chamber, the forty-seven-year-old Earl of Gloucester and the forty-two-year-old Earl of Hereford, trading remembered scenes like boys at a country fair.

'Damn shame he didn't ask me to ride. He was right, two humps, you couldn't fall off.'

'Those lynxes, or whatever they're called, did you notice their ears, the way they pricked?'

'It must have cost him a pretty fortune, shipping everything over – '

'And paying to have them caught in the first place. He said a jerboa. When we were out there, he pointed at something and said it was a jerboa. Do you know – '

'It's like a rat, with a long tail. It hops. You know, it holds its front paws so, tucked up against – '

'For the third time, my lords!'

They turned towards her, gave a wan smile and took their places at the table. She waited until they were seated, then told her brother, 'Please don't break any more furniture. If you disagree with me, say so, or leave, but let the chairs stay upright, yes?'

Bishop Henry listened with interest, enjoying Robert's discomfort.

They discussed the terms of Henry's submission.

Winchester was the repository for the royal treasure, the crown, and a mass of important documents. Matilda requested that these be handed over, and that, until her coronation, she be accorded the correct title of Lady of England. She would decide later which of the bishops were to have a hand in the conduct of the service.

Henry pushed himself to his feet, pressed his belly against the table edge to hold the parchment in place, then delivered his reply.

'My brother,' he said, 'Stephen, your captive, stands condemned of many ills, and God has executed His judgment upon him. Stephen failed to honour his Church, as he failed to honour his crown. We know this will not happen again. We shall prevail upon the Lord God to assist us, and under his protection we shall elect you, Empress Matilda, the Lady of England. Your claims are justified, for you are the rightful daughter of the glorious, pacific, wealthy and noble King Henry, a monarch without peer, all his life a just defender of the people. You will receive the full support of the Church and be elected by a council of bishops –' He caught her eye, waited for her to nod acceptance, then added ' – whom I shall appoint.'

Her head came up sharply. She brushed a strand of hair from

her face. 'You cannot have heard me, Winchester. I said *I* would decide – '

'No, Empress. You have enough work to do. You must allow me to choose the council.' He let his gaze roam along the table, and let them know by his voice that he had rehearsed his terms. 'I shall choose the council. And all matters of chief account in this country, with special emphasis on the bestowal of bishoprics and the like, shall be subject to my decision. This being so, we will receive you into the Church, and remain ever loyal to you. It's for the best, I assure you, *Lady of England*, how nice that sounds. Yes, it is for the best, for no monarch has yet ruled successfully without the support of Holy Church.' He had recaptured his benign smile, and, when he saw the chagrin in her face, the smile widened.

A long time passed, and then she murmured, 'As you say.'

They thought he would resume his seat, but Henry of Winchester debated as he ate, tasting everything on the table.

'There's a man outside,' he said. 'He insists on delivering a note, a letter, something of the sort to you. Excuse me a moment. I'll fetch him in.' He bowed, squeezed himself between the chairs, and left the room.

The man was waiting, and the conversation between them was brief. Henry scooped the parchment from beneath his tunic, handed it to the man and hissed, 'You're well paid to do one thing only. Read this aloud. I shall remonstrate, so will the others. Ignore us. Just read it, clear and loud, then pass it to me and get out. Is that clear?'

'I'm to read it come what may, put it before you and leave.'

'Just so. Now, tell me again. If she asks who you are?'

'I'm an emissary from King Stephen's wife, bound to make a public reading before the Empress.'

'Exactly.' He touched the man on the arm. 'How long have you been in my household?'

'Two years, Lord Bishop.'

'Yes, well, you do this properly and I'll bring you to the top.'

The man started to bow, but Henry guided him through the door and into the chamber.

Matilda, Robert, Miles and the others studied him, as yet

THE LADY OF ENGLAND

without rancour. Bishop Henry waved the man forward, then lowered himself into his chair. He told Matilda, 'Here he is. He won't identify himself, and he'll only address you direct.'

Matilda looked at the man. He was quite a handsome lad, a change from the usual travel-weary types. His clothes were clean, and there was no blueness in his face. She guessed he had been waiting several hours.

'Who are you?'

He gave his name and station, as Henry had instructed, and said he had been sent to read her a letter from Queen Matilda.

'Why not read me history?' the empress snapped. 'My name-sake ceased to be queen at Candlemas, when Stephen was taken. Read her letter, but don't call her queen.'

The emissary nodded, unfolded the belly-warmed parchment and intoned:

'From Matilda, Queen of England and Normandy – '

He hesitated, but the damage was done, so he went on:

' – to the Dowager Empress of Germany and Countess of Anjou – greetings. I have heard how you, and your ad-herents, are treating my husband, the king, and I entreat you to release him from the damp and filth to which he has been committed. I ask this as a woman to a woman, but I do not ask it as your subject. You must know that I control and command the entire county of Kent, and the city of London and its river approach. You must also know that – '

'That's enough!' Matilda shouted. 'I do not abide by threats. I'll hear no more.' Robert waved the man away, and Miles told him he had done his duty, and no blame would attach to him if he left now. The messenger glanced down at Henry, who slammed a chubby fist on the table, and exclaimed that such a letter was no way to make peace. After which, the man took a deep breath, raised his voice and continued:

'You must also know that I am aided by William of Ypres and a formidable army from Flanders. I control the water between England and Normandy and will, if necessary, blockade London and the south. Remember, too, Countess, that although you have my husband, the king – '

'Countess?' Matilda raged. 'This is too much! I am – '
'Lady of England,' Henry smoothed. 'You are Lady of England.'
'So I am, and I will *not* be addressed by inferior titles! Least of all by Stephen's sow!'
By which time the emissary was reading again:

' – although you have my husband, the king, I still retain the loyalty of these various nobles; the King's Constable, Robert de Vere; William, Earl of Surrey; Robert, Earl of Leicester; the Earls of York and Derby; Geoffrey de Mandeville, Constable of London; Simon de Senlis, Earl of Northampton, and many others. We will visit war upon you, and upon yours, until you return my husband, King Stephen of England, and make arrangement with us.'

He stopped, let the letter fall as though by accident in front of the bishop, then withdrew from the chamber. The men stared after him with grudging admiration; he'd taken quite a risk, defying Matilda. The empress stretched out her long, elegant fingers and watched Henry take the letter and tear it into shreds. Before she could speak, he said, '*That* for the vindictive Queen of Kent! I'll not have you even look at it. It's too upsetting. But – ' He lifted his heavy shoulders. 'But it might make sense to dry out Stephen's cell. Why maltreat him? He is no longer a danger to you, Lady of England, and you can only increase your popularity with mercy.'
She trembled. The temptation to smile was almost irresistible. He was perfect, this fat, self-seeking prelate. In less than an hour he had secured his position as senior churchman and influential baron. Without his cope and mitre, she would not be made Lady of England, however much he enticed her with the title. And without his silvered tongue she could not hope to win over the mass of the people. Some would have expected Henry to defend his brother, while others, who remembered how he had been denied the see of Canterbury, would have

anticipated his taking revenge on Stephen. Instead, he had admitted the king's failings, condemned the queen's arrogant demands, reiterated the authority of the Church, and requested more humane treatment for the captive. He had turned party defeat into a personal victory, and had somehow emerged as a devout, peacock-loving moderate, whose only desire was to see Church and country bathed in a peaceful light. His submission could be more accurately termed an ultimatum.

For the first time since she had set foot on English soil, the widow of Germany and wife of Anjou acknowledged her equal. Like Stephen, he was her cousin, but in no other way was he like Stephen.

'With your permission,' Henry asked. 'Shall I visit him, so that I may tell the council he is well cared for? I know it is something they would want to hear.'

'Yes,' she hissed. 'And whatever your next fifty questions, the answer is yes.'

'Now, now. I cannot take all the responsibility, else you would have to call me king! I'm anxious to play my part, that's all.' He stood up, smiling to reach his ears. 'I do have one more question for you though. If your blood is warmed through, will you come and see the peacocks?'

*

Edgiva knew the truth, and, because he was her husband, Sergeant Morcar knew it. A physician from Wallingford knew it, and had kept it to himself. These three were the only ones, and it fell to Morcar to tell his suzerain what had happened.

The young sergeant had learned much from Constable Varan over the years, but the ugly Saxon had never taught him to nurse his words. If a man died, Varan would say so. No one was ever 'transported to Heaven', or 'sleeping', or 'taken into the House of Angels'. Had he tried to use such phrases, they would have stuck on his tongue. It was the same with Morcar. One did not swaddle the truth.

Nevertheless, it was with considerable trepidation that he welcomed Lord Fitz Count and constable Varan back from

Lincoln, and told them that the Lady Alyse had tried to kill herself.

For a moment, Morcar mistook the import of Brien's first question. 'Who knows of it?'

'Only Edgiva, sire, and the physician I brought in from the town.'

He nodded once and strode through the yards. They realised now that he was keeping himself in check; he wanted to run to her, but if he did so it would excite curiosity. They kept pace with him, and Morcar said, 'It happened last night. Since you left, Lady Alyse has been – well, withdrawn from us. She has remained in her chambers, and my wife says she has eaten nothing but the odd crust of bread.'

'What did she do?'

'At first we thought it was because you were gone from her. She told Edgiva she had been sleeping badly and – ' He hesitated, then flinched as Brien snatched at his shoulder.

'For Christ's sake, man! I'm not here to apportion blame. Tell me what occurred!'

'She asked for a sleeping-draught. It was a concoction of hemlock and hyoscyamus, some opium and ivy, and berry juice of some kind. Edgiva found the ingredients in town and made it up for her. Next morning, Lady Alyse said it had had no effect, so she made some more. Then again the third night, and the fourth. My lord, my wife couldn't have known what – '

'No more do I, yet. So Lady Alyse took the draught for four nights, is that it?'

'No, sire. She stored them up in secret, and then, last night she drank the lot, together with a stronger fifth draught. Edgiva believed her, you see, and it wasn't until she heard a noise – she went into the chamber, and discovered Lady Alyse on the floor, senseless.'

'How is she now?'

Morcar swallowed hard. 'She is near death, I fear. The physician says that if he bleeds her, the poison will escape, but Edgiva won't let him. You may not believe me, my lord, but she does know about country medicine.'

They crossed the drawbridge and entered the keep. Varan and Morcar waited in the lower hall, while Brien, freed of constraint, sprang up the steps. As he ran, he threw off his helmet and snapped the hasp of his travelling cloak. The helmet clattered down to the lower floor, while the cloak fell in a heap on the steps. His head was still bandaged, and the effort of climbing re-opened the cut on his leg. Edgiva appeared in the doorway, then stepped back to allow him into the solar. He found the breath to say, 'I heard what happened. There is no blame,' and saw her shudder with relief.

'Thank God you are back safe, my lord. She is there, in bed. The physician's name is Lemos. He wants to bleed her, but I think he's wrong.'

Brien glanced at the man, who stepped forward, one hand pressed against his felt skull-cap. 'It is the girl who is mistaken,' Lemos said. 'But I can do nothing, so long as she opposes me. I must tell you, she has made threats.'

Brien said, 'In a while,' and moved quietly to the bedside.

Alyse seemed diminished by the drug. Her face was hollowed, her lips dry and parted, her breasts scarcely moving. He knelt beside her and lifted her hand. It was colder than the weather. He thought, I don't know what to do. If it was a wound, yes, or if she'd fallen in the river, but I know nothing about hemlock, or opium, or hyoscyamus. And she has taken five times the measure . . .

He looked at the indignant physician. 'Tell me why you would bleed her, Lemos.'

The man studied the patient, then in a lecturing tone said, 'Everything we eat or drink is changed into one of three things: blood, flesh, or bone. Fish and meat become flesh. Bread, certain vegetables and most fruits are transmuted directly into bone. Wine and water, indeed almost any liquid, runs through channels from the stomach and into the veins in our body. Bleeding is without exception beneficial, Lord Fitz Count. The dizziness that comes with too much wine can be relieved with bleeding.' He gave a small, out-of-place chuckle. 'I daresay even you must at some time have welcomed the chance to lose the poison from excessive drink.'

In a quiet voice Brien reminded him, 'We are discussing my wife, and an over-draught, not a celebration.' He turned to Edgiva. 'Why do you disagree with the physician? What he says makes sense.'

'They would bleed stones,' she said. 'It is their, ah – '

'Their panacea? Their cure-all?'

'Yes, my lord. Look at Lady Alyse. She is weak from lack of food, weakened still further by the over-draught, and Lemos wants to cut her arm, or at best suck her with leeches.' She faced the physician, and repeated what she had already told him. 'You scoff at my suggestion, but it's a sight safer than yours. I have a lot to reproach myself for. I should have stayed by, to see that my lady took the draught. I should have been suspicious when the glass was returned empty, each morning, for it's rare to swallow the entire concoction. But I mixed it, not you. And I know the remedy.'

Lemos shook his head, wise and pitying, embarrassed at being contradicted by a serving girl. 'You have almost killed your mistress. You must leave it to those who know, to save her.'

Tears coursing her face, the girl sank down and wept her advice. 'She must be in fresh air, my lord, but her body kept warm. She needs fennel juice, I have some ready crushed. It's what we use. It's what we have *always* used, to wake someone from a herbal sleep. I would have applied it before, but I did not immediately discover what she had done. Then the physician arrived, and he – he said he would cry murder if I tried. Please, my lord! Maybe I *have* almost killed her, but his way will make it certain.' She buried her face in the sheepskin coverlet, and Brien found himself holding two women by the hand.

'Be calm,' he murmured, then, above her head, 'Do you enjoy such cruelty, Lemos? Must your fraternity admit to nothing but superior knowledge? If fennel is a practised remedy, why not let her try it?'

The physician tilted his head to the side. How difficult it was to impress the ignorant. The patient was there, full of poison, and all he had to do was make an incision from wrist to inner elbow, and out it would come. Why did they call him, if it was only to argue?

Brien squeezed the girl's hand. 'Fetch the juice. Apply it as you think fit. If it does not revive her, we will do as Lemos says. Go on now. Don't be afraid. I know Lady Alyse loves you like a – '

Like a daughter . . . A son . . . Matilda . . . Young Henry, he's seven now, but you would know that. Ah, God, and that is why she has tried to kill herself . . .

He pressed his lips against her hand, and stayed there until Edgiva returned with the fennel.

It smelled of liquorice and made their eyes water, and Lemos retired to the window. The maidservant dipped her fingers in the juice, then touched them to Alyse's nostrils. There was no reaction.

She drew a dripping finger across Alyse's upper lip, asked Fitz Count to raise his wife's head, then smeared more of the stuff around her nose.

Brien felt her body twitch. 'Go on,' he urged. 'There's some movement. Go on with it!'

Lemos coughed and edged into the window seat. The smell pervaded the chamber. Brien blinked, couching his wife's head. He heard Lemos cough again and started to say, 'Christ, you are not the patient!' then realised that it was Alyse who had coughed. Her body jerked spasmodically. He rested her head on the pillow, and Edgiva said, 'She must have some air.' Brien nodded obediently, crossed to the stairs and bellowed down to Varan and Morcar to come and help move the massive bed. Then he waved Lemos from the alcove and the men set the bed between the stone window seats, where Alyse could wake and gaze out over the fields and the river and watch the first stirrings of spring.

Edgiva looked at the physician, then went to wash the fennel juice from her hands.

*

They stayed together next day, and Brien admitted his guilt, though he realised that his wife had already forgiven him. He, long ago, had behaved adulterously with the Empress Matilda. But nothing he had done could compare with the severity of her attempted self-murder. In that time there was no greater sin, save to deny the existence of God, and no one who had tried to take his own life could condemn an adulterer. Thus, by committing so grave an act, Alyse had surpassed his guilt and ensured that they would be together, if not in heaven, then amid the flames and fumes of hell.

She was glad she had failed to die. Now she could spend the rest of her days with the man she loved, fearing nothing until the Final Judgment.

*

In June, Matilda reached London. There she met Geoffrey de Mandeville, the only man who could match Ranulf of Chester in ferocity and the desire for personal aggrandisement. He cut a terrifying figure, tall, lean-faced, so deep spoken that he seemed to draw the listener into an echoing, unplumbed pit. One would lean forward, seduced by the voice, content to fall in with his wishes.

The year before Lincoln, Stephen had made him Earl of Essex. Matilda now added the titles of sheriff and chief justiciar, and confirmed him in his constableship of London, and as master of the Tower.

The additional grants all but doubled his income and mapped the path for other ambitious barons. They saw how the empress had rewarded Earl Geoffrey, and they arrived at Westminster to hum-and-haw and to set a price on their loyalty. Stephen's supporters were dispossessed, or banished, or imprisoned. Castles and fiefdoms changed hands, and the race for power became a stampede. Neighbour turned on neighbour, each accusing the other of treasonable conduct towards the Lady of England. Matilda created six new earldoms, though one name remained conspicuously absent from the list – Brien Fitz Count.

Still at Wallingford, he learned, and did not care, that Matilda meant what she said. For him the cauldron of preferences and promotions had already boiled dry.

Throughout this period, Matilda was accompanied and advised by Robert of Gloucester, Miles of Hereford and the indispensable Bishop Henry, who had not yet found the time to visit his imprisoned brother. Unfortunately, their advice was rejected, and they watched her become more arrogant with each passing day. They were, themselves, vain men, secure in their nobility and position. But Matilda chose to rebuff them in public, and no longer rose to her feet in response to their bow. On more than one occasion, Robert and Miles walked out on her, as they had done at Gloucester. But Henry remained, ever watchful, content to watch the current.

If Stephen died tonight, the bishop was secure in his support of the empress. If an assassin entered the Great Hall at Westminster and ran a dagger into Matilda, Henry could arrange his brother's release and be known as the man who had sought better treatment for him, and rescued him. But, he reminded himself, I *must* get to Bristol and pay him a visit.

The aldermen and elected officials of London were summoned to Westminster, where they pleaded for a relaxation of taxes, claiming that the war had impoverished them. This was an ideal opportunity for Matilda to put Henry's advice into practice, and to increase her popularity with mercy. She was without doubt one of the most beautiful women in the world, and on the threshold of being crowned Lady of England. Not since the landing on the estuary at Arundel had there been such an ideal moment in which to win over the people.

However, it was then that she chose to mutilate the leopard.

Her face contorted with anger, she strode among the delegation, screaming in their faces, marking on her fingers the number of times they had raised money for Stephen, and contributed to his cause, and joined in a city-wide conspiracy against her, and done all they could to hold her at bay.

'And now you come here and complain of poverty. Crucified Christ! I'll give you grounds for complaint. You will pay what you owe, on the hour of the day you owe it, and you will also find fifty thousand marks as compensation for your treason! That, too, you can pay, the same hour, the same day, or they'll be calling London the Ruin-on-the-River! Now dig around, or watch for the fires to start!'

The members of her court stared in silence as the delegation gathered their best cloaks around them and bowed themselves out. Henry rubbed a hand over his face, then glanced across at Matilda's brother. Robert passed the look to Miles, who was far enough behind the empress to risk a shake of the head.

Matilda turned, her expression settled again. 'Isn't it remarkable,' she told Robert. 'They have been my enemies since the beginning, and now they approach me as friends.'

'No fear of friendship,' Robert said. 'You've seen to it that they'll stay as they were.'

*

They came through the county of Kent, surrounded the city, infiltrated the outskirts, drove like daggers towards the centre. They were led by Stephen's wife, and the mercenary captain, William of Ypres. They met with no resistance, but were cheered on their way, and their ranks swelled by infuriated citizens. Then, with London retaken, the army swept eastward towards Westminster, where Matilda was enjoying a late dinner.

Men burst into the hall, shouting at her to flee for her life. She heard bells ringing, sounding the alarm, and then Robert was beside her, pulling her to her feet, telling her that the enemy was less than a mile away. Panic ensued, and she was hustled from the long hall, lifted on to a horse, all the while deafened by the bells and the chaos of flight. Horsemen thundered past with swords drawn, but she could not tell if they were friend or foe. Bishop Henry appeared, towing a string of rounceys, each horse laden with altar candles and crosses and clerical vestments. She saw Miles of Hereford lean over and grab at her bridle and urge her forward. 'They are in the street!' he roared. 'Kick in, lady, kick in!'

The horse jerked beneath her, and then they were riding into the darkness, rung out by bells.

They passed the cathedral, the riders following the route Brien Fitz Count had taken six years earlier, when he and

174

Alyse had left Stephen's coronation feast. But there was a difference, for on that night the building had served its purpose, and a king had been crowned there.

As Matilda rode alongside the vast, echoing structure, her fear of capture was overlaid with a more ominous foreboding. She wanted to reach out and brush her fingers against the cold stone, for she sensed she was as near to it now as she would ever be. She was still Lady of England, but nothing had been settled, least of all the crown upon her head.

CHAPTER 10

THE SNOW ROUTE
July 1141 – December 1142

THEY deserted her like fleas from a drowning cat. Many of those same barons who had fled from the field at Lincoln now abandoned all pretence of loyalty to Matilda and adopted the expedient motto – *Sauve Qui Peut*! As news of her expulsion from London spread throughout the country, knights and nobles slammed their doors, or offered their services to Stephen's queen.

As the first peal of bells rang out from Westminster Cathedral, Bishop Henry reverted to his brother's cause. He had had enough of this arrogant Lady of England. She had insulted her advisers, antagonised the people, even dismissed his peacocks as 'less colourful than I imagined; they're quite bedraggled, your birds'. Well, maybe so, but they were better company than the beautiful virago, who saw fit to treat her leaders like mindless peasants. What would the poet have written about her? 'Before the crown is placed, she struts'? Something like that, for she shared with Stephen the same fatal impetuosity, the same desire to let the cart drag the horse.

Between Windsor and the Chiltern Hills, the bishop left the fleeing convoy and turned south to Winchester. There he fortified the palace and castle, then wrote to Stephen's wife, offering her the city. 'But hurry,' he pleaded. 'The empress is nothing if not quick to repay hostility.'

Within two weeks he was proved right. Matilda summoned him to Gloucester and, when he refused, decided to make an example of him. The rebel army swept out of their West Country strongholds. On the way they were joined by Ranulf of Chester, and a day later by Brien Fitz Count, who had a personal interest in rejoining Matilda. He wanted to ask her a question; the most intimate question a man could ask a woman.

However, the speed and confusion of the advance prohibited privacy. The empress welcomed Greylock back among her leaders, and they met during the daily war councils. She asked if Lady Alyse had recovered from her fever – 'It must have been remarkably grave, to drag on for half a year' – then turned to more urgent, military matters. He played his part as one of the four senior commanders, and awaited his chance to speak with her, alone.

The army surrounded Winchester and demanded the surrender of the turncloak bishop. An unseasonable mist blanketed the city, and Matilda fretted impatiently in her pavilion.

'Cowardice keeps him in now,' she said, 'but when the mist burns off, and he sees the extent of our army, he'll come waddling. And this time *I'll* take *him* on a tour – of the dungeons at Bristol.'

Brien asked to speak with her in private, and was told, 'Don't worry, Greylock, I'll find some reward for you. You've come too late for the ripe pickings, but you won't leave empty-handed.'

'I'm not here to be enfeoffed, Empress. I want a moment alone with you, that's all.'

Matilda smiled at Robert and Miles and Ranulf and the others who crowded the pavilion. 'He *is* after a reward,' she joked. 'He wants me to send you all out into the mist, to catch a death chill. Then he can choose from your properties!' There were a few laughs, though none of them believed her.

The mist was not burned off by the summer sun, but blown away during the night. So it was not until the first light of dawn that the defenders saw the encircling force. When they did so, they pounded the battlements and cheered themselves hoarse. The rebels glared up at them, amazed by the strange reaction. Then, their spines crawling with fear, they turned around and gaped at a second army, spread out over the low hills to the east. Even as they watched, the banners of England, Normandy and Ypres were unfurled, then the county standards of Leicester, Surrey, Hertford and Northampton. One of the last to be raised was that of Geoffrey de Mandeville, Earl of Essex and master of London. Matilda called out from her pavilion, shrieked invective at the man she had so recently honoured, yet clearly failed to buy. 'May the maggots eat you alive, you purulent bastard! Blink while they burrow in your eyes! You vile, dripping – '

Brien caught her by the arm, swung her round and told her the plan was set. 'You'll come with me. Earl Robert is sending you back to Gloucester in my care. He and Miles will command the rearguard. Make a move, Empress. You are on the run again.' He led her, none too gently, to where Varan was waiting with the horses. Beside herself with mortification, she tried to pull away, screaming at Brien to let her lead her army. '*You* run! Scurry home to Wallingford and your sickly wife, but don't enlist me – '

'I won't,' he told her. 'This is Earl Robert's scheme to save you, not mine. For the way you treated Alyse, and the cruel hints you made when you visited us, I'd be happy to see you captured. But I made a vow to your father, a long time back, and I have held to it ever since. I said then that I would see you crowned, and I have always honoured – '

'Always?' she challenged. 'You told pretty Alyse how we had been together? No, I don't think so. In your dreams you might, but – '

He jerked out his arm, stiff as a pole, then bent it again, snatching her to him. The beautiful eyes were malevolent, the russet hair tangled about her face. Her mouth twitched as he turned his years of guilt upon her and burned her with his breath. 'Yes, Matilda! Yes! Yes, I told her what we had done! She all but died from it, but you didn't know that. It was not what she expected of me, but what choice had I, after you had spread the germ? She knows of my adultery, and that I am a father, and worse, that you are the mother. She knows *everything*, Lady of England, so you have lost your power with me. Now get mounted.'

He pushed her back, and she stumbled and steadied herself. A strange, discomforting smile shivered along her lips. 'My, my,' she whispered, 'is that what you told her?' Then she swung away, pulled herself into the saddle, and set the palfrey running from the camp. Varan glanced at his master, saw he was not yet ready to move, and spurred after the empress.

Brien stood for a moment, his fists clenched at his side. *Is that what you told her?* The smile had unnerved him. It was too knowing, too confident, too much the property of someone with an unfathomable secret. *My, my, is that what you told her?*

As though from a distance, he heard the clangour of battle. Shapes flitted across his vision, and arrows stabbed the ground around him. What else could he have told Alyse, when Matilda had all but admitted their adultery, when time and place fitted so perfectly with the child's conception? So why the smile, and the enigmatic question? What else could he have told her, if not the truth.

He felt someone push him and wheeled round, his sword out. He saw Ernard, the young soldier who had witnessed the arrest of the bishops at Oxford. 'Have a care!' Brien snarled. 'It's the wrong time to shove.'

Ernard decided not to tell his suzerain that, had he been an enemy, he would have killed instead, but gulped an apology and hurried, 'You're too much in the open, my lord. You should have a helmet.'

Brien glanced at the tethered horses. His plain, acorn helmet hung from one of the saddle pommels. He asked Ernard, 'Are you still with that girl Eadgyth?'

Startled by the question, he replied, 'Yes, my lord. She's happy at Wallingford. I have not been keeping her against her will. She's free to leave, but she prefers – '

'Take one of the horses. You're riding with me.'

'But I'm expected to fight for the empress.'

'Not today. This time we'll save you for Eadgyth.' He read Ernard's expression – more than he'd been able to do with Matilda – and snarled, 'Hell, boy, we're not running. The empress is ahead of us on the road. We're detailed to see her to Gloucester. Come on. I'll need your help.'

His life and honour saved, at least for the moment, Ernard ran to the tethered horses, waited for Fitz Count to don his helmet, then accompanied him in pursuit of Matilda. Behind them, Robert and Miles stayed to command the rearguard.

*

The result surpassed their worst fears. Miles of Hereford reached Gloucester in late September, bereft of his armour, his face and hands torn by briars, a livid cut already healing across his chest. He described how the rebel army had been routed, and how he, himself, had been captured, and had escaped. Weighed down by his link-mail hauberk, he had thrown it away, along with his sword, helmet and leg-guards. For five days he had walked, half-naked, across country, thus the scratches, and had eventually bribed a carter to conceal him amongst a load of rotting vegetables. The carter was outside now, and the exhausted earl implored Brien to pay the man well for his help. Then he sank into a chair and fell asleep.

Miles did not know the worst of it, for while he was blundering through the undergrowth, Matilda's brother had been dragged from his horse on the banks of the River Test, a few miles east of Winchester.

The two male rivals, Stephen and Robert, had now been captured, and the two Matildas, queen and empress, gazed at each other across the width of England.

They needed someone to act as a go-between, someone with a grasp of politics and a fine sense of cunning. The choice was obvious, and they both contacted Bishop Henry, remembering to inquire after his peacocks.

*

He was in his element and, during the latter half of the year, he rode between London and Gloucester, arranging the intricate details of exchange. He made an extravagant show of impartiality, first praising the queen for having caught up the reins dropped by Stephen, then, on the other side of the country, encouraging Matilda to pursue her rightful cause. To both of them he offered arbitration by the Church, and his own good offices with the Pope. The women told him to get the exchange made; then they'd decide whether to go before the council or fight on.

In prison in the royalist castle at Rochester, Earl Robert was offered the chance to change sides. The go-between told him that, if he agreed to abandon his sister, the king and queen would make him the most important magnate in the land. He would be second only to Stephen, and could create his own title.

Robert refused without hesitation, reminding the bishop that, like Brien Fitz Count, he intended to honour his oath.

In prison at Bristol, Stephen was offered an absolute pardon and a substantial pension if he would renounce his throne. His throat had healed sufficiently for him to bawl his brother from the cell.

When the details of the exchange had been set out, Robert refused to be released. He claimed he was less important than the king, and that other captured rebels should be used to balance the scales.

'Stephen's party would, no doubt, like to make this tit-for-tat. But he *is* a king, and I'm no more than an earl. I want all my compeers released. Surely a king is worth a dozen nobles?'

Queen Matilda rejected the condition. 'That's a fine trick,' she told Henry. 'We get back one man, while the Angevin bitch restocks her nobility. No. I want my husband returned, but as one for one with Earl Robert. You ask the king what he thinks about it. I am sure he would rather be a prisoner for life.'

The message was conveyed to Stephen, who echoed his wife, then again drove Henry from the cell.

Eventually, the empress convinced Robert to accept his release, and in late October he was taken from Rochester to the exchange point at Winchester.

The queen then rode to Bristol, as hostage for Stephen, who was also conducted to Winchester.

In an atmosphere of general mistrust, Earl Robert made the reverse trip, leaving several members of his family as hostage, this time for the queen.

Then she, too, was released, and on her arrival at Winchester, Robert's family was freed.

It took ten days to complete the transaction, and the winter was on them again. The rival factions immured themselves in their castles, Stephen and his party in London and the east, Matilda and her supporters in the West Country. Brien Fitz Count, who commanded the tip of the rebel spear, returned to Wallingford and Alyse. All was well between them now, though he had only to pause and listen for Matilda's words to scratch at his ear. *My, my, is that what you told her?*

*

Snow melted on the branches, and they lost their skeletal appearance and were clothed in leaves and spring blossom. The land warmed, and the sun learned to hang hot in the sky, and there was no longer the need for surcoat or woollen tunic. Water was sucked up from the Thames, and one could cross the ford and remain dry. There were thunderstorms, and a night of hail damaged the spring crop, but it was a time to be out of doors and to eat by the river. Men and women grew brown in the face, while the children ran naked, pulling up short to watch the jugglers, then running on again to steal vegetables from the fields, or thrash their way downstream, or race each other alongside the castle moat. The air hummed with insects, and was enlivened by birdsong and the occasional plaintive sound of flute or lyre.

And between these pastoral scenes rode armoured columns, and cartloads of prisoners, and single envoys, ploughing a furrow of dust across the country.

The war might be gone from a district, but it was not forgotten. Somewhere, they could be sure, a skirmish was in progress, a castle besieged, a cell door slammed shut. Somewhere the royal army was subduing a fortress, the rebel troops investing a stronghold. There was peace and there was war, in any village, in any week.

As king restored, Stephen was in the north. His avowed intention was to settle the affairs of his kingdom and put an end to wickedness. If it entailed hanging and burning, so much

the worse for those who died on the gibbet, or under the
torch. He did not ride with murder in his heart, but he had
experienced the ministrations of Cousin Matilda, and he had
no intention of being recaptured. He had fought hard at
Lincoln, and would fight harder now. And next year, if she
was still at liberty, he would make his present efforts seem like
overtures of peace. He would do what he had said, and put an
end to wickedness, personified by the Empress of Germany
cum Countess of Anjou cum Lady of England.

To hell with her high-flown titles. She was an arrogant
and merciless woman, an intruder at the feast of England. She
would be evicted, or unmasked at the table. It did not matter
which, so long as the country was made aware of her vicious
nature.

He had once been troubled by the rightfulness of her claim
and had questioned his own motives for taking the crown. But
no longer. Now he saw her for what she was, and, if he had
been wrong before, time had proved him right. Under his
guidance, England would survive and prosper. Under Cousin
Matilda, it would die of a thousand wounds.

Needless to say, the empress saw it differently. She was the
daughter and sole legitimate issue of King Henry of England,
and the English and Norman nobility had thrice sworn to
support her. Many had reneged, but that did not make the
oath less real. Nor did it pull her back into her mother's womb,
or stay King Henry's seed. She *was* his daughter, and she *was*
the rightful heir, and nothing Stephen could say or do would
change it. He could hedge and hinder till Doomsday, but he
would never be more than an actor, playing at king. And even
as an actor he was a joke. Dear God, it would have been better
to employ one of Bishop Henry's animals and stick on a
horsehair moustache. Then, at least, the courtiers could laugh
openly, whereas they now sniggered behind their gloves.

And so the year grew hot, and then cooled, and all the while
castles were razed, towns sacked, ambushes sprung. Cirencester was burned to the ground by the royalists. The empress
replied by laying waste vast areas of Leicester and Northampton. She herself was leading the army, for she had sent

Earl Robert to Normandy, to seek help from her husband, Geoffrey of Anjou. In Robert's absence, she rode south to Oxford, and was there when Stephen launched a surprise attack against the city.

This important stronghold boasted a river-fed moat and a palisade and a strong, stone castle. The bridges had already been destroyed, and there was no easy way across the moat. So Stephen set up camp around the city, content to starve his enemies into submission. It could take a week, or a year, he didn't care. Sooner or later the defenders would feel their bellies contract, and their throats swell. They would demolish the houses for firewood, then suck leather straps for sustenance, and finally, when there was nothing left, they would stagger out, weeping dry tears.

He settled down, sword at hand, to await the outcome.

*

The bitter Normandy winter did nothing to cool Earl Robert's anger. He had arrived in the duchy in August, and it was now October, and he was still there, waiting for Count Geoffrey to act. News of Matilda's plight had reached them, but had failed to elicit any response from her husband. He offered one excuse after another, all of them variations on the same theme. He and his wife had agreed on a plan; she would go to England and lead her supporters against Stephen, whilst Geoffrey remained on the other side of the channel, protecting Anjou and attacking Stephen's castles in Normandy.

'Good God!' he exploded. 'If I was captured, do you think my wife would leave England and come to *my* aid?'

'That is not the point,' Robert said. 'Empress Matilda is not famed for her rescue attempts. There were many occasions in the past when she might have sent help, or led a rescue-party. But this is different, and you know it. She is about to be taken, and if that happens, the cause is lost. Immaterial that you have gained half of Normandy. Stephen will be once again an unquestioned king, and will come against you with a united army. Those parts of Normandy that have remained loyal to him will rise at his command, and I would not fancy your chances. Take the war to his doorstep, Count Geoffrey, before he brings it to yours!'

'You force my hand,' Geoffrey complained. 'I'm expected to fight on two fronts at the same time.'

Robert stared at him. 'I force your hand? Christ in Heaven, the situation forces your hand! Yes, you are expected to fight on two fronts! Or ten, or twenty! But you are also required to assist your wife and our future queen. Look, come over and help lift the siege at Oxford – '

'No, that's impossible. My presence is needed here. But I'll do this much. I'll lend you fifty ships, and four – three hundred knights. They'll supply their own sergeants and foot-soldiers. And for a rallying post, take our young son. He's a bright boy. The barons will fight for him.'

Robert struggled to keep his temper in check. He was taller than Geoffrey and dominated him as he queried, 'My nephew Henry? Is that whom you mean? A nine-year-old? Where shall I put him, in the front rank with the archers?'

'It's the best I can do, Gloucester, and there's no call to lean over me. If you don't want the boy, then don't take him. But I say it will hearten Matilda, and please the barons to know they are not merely fighting for a woman. That's what helped Stephen to power, isn't it? That he was a man? Well, let them see Matilda's heir. I tell you, Gloucester, he's a likeable boy. And it's time he travelled.'

Robert curled a hand around his jaw. Fifty ships, he thought. And three hundred knights. And perhaps a thousand foot-soldiers. And the boy Henry, who would probably insist on bringing his toys and games. He was not being lent a rescue force, he was being given charge of a nursery!

But he knew it was all he would get from Count Geoffrey, and he grunted acceptance. Then he assembled the knights, took his garrulous, wide-eyed nephew by the hand, and led the borrowed fleet back to England. Buffeted by storms, the reinforcements landed at Wareham in Dorset, and immediately laid siege to the castle there. Robert sent men into the surrounding countryside to spread the word of the landing. He wanted Stephen to hear about it, and take retributive action.

The impetuous monarch would withdraw from Oxford and lead his army south-west to the relief of Wareham. The Oxford garrison could then break out, enabling Matilda to escape. That was the plan, an invitation that Stephen would find impossible to resist.

But the dog had already treed the cat and had no intention of being drawn away. Wareham would have to stand or fall by itself. As, by God, would Oxford.

*

By December the king had grown impatient, and his troops had overrun the city. They had managed to bridge the freezing river-moat and had set up their siege machines in the squares and side-streets. Houses had been torn down in order to give a clear field of fire, and the rectangular castle shuddered beneath a constant bombardment of missiles. The royalist archers sent their shafts high into the air, where they disappeared in the overcast. Then, unseen, the arrows and crossbow quarrels reached the peak of their trajectory, turned and fell on to the open towers and wall-walks. The deadly rain continued, day and night, and drove the defenders from the battlements.

In the nearby streets the catapults were tilted so that they too sent their missiles on a near vertical path. There were accidents, and some of the massive rocks crashed back on the attackers, but each morning revealed fresh cracks in the walls, old fissures widened, watch towers wrecked. Stephen's military advisers estimated that within two weeks the castle would be breached, though there were already signs that the garrison had run out of food.

'No matter,' he told them. 'Keep up the bombardment. They'll soon tire of living in a dice-cup.'

His description was accurate, for the impact of the half-hundredweight rocks was enough to send a tremor through the castle. The shell of the structure was still standing, but the wooden roof had been smashed to splinters, and the rocks had continued down, tearing jagged holes in all five floors. It was now possible to peer down through the centre of the building and see the pile of spent rocks and broken beams and bodies that filled the cellars, sixty feet below. The well, their main source of water, lay buried beneath the debris.

The defenders lived on the outer edge of the floors, and in the mural chambers in the wall itself, and on the broken stairways. They shot arrows from the loopholes, but even if it had been safe to man the battlements they could not have done so, for the upper stairway had been destroyed. Their only vantage points were the arrow-loops, allowing them slices of the scene below.

Matilda's left hand had been pierced by a splinter of stone. The fragment had been removed and the hand bound, but the slight wound had left her depressed and sullen. Until now she had urged the occupants to resist, assuring them that Earl Robert would return from Normandy at the head of a relief force, or that Brien Fitz Count would cover the fifteen miles from Wallingford, or Ranulf of Chester sweep down from the north. She had nursed the injured, eaten no more than her ration of food, even gave up her swansdown mattress to ease the last hours of the dying. Thereafter, she had slept on a straw-filled sack in one of the mural chambers, shivering as the snow blew in through the arrow-loops.

But the wound made things different. It acted as a painful reminder that she stood as close to death or disfigurement as any of the beleaguered garrison. The rocks and arrows were no respecters of rank. They crushed or transfixed anyone in their path, infant or empress.

She imagined her face seamed with scars, an arm torn away, her sight gone. Deprived of her greatest asset, her beauty, she would be disowned by her supporters and sent back to Anjou as a hideous example of divine judgment. The thought drove her to the brink of panic, and she determined to escape.

She summoned the garrison commander and three of the knights who had accompanied her to Oxford, and told them to formulate a plan. One of the knights suggested a sortie, under cover of which the Lady of England could lose herself among the side-streets. If she donned disguise –

'No. I'll probably be killed at the gate, or live to be captured by mercenaries. In which case I'd rather take an arrow. Think again, messires.'

Hugging herself beneath her stained, squirrel-skin cloak, she glanced out through the arrow slit. Below lay a jumble of snow-covered rooftops scored by dark alleyways. A narrow street led into a small, open square, and she gazed down at one of Stephen's infernal catapults. Men were filling the bowl of the machine with rocks, stacking them in the shape of a pyramid. A moment later the winding mechanism was released. The arm of the catapult jerked upward, and the empress flinched as the rocks blossomed in the air. They shattered below the window and she felt the wall tremble. The garrison commander said, 'Stay clear, my lady. You'll not see the one that comes for you.'

'Have you thought me out of here yet?'

They admitted they hadn't, and she turned back to gaze morosely out of the window. She no longer believed anyone would come to her aid. Indeed, she wondered if she had ever believed it. Fitz Count despised her for having provoked his admission of adultery. Robert and Miles were still smarting from the insults received in London. Ranulf seemed content to stay in the north and see which way the wind would blow. Geoffrey de Mandeville had already rejoined the king. So had Bishop Henry. So had a hundred others.

No, nobody would come to her aid, because nobody cared to.

Escape reclaimed her thoughts, and she faced the knights and said, 'That far wall fronts the moat, doesn't it?'

The men frowned at her and nodded.

'Is it frozen over?'

'Yes, it's been solid for several days. There's a pipe comes in from the river, and I've had men down there, heating it to turn it back into water. That's where we're getting what little we have. If the ice gets much thicker Stephen will send men across to undermine the wall.'

Matilda ignored the information. 'On the first-floor level there's a good-sized window, I remember.'

'There is, but it's boarded over against arrows and – '

'The boards could be taken down – '

'Yes, I suppose – '

' – and a rope let down to the ice.'

Now they understood, and rushed to dissuade her. 'You'll be seen, even while you are in the window!'

'Not at night.'

'Then you'll fall. It's twenty feet or more, and the wall's as slippery – '

'I won't fall if I'm tied. I can be lowered down.'

'It's possible. But you'll still be spotted on the ground.'

'That's the risk,' she snapped. 'But considerably diminished if I'm dressed in white. The ice will bear my weight, and I'll wear a summer gown, a winding sheet, I don't care what. The milled wheat came in white sacks, didn't it? Very well then, I'll dress in sackcloth.' She waved away further argument, and told the knights they would go with her. 'We'll leave when it's dark. The moon is down to the rind, so the pickets need not see us.' Indicating the garrison commander, she said, 'You, master. Hold on here a day or two, then surrender. Stephen may think of hanging you, but he won't do it. It will make him look too vengeful. One doesn't break the eggs because the bird has flown.' She glanced at the knights again and repeated, 'When it's dark. Go on now and loosen the boards, so they can be removed later. And find some strong rope, and a team to lower us. I'll fit us out with the sacks.'

'May I ask?' one of them said. 'When we have made our escape, where are we headed?'

'To the nearest safe refuge, where else? To Brien Fitz Count's place at Wallingford.' She managed a smile, and added, 'If he allows us in.'

The men laughed, aware of Greylock's love for the empress. If he allowed her in? That was good. What she meant was, of course, if he ever allowed her out again.

Matilda chose not to disillusion them.

*

Dusk, and they waited for the time candle to burn down. When it had melted three of the black rings that marked the hours,

Matilda handed out the rolled sackcloth cloaks. The escapers groped their way down the littered steps and around the edge of the floor. The men who would lower them to the frozen moat were already easing the boards from the window. No one spoke, and for a while there was only the fitful sigh of the wind and the creak of obstinate boards. One by one they were removed and stacked beneath the window to form a step. Then one of the knights slipped a loop of rope around his waist, climbed cautiously into the arched window and knelt there, his back to the moat. He braced himself with one arm, his other arm pressed tight against the sackcloth bundle. The hastily-made surcoat would be put on when he reached the ground; it would not do for the enemy to see four pale phantoms float down from the window.

The knight nodded, and the men took the strain, grunting as he slithered from sight. Matilda listened, half expecting a shout of alarm, a howl of pain as an archer let fly at the dangling man. But there was only the rasp of the rope against the sill, and the continued plaint of the wind. Then the rope went slack, and the lowering crew grinned at Matilda. The first one was down.

The garrison commander balanced himself on the step, pressed his hands against the sides of the window and leaned dangerously far out. He could not see the knight, but that was just as well, for it meant the man was huddled down under the wall. The rope was hauled in, and the commander stepped back into the room.

Another knight went next. He copied the leader, kneeling with his back to the moat. Then, as the garrison commander moved to help the lowering crew, the knight slipped from the icy sill. The men grabbed at the rope, cursing as it burned their hands. They caught it in time and it jerked taut. Ten feet below, the knight squirmed with pain, his feet kicking against the stone. They lowered him quickly and his companion released him and pulled him into the lee of the wall.

'Are you hurt?'

'Christ,' he hissed, 'I'm snapped in half!'

'Ssh – You'll live. Lie on the ground. Give me your white –

that's it. I'll lay it over you.' He watched the loop rise again,
then peered anxiously across the ice. There were lights on the
far bank, and the silence was suddenly broken by the blare of
trumpets. He hunched down, still as death, then relaxed a little
as he realised the sound had come from somewhere in the
town. Out here there was nothing but the scattered camp-fires
and the gaunt trees and the countryside, blanketed by snow.

Matilda was lowered without mishap. She dragged the loop
over her head, then leaned against the wall, looking down at
the prostrate knight. 'Do you want to be taken back?'

The man shook his head. 'It's not as I feared, Lady. I'll be
ready.'

'Are you sure? If you're injured, you'll be better off inside.'

'I thank you for your concern, but – '

'Concern for all of us,' she said. 'I don't want to be slowed.'

The man swallowed his gratitude, eased himself upright
and wrapped the white cloak around his shoulders. As he did
so, the third knight swung to the ground. The lastcomer
freed himself from the rope, and it hung for a moment, offering
them a final chance to retreat. Then it was hauled up, and they
donned their crude camouflage.

The heaviest knight went first, to test the ice. It creaked
under his weight, but held firm. He hurried across, stooped
over, and the others followed, moving in line abreast. They
reached the far bank and scrambled up. Matilda glanced back
at the castle. The rope had gone, and there was nothing to be
seen in the window.

They went on through the trees. They saw a dozen camp-
fires, and on three occasions they huddled against snowbanks,
waiting for patrols to pass. They were astonished at the depth
of Stephen's lines. Small wonder no one had come to their
rescue. It would have taken an army at full strength to cut the
besieging belt.

They emerged from the trees to face a new hazard; open
fields that seemed to magnify the sliver of moonlight. For a
while they kept to the hedgerows, adding miles to their journey,
but the cold began to bite into them and they knew they would
have to move faster, or freeze in their tracks.

They decided to risk discovery and cut straight across the fields. It would take only a sleepless farm dog, or one of the numerous road patrols, or even, God help them, a startled poacher, and the hunt would be on. But they could not continue skirting every field, not if they were to survive the night.

So they trudged south, four wraithlike figures, their arms wrapped around them, their breath swept away by the wind. The injured knight began to lag behind, and one of the others pulled him forward by the hand. Matilda felt her legs grow heavy, and then, crossing one of the furrowed fields, she tripped and fell on her pierced hand. The leading knight lifted her, grunting encouragement. 'We must have covered five miles, near enough. Abingdon's over there, if I've led us right. If we can reach it, we'll ride the rest of the way.'

'Ride? How?'

'Leave it to me, Lady. Will you allow me to assist you?'

'Yes,' she nodded. 'Until the next field.'

They stumbled on, pausing now and again to let the air warm in their lungs, then continued their flight. They skirted iced-over ponds, crossed ditches and banks and the occasional rutted cart track. The leading knight still supported the empress, and then he fell, bringing her down with him. She lay, half buried in the snow, wishing nothing more than to sleep. The frozen pillow was quite soft, and there was something comforting about the pale light that suffused the field . . . It was easy to close one's eyes, while the snow deadened all pain . . .

The knight pulled her to her feet, and she felt his arm around her waist, a metal hook that dragged her forward across the uneven ground. She tried to walk, but her feet twisted under her, and she heard him say, 'Rest yourself. We're not far off.' She murmured something and then her head sank forward, her face framed by a dripping curtain of hair . . .

Black fingers reached down to strangle her, and she twisted violently in an effort to escape. They were all about her, moving in for the kill, grotesque monsters disguised as – ah, yes, of course, just trees.

The injured knight crouched beside her. 'Be still, Lady.

You're quite safe. We are in a small grove, near Abingdon. There's a farm across the way. The other two have turned robber.'

'I don't understand.'

'They've gone to find some transport for us.'

'I'm cold . . . I'm so cold.' She squinted at the dim, hunched figure and said, 'Lend me your white cloak for a while.'

'I would, Lady, but I'm none too warm myself – '

'Damn you, I am the empress! Do you expect me to freeze?'

' – since I gave it to you some time ago.'

She looked down, plucked at the two layers of sackcloth, then blew angrily on her hands. The knight gazed at her, acknowledged that she was quite unrepentant, and pushed himself to his feet. Matilda heard him fumble with the clasp of his own squirrel-skin cloak, then watched it swirl like a giant bat and settle over her legs.

'You would not want my armour,' he told her. 'It's the wrong size.'

She made a note of his sarcasm, but said, 'You'll be rewarded for this. I promise you. As soon as I'm safe back at Gloucester – '

'What will you give me, Lady? A warm grave?' He moved to the edge of the trees, then called softly to her, 'They're coming back.'

Swathed in the cloaks, she went out into the moonlight and watched the two knights lead a horse and cart away from the silent farm. Their injured companion asked, 'Were you spotted?'

'Some old man. He started shouting at us from one of the windows.'

'Yes. So you – '

' – took care of it. Yes.'

Matilda glanced from one to the other. 'I hope you left them well tied. It won't help us if they break free and raise the alarm.'

The senior knight held out a hand and helped her on to the cart. 'Don't worry,' he told her. 'The dead aren't known to shout.'

*

They stayed clear of the river-path and made their way around Abingdon, then along snow-silted side-roads. It was a slow and indirect journey, and the sky had taken on a grey pallor by the time they reached Wallingford-on-the-Thames.

They were challenged by a gate guard, and the knights heaved themselves to their feet. Matilda had fallen asleep during the ride, but had woken a mile back. Now she said, 'Let me answer him. Help me up.' Then she raised her voice and called, 'I am the Empress Matilda, Lady of England. I have arranged my own escape from the castle at Oxford. Tell Lord Fitz Count I request shelter for myself and my men. Add that he need not fear the cost this time. There are no more of us to come.'

It was as though the courtyard had been set alight. Every available torch was lit, and the yellow glow flooded over the walls, turning the snow to sand. The gates were swung open and the cart rolled in. Soldiers ran to kneel before their empress, and they implored her to warm herself at one of the fires. But she stayed in the cart, her eyes on the inner gate. She would descend at Greylock's invitation, and allow him to escort her into the warmth.

Flurries of snow spat on the torches and settled on the waiting figures. Matilda thought of her two previous flights, from the dining-table at Westminster, and the battlefield outside Winchester. And now from the castle-turned-prison at Oxford. Three times God had delivered her from her enemies, though He had made each successive escape more difficult. No matter. He was clearly on her side, and would not see her taken by Cousin Stephen.

She brushed snow from her eyes, peered again at the inner gate, then frowned as Alyse walked towards her. She had not expected this. Nor did she want it. She wanted Fitz Count.

Alyse made her way across the yard, neither dawdling nor hurrying. She came level with the cart, looked up at her exhausted visitor, then bowed. Again, it was neither subservient nor scornful.

'My husband is not here, Lady. He is at Wareham, with your brother, Earl Robert. You've called on the wrong night.'

'I have come when providence allowed, Lady Alyse. To ask for a bed, and food, and a fire, that's all. And perhaps, when I have slept, the chance to speak with you.'

'That's only half the battle,' Alyse countered. 'The other half is to make me listen, and that I am not willing to do. Anyway, you surprise me; I'd have thought you eager to get on to Wareham.'

'I am, but I'm sure my brother has things in hand, and – '

'I don't mean the earl.'

'Well, if you mean Fitz Count, there's no special reason – '

'No, nor him. I mean your son Henry. Earl Robert brought the boy over with him, hadn't you heard? And Lord Fitz Count has gone there to greet him. After all, one of you should be there, don't you agree, the mother or the father?'

Matilda leaned against the side of the cart. She had no strength left, but managed to say, 'Let me sleep, Lady Alyse. Let me sleep, and I will repay you with the truth.'

Alyse nodded slowly. She had already ordered her servants to prepare food, set out mattresses on the ground floor of the keep, and bank the massive fire. Even so, she doubted that Matilda could honour her part of the bargain.

CHAPTER 11

TRUTH AND CONSEQUENCE

December 1142 – December 1143

FOR the first time in his life, Constable Varan bowed to the weather.

The wind that keened across the marshes around Wareham could not compare with the howling blizzards of Cilicia. Nor did the driven snow contain the cutting-edge of a German winter. The dampness that mildewed clothing did not approach the rotting, irritating humidity of the Syrian coast, and the countries of the West would never be scoured by sandstorms, or crushed beneath the golden heel of an Arabian summer.

Varan had experienced all these, and suffered them without lasting ill-effect. But the left side of his body was now stiff and unresponsive, and he felt chilled from within, as though ice encrusted his bones. He blamed the weather, for his pride would not allow him to admit the truth. He was sixty-three years of age; an old man.

He had accompanied Brien Fitz Count from Wallingford, and they had reached Wareham to find Robert of Gloucester in the act of accepting the surrender of the castle. The purpose of their visit was to advise Robert that King Stephen would not be drawn from Oxford, whatever the lure. He had Matilda trapped in the keep there, and seemed content to demolish the building, block by block. The contingent at Wallingford was not strong enough to launch an attack on the royal army, but if Robert would sound a general call-to-arms they might yet be in time to save the empress.

Standing with them on the churned ground outside his tent, Robert said, 'I appear to have misjudged the man. Stephen was never the easiest creature to predict, but I was sure he would come. You've heard, I suppose, that I brought Matilda's son over from Normandy?'

Brien looked at him for a moment, but read nothing in his expression. Did Robert know? Had Matilda ever let slip that the boy's father was not Geoffrey of Anjou but her loyal supporter, Greylock of Wallingford? Indeed, was it not obvious that young Henry lacked his parents' red hair? It might not be conclusive, of course, but when red squirrels mate, the offspring are rarely grey.

'Yes,' he said, 'I heard. And Stephen must also know it, which shows his steadfastness. He wants Matilda. And he'll have her unless we make a move.' With studied nonchalance he added, 'By the way, where is the boy?'

Robert jerked his head in the direction of the castle. Brien decided that the food-stocks in Wareham must have been very low, for the Angevin invaders had only managed to assemble three or four siege machines, and the castle was largely undamaged. He heard the earl say, 'I sent him on a tour of inspection. He's taken one of Count Geoffrey's banners with him; says he's going to climb to the highest turret and unfurl it there. I'm to wait here and wave to him when it's done.' He grinned like the distant uncle he was. 'He's a lively boy, our young Henry. But by God, he has a temper to match his looks.'

Brien frowned. It seemed a strange thing to say. How could a nine-year-old have angry features?

He was about to query the remark when the men heard a shrill cry and saw the boy signalling to them from the turret. Snow was still falling, and it was impossible to discern more than a skinny arm, and the taller, conical shapes of guards, sent up there to keep watch over the prince and the surrounding countryside. Then the Angevin banner was unfurled, and Earl Robert returned the boy's wave. 'Let's go in,' he said. 'There are still some formalities of the surrender to be observed.'

They made their way across the flat, frozen marshland. Varan followed at a distance, favouring his stiff left leg.

As they approached the snow-capped walls, Brien asked, 'Who's the castellan here?'

'A rather gaudy young man,' Robert said. 'We've had him

in our hands before, at the Battle of Lincoln. Name's Gilbert de Renton. His father bought him back with an extremely ill grace, and now Gilbert's been telling me there's no point in my holding him to ransom again. He says this is the third time he's been taken, and that his family have already refused to reclaim him.' He chuckled quietly. 'You know what he did with his money instead of laying in food? He bought tapestries for the walls, and had embroidered cloaks made up for his guards. I wish all our enemies were as house-proud.'

*

The boy ran to the head of the turret steps, leaned forward and shouted into the darkness. 'Clear the way! I'm coming down! I have taken this castle in the name of my father, Count Geoffrey of Anjou, so make way for me!' Then he clambered down the circular stairway, feeding the echoes as he went.

Robert of Gloucester had assigned a permanent escort to the young prince, and these burly knights clattered muttering in his wake. Damned jumping flea. Couldn't he hold still long enough for them to catch their breath? Up the stairs, down the stairs, how does this work, what does that do . . . On and on, from the moment he'd been put in their charge, and they were getting damned tired of his piping and prancing. The sooner Earl Robert sent him back to Anjou, the better they'd like it . . .

The capture of Wareham had not been entirely bloodless, but both garrison and castle had been spared the usual ravages of defeat. Gilbert de Renton's sense of priorities had ensured that starvation quickly overtook his men, and they were now hunched in three shivering lines, awaiting their fate. Their young overlord stood a little apart, his polished helmet in hand, his head covered by the hood of his link-mail hauberk, the hood capped with snow. The six or seven knights who had agreed to accompany him to Wareham – his first fiefdom – glared at him from the far side of the courtyard. They wanted their captors to see that they disassociated themselves from their spendthrift master; not for them the tapestries and embroidered uniforms, and never again service under the fashionable de Renton.

The boy erupted from the doorway at the foot of the tower, saw that everybody was still standing about, and ran off in the direction of the squat, round keep. His guardians lumbered after him, while Brien glanced too late in their direction. He wanted to see Prince Henry, very much wanted to *see* him, and he started towards the keep.

'One moment,' Robert said. 'I'll hurry this along, then we can all get warm.' He strode forward, exchanged a few muttered words with de Renton, then allowed the young nobleman to kneel and make his submission. As he came to his feet again, he brushed snow from the hem of his gown and said, 'I must repeat what I told you, my Lord of Gloucester. You won't get a penny from my family. They warned me of that before I came here. You see, they bought this place for me from King Stephen, and they allowed me five hundred silver marks and told me to make the most of it. I must say it seems unfair, just because I'm prone to capture.'

It was impossible to dislike the man. He was effete and narcissistic, and he had an extraordinary sense of values. But at least he made a change from the sweaty, brutal self-seekers who dominated both parties.

'I'm curious,' Robert said. 'Your food-stocks were so low – How did you expect to see out the winter?'

'I'd have sold off the tapestries, one by one.'

'But you can only have had them a short while.'

'Yes, that's true. However, I have had them.'

Robert looked at him, then shook his head, bewildered. 'Am I to believe what you said about your family?'

'Yes, my lord. They have never found much time for me. And now their limitation includes coins.'

'Then what am I to do with you? You've made your submission, but that doesn't mean you'll fight for me.'

'In truth,' Gilbert said, 'I'm tired of fighting. For some time now I've had it in mind to become a pilgrim. There's so much of the world to see, and I have no wish to travel with packhorses and armour. If you imprison me, well, I suppose I could study – '

'And if I let you run free?'

'I'll visit Jerusalem. I can sail from here.' He smiled. 'Even if I were to break my word, and take up arms against you and the empress, you know how incompetent a soldier I am. I'd probably do King Stephen's cause more harm than good.'

'I must admit,' Robert nodded, 'I'd like nothing more than to see you elected Constable of London. We'd have the city in a week.'

Arrangements were made whereby those knights and soldiers who were prepared to swear fealty to Matilda, as Lady of England, were allowed to do so. The rest were imprisoned in Wareham itself, the knights to be held for ransom, the soldiers to be sold-off as slaves.

With the exception of one small tapestry, the castle and its furnishings became rebel property. This single decorated hanging was returned to de Renton, with instructions that he sell it to raise his fare to the Holy Land.

'Not de Renton,' he requested. 'Brother Gilbert. It sounds rather promising, don't you think?' Again he knelt at Robert's feet, this time in gratitude, then bowed to the Angevin barons and to Brien Fitz Count. As he did so, he caught sight of Varan. He remembered seeing him at Lincoln, but he was sure they had met before.

His duties at an end, he started for the gate, taking care to keep the tapestry dry. When he reached the constable he stopped and asked, 'If I may, master. Do you recognise me?'

The Saxon looked past him, gauged that Brien was out of earshot, and growled, 'I know you.'

'Tell me from where. I shan't see you again, and it will haunt me – '

'No need for that. I wore a shopping bag as a hood, you remember?'

'A shopping – Yes, of course! On the Dorchester road! I thought you were a demon, fresh out of the ground.' He nodded without animosity. 'It was a good trick. A shopping bag? Well, no one took home so much money before in a shopping bag.' He turned towards the gate, then felt Varan's hand on his arm.

'Brother Gilbert? When you reach the hot countries in the

East, always carry water with you. Always.' He shrugged, but only his right shoulder would move. 'I was out there. I offer the advice to you. You'll stay alive longer.'

The young, would-be pilgrim gazed, deeply moved at his kidnapper. 'I'll remember,' he murmured. 'And thank you, master. I feel well-sent.' Then he went out through the gate, wondering what colour tassel to buy for his travelling robe.

*

Brien waited for his son. He stood on the ground floor of the small, moatless keep and let his gaze roam incuriously over the broken furniture and rubble-strewn floor. What little damage the castle had sustained had been inflicted on the north-eastern face of the keep. Here a section of the wall had been breached, and two of the missiles had carried on across the circular chamber, smashing chairs, tables, benches, chests and weapon racks. Brien stooped and picked up a snapped-off sword pommel. It had once held a coloured stone, perhaps a jewel, perhaps merely glass, but it had either been dislodged by the impact of the missile or gouged out by a sharp-eyed defender. Hefting the broken hilt, he thought of the craftsmanship that had gone into its construction. It had been made, of course, as an instrument of death, yet it somehow seemed unjust that it should have been so thoroughly and easily destroyed. Today it was the slings and catapults that reigned supreme. Tomorrow those self-same mangonels might be blown over by great blasts of directed wind, or turned to ashes by man-made dragons. The ingredients of warfare would always be drawn from the elements; fire and air, the earth and the water. But whatever the mixture, there would always be a need for men with jewelled swords.

Robert came into the chamber and asked, 'Where is he?'

'Henry? Upstairs somewhere.'

'Under supervision, I hope. He's only to fall and break his neck – '

'Earlier, you said something about his having a temper to match his looks.'

'So I did,' Robert grinned, 'and it should hardly surprise you, friend Brien.'

Testing the words before he spoke them, Brien asked, 'Why do you say that? Why should I be specially aware?'

The earl kicked a path through the rubble, found an unbroken bench and dragged it against the wall. Then he sank down on it and stretched out his long legs. He yawned widely, rubbed a hand around his jaw and pushed back the hood of his hauberk. 'You're in an inquisitive mood today. Why did I say he has a temper? Why should it not surprise you? Because you know the mother, that's why!'

'Matilda told –'

'What? You know what she's like when she's aroused, that's what I'm saying . . .'

Aroused, Brien remembered. Yes, she was aroused that one time, that one single time.

'. . . like mother, like son. Told me what? What might she have told me?'

Brien shook his head, then persisted, 'In appearance, is he –'

'See for yourself,' Robert pointed. 'Those are his cloven hoofs on the steps.'

They listened to the clatter, the shrill cry 'I'm *not* in danger of falling!' the guttural response, and the further 'Let me *be*! If I *do* fall, it'll be because *you* pushed me!' And then the nine-year-old came twisting and squirming into the chamber, and Brien Fitz Count saw the diminutive mirror image of Count Geoffrey of Anjou, and the red hair that curled to his neck, his appearance matching his temper, and there was not a single fleck of grey anywhere on his head, nor anything else about him that would suggest he was the son of Wallingford. So there had been no need to tell Alyse.

The revelation carried the force of a blow. Brien felt himself slip, heard his own voice blurt 'A loose footing,' then stayed down until his mind had cleared. One of Henry's guards came forward to help him, and the boy followed and asked, 'Are you Greylock? Is it all dead, your hair? My mother, Matilda, Lady of England, said you are one of her most faithful liege-lords.' He nodded, pleased that he had remembered it correctly, then added, 'It looks dead.'

Still on his knees, Brien gazed levelly at him. There was no resemblance. Nothing. *Nothing.* And she had always known there was nothing, the beautiful, venomous Matilda. It had not been enough for her that he had been unfaithful to Alyse. Nor that he had fought for her and impoverished himself when others had grown rich by defection. Nor that he had guided and counselled her throughout the years and delivered her to within armstretch of the crown. Oh, no, that had not been nearly enough for Matilda. She had found it necessary to test him still further, her loyal Greylock, so had visited upon him the blessing and the curse of paternity.

And it had been a monstrous lie, a mirage constructed of hints and half-truths, fears that were without foundation, chance remarks that had been most skilfully intended. And when it was done, and he had told Alyse, and she had tried to kill herself, then there had been the enigmatic smile and the haunting 'My, my. Is that what you told her?'

Brien said, 'You know what we must do, young Prince? We must gather our forces, and rescue your mother the empress – '

'The Lady of England.'

'Quite. And then I shall personally conduct you to her. I assure you, Henry, even if she has heard you are in this country, our mutual appearance will astonish her. And, no, my hair is not dead. Here. Tug it if you will.'

*

In the warmer, undamaged solar at Wallingford, Alyse and her maidservant discussed the departure of the Lady of England.

'She could not have slept for more than an hour,' Edgiva said. 'Certainly not as much as two.'

'Did your husband check with the gate guards?'

'He did, my lady, but you know what they're like. Their time candle had burned out, the one they keep in the guard-house, and they hadn't replaced it, so all they could say was that the empress and her escort left a while ago.' She clicked her tongue, and Alyse turned away to smile. Edgiva's marriage to Sergeant Morcar had made the girl critical of the men who had once been her everyday companions. If she had married Constable Varan – an unlikely thought – she would have been the very devil with the garrison, Morcar included.

'No matter,' Alyse said. 'She's gone, and I think I know where. Her son – ' should I not rather say Brien's son? ' – he was brought over from Anjou, or Normandy, anyway brought over by Earl Robert, so I imagine Matilda has gone to Wareham to collect him.'

'Wareham?' Edgiva queried. 'Isn't that where Lord Fitz Count – '

'Yes.' She moved in her chair. 'There's not much to be done in this weather. Why not try another reading lesson?'

Edgiva nodded without enthusiasm and went to fetch one of the scraped skins from the library box. Long ago, before she had married Morcar, she had been willing to struggle with the written word. But in those days she had harboured dreams of marrying a clerk. Morcar was all very well in his way, but he had no desires, outside bed or the bailey. However . . .

*

Matilda and Brien passed each other *en route*. It would have been surprising if they had met, for the empress and her three companions kept to the side-roads, whilst Brien and Robert zig-zagged from one friendly stronghold to the next, gathering support as they made their way north-east towards Wallingford.

But the rebel army was still some way short of the Thames-side castle when they heard of Matilda's remarkable escape. They heard, too, that Oxford had surrendered to Stephen, and that the furious king was massing his troops for a spring drive against the rebellious outposts.

The march on Oxford was abandoned. Earl Robert took his young charge with him to Bristol. Brien and Varan continued homeward. The other rebel leaders went their ways. They would follow the established pattern of warfare, holding their castles through the winter, then reforming in the spring. Pitched battles *had* been fought in the snow, and Lincoln was a prime example, but they were the exception rather than the rule. Spring was the testing time, spring and summer and autumn. Winter was supposedly the peaceful season.

*

None was more grateful for the lull than Brien Fitz Count. The news he brought to Alyse was mortar for their marriage. He was not Henry's father, so it could not be concluded that Alyse was barren. No physician could say she was unable, not yet, whilst there was still hope.

*

The new year set the example for those that were to follow. And, in the same way that a wounded man will fight for life in the morning, singing and praying on his sick-bed, then die blaspheming at nightfall, so the people of the island chose this year to sound the death-rattle of discipline. They had lived near the edge, peasant and patrician, and their bellies had contracted with hunger. The coffers were empty; the grain barrels had gone unfilled. Throughout the country, on marshland and mountain, in forest and valley, in the teeming cities of London and York and Bristol, and in the towns and villages and hamlets between, the twin plagues of hunger and violence had gone unchecked, and the population had reached the brink and clung there and were now ready to fall. The war ebbed and flowed across the country, a flood of fire that consumed crops and houses, immolated entire families, turned peaceful communities into bands of roaming brigands. The peasantry adopted the motto of the landless nobles and disinherited barons – *Sauve Qui Peut!* Each man for himself!

Castles were taken and recaptured. Highway robbery became commonplace, and, as the crimes of violence increased, hastily-formed groups of vigilantes reacted with equal ferocity. For every murdered traveller who lay denuded in some roadside ditch, a convicted felon swung from the gibbet. But the vigilantes were as indiscriminate as the brigands. Innocent men were hanged along with the guilty, and it was not thought extreme to deck the gallows with women and children.

The country was now like a crudely-made quilt, its divisions marked by track and stream. Barons emerged from their strongholds to lead raiding parties against the surrounding settlements, and the villagers replied with ambush and assassination. There was no form to the war. Rumours were believed, authentic reports disputed. Today's ally was tomorrow's enemy, so the time to strike was now.

The rival leaders faced each other once that year. On 1st July, King Stephen was surprised in the act of besieging Wilton castle. The battle was a repetition of the debacle at Lincoln, and the royalist troops were routed. The king and his bishop-brother escaped, though a number of his senior knights were captured, men he could not afford to lose. He retreated to Kent, his one sure base, where his wife greeted him with further disquieting news.

Be it fact or rumour, she had received repeated warnings that Geoffrey de Mandeville, Earl of Essex and constable of the Tower of London, intended to renounce his king. If this happened, the counties of Essex, Middlesex and Hertfordshire would most certainly go over to the empress, for de Mandeville was their justiciar. He had to be stopped, before he started.

But if there was one man of whom Stephen was truly frightened, it was Geoffrey de Mandeville. It was easy enough to say he must be stopped – one could say that of an armed lunatic, or a wild boar – but it was not so easy to achieve. He was never seen outside the company of his bodyguards and, if an arrest was attempted in London or Westminster, the court would probably be stormed by his loyal townsfolk.

It had to be done, yes, but not on Geoffrey's home ground, where he might turn the tables on his nervous monarch. But neither could the venue be so alien as to deter him.

Accepting the advice of his queen, Stephen arranged to hold his autumn court at St Albans, twenty miles north of London. Situated well within the borders of Hertfordshire, the once Roman town seemed to offer Geoffrey the security he demanded. Nevertheless, he kept company with a dozen hard-eyed knights.

*

Such councils were evenly divided between prayer, the planning of military strategy, and snarling ill-humour. The court met together on several occasions; groups whispered in private; individuals sought an audience with the king; committees were formed, or disbanded. It was an opportunity for the leaders of the party to test the wind, and for Stephen to revise his lists. In the matter of Geoffrey de Mandeville, the lists balanced, for and against. The general sessions rang with accusation and rebuttal, though Geoffrey chose to make light of his alleged treason. He neither admitted it nor denied it, but told his compeers to wait and see.

His deep, seductive voice flooded the chamber as he told them, 'I shall do as I think fit. I may be the most loyal man here. Or maybe not. But since none of you have ever shown the gift of prophecy, you must await events. Hindsight you have, by the bushel. But you cannot say what I shall do next – see, I scratch my arse, but you did not foretell it – so why not shut your mouths and cease blathering!'

His remarks were greeted by a storm of approval, and an equal outburst of abuse. His supporters roared that he was stopping the rot. If they did not trust the mighty Earl of Essex who in hell would they trust? His opponents accused him of vile deception, and of daring to ridicule the truth. His intentions were as plain as day, yet he had the impertinence to tell them it was dark outside.

They were so preoccupied with their squabble that they did not see Stephen exchange a surreptitious glance with the guards at the door.

The meeting ended, as so often, with nothing resolved. The barons bowed perfunctorily to their king and made their way from the chamber. Geoffrey found himself held in conversation by some of his accusers, whilst his allies filed out. Then, surrounded by his dozen knights, he strode to the door. As he reached it, Stephen called, 'Essex! Give me a moment.'

The earl turned, and his accusers swept past him, right and left, shouldering the bodyguards from the building. Then they jumped back, and Stephen's guards dragged the doors shut and dropped the bar in place. Geoffrey's few remaining knights stood where they were, their chins raised by sword tips. The manœuvre may have lacked style, but it had worked.

Stephen stepped from his chair, pumping anger into his voice to dispel the fear. 'You are arrested, Essex, as a potential traitor! I was never fooled by your dissimulation! You plan to defect, and we know it. You've risen up by swinging from one tree to the other. Whatever I gave you in the past, my cousin Matilda has doubled. Then you came back to me, and I gave you more. And now you intend to swing again. Well, sire, I tell you this. The next swing you make will be at a rope's end!'

The doors shook as the excluded bodyguards pounded on them. Geoffrey pressed back against the wall, swords aimed at his throat and belly. His lean cheeks were sucked in, and his eyes blazed with fury.

Invisible weights seemed to hang from the corners of his mouth as he snarled, 'Petty little king . . . You'd catch a chill and swear the wind was against you . . . Christ weep for the miserable thing you are . . . A pathetic, mindless doll, frightened of the dark, and of the shadows the nightlight throws . . .'

He snatched at one of the sword blades, and blood ran from his hand.

'Stand off!' Stephen commanded. 'We have him safe. Chain his knights.' Then he drew his own sword – one does not go unarmed against a wild boar – and delivered the speech his queen had taught him.

'If you have not yet acted treasonably towards me, and I say you did when you first let Matilda into London, it is in your heart to do so. Your past speaks for itself, for you have changed sides more times than a dice. If you think I have ever trusted you, Geoffrey de Mandeville, I'm pleased, for it means I have deceived you. You are a self-seeker of the worst kind, for you do not even make provision for those who ride with you. To be your friend is to bare one's back for the knife, which is why I have never presented such a target to you . . .'

He frowned, hoping he remembered it right, then went on, 'Now. This is my offer. You will surrender to me all your castles, manors, holdings, shrievalties, offices and honours, and leave here a destitute man, or you will retain them for the time it takes to lead you to the gallows. Arrangements for your hanging are complete. You'll be gone within the hour. I shan't dither with you. I'll take your answer now, and it will be stamped as final. Divest, or die; which is it to be?'

The malevolence of Geoffrey's expression concealed any satisfaction he may have felt. So Stephen did not realise that he had made yet another serious mistake. To offer a hideous death on the gallows, or the surrender of all property, was to offer no choice at all. But with surrender, the king had offered freedom. Leave here a destitute man, he had said. Unfortunately, it was not what his queen had told him to say. Time and again she had rehearsed him, not to offer death or freedom, but death or imprisonment. That was what he should have said, but the demoniacal Earl of Essex had confused him.

Geoffrey licked foam from his lips. Then he nodded. 'You seem to have me, and I don't like the feel of rope. So I divest. Take everything, well, naturally you will. But if I were you, I would not give it away. Not for a while. Just keep it for me, hmm?' He rested his head against the wall and closed his eyes. The muscles tightened, and his eye-lids creased and shrivelled. Then he opened them again, and they were twin orbs of fire. To touch the eye-ball was to be burned. Stephen stepped back, horrified.

His voice again deep and beckoning, Geoffrey asked, 'Well, why am I kept here? You do not usually allow commoners in your court.'

Stephen motioned to his barons and they sheathed their swords. The hammering on the doors had died away, and the bar was lifted. Geoffrey de Mandeville moved into the entrance, looked at his armed accusers and the royal guards, then slowly stretched out his long arm and uncurled his bloodstained fingers and pointed at the king. No more than that, though he might as well have loosed a crossbow bolt at Stephen's skull.

Then he stepped backwards, remembering the step, and was gone from sight.

Stephen slid his sword into its scabbard, and rubbed angrily at his forehead. But it continued to itch most of the day.

*

The murderous, piecemeal war continued. Snow revisited the country, and the barons retired to their castles, the villagers to their ruined homesteads. At Wallingford, Varan again felt the left side of his body stiffen in the cold, and he grew sullen and uncommunicative, for this year it had stiffened earlier, as though in anticipation of the first snowfall.

Brien and Alyse had recaptured the happiness of their early years. But the chatelaine was now thirty-seven years of age, the warlord forty-three, and they were still childless.

The younger couple, Edgiva and Morcar, doted on their young son Alder, and did not object when, from time to time, Lady Alyse offered to watch over the boy. Indeed, they were flattered, and seized the opportunity to roam along the river-bank, scene of their earlier amorous encounters. In their absence Alyse played a gentle game, in which Alder answered to the unspoken name of Brien.

On Christmas Eve, Fitz Count's closest friend, Miles of Hereford, led a hunting-party across the Severn estuary and into the snowbound Forest of Dean. The hunters started a number of boar and red deer, and were out to break the record for a winter kill when a stray arrow ricocheted off a tree and transfixed Miles through the neck. He was dead when the hunters caught up with him, still in the saddle, his horse puzzled by the sudden lack of direction.

The leadership of the rebel party now devolved upon Robert and Brien, and the latter was not at all sure he wished to go on with it.

CHAPTER 12

VILLAINS OF THE PIECE
January 1144 – December 1146

IN the event, Brien's decision was made for him.

Within a few days of the death of Miles of Hereford, the empress accompanied her young son to Anjou. She had by no means abandoned her cause, but she had not seen her husband for three and a half years. In that time he had conquered most of Normandy, though he still showed no inclination to visit England. So, if he would not come to her, she must go to him. It was less the act of a dutiful wife than of a general demanding a war council. She had much to tell the count, and all of it could be said outside the bed-chamber.

Nevertheless, Matilda's departure sucked the wind from the rebel sails. Trumpets still sounded, and castles were strengthened, and patrols sent out. But neither side invited battle, and the leaders avoided any direct confrontation. Robert of Gloucester stayed in the West Country, awaiting the return of his sister. Brien Fitz Count remained at Wallingford, polishing the tip of the rebel spear. Letters passed between them, and Robert forwarded enough money for Brien to pay for a sixth watch-tower. This was erected above the existing gatehouse, overlooking the Thames. It was called Alyse's Tower, a guarantee that it would be defended to the last grey stone.

With the rebel leaders holding their ground, many of the minor barons became restive. They found this war without battles irksome and unprofitable, and they again took the reins into their own hands. With the first stirrings of spring, they emerged from their strongholds to continue their policy of aggrandisement. But they were as faint shadows compared with the two spectres who arose among the fenlands of East Anglia, and the rocky fastnesses of the north.

The first of these was the dispossessed and vengeful Geoffrey de Mandeville . . .

*

He had been joined by one of the most accomplished turn-cloaks of the day, Hugh Bigod, Earl of Norfolk. It was Hugh who, nine years before, had ridden pell-mell from the Forest of Lyons to Boulogne to inform Stephen of Blois that King Henry was dead. And it was Hugh who claimed to have over-heard the dying king name Stephen as his heir and successor. This had involved a remarkable feat of eavesdropping, as Hugh had been outside the hunting lodge at the time.

Since then he had fought for and against the king, and was now delighted to join Geoffrey de Mandeville in open rebellion. His pleasure was sharpened by Geoffrey's assurance that they would be fighting for themselves. 'You will be loyal to me,' he told Hugh, 'as I will be to you. It need not go beyond that.'

So, freed from all restraint, they set out to plumb the depths of depravity, well aware that it was a bottomless pit. It worried Hugh at first. He wondered why he had not thought of it before.

Geoffrey chose as his base the stone-built monastery of St Benedict at Ramsey. This isolated collection of buildings, complete with its orchard and vegetable garden, stood on an island, deep within the fens. On the way there, he attacked and plundered the city of Cambridge, never his enemy. His troops, recruited from unemployed bands of mercenaries and unhung brigands, ran riot through the city. They murdered whomso-ever they saw, hacked their way into the churches, stole the ornaments, defiled the altars, then set the buildings alight. They were in no mood to take prisoners, so they castrated those merchants who were slow to surrender their money, or used women as keys to the coffers. Geoffrey's men brought a wealth of experience to their work, and treated the citizens to a week of indescribable invention. Then they rode on into the fens, their trail masked by smoke from the burning city.

One could enter the fens and be hidden in a moment. Reeds and osiers grew higher than a man on horseback, and were resilient enough to part, then sway back into place. The real danger was not of discovery but of losing one's way, or drowning in the deepwater pits, or being sucked into the glistening black mud. It was difficult enough to navigate the marshes in daylight, impossible at night. So Geoffrey led his men due north and along a narrow causeway to the island of Ely, centre of the eel fisheries. He reached the low-lying island at dusk and turned at the end of the causeway, repeating over and over to the men who filed past, 'We'll have these people for friends . . . Leave them alone . . .' He had no need to say more; the sound of his voice and the expression on his face were enough.

They camped around the shores of the island, not even daring to enter the town. But the night was not without incident, for there are recidivists in any army, however severe its commander. A dozen men did barter at the town walls and come away with wine or mead and stagger roaring about the camp. And a few stones were thrown, and shops looted, and fishermen clubbed as they came ashore.

But the morning light revealed Geoffrey's sincerity. It was hard to imagine an atrocity that had not been performed upon the malefactors. Their bodies were on display beside the causeway, and anyone who had the stomach to ask was told, 'No, you heard no screams. They were executed first. This time.'

After that, Geoffrey de Mandeville and Hugh Bigod commanded one of the most obedient armies in Christendom.

They left the inhabitants of Ely to gape at the bodies and stare south at the pall of smoke that rose from the still-burning city of Cambridge, and headed due west across the fens towards the chosen base at Ramsey. They did not reach it in one day, and were forced to spend the night in the marshes, each man huddled in his place, not daring to move for fear of drowning, or of being smothered by the liquid peat, or of catching Geoffrey's eye. They were hard men, this collection of murderers and rapists, but they crouched like children among the reeds, imagining every footfall to be the work of de Mandeville. The moon allowed them to see eels and snakes, and to watch

THE VILLAINS OF THE PIECE

spiders climb the rushes an inch from their eyes. But they did not stir, not when they could still remember the latticed corpses by the causeway.

And then, stiff, wet and exhausted, they clambered to their feet and staggered away from the rising sun. By now the amusements of Cambridge were forgotten and, like the retaliatory creatures they were, they wanted repayment for their sufferings on the marsh. Geoffrey knew this, and had arranged it, for he could easily have taken them on a detour and let them pass the night on one of the nearby islands. But he needed to reawaken their animosity, then direct it against his next adversaries, the monks of St Benedict.

Even he, who had once told his friends, 'God holds no terror for me, though it may possibly work the other way about,' was not prepared to lead even-tempered men against the monastery. He required the worst, if he was to achieve the worst.

*

The black-robed Benedictine peered from beneath his cowl, at first interested by the appearance of the horsemen, then alarmed as they led their mounts through the budding flower-beds. He hurried forward, one hand raised in warning. 'Take care! You're trampling bulbs! Messires, I beg you, control –'

The arrow passed through his shoulder and he spun round. Some unexplored sense of preservation made him stagger away from the monastery entrance, and he fell senseless against the ivy-clad wall. The angle of the shaft and the folds of his voluminous robe gave the appearance of a chest wound. His eyes were closed, so the invaders judged him dead and ignored him.

They thundered across the laid gravel and into the monastery yard. They loosed arrows as they rode, killing monks and pigs and chickens. Cell doors slammed shut, to be broken open a moment later, their occupants slain. The sound of chanting faltered and died away, and more monks emerged from a side door in the chapel. They were greeted and murdered by a flight of arrows.

Geoffrey and Hugh reined-in beside the building.

'I want no looting,' Geoffrey said. Then, before Hugh could voice his astonishment, he clarified, 'I want it piled here in the yard. This is not like Cambridge, where there was enough for everyone. We'll share what we find.'

The pock-marked Earl of Norfolk nodded, partly with relief. He had not been anxious to attack a monastery, at least not one that was so obviously defenceless. He had looked to Geoffrey to lead the way, but for a moment he had thought de Mandeville meant – well, no matter. He didn't.

'I'll see it's done,' he said. 'I'll see no one keeps mementoes.' He looked round to make sure he was not stepping into the path of an arrow, then dismounted and plunged into the building.

Sounds blended into a traditional requiem. Shouts and screams, the splinter of wood, the chink of metal. The squeal and flutter of livestock, the shattering of glass, the rend of fabric. And then, stopping the invaders in their tracks, the sonorous tolling of a bell. Its sound carried across the marshes to Ely, to Cambridge – Christ in His grave, it would alert the country!

'Still that noise!' Geoffrey roared. 'Cut the ringer! And the rope! Do it, one of you!'

Men ran forward, swung their heads to locate the bell-tower, then charged through one of the low arches. The tolling continued, then rang twice, out of rhythm, then stopped. Geoffrey sighed with relief and waited for his men to reappear.

By this time the monks of St Benedict had either fled, or been killed, or were huddled in a group against the south wall of their refectory. The invasion seemed complete, so there was no reason for those who had rushed to silence the bell to stumble backwards into the open air.

But they did, still holding their knives, and Geoffrey leaned forward in his saddle, uncomprehending.

At the end of the line, driving the invaders before him, came a thin, wizened monk. He was not an old man; in the middle of his life perhaps, and at second glance he was more than a monk. His white robe and black cowl proclaimed him to be the abbot of St Benedict, and his weapon, a heavy silver cross on a chain.

He did not hold the cross rigidly before him, but lashed out with it, this way and that, as though it emanated flames, or was the hilt of an invisible, ten-foot sword. Whatever its properties, it forced the invaders to retreat, their free hands raised to ward off a blow, their sword arms limp.

With a mixture of interest and apprehension, Geoffrey watched the abbot repel his troops. Then he spurred forward and the line broke.

'Now, now,' he said, his voice deep and attractive. 'I need you in my vanguard, Abbot. Fifty of those crosses and I would be invincible. What name shall I tell them to put on your grave?'

The skinny priest let the cross fall against his chest. He pushed back the cowl of his robe, smiled encouragement at his huddled monks, then banished the smile as he answered the horseman.

'Tell them what God allows. Daniel, Abbot of St Benedict. Anything else will be your own invention. And in return, how should I instruct the devil?'

'Geoffrey de Mandeville, Earl of Essex.'

The abbot reclaimed his smile, then achieved a very rare victory. He laughed in Geoffrey's face. 'I've heard of half of you, Geoffrey de Mandeville. But were you not relieved of your earldom? Do you think we are deaf because we are distant? We heard what happened to you, and if we ever doubted it before, we cannot doubt it now. An earl become a marsh rat? No more the Tower of London, or the manor house, or the castle. Just reeds and streams, eh, de Mandeville? Just the company of murderers and despoilers. Oh, dear; there's little I can tell the devil that he won't already know.'

'Did you ring that bell?'

'Did you slaughter half my monks? Did you kill those pigs, that dog there, those trampled chickens?'

'I want this place, cleric – '

'Then ask God for it. It is not mine to give you.'

' "*Ask, and it shall be given . . . Knock, and it shall be opened*

216

unto you . . ." Yes, I remember something of the kind. However, I have my answer. And you have the time it takes me to count my fingers. Collect your brethren and run out of here, run from this place or I shall take it over as a graveyard. One . . . Two . . . Three . . . Four . . . A thumb . . .'

Daniel beckoned to his surviving flock, then quietly told them, 'Hurry on. You know where the boats are. Get going.'

They hesitated for an instant, but he threw up a hand and they lifted the skirts of their robes and ran for the gate. He followed them, walking, listening to Geoffrey's deep-toned count.

'. . . Second hand . . . One . . . Two . . . Three . . .'

Daniel raised his cowl against the spring wind, then stooped to adjust the thongs of his sandals.

'. . . Four . . . And the thumb . . .'

There was still time to run. He was within the arched entrance. There was time to step aside and dash for the boats.

He turned to face the yard, and raised his chained cross and told them they were excommunicated. They would die without salvation, and their bodies would not be received into holy ground, and they would be forever damned, each and all of them, separately and severally damned, throughout all eternity, and beyond.

Geoffrey said, 'Bring him down.' But no one moved, or let fly at the abbot. He did not repeat the order – once, and once only from de Mandeville – but he dragged his horse sideways, then leaned down and snatched a loaded crossbow from one of his men. He shushed the nervous palfrey, pressed the butt of the crossbow against his shoulder and tripped the catch.

The skinny figure of Abbot Daniel was hurled back on to the gravel path.

Hugh Bigod hurried out of the chapel. 'Everything's accounted for. It's a haul, I tell you, brother. Crosses, candles, gold mugs, chains of – What's the matter? What happened?'

Geoffrey de Mandeville shook his head. Nothing was the matter. Nothing had happened. He tossed the weapon down to the bowman.

*

They fortified the walled monastery, and linked the out-lying guest houses with a wooden palisade. In area, the base exceeded that of most castles, and every day saw the arrival of a dozen mercenaries, a gang of cut-throats.

The monks who had escaped by boat raised the alarm at Peterborough and Hungtingdon, though news of the sack of Cambridge had already reached the capital. Stephen reacted true to form. He rushed north at the head of an army, only to be checked by the treacherous nature of the fens. His siege machines sank in the ooze and had to be abandoned. His troops lost their way and let fly at one another through the reeds. Scouts, planted by Geoffrey, guided the royalists into ambushes or quagmires, or left them stranded among the rushes, which were then set alight.

The king challenged the disaffected earl to single combat, then threatened to hang every last member of the de Mandeville brood. But he might as well have asked one of the reeds to uproot itself and walk on dry land, for all the effect it had. Geoffrey was happy where he was. Ramsey was now only one of several bases, and he had taught his men to respect and therefore understand the ways of marsh life. They learned how to pole the flat-bottomed boats, and how to exist on a diet of raw eels and rainwater. They developed a crude sign language, and treated the reeds as though they were made of glass. In this way they could tell where Stephen's men had passed, and in which direction, and at what hour of the day, whilst they themselves left no marks of passage.

During the summer months the brigands struck out beyond the confines of the fens, riding east to pillage Hugh Bigod's earldom of Norfolk, and south to plunder Geoffrey's confiscated territories in Essex. The entire eastern shoulder of England fell beneath the shadow of the sword, while the king flailed aimlessly at the waving rushes.

Bishop Henry came up from Winchester to repeat the advice he had given his brother eight years before, when Stephen had first quarrelled with Brien Fitz Count.

'Hem them in, and starve them out. Don't chase after them. De Mandeville is no farm girl, and the fens are not cornfields.

If you know your history, you'll know about the man the
Saxons call Hereward the Wake. He set up here, in the fens,
and it took our ancestor, the Conqueror, five years to reduce
him. But King William was doing what you're doing now,
thrashing about as though he could cut down every stem.'

'Hem them in with what? How long do you think it will take
to build a wall right around – '

Henry hissed with exasperation. 'You don't need a wall. Seal
off the main entrances to the marsh.'

'That won't stop them getting out.'

'Brother, brother . . . I'm overweight, and I tire easily, so
don't make me talk myself breathless. Be a little sharper, I
implore you. No, you will not stop them getting out, a few
at a time. But you will prevent supplies getting in. They may
be inventive, but they are common soldiers in there, not millers,
or fletchers, or stone-masons. They need food and weapons,
fresh horses, firewood, a thousand things the fens do not
provide. Build some castles and sever their supply routes. If
they want to stay in the fens, then let them. Just make sure
they are discomforted, that's all. Speaking of which, should I
have brought my own wine cask with me?'

Stephen hurried to be hospitable, while his brother looked
around for somewhere to sit.

*

During the next twelve months, Matilda's party supplied
further proof of her personal magnetism. But they did so in
an extraordinary way, by remaining exactly where she had left
them.

Stephen's army was mired down in the fens, committed to
the destruction of Geoffrey de Mandeville. It offered the rebels
an ideal opportunity to snatch the initiative and move against
London and Winchester. But they did not take it, preferring
to await the return of the Lady of England.

For the first time in a decade, farmers in the south and west
were able to harvest their crops. Villagers nervously rebuilt
their houses and dared to travel from one settlement to the
next. It was as if the poison in the body of England had

centred in the inflamed eastern shoulder. The body was still diseased, but seemed to be improving with rest and a more substantial diet. It only remained for the patient to stay quiet, and the poison to be drawn from the infected wound.

*

One of Stephen's encircling castles was at Burwell, a few miles from Ely. It barred access to the marshes from the south-east, and its garrison had successfully intercepted a number of supply columns. Geoffrey de Mandeville and Hugh Bigod had survived one winter in the fens, but they were beginning to feel the pinch. Burwell would have to be attacked and destroyed, that much was clear.

So, in early September, the disaffected barons emerged from the reeds and laid siege to the castle. They lacked slings and catapults, so went at the walls with flexible ladders and crudely forged grappling irons. Geoffrey led the first wave of a hundred men, and was one of the nineteen who survived the retreat. Hot and sweating, his expression modelled on a river demon, he threw off his helmet, flung back the hood of his hauberk, and roared at the next hundred to scale the propped-up ladders.

'The door's open for you! Get up there and deal with them! Norfolk, lead them in!'

Hugh hesitated, and an arrow flew from the castle and slashed the side of Geoffrey's head. Blood ran around his ear, and Hugh put out a hand to steady him.

Geoffrey slapped the hand away. 'It's nothing. Leave it. You see!' he shouted, 'we have them so terrified they – we have them so terrified –' He lurched drunkenly. Hugh caught him and was again pushed away. 'They cannot even aim straight. I've been standing here in the open, and –' He stamped to keep his balance. '. . . I think I've caught the sun . . .' He sat down hard on the ground, blood pouring from the wound.

Near to panic, Hugh said, 'It's the impact of the blow. You're not badly cut.'

Geoffrey lolled forward, his head between his knees. 'I know it,' he snarled. 'It's the sun and the blow. Christ, if my head would clear I'd – ' Then his words ran into a long, chilling scream, to show his brain had been destroyed, and he arched backwards, his eyes staring at the incurious sun.

Hugh stood over him, not knowing what to do. Geoffrey wasn't dead, not from so slight a thing. *He couldn't be dead!* He was Geoffrey de Mandeville, the most terrible of scourges . . . Fate would not allow a stupid, glancing blow . . . yes, one aimed in such fright that it was not even straight . . . not allow it to snuff out the bitter flame of . . . Oh, God, he was so still!

He's become senseless with pain . . . He needs, what do I do, dare I lift him, he must be bandaged . . . He needs, that's it, yes, shelter from the sun . . .

A mercenary crouched beside Geoffrey, turned the bloody head from side to side, pressed fingers over his heart.

'He's dead. Hey, Bigod, you're in charge now. Earl Geoffrey is dead. Is that his only wound?' He went away without an answer, spitting disapproval. He'd always thought de Mandeville immortal. It just went to show.

The reign of terror was over. Royalist troops swept the fens and found nobody. The brigands had never respected Hugh Bigod, and anyway he had not stayed around to regroup them. So they had made their way out of the marshes, sniffing the air for the scent of blood.

The body of Geoffrey de Mandeville was claimed by a group of Templar Knights. The earl's excommunication had been echoed by the authoritative Bishop Henry, so they laid his body in a lead coffin and had it carted to London. There it was attached to the branches of a tree in the Temple garden.

It was to hang there, denied burial, for twenty years, suspended between earth and sky, between the heaven he had scorned and the hell that so much wanted him.

Meanwhile, the scent of blood drew the brigands north, where the second spectre was ready to snatch up the banner of insurrection. It was gripped by shorter, thicker fingers than those of de Mandeville, and the wandering brigands grinned with anticipation. They would not like to say which was the stronger, the more merciless, the closer to Satan – Earl Geoffrey or his successor, Ranulf de Gernons, the Moustache.

*

It was a world that believed in miracles. They happened every day. If a man was asleep, and his house caught fire, and he woke in time to save his family and livestock, it was a miracle. If a farmer prayed for rain, and after five weeks of prayer the clouds were torn, it was a miracle. It was a miracle to find a coin in the street, or to be cured of sickness, or to discover love requited. Priests traded in miracles, and the artifacts that would make them happen were sold for a high price. So what occurred at Wallingford was judged a miracle, even though it had taken fifteen years of prayer and intimacy.

Alyse was pregnant. And, had she already given easy birth to ten children, it would still have been miraculous, for her condition was confirmed one week short of her thirty-eighth birthday.

The townsfolk of Wallingford thought the civil war had ended, judging by the clamour within the castle. But they accepted the announcement as the next best thing, which it was.

Alyse felt sick, her body churned by achievement, and she cried openly, knowing she had justified two lives. For his part, Brien Fitz Count contained himself within the boundaries of pride and protectiveness. It was only in private, alone in the chapel, or beside the swift-flowing Thames, that he allowed the tears to come. It *was* a miracle, and it broke the last strands of Matilda's web. Brien was neither Henry's father nor was he unable. He was the father of Alyse's child, the next Lord of Wallingford, or a Lady of Considerable Beauty, it did not matter which.

Edgiva sought out her mistress and recited a poem it had taken her a month to read and memorise.

Varan debated for a long time, then accepted that he would live and die at Wallingford, and spent his life savings on a wooden statue of three figures, a lord and lady, holding a child. The carving was crude and dominant, because the constable had stipulated a lifesize representation, but had only allowed the sculptor an occasional, secretive glance at the subjects. Nevertheless, the message was clear, and the massive group was given pride of place in the solar.

Sergeant Morcar journeyed beyond the borders of Brien's land, and poached a well-fleshed deer from the neighbouring forest. This he presented to his master, with an extenuating explanation.

Presents arrived for Alyse from Robert of Gloucester, Baldwin de Redvers, and from Miles of Hereford's widow. Trinkets and sweetmeats were delivered by villagers and towns-folk, and the members of the Wallingford garrison presented their liege-lord with a complete suit of armour. It did not matter that Lady Alyse might give birth to a girl, or that, in the event of its being a boy, the armour would only fit him when he was seven or eight, not before or after. None of that mattered, for they were saying we will protect your child, we want to see him safe.

Who could say it was not a miracle, and well deserved . . .

*

The disease, cured in the shoulder, now infected the throat. Earl Ranulf was only too pleased to welcome the brigands from the fens, and he set them to ravaging the northern counties, again engaging Stephen's undivided attention. In May 1145, the month in which Alyse gave birth to a perfect male child, naturally named Alan after Brien's father, Alan Ironglove, Ranulf the Moustache attacked York. He showed himself as experienced in depravity as the deep-spoken Geoffrey de Mandeville, and better placed in his search for money and valuables.

One of his favourite methods was to warm the truth from the citizens. This entailed hanging them by their feet from a pulley over a blazing fire, or reversing the process, so that their bare feet blistered in the flames. It never failed, for even if the human venison possessed nothing, he would quickly name his friends and neighbours.

Those who disobeyed the Moustache, be they soldier or civilian, were usually garotted, or their skulls squeezed inside a circle of knotted rope, or were lowered into a pit already occupied by snakes. If their crime fell short of the ultimate penalty, they were nailed up in a box that was just too small in which to sit, just too short in which to lie. A week of that, and they had managed to deform themselves. It kept the army in line, and made the ensuing months the most profitable of Ranulf's career.

In the autumn, Empress Matilda returned to England, this time without her son. She was infuriated by her party's stagnation, and personally visited most of the rebel-held castles. One fortress she did not visit was Wallingford-on-the-Thames, though she wrote to Alyse, congratulating the chatelaine on the birth of her son.

'There are those who conceive in tranquillity, and those who do so in the first fever of desire. You must never think my adoring Greylock loves you the less, because his seed had taken a while to flourish. I, too, would have been patient, had my husband, Count Geoffrey, suffered the torments that so easily beset our men.'

Alyse showed the letter to Brien, who asked, 'Yes?' and, when she nodded, tore it across and across, until his fingers ached.

The rebel leaders broke the rules of winter and stirred themselves into action. They captured a number of royalist castles, and contributed to a fund to purchase Ranulf of Chester's allegiance. But he was doing well enough by himself, and had no need of the snow-bound southerners. He had conquered almost one-third of the country, and suddenly saw himself in contention for the throne. Now that would be something, he thought. Ranulf of England.

CHAPTER 13

THE LAST LEADER
February 1147 – January 1148

HENRY of Anjou had changed, and become an imitation man. He no longer clambered up and down stairways, pursued by bulky knights, or yelled in the corridors, or pestered the courtiers with endless, unrelated questions. He measured his tread where earlier he would have run, and expended his energies on riding, tilting at the quintain, and sword-play.

He already showed extraordinary physical prowess. No one of his own age dared compete with him, and he delighted in unhorsing his seniors. He kept his red hair cropped short, for he preferred to hunt without hood or helmet, and thus risked catching his hair in the briars. Whenever he returned from the hunt it was with his face mapped by scratches and, as often as not, one eye closed by a low branch, his forehead purpled with bruises.

His chest and shoulders were filling out, his voice deepening, his temper as splenetic as ever. He mixed unquestioned with Angevin nobles in their early twenties, and enjoyed the deception, as would any thirteen-year-old.

In one week's time it would be March, and on the fifth of that month his fourteenth birthday. He decided to celebrate it in England, his future kingdom.

*

Stephen was still engaged in the drawn-out conflict with Ranulf of Chester when he heard that Matilda's son had landed at Wareham with fifteen thousand men.

'He has also brought a galley-load of treasure, and a thousand Arab chargers donated by his father. His army is moving northward to Salisbury, and seems all set – '

Stephen stilled the flow of bad news and glanced at his

brother. 'We'll have to get down there before he joins forces
with his mother and Earl Robert. I'll give the order to strike
camp, and then – '

'One moment,' Bishop Henry cautioned. 'Before you lead
us in hectic flight, examine it again.'

'Does it need further study? If there is an invading army on
the south coast – '

'Yes, *if* there is.' He pointed a bejewelled finger at the
messenger. 'Tell us again. How many men?'

'Fifteen or twenty thousand, my lord. Their lines extend – '

'You've seen them?'

'Not I, personally, but I've heard – '

'And the horses? Those you've seen?'

'No. My brother rode up from the south, and he told me.'

'Ah . . . Then *he* saw this array, did he?'

'He was nearby when they landed – '

'Near enough to hear about it – '

'Yes, my lord bishop.'

' – but not to see. So we have it at third hand. Precise
numbers, even the breed of horses. And one galley-load of
treasure, not two, or five.' He let his hand droop and flapped
the messenger away. 'Too neat,' he murmured. 'Much too
tidy. You're being stampeded, brother. You're being asked to
put weight on your own weak spot.'

'Many thanks. And what is that?'

'To act first, and think second.'

Stephen scowled at the truth. 'And if you are wrong?' he
queried truculantly. 'If the prince overruns the south of
England?'

'Then the chroniclers will record that you employed the
most inept spies in the history of the world. Fifteen thousand
Angevins? From where, may I ask? Since when could the
Count of Anjou call on such forces? If he had them, don't you
think he'd have sent them over years ago? And if he has them
now, which he does not, would he really entrust them to a boy?
And what source these mythical Arab stallions; you know how
much they cost apiece? As for the treasure ship, it's not quite
the thing to place at the mercy of spring storms. No, King, no.

The invasion is imaginary. It's a tale that grows with the telling.'

Much against his will, Stephen agreed to wait a week. In that time, a stream of messengers entered the royal camp, among them several who had actually seen the invading force. It was true that it was led by the young red-headed prince of Anjou; they were all agreed on that. But the estimated number of troops varied – between thirty-five and sixty. There was, of course, no treasure ship, and the forty or so horses were commonplace palfreys and destriers.

Stephen did his best to smother his embarrassment, though he all but plucked his moustache in the process. The corpulent bishop was content to breathe on his rings and polish them on the hem of his embroidered cope.

*

The Prince of Anjou's presence in England caused Empress Matilda and Earl Robert acute anxiety. It transpired that the fourteen-year-old had left his father's court at dead of night, without permission and without stating his destination. On his way to the coast he had recruited a motley group of knights and mercenaries, promising them excitement and the highest rates of pay.

The adventurers had made the crossing from Barfleur in three fishing boats, and young Henry had financed the passage with a promissory note, to be delivered to Count Geoffrey's court.

They had landed at Wareham, ridden north towards Salisbury, then by-passed it and managed to lose themselves among the oaks and beeches of the great Savernake forest. Henry's ability as a hunter saved them from starvation, but when they emerged at the eastern edge of the forest, four of the party were missing.

The sense of adventure soon deserted them. They launched a series of unsuccessful raids in the district around Cricklade, then fled back to the forest. News of their activities reached the empress, and she immediately told her son to join her at Bristol. While she waited, she raged at Robert, reminding him that Miles of Hereford had died from a stray arrow in just such a forest.

'I don't know what excuse my husband will offer, but it will be insufficient, whatever it is. How could he allow our son to be so jeopardised? Good God, if one of Stephen's local barons discover him, they'll hold him for every penny we possess! Or Henry's group will run foul of some real brigands, and then who'll be left alive? Get some men out to Savernake, Robert. Retrieve the boy, lest England loses her future king.'

'And you your beloved son, eh, Matilda?'

'What? Yes, of course. Get on with it.'

But the most serious threat to Prince Henry came from within his own group. They were tired of skulking in the forest and asked to be paid off. He stalled them for a while, but their suspicions hardened and, one night, while he slept, they rifled his saddle-bags. As they had suspected, he was penniless.

They hauled him to his feet, tall, brutish men who had anticipated a more rewarding adventure than this. Prince of Anjou he might be, but he was also a lying little whelp. Pay up, they told him, or the outing will end badly for you. And have no doubts about it, pauper; we keep our word.

He told them he would appeal to his mother. They'd have their money in a week.

Perhaps he did not make the content of his letter sufficiently urgent, or perhaps his demands were excessive. Whichever, Matilda and Robert decided not to comply, thinking it would bring the boy to Bristol.

Among the gnarled oaks of Savernake, the Angevin adventurers were fast losing patience. They discussed selling the prince to King Stephen, or Ranulf of Chester, or whoever would pay the most. Henry pleaded with them to allow him one more try, and racked his brains for a likely donor. He thought of Brien Fitz Count, then dismissed him, aware that he was permanently impoverished. So were most of the rebel leaders, that was the trouble.

But there was one man who could afford to pay, and the prince wrote him a long and persuasive letter. In part it said:

'I implore you to look with pity upon my situation. I have been headstrong and foolhardy, though I sincerely repent my ways. Poverty weighs upon me, and casts doubt upon my honour. In short, I am at a loss as to how I can keep my word. I shall leave this country as soon as possible, for I have caused enough trouble here. You and I are bound by close ties, and, so far as my personal feelings go, I am well disposed towards you. I have always admired your courage in battle, and many of my countrymen still speak of you with awe. If you choose to help me now, I shall not forget it. Nor, I am convinced, will God, or my mother.'

Moved by the penitent and respectful tone of the letter, King Stephen forwarded the money to his enemy's son.

*

This astonishing display of gallantry was, at first glance, one of Stephen's most reckless mistakes. He had had the young prince at his mercy, and could have bought more with his money than a promise of departure. But a calmer study of the act revealed the king to be more devious than any of them had thought. Bishop Henry in particular was impressed. His brother had shown rare understanding of a young man's waywardness. He had allowed Prince Henry to retire with honour and, at the same time, had branded Matilda as a callous mother, and Earl Robert as a miser. On a more general level, the king was seen to be wealthy and generous, even indulgent, whilst the rebel faction were wrapped in the tatters of poverty.

The feuding barons knew where their future lay, and trooped north to beg forgiveness of their king, and renew fealty to him.

On yet another level, Matilda's miscalculation hastened the end of the war, for it cast the ageing Robert of Gloucester into deep depression. He was not a miser, nor were his coffers completely empty. But like so many of the rebel leaders, he had allowed the empress to direct him. It was *she* who had told him to disregard Henry's appeal, and *she* who had convinced him the letter was unimportant. Since she was the boy's mother, she should have known.

But none of them could have known that the young prince would beg money from their rival, or that Stephen would have the intelligence to lend it. So the respect that Earl Robert had earned over the years was lost, and people spoke of him as a poor man, unable to pay his way.

He became sour and spiteful, quick to take offence, eager to parade his existing wealth. He squandered his money on clothes and jewellery, threw lavish parties for his shrinking circle of friends, then thrust out his long jaw whenever Matilda intruded.

'I am correcting a misconception, sister! You would do better to repaint your own portrait than to criticise mine. Remember, *you* are the one who would not rescue her son. I am merely made mean in your shadow. If you tell me how to spend my money, you must let me tell you how to treat your family.'

'You are being ridiculous. Do you think your so-called friends are impressed by your vulgar displays? They'll drink you dry, and the fur clothes you give them will keep them warm all the way to Stephen's camp. For God's sake close your purse. Your friends have long since closed their hearts.'

'Ridiculous?' he snapped. 'Yes, maybe I am. But say this. Say I have been made ridiculous, then look at yourself in the mirror.' Stalking the room, he told her, 'I am your brother. A bastard brother, but nevertheless your kin. I'm the one who laid the foundations for you here, in England, and fought for you before you landed, and led your party, and made your arrival possible. I don't say I did it alone; I had Miles of Hereford, and the man who once worshipped you, Brien Fitz Count, and Baldwin de Redvers. We all worked on your behalf, without recompense, and for the most part without thanks. We never saw a day when we had too much money, and there were few days when we had enough. But we kept up the pretence, as we would have pretended health when we were ill. And now you deny your son a few silver marks, and make us out to be a nobility of beggars!

'How dare you find fault, you who have always worn your purse on your face? How much has your beauty earned you, Matilda, tell me that? How many honest men have ruined themselves for your smile, or died with your image in their eyes? You are not ridiculous, as you say I am. You are greedy and demanding, believing that because God made you a woman, and gave you such perfect features, you have the right – yes, you think it the right – to take all and withhold all.

'Are you generous, would you say? Do you have a warm heart? Is there any compassion in your blood? Do you own to your friends, and care for them, and ache when they are wounded? No, I think not. I think you have traded your God-given looks and men's oaths, and seen yourself as an angel, lent by heaven. You live in a niche, set apart for you, above the horrors of the world. We mortals are here to succour and amuse you, and to set you on the throne of England. That is what I think. Ridiculous, you say?'

She watched him for a while, and he ceased to be the tall, dominant, jut-jawed architect of her plans. Instead, he became an emaciated, querulous old man. Fifty-three was he? He looked sixty-three. Vain and unfulfilled, with a chin that threatened to bang against his knees.

'Yes,' she said. 'Ridiculous, and becoming more so.'

*

They tore at each other throughout the summer. There were a few interludes, during which Robert goaded his party into action. A royalist castle was taken, a river crossing established, a wooden lookout tower built in some stretch of the forest. He exchanged letters with his friend, Brien Fitz Count, and became so envious of Brien's austere existence that he thought of retiring to one of his smaller castles and holding it in faith, as Greylock was doing.

He knew that the Lord and Lady of Wallingford were desperate for money, and that they had bankrupted themselves, time and again, in the service of the empress. But even so, they were together, and Lady Alyse had given birth to a son, what was his name, yes, Alan, and Brien had freed himself of Matilda's spell.

But Robert had not. He snarled at his sister in June and August and October, and in that last month strode towards her to deny some accusation or other, and felt his chest explode, and walked on, drowned in pain, and heard screams and shouts as he crashed headlong into the wall.

He saw faces and swirled sleeves – *did I give them those clothes* – and his chest heaved again, and his heels and the heels of his hands drummed the floor and his heart burst. Or, as some thought, it broke.

It did not much matter which, for he was dead, and Matilda's party was beheaded.

*

An immense stillness blanketed the land. Robert of Gloucester had been more than the leader of the rebel party, more than King Henry's eldest bastard son, more than Matilda's brother. He had been a sincere, moderate, somewhat unimaginative example of an honest man. There had been little about him that glittered, but he had held the reins for ten years, more than ten, and had proved himself worthy to be called the son of a king. His sudden death drew memories to the surface, and his friends and enemies alike paused to see him in their inner eye.

They hoped he would be buried with the fullest honours, and King Stephen sent an anonymous sum of money to help pay for the funeral. Happily, it was used for that end, and Robert was buried beneath the wave-lapped walls of Bristol Castle.

Then, slowly, the adversaries rose from their knees and resumed their war.

*

Alyse knew better than Brien what would follow. He had been unable to attend Earl Robert's funeral, and this had heightened his sense of grief at the loss of his last good friend. But he had not dared absent himself from Wallingford, for his scouts had reported large detachments of royalist troops in the area.

Stephen's campaign in the north had been neither won nor lost, for the death of Robert of Gloucester had caused Ranulf the Moustache to think again. The brutal warlord had never seriously seen himself as a candidate for the throne, but he had every intention of becoming England's senior magnate. Indeed, with Robert out of the way, he was already the most important landowner, and he determined to secure by law everything he had gained by force. The way to do it was simple, if disagreeable; he would make peace with Stephen, and help rid the country of the hated Angevins.

Naturally, had Stephen died in place of Robert, Earl Ranulf would have thrown his weight behind Matilda, beloved Angevin. Either way, the price would be the same.

So with Earl Robert's body scarcely cold in the ground, the king found himself with an unexpected ally, and free to turn his attentions to the south. He made his first target Wallingford-on-the-Thames for, like Alyse, he sensed what would follow.

'She'll come here now,' Alyse forecast. 'She has to, for you are the last of the triumvirate.'

Brien shook his head. 'She knows better. She has steered clear of me ever since – since the day I saw the colour of young Henry's hair. She knew then that I would want no more to do with her. Besides, there are others she can approach. Baldwin de Redvers – '

'The empress may not wish to see you, but I repeat, she has to. Baldwin's a good man, though whenever I hear of him he's dug deeper into his holdings in Devon. He's become a creature of property, and he'll only fight if he is directly threatened.'

'And we have not, eh, my love? We remain unhampered by an extensive domain, or an embarrassment of riches.' He gave a wry smile, and accepted her nod.

'It's true, we have hardly prospered. But that alone should prove to you how important you are to Matilda. She will come to you, not because you have the wealth and weaponry, but because you are the only man with the power to raise flagging spirits, and remind them why they fight.'

Glancing out of the solar window, Brien said, 'Those are snow clouds. I hope they break soon. A good deep fall might block the roads.'

'Whom do you wish to deter, Stephen or Matilda?'

'Both of them. Everybody. Wouldn't that be satisfying?

No visitors, all winter. Just us and a blazing fire. I swear, if we were not interrupted, we could teach Alan to read by February.'

Alyse put a hand on his arm. 'It's an attractive picture,' she said, 'and I feel as you do. But she *will* come, husband. You may as well make ready for it. I have. At least, I've made the attempt.'

Brien lowered himself into one of the box chairs. 'Yes,' he sighed, 'I'm not blind to it. And it's not her arrival that worries me. Nor even the demands she'll make. It is the answer I'll give her that matters.'

Alyse nodded and looked down at the rush-covered floor. 'Can you say what it will be?'

'I don't know yet.'

Alyse thought, yes, you do. And so do I. And so does Matilda. That's why she'll come.

*

Varan limped across the bailey. He saw Sergeant Morcar and forced himself erect, but there was too much pain in his left side, and he let his shoulder droop again.

'What in hell are you staring at?'

'Nothing, Constable, nothing. I heard the alarm bell. I'm on my way to the gate.'

Varan snarled something under his breath, furious that Morcar had slowed to keep pace with him. The sergeant asked, 'Do you think it's Stephen? I mean, his men?'

'When I can see through walls I'll let you know. Yes, it's Stephen; no, it's not. How should I know?'

Morcar pressed a hand to his wind-chapped lips. Old Stonehead was in a vile mood today. And not just today. He'd been like this for weeks, since the advent of winter. It must be because his muscles had stiffened. It happened to old men, and Varan – *Constable* Varan – was nearing seventy. Christ, he must be one of the oldest men in the country, apart from a few lame priests. Anyway, it gave him the right to bare his teeth.

The alarm bell tolled again. Varan and his protégé climbed

234

Alyse's Tower and watched the Empress Matilda ride towards them, bringing with her the first flurries of snow.

*

They faced each other for the first time in five years, the forty-five-year-old Lady of England, and the Lady of Wallingford, four years her junior. The last meeting had taken place in deeper snow, and Matilda had then been exhausted after her incredible escape from Oxford. The years since then had been long and arduous, but she had completely recaptured her looks, and Alyse could see why men chose to lay their lives, like horseshoes, on the anvil of her desires.

The empress looked ready to be courted, to be adorned with jewels, or set up in some fine, fire-warmed castle. Somehow she had evaded the marks of time, as one man always escapes unscathed from battle, as a single pupil goes unpunished when the entire class is chastised. She had been left out by age, and looked now as she had looked when she first set foot in England.

Alyse and Brien knelt before her, then escorted her into the keep.

'You remember this chamber?' Alyse asked. 'You slept here, for an hour or so, on your last visit.'

'I remember it clearly,' Matilda nodded, and proved her point by adding, 'The shields have been moved on to that other wall, and someone has woven you a new log-basket.' She smiled at Brien. 'You know the circumstances of my last visit, don't you, Greylock?'

'I know them, though I was away at Wareham. Greeting your son.'

'So you were. No doubt you've heard of his latest escapade.'

'Accounts arrive,' Brien told her. 'We heard how Stephen furnished him with money, and you did not.' Something within him clawed for release. He wanted to remark on her beauty, to let her know he still admired her russet hair, her carriage, her unrivalled *hauteur*. Images flooded his mind, and he could see her now, and on her first visit to Wallingford, when the garrison had chanted over and over, 'Mat-ilda! Mat-ilda!' and in Anjou, in the firelight of Count Geoffrey's castle, where she had stood naked before him, so long ago. This Matilda made room for that Matilda, moving and circling, allowing him to disrobe her, smiling because her husband was a fool to have imagined Fitz Count more trustworthy than any other man. Then he heard Alyse say, 'That's true, is it not? Empress Matilda once told us that her son Henry threatened to grow grey hair, you remember that? And now our own sweet Alan seems set to become a redhead!'

Brien assimilated the cheerful lie, and the images faded and he saw insincerity corrode Matilda's smile. 'Yes,' he said, 'indeed it is. Whereas we thought Prince Henry would be a miniature Greylock, we now see young Alan with the colouring of Anjou. It's strange how appearances can mislead, eh, my lady?'

'Isn't it,' Matilda managed. 'But time presses, and we must not reminisce. I shall leave before nightfall – '

'That's as well – '

'Oh, you welcome my early departure?'

' – with Stephen's troops in the area.'

'Ah, yes, I see. Well, Fitz Count, I've come to you with one object in mind; to advise you that you are now my senior baron – '

'But I am not. There are many earls ahead of me on the list. Baldwin de Redvers – '

'A yokel! A peasant baron, imprisoned by his own boundaries. What has he ever done for me? It's you who will lead – ' She saw Brien's raised hand, and the flat of his palm, and stopped.

'Let us all be seated,' he said, 'and then I shall answer you. Will you sit there, Empress, near the fire? Alyse, beside me here?' He indicated the chairs, saw his wife's faint smile, and Matilda's expression, alert and suspicious. He stayed on his feet, and thereafter ignored Alyse. He had been haunted long enough by the reality and the images of the magnetic Angevin, and now he would show his wife that he could stand close to the lodestone of his past and resist it. He might never again have the chance to say what he wanted to say. He might never again find the courage to say it. So the time was now, in his own house, in the warm.

'Three things,' he presented. 'First, you are in no position to advise me, which in your terms is to command. Like a good miller, I have sifted the accounts and rumours that have reached me during the past year. I think I know as much as you about the travels and travails of your son, Prince Henry. I know what he did, and where he went, and how ill-prepared he was for his escapade. I know, too, that he found himself threatened by his companions, and appealed to you for money, but received neither coin nor care. I know that, throughout the year, you and Earl Robert savaged each other, and that you finally broke him, your greatest disciple, your own brother. He died quickly, thank God, for he had suffered long. So do not advise me of my duties, Empress, for I am well aware of them, and no longer react like an enchanted simpleton.'

'Arrest yourself a minute! I have never so much as dreamed that you were – '

'I am still speaking.'

' – enchan – *what*?'

He stepped forward, placed his hands on the arms of her chair and told her to keep her mouth shut, he was still speaking. Her head jerked back against the high, carved board, and her expression accommodated her most unwelcome tenants – fear and indecision. Her brain screamed at her to reject him, this poverty-stricken, one-night lover, but she was nailed to the chair, and could say nothing.

'Such a creature,' he continued, 'would bob and bow and be unhampered by experience. But I know what has happened, best of all to myself, and am no longer receptive to your orders. *Ask*, if you will. Say what you would *like* me to do. But do not tell me what part to play, nor whereabouts on the stage I should stand.'

Matilda looked across at Alyse. 'Fitz Count's memory fails him, along with his loyalty. He forgets that I am still Lady of England, and as such – '

'You were,' Brien said, 'but you must not keep titles you no longer deserve. England is split, you may have noticed. The

THE VILLAINS OF THE PIECE

north belongs to Stephen, through Ranulf of Chester. The east belongs to him through his own efforts. London and many of the southern counties belong to him through the diligent efforts of his wife, your namesake. And what belongs to you, east of Wallingford? Nothing. You – we – the few who have held true to their vows control nothing but the middle south and the west. So you are the Lady of Ten Counties, maybe less, and a long way from the throne.

'The title, *Lady of England*, was never more than a courtesy. It showed our optimism and our ambition, but it also admitted our failure to get you crowned. And since you antagonised the citizens of London, and were driven from Westminster, it has seemed less and less appropriate. Times have changed, my lady. You're bound to ask for help now, not demand it.'

Alyse sponged up the words as though they were the elixir of life. She had heard Brien defend the empress, endorse her actions, commend her beauty, deliver countless tributes and laudations. But she had never heard him speak as he did now, an impoverished, all but landless noble, yet, more than he had ever been, a voice to be heard. He, Brien Fitz Count, was telling Matilda the truth, and Alyse buried herself in her chair, praying that he would tell it all.

The empress felt otherwise. But recognisable truth has a fascination of its own.

'The second thing,' he said. 'Baldwin de Redvers is neither a yokel nor a peasant. He is, and has always been, one of your staunchest supporters, and by controlling the county of Devon, he has done more than most. Don't criticise him to me, lady, for I know him better than you. Also, it makes me think you would speak ill of Wallingford in his house.'

'No,' she denied, 'not so. He knows you are an exceptional man.'

He approximated a smile and told her, 'Indeed I am. For one thing, I'm penniless. And for another, I am one of the few to have extricated themselves from your web.' He salted the smile and went on, 'Do you know, I could almost wish your father had died before he did. He was a great man, King Henry of England, but if he had died young I would not have been asked to swear allegiance to you. If I could think back that far . . . If the thrice-made promise had not been made . . .'

'But it was.'

Lost among those earlier times, Brien mused, 'Stephen and I were as close as men could be . . . What did he call me, his lifelong friend? If I had earned that title, I would have been second only to him in this country, or anyway, on a level with his brother bishop . . . I could have given my son such an inheritance . . .'

'You made your choice,' Matilda said tonelessly. 'And you repeated it again and again.'

'Yes!' Brien roared, making both women flinch. 'Yes, I did! But I swore fealty to his daughter, not to you!'

'I *am* his daughter!'

'You think so? Do you think so by a single action? King Henry's daughter? You?

'No, sweet Matilda. You are his daughter because we have said so. Stephen made himself king with less. But you, who have had blood and lineage and the help of thousands, you are no more his daughter than I am, what? The father of your child?'

She drew herself erect in the chair. 'So now we come to it. This extraordinary delusion of yours. This earnest, indeed supremely arrogant belief that I should have chosen you to father my son. You have already told me that Lady Alyse knows all there is to know, so I shall not be causing her any distress. But you and I, Fitz Count, we had our night, and you were happy enough to thrust forward then, I remember, and it was over and finished. Or so I thought.'

Brien glanced at his wife. She smiled at him and said, 'I enjoy a well-told tale.' Then, to Matilda, 'Pray continue, Empress. I am as anxious as you to understand my lord's delusions. And my own, for I shared them from the start.'

'Think what you will,' Matilda dismissed. 'I made passing mention of the colour of my son's hair – '

'Which was what it is now. Red. A strong, bright red. It was never grey,' Brien pressed. 'I've checked. Nor was it green, or black. Henry was always a redhead, and the only

239

reason – if reason is the word – the only reason you invented the story was to arouse my wife's curiosity and test your power over me. But what did you hope to gain? Did you imagine I would come clamouring to you at Bristol? Did you think you would make a wound that could never be healed? What *did* you think, Empress, when you, yourself, say it was over and finished between us?'

'He did have a few grey strands, at the start.'

'No, he did not.'

'As his mother, I should know.'

'Yes, you should. And I grant you this; you knew what you were doing, and what you were saying, and what you expected to achieve. You have always known, that's the tragedy. No one can ever say of you that you made a mistake through ignorance, for you are altogether too knowing. Your cousin the king – he blunders and falters, but there is something about him that encourages forgiveness. He's an uncommanding figure, and his moustache withers on his lips, and he needs to be chained to his advisers. But you are a horse of a different colour, Lady of England. You put yourself above such frailties. Not for you the slip of the tongue. You know what you have said before you say it, which is why, here, in this house, you are condemned out of your own mouth.' He gave a deep sigh and concluded, 'God gave you so much of advantage, lady. Why could you not have used it to the advantage of England?'

Breaking the long silence that followed, Alyse said, 'There was a third thing.'

'Not important,' Brien murmured. 'I would have mentioned that I was once in love with the empress, so find her cruelties all the more wounding. But it's valueless talk. There's no sack so flat as the one emptied of affection.'

Matilda sat rigid in her chair, her face sallow with strain. The flicker of flames mingled with the shadows and with Brien's shape as he moved to the half-open door. He stood there, seeing nothing beyond the smudges of torchlight on the walls. Then he heard Matilda's voice, low-pitched and anxious. 'Well, my lord? Will you take charge for me? After all you

have said . . . As you see, I am asking, not commanding . . .
Will you – please – further the cause?'

'It's an unnecessary question,' Brien told the darkness. 'You
know I must. So you know I will.'

*

In the first few weeks of 1148, Empress Matilda sailed for
Normandy. She bade her supporters *au revoir*. But that was
inexact. She should have said *adieu*.

CHAPTER 14

ALONE

February 1148 – February 1150

THE expected attack did not materialise; at least, not then. Stephen's troops patrolled the roads around Wallingford and set up watch-towers along the southern ridge of the Chiltern Hills. The king sent the rebel leader several ultimata, all of which Brien Fitz Count rejected.

'The situation is now as it has ever been. You may think that because we have lost Robert, Earl of Gloucester, and Miles of Hereford, we are unable to go on. You may think that because Empress Matilda has left England we are unwilling to go on. You may think, in short, what you will. But the situation maintains, and the war will end when you surrender the crown. Until then, we will hold what we have, trusting in the Lord God and the righteousness of our cause.'

It was a brave response, and was circulated among the rebel barons. But it was not entirely accurate, for Matilda's departure seemed dangerously akin to desertion, and a number of her party switched sides. Brien tried to convince himself that she had gone to raise help, and would soon return, accompanied by her husband or young Prince Henry. The belief flickered for a while, then died. She would not return. She had no intention of returning. The fight – that others had carried on in her name – had gone out of her.

But if Matilda had lost heart, her supporters had by no means lost the war. They still controlled all but half the country, and Stephen ranged the length and breadth of England, damping the fires of insurrection. Time after time he prepared to launch an attack against Wallingford, only to be distracted by other, more urgent outbreaks. His inherent weaknesses rose to the surface, and his sleep was once again riddled with suspicion and mistrust. Men who thought him their friend found themselves under arrest, their lands confiscated, their wealth appropriated by the royal treasurer. He spurned his brother's advice, and the tempestuous pair parted for the hundredth time in their lives. Bishop Henry withdrew to Winchester, where he devoted himself to his menagerie and his enviable collection of European statuary. Brother Stephen could run himself ragged, chasing real and imagined enemies. Or he could come cap in hand and beg forgiveness. It was up to him. He was, after all, the king, and free to choose.

So the year turned, and Wallingford remained unassailed. It withstood the natural onslaught of winter, and the snow melted, and the country made ready for its fourteenth year of civil strife . . .

*

In April 1149, Henry of Anjou – now better known as Henry Plantagenet after the sprig of golden broom, the *Planta genista*, he had taken as his crest – returned to England. He was sixteen years of age, already bow-legged from riding, his temper sharpened by the knowledge that his earlier visit had ended in failure. On that occasion his enemy had paid his fare home; this time he made sure he arrived with a full purse.

There were two reasons for his visit, the first that he had come to receive the buffet of knighthood from his great-uncle, King David of Scotland.

It was now generally accepted by the rebel party that Empress Matilda had abandoned all hope of becoming queen. Instead, she, and they, would support Henry Plantagenet and offer England a new king. Those barons who had always been averse to a female monarch could transfer their allegiance to Henry and still honour their thrice-made vows. He was young and headstrong, but he had the makings of a king and he compared favourably with the precipitate Stephen.

Thus the show of unity with the hard-voiced David. His formal acceptance of Henry allowed the barons to press forward with a clear conscience. Like mother, David told them, like son.

The second reason for the visit had been a close-kept secret, and it was not until Henry had travelled the length of England to join King David at Carlisle that his suspicions were allayed. What he had heard had seemed so unlikely, so far-fetched, that he had treated it as nothing more than a wishful rumour. But it was a fact – the brutal and powerful Ranulf of Chester had once again decided to change sides.

Earl Ranulf, the Moustache, had had quite enough of King Stephen. Or, put another way, he had had nothing of him. For the last two years he had fought alongside the king, and safeguarded his own vast territories in the north. And his reward? Effusions of praise, and the odd, two-a-penny trinket. No lands, honours or concessions. No rights or shrievalties. Not even a sack of coins, or a set of plate. Just words and smiles and promises as hollow as a drainpipe. We are grateful to you, Lord Ranulf, and accept this token of our esteem, and we will assuredly advance you before long . . .

Ranulf cast his memory back eight years, to that snow-swept day at Lincoln, when he and Stephen had faced each other beneath the castle walls. The earl's prismatic memory had distorted the incident, and he conveniently overlooked the fact that Stephen had knocked him off his feet with a borrowed axe. Instead, he saw himself as the victor, and regretted that he had not finished the king, there and then.

Fortunately, the mistake could still be remedied. If not there and then, some other place, and soon.

So it was that the two redheads, Henry and Ranulf, came together under King David's roof. On 22nd May, the young Plantagenet was knighted by the king. Next day, Henry and Ranulf swore homage to David as Lord of Carlisle, the town that Ranulf had always regarded as his, by inheritance. In return, the Scottish monarch gave Ranulf the honour of Lancaster. To seal the bargain, one of King David's granddaughters was betrothed to Ranulf's son, and both men then affirmed their support for Henry, as future King of England.

Each of them had profited by the agreement, and the meeting degenerated into an orgy of fellow-feeling. Pounding the tables, the wine-warmed trio decided to put their drawing power to the test. They would raise an army and move against York, Stephen's northern stronghold.

'He's been singularly unsuccessful in the south, where we lack any leader except Fitz Count of Wallingford, so how will he do up here, with us three against him? He'll soil his legs at the sight of us!'

'You'll be king by autumn, Henry.'

'And you, my dear Ranulf, will pick and choose your rewards.'

'When do we show ourselves to the people?'

'Soon,' David growled. 'As soon as we hear the cellar's run dry.'

*

Brien waited for his four-year-old son to finish a long and exaggerated description of a juggler he had seen in town, then asked Alyse, 'Will you give him to Edgiva again? I want your views on this.' He held up a letter, and went over to re-read it in the window alcove. Alyse steered the chattering child to the solar entrance. The maidservant emerged from her room at the head of the stairway and grinned down at the boy. 'What now, master Alan? Am I to bear out one of your stories?'

Alyse said, 'If he has not entirely exhausted you, will you take charge of him for a while longer?'

'Did he tell you about the travelling fair?'

'In detail. I doubt if their performance has ever received such rapturous acclaim. Did the juggler really spin silver dishes on the point of a spear?'

'What?' Edgiva laughed. 'Is that how he saw it? He'll be a troubadour, your son. He'll tour the courts of Europe, telling his tales. The silver dishes were only clay plates, and the spear was a stick. But, yes, he did spin them.' She shook her head, bemused by the boy's inventiveness. Her own son, the ten-year-old Alder, was as much like his father as Morcar was like Constable Varan. Alder never embellished, but rather stripped the embroidery from life and redressed it in plain garb. If he saw a high-stepping Arab stallion, he called it a horse. If Alan saw a farmyard pig, he told how he had escaped from a wild, tusky boar.

She took the child by the hand, and Alyse thanked her and went back into the solar. Noting Brien's serious expression, she closed and barred the door.

'What is it, husband? Another of Stephen's final warnings?'

'In a sense, though it is not yet directed at us.' He stood facing the room, the summer sun on his back. 'This is from a man I know in the north. He has always proved reliable before, so I believe him now.' He read aloud, relaying the writer's account of the union between King David and Prince Henry and Earl Ranulf. But that was only part of the letter. The rest, the all-important section, described how the trio had raised an army and advanced on York.

'You might think, Lord Fitz Count, that with three such leaders, all opposition would crumble. And it would have done so, had they buttressed their talk with action. But they are mules, these three. They bray and kick, but they don't go down the road.'

'He's very obtuse,' Alyse commented. 'What is he trying to say?'

Brien discarded the letter. 'You're right; he does decorate. But what he is saying, in his own way, is that the King of Scotland, and the Plantagenet, and that turncloak Ranulf gave ample warning of their intentions. By the time *they* had assembled their army, Stephen had assembled his. And his was twice the size.'

'And the attack on York?'

'They never reached it. Stephen got there first, and confronted them with an overwhelming force.' He referred to the letter, hoping that he had mis-read it. But it was all there, penned in dark green ink.

'They were never even brought to battle. King David has withdrawn to Carlisle, and there's talk of him going back over the border. Ranulf has retired to Chester. The Plantagenet has fled to Bristol. Fled; that's the word used here.' He turned the

246

letter in his hands. 'A short-lived resurrection, wouldn't you say?'

Almost twenty years of marriage to Brien Fitz Count had given Alyse a clear understanding of military strategy. 'So he's broken our back in the north, and now he'll come against us here.'

'I believe so, yes. For once in his life, Stephen's impetuosity has worked in his favour. I don't know what those three had in mind, but they seriously underestimated the king. My God, they must have been shaken to the bones when they saw the size of his army.'

Alyse crossed the room and stood, dwarfed by the statue Varan had commissioned. She ran a finger over Brien's wooden shoulder, then over the wooden child in her arms. 'What do we do now?'

'We keep our eyes wide, that's what. We've waited long enough for it, and it's about due.' He tossed the letter on to the window seat and came forward, as though jealous of the crudely-carved replica. He took Alyse's hands in his and said, 'I wish I could find some easy way –'

'There isn't one,' she told him. 'Anyway, I don't want my coffin greased. Tell me as you would tell Varan or Morcar. All I ask is that you tell me first. You say he will come for us?'

'Yes.'

'And in earnest?'

'He must, if he is to follow up his success. He has never been so well placed before. The other leaders are scattered. Worse, they have been defeated without a fight. And, however powerful David is in Scotland, or Ranulf in the north, they will not unite again. As for Henry, he'll probably go home and tell his mother.'

'I see. Then it only leaves us.'

Brien turned away abruptly. Us she had said, and that was right, for whatever happened to him would happen to her and Alan.

Shielding his emotions with a smile, he echoed, 'Then it only leaves us. We've been hemmed-in here a damn long time, but the south looks to Wallingford for leadership, and always will. Every day we resist, the south resists, and the cause is kept alive. And if we fall – ' He shrugged.

'He tried it once,' Alyse said. 'Do you remember? We burned his siege machines, and Miles of Hereford came along and destroyed his watch-towers.'

'I remember, but he'll not fall into the same trap again. And there's no Miles of Hereford to dig us out. An arrow bounced off a tree . . . Jesus, that was a tragedy . . .' He released her hands and said, 'It might be as well for you to take Alan to Bristol. The place is impregnable, and – '

'I pray you, don't go on. I, too, have waited overlong, but I do not intend to be absent when the king calls.'

'I'm serious,' Brien said. 'He'll do his best to kill us. There'll be no parleys, or offers of friendship. He'll flatten this place if he can. He must, for whether we like it or not, we are the last symbol of resistance in the south.'

'And the very first rock may catch Alan, is that what you fear?'

'Or you.'

'So I'm to run away from that, and from you, and from this place where I've lived all my life. You say you're serious, and I know you are. But I also know I've earned your respect through the years – '

'You had it from the first day.'

'You have never made me act against my beliefs.'

'No, I trust – '

'Then you've waited too long to start now.' She moved away from the statue and went over to study their other valued possession, the hammered silver mirror bequeathed to Brien by his father, Alan Ironglove. Again, she touched it with her fingers, tracing the engraved border. 'We have built up to this meeting,' she said. 'It comes as no surprise to us. We are against the king, all of us. So either we stay, you and I, and Varan, and Morcar and his wife, and that up-and-coming soldier Ernard and his woman, yes, *and* Alan and Alder and the other children, or we leave the place empty and in flames.'

'Is that your last word?' he asked gently.

'It was my last word,' Alyse told him, 'from the first.'

*

Stephen's show of force at York brought his brother hot-foot from Winchester. Careful to conceal his astonishment, Bishop Henry congratulated the king and attempted to patch up their latest quarrel.

Making light of it, Henry said, 'You no longer need my advice, it seems,' and was promptly told, 'No, I do not. I grant you, you were of value in the early years, and I have not forgotten that it was you who laid the path to the throne. But it's as well that we understand each other. You have always told me to ponder on my actions, to test the water as it were. But I plunged in this time and have emerged victorious. It shows – '

'That you were lucky,' Henry snarled, 'nothing more. I came here in good faith, to re-establish fraternal friendship with you, and I find you smitten with the plague of arrogance. You were *lucky*, brother! They gave you too much warning, and you had time to assemble your army. I'm surprised by your success, but not by your reaction. It's typical of you, and one time out of twenty it has worked to your advantage. But don't let it go to your head. You are no peerless general, and we have yet to see you show any tactical sense. We've been at war with the Angevins for fifteen years, and they still run half the country. Capture the Plantagenet, or the dogged Fitz Count, and then we'll let you preen and prance. Until then, think yourself lucky, for that's all you are.'

Stephen no longer worried his moustache. That nervous mannerism had been mastered. Instead, he treated the bishop to an expression he had practised in the mirror; that of the brilliant pupil made bitterly aware of his tutor's shortcomings.

'If you have nothing better to offer than selfish recrimination, I suggest you go back to your ostriches. Or are they peacocks?'

'Both,' Henry retorted, 'and each with more right to preen than you will ever have. My sweet brother . . . Mistaking the taste of Luck, which has always been in your mouth, with the

THE VILLAINS OF THE PIECE

untried fruit of Success. Should you need me, send word to Winchester. If I am not otherwise engaged, I shall be happy to correct your mistakes.' His bow-like mouth twisted into a sneer, the corpulent bishop hurried for home.

In truth, Stephen was glad to see him go. He felt his brother had dominated him long enough. Now, armed with the victory at York, he would start south and deal a death-blow to his most determined enemy, *his lifelong friend* . . .

*

The two men stood on the crenellated turret of Alyse's Tower. They were both wrapped in wolfskin cloaks, their hands buried in fur-lined mittens, their heads concealed beneath woollen hoods and the metal hoods of their hauberks and plain pot helmets and outer cowls, again of wolfskin. Even so, they shivered with cold and blinked tears from their eyes.

They peered eastward across the river and over the snow-capped forest. Ernard waited for the flurries of snow to clear, then, taking an arrow from its quiver, pointed with it and said, 'There. Where the gully ends. They're clearing the ground.'

Brien squinted along the shaft. 'I see it.' He straightened up as a fresh flurry obscured the view. 'Why've they stopped there?'

Ernard shook his head.

Throughout the past month, the first of 1150, the occupants of Wallingford Castle had listened to the rhythmical thud of axe on wood and the splintering crash of felled trees. They had soon traced the sounds to that section of the forest due east of the castle and directly opposite the gate tower. Two scouts had been sent across the river to learn what they could about this mid-winter industry. Only one of the men had returned, mortally wounded, but he had lived long enough to deliver his report.

Out there, he had gasped, a mile beyond the east bank of the Thames, Stephen's troops were cutting a wide road through the forest. From what he had seen, the enemy were advancing more than fifty yards a day. He wished he could give Lord

Fitz Count a fuller description, but he and his companion had been spotted by royalist archers, and it was only by the grace of God that he had managed to get back across . . .

The road-makers were now within three hundred yards of the riverbank. If they maintained their remarkable rate of progress they would be through the forest in a week. So why the clearing? And why there?

Brien brushed irritably at his eyes, and leaned forward as though the few inches would clarify the view. He told Ernard to wait for a break in the snow, then loose an arrow at the new-made road. 'See if you can overshoot the clearing.'

They lost sight of the arrow as it dipped towards the trees, but it told Brien what he wanted to know.

'That's why they've halted there, to widen out. It's for protective missiles.'

'My lord?'

'The woodsmen – they are almost within arrow range. They'll need protection if they are to cut right through to the bank. The clearing is to make room for a line of catapults.' He expelled his breath as smoke. 'We'll be under attack by to-morrow, soldier, unless we foul their nest.'

Ernard made a vague gesture towards the north. 'Why doesn't the king place his machines out there? Flat fields – '

'He remembers what happened to him at Lincoln, when he was caught in the open. No, he's doing the right thing. I'm the one at fault. *I* should have remembered it.'

Eager to commiserate, Ernard said, 'Well, even if he lets fly at us from the forest, and his men do cut through to the bank, how will they get across the river? The road is a long way north of the ford.'

'It is, but he has the materials at hand. He'll use the felled trees to make rafts, maybe even a floating bridge. If he attacks us from all sides . . .' His thought swallowed his words, and he turned his back on the scene.

If they come from all sides . . . But he will not be caught in the open . . . He'll launch his main attack through the forest . . . Yes, we'll probably see a complete bridge, run forward on rollers . . . Christ, I'm marked down for this . . . I should have sensed it . . .

He prowled back and forth across the gate tower, and for the next few moments used Ernard as a sounding board.

'We'll go out tonight. How many bladders and waterskins are there in the place?'

'I suppose, uh, two or three to each man. Some extra ones in the stores.'

'Fill them with pitch. I've seen some barrels of that around. Set up a cauldron in the yard, so the pitch can be heated and pour easily. Nice warm work on a winter's night. Now then, how many men? We must keep the noise down. Twenty, would you say?'

'In the sortie, my lord?'

'Not more, or they'll hear us coming. And rags around our feet.' He looked at Ernard without seeing him, and asked, 'When were the boats last tested?'

'Constable Varan had them in water a week ago.'

'That's good. Can we get ten in each boat?'

'We've had as many as twelve – '

'And torches. And flints. We can't take a light with us.' He stopped pacing, re-examined the plan, then told his bewildered companion, 'This is what I want. Find Varan and Morcar and send them to me. I'll be in the conference chamber in the keep. Then make a collection of skins and bladders; wine or water, it doesn't matter. Have the barrels and cauldron set up in the outer yard, and detail some of the kitchen servants to fill the skins. They should know what they're doing, they've poured soup often enough. Any women you see, tell them to tear strips of rag and pile them beside the barrels.'

My own woman, Ernard thought. Eadgyth. I'll put her in charge.

'Bring the boats out of store,' Brien continued, 'and bind the oars and rowlocks with rags.' He drummed a fist against his mittened palm. 'What else?'

'The torches and – '

'Yes, well done. Torches and flints, a dozen of each. I want the torches well soaked in pitch, so they catch alight at the first spark. Right, that's it.'

Like the reliable soldier he was, Ernard repeated the orders, then hurried down the steps. He was not quite sure what Brien Fitz Count intended, but whatever it was it had a decisive ring.

*

At dusk the raiding-party assembled in the outer bailey. During the afternoon the constable and sergeant had chosen the seventeen who would go with them. Now, joining them in the yard, Brien realised there had been some misunderstanding.

He beckoned to Varan and Morcar and led them away from the waiting group. The seventy-year-old Constable of Wallingford limped after his master. It was as much as he could do to walk in a straight line, for his left side was almost paralysed. Beside him came Morcar, less than half his age, strong and muscular. Sergeant Morcar, impatient to try on Varan's shoes.

'This is wrong,' Brien told them. 'We three cannot all go. I know each of you is as anxious as the other to strike a blow, but if the boat sinks, who leads Wallingford?'

'You should stay,' Varan said flatly. 'You've told us what to do, and we're able to do it.'

Morcar gazed pointedly at his mentor's deadened leg. 'With respect, Constable, it's you who should stay. Climbing in and out of the boat, then having to creep about among the trees – ' He broke off as Varan lurched towards him. 'You think I'll alert the enemy, eh? A touch of cramp, and you judge me infirm? Why, you natural know-nothing, I'll be the one to pick *you* up when you've stumbled!'

'Enough of this!' Brien snapped. 'No one said you're infirm. And you put a foot on your opinions, Morcar.' His gaze swung from one to the other, though he already knew in whose favour he would decide.

He looked at Varan, the man who, at fourteen, had accompanied Brien's father, Ironglove, on the first Christian Crusade. For twenty-five years the Saxon had ridden at Ironglove's shoulder. And for twenty-five years after that he had devoted himself to Wallingford and Lady Alyse and Count Alan's bastard. It was a long time.

He looked at Morcar, another Saxon who, through his own abilities, had risen from the ranks. True, it was Varan who had singled him out for advancement, but Morcar had proved himself worthy of selection. Brien would be pleased to have him as constable, one day.

Varan again. A touch of cramp? No, something far more serious. In his absence, members of the garrison called him Stonehead, but there was no longer any humour in the title, for the left side of his body did, indeed, seem to be turning to stone. Each year it grew worse. Each winter the immobility came earlier, and stayed later with the spring. Only in the hot, mid-summer months did Varan recapture his stride and find a use for his stiffened hand.

Morcar again. No such problem there. He'd move silently among the trees, quick and sure-footed. No real chance of him stumbling, or shouldering snow from the branches.

But fifty years was a long time. After that a man deserved to choose how he would spend the night.

Brien nodded at Morcar. 'You'll command here while we're away. If the castle comes under attack you will set the pitch barrels alight. We should see the glow, even in the forest.' He nodded again, this time in dismissal. Morcar snatched the edge of his cloak, as though slamming a door, then plunged away into the darkness. Later he would accept Brien's decision. But later Brien himself would be consumed by doubt.

The raiding-party had wrapped the rags around their boots. They had discarded their link-mail hauberks for fear they would chink and rattle, and were now shivering in plain woollen tunics and short, rabbitskin cloaks. They carried no bows or crossbows, and Brien told a few of them to get rid of their spears.

'Knives only at this meal. Right; we've found you four bladders apiece. Hang them around your necks, so you can keep one hand over them. Twelve of you collect torches and flints. The rest carry out the boats. And I'll say this once. The only voices you'll hear will be mine or Varan's. I won't be gentle with anyone who speaks.' He unbuckled his sword-belt and handed it to one of the remaining garrison. Then he looped his share of the pitch-filled bladders around his neck and signalled to the gate guards to open up.

The boats were carried out and lowered on to the river. The ice cracked beneath the hulls. One by one the soldiers lowered themselves into the broad-beamed tubs. One of the last men in caught a wine-skin on the edge of the boat. The skin split and warm pitch oozed across his chest and dripped on to his bare knees. He stifled a curse, whilst those beside him grinned at his discomfort.

Brien and Varan joined their crews. The boats were pushed away from the bank, and the chosen oarsmen swung the craft in mid-stream, so the leaders would be first ashore. The current swept the boats down river, but the Thames was less than sixty yards wide along this stretch, and they quickly bumped against the east bank.

Brien clambered out, then glanced surreptitiously at Varan. The constable had straddled the bow, but he could not raise his left leg quickly enough and the boat began to drift away from the bank. There was a splash and a sharp hiss of suppressed anger, and he hauled himself ashore, his body soaked below the waist. The crews followed, peering in among the trees.

However, they were first made to haul the craft upstream, well past the castle. Now, if they were forced to retreat in a hurry, the current would, with luck, carry them down to the launching point. The boats were moored to deep-rooted trees, and the raiders moved inland.

Snow, which had over-laden the upper branches of the trees, fell like cold phosphorus, breaking apart as it hit the lower limbs. It caught some of the men as they passed underneath, but the constant falls covered the sounds of advance. Brien leaned close to Varan to mouth instructions, and the raiders spread out. The warlord had counted his steps and estimated the line was now one hundred yards from the clearing. It was again time to divide the force.

Leaving Varan to pass on his instructions to the right-hand section, Brien edged over to the other end of the line. There he told four of the men to continue on another five hundred paces, then move across and block the road. Five hundred paces would take the men past the clearing and, with Varan's four, the detachment would cut off all escape. They went forward, each wearing an extra cloak of snow.

The main group continued in the direction of the clearing. They saw a light ahead, half hidden by the undergrowth. A camp-fire. The men looked to their leaders, but Brien slowed the pace. The detachment had to be given time to get into position. The firelight beckoned, an oasis of warmth in the snowbound forest . . .

Brien no longer counted his own steps, but estimated the progress of the detachment. Two hundred and sixty . . . sixty-one . . . sixty-two . . .

Varan touched him on the arm. 'There's a dozen or more of them around the fire. They're protecting something – '

'I hope so. Materials for their rafts, or bridge, or whatever they're going to use. We're close enough now. Halt your end of the line. Tell them to make ready. I want the torches lit together, then straight through to the clearing. We have to be quick, or at least one of them will raise the alarm.' He felt Varan turn away. He wanted to ask his friend if he was well enough. The cold water must have shocked him, and thickened the blood in his one good leg. But he could not insult the old man with such a question. Of course he was well enough. He'd once walked through Siberia on branded feet, hadn't he?

The men produced their torches and tucked the wooden shafts under their arm. They held the flints close to the pitch-soaked heads and watched for Fitz Count's signal fire.

He had passed five hundred . . .

He struck the flints and the sparks jumped on to the torch and he pushed it away from his body. Fires sprang up all along the line, illuminating the cage of trees. 'Now!' he roared. 'Now!'

The raiders padded forward, swerving between the trunks. They drew their knives as they ran, and the line of flame swept through the forest and converged on the clearing. Fire-drugged guards lurched to their feet, their minds assailed with thoughts of phantoms and hellhounds. They glimpsed creatures with bouncing breasts and huge feet, wrapped in rags, and then the monsters were among them, stabbing them down.

A few of the guards managed to loose ill-aimed arrows, or snatch up their spears in time to out-reach their attackers. A few panicked and dashed back along the road – and on to the waiting blades. A few offered to surrender, a suicidal gesture on that particular night. And one, the one Brien had feared would escape, ran into the shadows at the edge of the clearing and raised a curved bull's horn to his lips. Three mournful blasts rose above the forest, to be immediately answered from the far end of the road. The raiders hesitated, and the man slipped away among the trees.

Several of the raiders started after him, but were called back by Varan. Meanwhile, Brien had crossed the clearing in search of wood. He found it stacked in two great pyramids, one on either side of the road entrance. Alongside the nearer pyramid was a low wall of sacks, almost certainly containing tools, and tarred rope with which to bind the bridge. He looked round, saw that only two or three of the guards had yet to be accounted for, and shouted, 'Over here! Unsling the skins!'

His men came running, and he told them to jam their torches in the base of the pyramids. Then, setting the example, he hurled his pitch-filled bladders at the flames. The swollen skins split on impact, spraying the pitch over the logs. The flames spread, and the remaining torches were thrust among the sacks. They, too, caught alight, and the eight men who had been sent to block the road came running between the pyres.

Brien made a check of his losses. One man had been killed by a chance arrow, two more impaled on spears. Four or five had been wounded, though these could still walk, or be led. He glanced at the pyramids again, satisfying himself that they could not be extinguished. Then he waved his men back towards the river.

He waited until they were among the trees before following them, so there was no one to warn him of the guard who rose, like some bloody apparition, in his wake. He never saw his assailant, for the hurled dagger sent him stumbling from the clearing, his back arched, his eyes squeezed tight with pain.

Behind him, the guard flopped down again, dead beside the fire. He had been a good soldier; he had known the Lord of Wallingford would stay till last.

Brien staggered blindly into a tree, reeled away from it and felt himself falling. *God, not on my back! The blade will transfix me!* He twisted violently and crashed down in the undergrowth.

He lay there, his breath melting the snow. Now, he thought, all the doors of death are open . . . If I don't bleed white, I'll freeze, or be here for Stephen to turn over with his foot . . .

How deep did it go in?

Well, well, we are never too wise to learn . . . It must have been one of the dead men . . .

Who said we should not wear hauberks? I did . . . It was my brilliant instruction . . .

How deep *is* it? Dying is bad enough, but not stuck like a pig. If I can reach round far enough to – '*Aagh, Jesu!*'

The cry was in response to whoever had pulled the blade from his back. He felt a hand slide under his chest, and then he was lifted to his feet and turned and swung forward, off the ground. The movement opened the wound, and the pain made the earlier pain seem gentle. Tears dripped from his eyes and he hung, head down, a sack of oatmeal, gnawed by rats . . .

*

He saw a face he recognised. It was not unlike his own, though the skin was more pink and shone with rubicund health. The figure stood ominously still, as though at a graveside. The image annoyed him, and he growled, 'What? Are you in a hurry to see me off?' Footsteps approached, but the mourner did not move. Pious brute. Doesn't it astound you when the dead awake?

When the dead awake and come from behind with knives . . .

He moved to show he was alive, and discovered he was strapped down. A woman's voice said, 'Lie quiet. Give yourself time. You're quite safe, you're at home. Lie still.'

He felt a hand on his forehead and blinked, clearing his

vision. Then he treated the painted statue – of himself and Alyse and the baby Alan – to a wry smile. 'That's no way to come awake, and find oneself mourned by one's effigy.' Turning his head he saw the real Alyse and made to reach up to her.

'Oh, these damned straps! Are we prisoners here? Has Stephen – '

'Stephen is miles away. There's no sign of him. The straps are to let your wound close. The physicians say your spine was nearly severed. You must lie still.'

'At least free my arms. Am I not even allowed to embrace my wife?'

She spoke to somebody he could not see, then released him. 'We knew you wouldn't be restrained. But please, my love, let the wound mend.'

He asked, 'Have I been here long?' He could see her clearly now, and the hollows around her eyes were answer enough. All the while he had lain senseless she had stayed with him, rejecting sleep. 'How long? A week? More?'

'No, no, a few days, that's all. You came to your senses from time to time, but it was thought better to drug you – '

'While the enemy pressed their attack?'

'No, they've done nothing since that night. Morc – we sent some men out to see what – '

'Morcar? Is he in command? Why not Varan? Oh, God, don't tell me the sortie froze his blood.' He summoned another wry smile. 'Well, you *are* hard-pressed, even though the enemy are quiet. If you think I am a surly patient – '

'He's dead, Brien.'

' – you should try ministering to – What did you say? What did you say?'

'I'm wept dry, so I can tell you. The constable is dead.'

'No.' It came flat and positive. 'No.'

'We searched for his body – '

'You haven't found his *body*? Then he's not dead. God's crown, you had me on the verge of believing you! A monster like Varan – '

'It's true. When I tell you what happened – '

'Yes,' he said, 'tell me. I need the gap filled.'

*

. . . He felt a hand slide under his chest, and then he was lifted to his feet and turned and swung forward, off the ground . . .

One hand only, for that was the best Varan could do. All the strength had gone from his left side, and he had watched the others pad ahead towards the boats. But he had not seen Fitz Count. Dragging himself away from the clearing, he realised that the suzerain should have come level with him by now. The men were no longer spread out, but were running forward, stamping a direct path to the boats.

Had he missed his master? *Had* Brien gone past unseen, farther to the left or right? If so, he would be almost at the bank. But, if not –

Varan put his weight on his good leg, then dragged the other in an arc, turning the trampled snow. He faced the clearing and started back, correcting himself every few yards, zig-zagging through the forest. He saw the burning pyramids and heard more alarums, and then he saw the body and the hilt of the knife, shining in the firelight.

He braced himself against a tree, leaned down and withdrew the blade, straight and steady. Brien cried out, and Varan curled his right arm like a giant spoon and lifted Greylock to his feet. Then he turned him and draped him over his right shoulder and carried him away, lurching from tree to tree.

His progress was agonisingly slow, for the trees had not been planted for his convenience. They grew close, or sparse, and it was necessary to grope in the darkness, to change direction, sometimes to take a step on trust. But he managed it, and all the while he heard the distant trumpet blasts, and then the shouts, drawing nearer.

Stephen's men reached those who had been ambushed on the road, and the shouts became howls of anger. Then they entered the clearing and saw their dead comrades, and the howls were replaced by a close-mouthed desire for revenge.

A little way ahead, and as yet unseen, Varan staggered

through the forest. He did not know if Brien was alive or dead and, in truth, he did not give it a thought. His only aim was to reach the boats. After that, Ironglove's bastard would be taken away, and the rest left to the physicians, or the priests. Reach the boats, that was enough.

As he veered from trunk to trunk, he indulged in a private dream. Hardly the romantic, he had, nevertheless, seen himself as Brien's saviour in time of stress. It was no more exotic a dream than a husband enjoys. Thieves attack his wife, and he is there, defending her, his every movement instant and precise, whilst the felons blunder and run. It would be the same, friend for friend, the two of them ranged successfully against over-whelming odds.

This had long been Varan's dream, and now it had come true. He was saving the man that mattered most to him. But, unlike the dream, the reality was imperfect, for neither of them might survive.

A few moments, a few crutches later, ally and enemy came together. Five members of the raiding-party had hurried back to find their leaders, and now saw, over Varan's shoulder, his pursuers. It was a one-sided engagement, arrows against daggers. As the raiders dragged Brien from Varan's grasp, the king's archers let fly, using the constable's broad back as their target.

The effort of carrying his master had deadened so much of his body that he seemed impervious to the shafts. Released of his burden he lurched forward, grasping at the nearest tree. He covered thirty yards, moving parallel with the bank, before the wounds made themselves felt. Thirty yards, it was said, for they did not see him after that, but carried Brien to the boat and pushed it away from the bank. All the way across the river they shielded his body with their own. Then the boat touched, not far from the launching point, and they hurried him through the gate . . .

'Morcar sent men in search of him,' Alyse murmured. 'He went himself, more than once, but they could find nothing. Varan is dead, my love.'

'Then why . . . Why has his body not been found?'

'God has taken it,' she said. 'He would not let him lie there, in the cold.'

It seemed to Brien the most perfect thing she had ever said, and he accepted it. Alyse gazed down at him, then moved away, motioning the physician from the solar. There was no need for anyone to witness Brien's grief. They had already shared in it.

CHAPTER 15

WALLINGFORD-ON-THE-THAMES

March 1150 – November 1153

THERE were times when Alyse thought Brien would never recover. The wound suppurated, and his bed-ridden existence left him open to a variety of infections. Twice a day the physicians drained the poison from his back, and then, when they thought it safe, went to work with twine and long bone needles. The following night his entire body burned with fever.

Stephen had abandoned his river-crossing in favour of a landward assault on the castle. With Fitz Count laid low, and Constable Varan proved mortal, the king anticipated an easy victory. He had no wish to endanger the courageous chatelaine, so he offered to accept her surrender and avoid further bloodshed.

She asked for time. 'The physicians tell me that this period is critical. My husband will either show signs of recovery or he will die. You have waited fifteen years to defeat us. As a mark of compassion, allow us a few more days. If, during that time, you see a black flag hoisted above the keep, you will know I am widowed. Two days after that I will surrender the castle.'

It was all rather imprecise, as Alyse meant it to be, but Stephen was honour-bound to accept it. He had Wallingford at his mercy, and a few days would make no difference. 'Yes,' he said, 'we will let nature take its course, though I hope you will both emerge to seek forgiveness. Brien Fitz Count and I were once inseparable, and I shall not look eagerly for the raven's wing.'

Pleased that the world would again adjudge him generous and chivalric, he sat back to wait. He was not to know he had made the last serious mistake of his reign.

*

Nor, in the darkened solar, did Alyse realise it. She blamed herself for having told Brien of Varan's death, for the news had robbed him of all resistance, and each day the physicians grew longer in the face. Fitz Count was failing, both in body and spirit, and there seemed little point in postponing the inevitable. Indeed, they told her he should be removed from the dampness of the riverside and, though they were loth to admit it, placed in the care of more accomplished physicians.

'We are doing all we can, my lady, but the patient needs special medicines. We've dealt with such injuries before, of course. We are not out to give the impression that – '

'Just do your best. If he is to die, he will do so here, not at the roadside, or in some strange room. We have been granted a few days' respite; make the most of them.'

Yes, a few more days in which to sit beside the man she loved and feel his skin grow hot to the touch. Perhaps the physicians were right. Perhaps Brien should be carried out and laid at the king's mercy. If he recovered, he would probably be banished from England, or imprisoned for life in the Tower of London. But even that was better than death, wasn't it?

No, she thought, not for Greylock. And I will not be the one to commit him. Stephen has agreed to a few more days. We'll see what they bring before opening the gates.

*

The news had already spread through the country, and a strange question settled on the lips of the rebel barons. Each man phrased it in his own way, but it was provoked by the same, single thought.

'Is the illness grave? Is Fitz Count unable to take command? Is Wallingford leaderless?'

'Yes,' the harbingers said, 'and yes, and yes.'

The answers satisfied their most demanding emotion – pride. They were a race of leaders, if only as masters of their own small household and a few hectares of land. Ambition had driven many of them to change sides in the past, and to forget their thrice-made vows. But they were all rebels now, and the gravity of the situation at Wallingford gave them the chance to act with honour. Most likely the final chance.

Brien Fitz Count was *hors de combat*; worse, from all accounts he was on his death-bed. He had not asked for help but, as his compeers, they were free to offer it. In this way they could retain their individuality, for each would act according to his own dictates. Had Fitz Count commanded them, they might have obeyed. Had he requested help, they would have responded in their own good time. But he had said nothing, so the decision was left to them. Ironglove's bastard was at the king's mercy. And at theirs.

It was a wonder England did not tip off-balance with the numbers that poured from the West Country. They came from Devon and Cornwall, Dorset and Somerset, from the banks of the Severn and from the minor holdings in the south-west. Poachers-turned-archer, and freelance knights, and peasants with scythe and billhook, all of them swelling the hard core of mercenaries and garrison troops. It did not matter to the barons that they met others on the way. Each had answered the unspoken plea as though he alone had heard it, whispered by the wind.

The army had a hundred leaders, yet no commander-in-chief. It should have collapsed in a welter of acrimony, for it was unthinkable that such an assembly of warriors could work together. They had never done so in the past. Where was the strict order of seniority, where the queue for precedence? How could this baron ride in the wake of that landless upstart? By what right did this unproven knight lead the day's march?

These questions came to mind, but were denied a voice. The army swept eastward, one contingent overtaking another, the groups meeting and separating as they followed their own routes across country. The roads were choked with troops, and the earth was stamped flat where men and horses had pounded a path across open fields.

By tacit agreement, those who were first to arrive would await the others five miles west of Wallingford. Then, when the bulk of the army had assembled, they would announce themselves to the king. They would also make their presence known to Lady Alyse, and to Lord Fitz Count if he was well enough.

One last question remained. Who would carry the message to the castle?

The leaders hesitated, their tongues heavy with prerogatives. Each examined his claim, aware that the messenger would find a special place in Greylock's heart. Then the awkward moment passed, and they detailed one of Brien's neighbours. 'They'll know your face when you ride up. You tell them.'

*

Alyse hurried to share the news with Brien. Kneeling beside the bed, she told him his loyalty had at last been rewarded.

'Amply rewarded, for there is not another man in the country who could stir such feelings. They have come to save *you*, my lord. It's no party thing, this incredible response. It is a personal act of love. And unbesought, remember that. I have issued no appeal, nor even bruited your illness. They have heard about it somehow or other, and decided for themselves. Twelve thousand of them, so the messenger said, and more arriving all the time. I thank God that you have – '

'What?' he whispered. 'Lived to enjoy it? Don't be foolish, sweet. It was all a ruse. Now that I have lured them here, I can start my recovery.'

She nodded, playing the game with him. Then, looking at his sunken features, and the patches of pale skin where his hair had come away in handfuls, she said, 'You're too intense an actor, Brien Fitz Count. You overplay the part.'

*

Faced with the threat of pitched battle, Stephen withdrew his army to Oxford. His own features had taken on a greyish pallor, as though he realised the finality of the move. Bishop Henry rode up from Winchester, not to attempt a further reconciliation with his brother, but to ask him what kind of creature he was these days, a king at war, or some romantic figment?

'You had them in the bowl of your hand, the only pair with enough authority to unite the Angevins! You had them, and you let them go. Oh, yes, beloved lady, take time to think . . . I shall sit here and count my teeth with the tip of my tongue . . . And when that's done, I'll polish my crown, or cheat at chess. . . . Take all the time you need. Why not? This is only the spearpoint of the rebel line, commanded by my most efficient and implacable enemy . . . Now you must excuse me, dear lady. Someone has brought a tapestry for me to embroider . . .'

'Why don't you shut your mouth!' Stephen snarled. 'I was not to know this would happen. The Angevins have never stirred themselves like this before. Anyhow, it's not too late.'

'For what?' Henry queried maliciously. 'Not too late for what? To surrender the crown?'

'To meet them on the field, what else? Fitz Count is at death's door. He won't be there, and without a firm leader – '

'Then it's a widespread problem, isn't it?'

'What do you mean by that?'

'Well . . .'

'You think I am incapable of leading an army?'

'I think you were absent when we beat the Scots at Northallerton, at the Battle of the Standard. I think you were present when we were routed at Lincoln. No, you were not routed; you were captured. And I think it was only the size of your force that panicked King David and Earl Ranulf and the Plantagenet at York last year. In short, I don't like to think about it at all, for if you *do* fight here, and lose, it will be over for you.'

'But not for you, eh, you gross, self-opinionated – '

'No. Not for me. I can always make myself useful. You see, brother, I am not only a wealthy landowner, and well versed in politics, but also a man of God. And, if bad becomes worse, and I lose my position in the Church, I can sell my statuary, or write that book I promised myself, the one on wild animals. But I am no real danger to the Angevins, as they know. They'll keep me around, if only to do what you no longer let me do – advise and, what did you say, opinionate?'

'You *are* well prepared,' Stephen said.

Henry beamed, showing several fresh folds of skin. 'I always was, brother. One never knows when the weather will change.'

The king allowed himself a long, nervous sigh. He listened to the sounds of Oxford, given a harsh timbre by the influx of soldiery. His scouts had told him that the rebel force had encamped around Wallingford and were prepared to stay there until Doomsday. If the king wanted a fight, he would have to ride fifteen miles for it. After all, his adversaries had travelled a hundred miles or more from the West Country.

He glanced at Henry, spoke too quietly for the question to be heard, then asked again, 'Would *you* attack them?'

'I hope that's not a personal request!' Henry laughed. 'It's all I can do to get on a horse these days.'

'Bishop – '

'Yes, yes, there's no need to glower. I know what you mean. And don't torture your moustache. I thought you'd cured yourself of that.'

'*In God's name! Answer the question!*'

'No.'

'You refuse to – '

'No, I would not attack them. They are there for one reason or, rather, one person. You would be better advised to wait for him to die. Or, if you can arrange it, have him killed.'

'Send someone in to murder Fitz Count? Do you really think I would employ such methods?'

Henry shook his head. 'No, King, I do not. But that's another worry I have always had about you.' It was nearly midday, and he was hungry. He walked away in search of food, leaving Stephen to roll an uprooted moustache hair between his fingers.

*

After that, the current ran fast against the king. Brien Fitz Count did not die but, as he had promised, started to recover. He was fifty now, and terribly weakened by injury and illness. But he was determined to visit the rebel army and let them see that the patient was up and about. It would take weeks, perhaps months, for he dared not risk a relapse. But his compeers had already been to see him, two and three at a time, and had assured him they were in no hurry. They had worked out an elaborate rota system, whereby there were never less than eight thousand men around Wallingford. Supply routes were kept open from the south and west, and the contingents took it in turn to ride home and rest and till their fields. The presence of the army, so near Oxford, forced Stephen to match their numbers. The temptation to raid the unguarded western counties was almost irresistible, but he knew that if he deserted Oxford, the important crossing-point would fall to the Angevins.

However, he did not remain completely inactive, and launched a half-hearted attack against Worcester. He succeeded in razing the town – an act that typified his frustration – but failed to reduce the nearby castle. Nevertheless, he proclaimed it a victory, which it was, over civilians.

In July, Brien walked out of the gates of Wallingford and into the rebel camp. Men interrupted their dice games to cheer him, and bodyguards were hastily recruited to prevent the enthusiastic soldiers sweeping him off his feet.

He had lost a quarter of his weight, and henceforth it was rare to hear anyone use the term Greylock. It sounded too much like an insult, for his illness had left him tonsured, like a monk.

In a low-pitched voice he addressed the army, thanking them, not so much for having saved Wallingford, as for showing King Stephen and, yes, Empress Matilda and Count Geoffrey of Anjou, that the great and dead King Henry of England had not been forgotten, and that even in the midst of anarchy, there were men who honoured their vows.

He made no mention of the hundreds among them who had thought of changing sides, or done so. What was past was past. All that mattered was that the cause had been saved and that Stephen was still regarded as a usurper, fifteen years after he had snatched the crown.

'We have not yet won,' he told them, 'but we are as close to winning as we have ever been. We have been deserted and abandoned, defeated in battle, and taught to survive the loss of our greatest leaders. Many of us, even knights and barons, are as poor as wood-cutters. We did not expect this, nor are we happy about it. But we would be far poorer if we had traded our vows for money, or ploughed our loyalties into a gift of land.

'There are some who have prospered from the war, as they always will. But those creatures have a bubble of air for a conscience, and swill-water in place of honour. We are all fallible, God knows. I own one or two possessions with which I would not readily part, so perhaps I am not as impoverished as I make out. But there is a difference, I think, and your presence here illuminates it. You will get no money from this venture, and very few of you will be advanced. But you knew that before you started out, and still you are here. I tell you, though it will not bring the taste of wine to your tongue, or ripen the corn in your fields, you *are* rich, every one of you, for you have been true to your beliefs. So am I, *messires*, though I would ask you not to raid my larder.'

He climbed down from the cart on which he had been standing, and spent the rest of the day with the army. His army. He could say that now.

*

The next twelve months passed almost without incident. It was scarcely a time of peace, for both sides kept their hands on their swords. But the leaders stood, stooped over, leaning on the hilt. The civil war had occupied the greater part of their adult lives, and they were tired. Stephen and Brien were both over fifty. It was not an age that brought senility with it, and there were many, like Varan, who lived to be seventy and beyond. But at fifty a man glanced around for a chair, and edged over to the hearth. He thought of death more often, and conserved his strength.

But death, when it came, moved farther down the line to claim one of the younger protagonists.

In the autumn of 1151, Count Geoffrey of Anjou was

following the river road from Paris to his capital, Angers. The weather was hot and overcast, and every few miles he interrupted his journey to swim in the Loire. His companions declined to join him, though they denied it was because they feared water demons.

'Ah, you protest too loudly,' Geoffrey taunted them. 'Splash about, and they'll keep their distance.'

Two days later he was stricken with fever and, on 7th September, he died at home. He was thirty-five years old.

He left his son, the young Plantagenet, the vast inheritance of Anjou and Normandy; but Geoffrey had never set foot in England, the centrepiece of the struggle. Matilda and Henry saw him buried, then walked away, their arms linked, as though each was supporting the other in their hour of grief. Anyone who had had the ill-grace to eavesdrop on the bereaved pair would have heard them discussing the attributes of a woman named Eleanor . . .

*

In May 1152, two events occurred to sweep the current still faster against the king. The first struck a direct and personal blow against him, for on 3rd May his wife died. All her life she had shown constraint and self-discipline and, throughout her marriage to Stephen, she had helped curb his impetuousness. He had held the reins of power, but, more often than not, he had allowed his queen to draw them tight.

Understandably, her death unnerved him, and he embarked on a series of short-lived campaigns. He attacked Wallingford, and was beaten off, then by-passed it in an attempt to capture less well-defended castles. He achieved one or two victories – mere grains in the salt pot – but his disorganised forays were terminated by news of the second event. He heard that on 18th May, Henry Plantagenet had married the ex-wife of King Louis of France; the twenty-nine-year-old Eleanor of Aquitaine. This woman, who would one day bear two future kings of England – Richard the Lionheart and John Lackland – bestowed upon her new husband the vast duchy of Aquitaine, and so made him the most formidable landowner in Christendom. He was already Count of Anjou and Duke of Normandy. All that remained was to become King of England.

*

'One hundred and forty knights,' Brien said, 'and more than three thousand foot-soldiers.' He handed Alyse the letter, and she read the Plantagenet's message. He had landed, he wrote, at Wareham, and was on his way to Wallingford. The letter was dated 6th January, five days ago.

'Then he'll soon be here.'

Brien nodded, then stooped in front of the metal mirror. 'I remember the first time I met him. That was at Wareham. He was a squalling brat in those days, fighting with the guards, running around with lungs like bellows. He asked me if my hair was dead. I invited him to pull it – which he did – but I can't risk that again. One good tug and I'll be as bald as an egg.'

'You look fine,' Alyse told him. 'It's your vanity that shows, not your baldness.'

'Hmm . . . Maybe so.' He guided a few pale grey strands across the open patches, frowned at the result, then walked over to his clothes chest. 'We should dress up for this; the return of our future king.'

'Is that what you want?' she asked. 'Would you really welcome Henry as master of England?'

Brien raised the lid of the chest, then turned back to his wife. 'I don't know,' he mused. 'He has come a long way since we last met. And he is Matilda's son, so – ' He caught her eye, and a slow, gentle smile stretched his lips.

'Yes,' Alyse affirmed, 'he's Matilda's son. And so?'

'He has a direct claim to the throne. And now that he rules Normandy and Anjou and Aquitaine – Well, I think Stephen will be hard put to stop him.'

Alyse nodded, Brien thought reluctantly.

'Are you opposed to him? You never spoke of it before.'

'No, it's just that – ' She gathered her thoughts and continued, 'We speak of the throne and the crown, and of claims and lineage, but we so rarely mention the people. What if

Henry Plantagenet has inherited the worst of Matilda's traits? We know he shares her quick temper, so why not her arrogance, and her distaste of commoners? Do you remember how she alienated the Londoners, how she threatened to reduce the city to ruins if they did not pay compensation for having supported her cousin? You say Stephen will be hard put to stop Henry. What I fear is that we may *all* find it hard. Duke of Normandy and Aquitaine; Count of Anjou; King of England. That's a weight of titles.'

'You're condemning the horse before it runs.'

'No,' she told him. 'I have another animal in mind. I would rather say I am fearful that the offspring of a wildcat will also have claws.'

Brien lifted his best robe from the chest, then laid it over the lid to let the creases fall. 'Your fears may be justified,' he said, 'and I've nursed similar ones. But we both know the choice. Support those with the right to rule, and pray they'll be worthy of their position, or treat the throne – yes, I'm speaking of it again – as the goal for every self-seeker in the land. The people *are* at the mercy of king and court, and always will be. But how much better to put them under the guidance of a man like Henry, who has at least been trained and schooled in the ways of monarchy, than some power-hungry creature like Ranulf of Chester.'

'There is no choice, I agree. But can you say that the rightful heiress, Empress Matilda, would have been better than Stephen? He *might* have made a king, had we supported him from the first.'

'Yes, he might. And so might his elder brother, Theobald, or Bishop Henry, or Robert of Gloucester. Or I. But, if it had been offered to us, it would have been offered to Earl Ranulf, and Geoffrey de Mandeville, and God knows who else. As you suggest, in time and with our help Stephen might have attained some stature. But the truth is this. He had no right to try.'

'Someone's sounding trumpets,' she said. 'We'd better dress.'

*

They met Henry in the outer yard, and accompanied him on a tour of Brien's army. The Plantagenet was not yet twenty, though he looked twice that age. His passion for hunting had left its mark on his face and hands, and he was almost comically bow-legged. But no one smiled at his appearance, or gave more than a hastily-banished thought to his earlier visit, when he'd run short of money. The circumstances had been different then. He had been young and foolhardy, a truant from his father's court.

But it was his court now, and in it he had found the money with which to buy men. This time, they knew, his visit was more than an adventure. He had come as a married man, laden with titles, to claim the greatest title of all. There was nothing humorous in that.

He was dressed for battle, his stocky chest encased in a moulded iron tunic. Sensing Brien's curiosity, he said, 'Everybody asks about it. It's a revival of the Roman style. A crossbow quarrel will tear straight through the links of a hauberk, but it hardly dents plate.'

'It looks damned heavy.'

'It is,' Henry grinned, 'so it pays to keep fit.'

'What happens if you're knocked down? Isn't it impossible –' He stopped, warned off by Henry's angry glance.

'I've never been knocked down, Fitz Count, so I cannot answer you.' Having aired the boast, his expression cleared and he said, 'It wouldn't be so difficult.'

With a straight face, Brien said, 'If one was fit enough, eh, Prince? With sufficient strength in the arms?'

'Just so. You would roll over and push yourself up again. Anyway, it's the common thing among my men. You'll see several of them wearing plate.' He strode on through the camp, nodding at the soldiers, and occasionally plunged left or right to drink a proffered mug of wine. His red hair and briar-torn face marked him out, and he enjoyed rapping his fist against the breast-plate and recommending it to the attendant barons.

When he had quartered the camp he asked the leaders to accompany him to the northern perimeter. 'Can I see Stephen's force from there?'

'No,' Brien said. 'They're rooted at Oxford. We've been waiting for Stephen to attack, but he seems disinclined.'

'How far away is he?'

'Fifteen miles along the river.'

'Yes, well, I want a meeting. There. He can stand there, on the other bank. We'll talk across the water.'

'As you wish, Prince, though why not meet him half-way, or allow him into the camp?' As soon as he had asked, he knew the answer. Henry, with a voice that boomed, and Stephen, who employed other men to deliver his speeches. Vanity, he thought. Alyse is right; it shows in all of us.

Henry studied the open ground to the north, then looked in the direction of the forest. 'Arrange the meeting,' he said, 'and meanwhile lend me some guides.'

Not sure he had heard right, Brien queried, 'You want guards, my lord?'

'Guides,' the Plantagenet repeated. 'Someone to take me hunting.'

*

Within days of Henry's arrival at Wallingford, the Earl of Leicester defected to the Angevins. This was one of the men who had snarled at Robert of Gloucester across King Henry's death-bed in the Forest of Lyons, insisting that the king had named Stephen, and not Matilda, as his successor. Now, eighteen years later, he changed sides, offering some thirty-five castles as his dowry. He was received with open arms, and another tract of England was sown with the *Planta genista*.

Stephen began to despair. He ordered regular estimates of the rebel strength, and learned that it was on the increase. Men came to reaffirm their friendship with Brien Fitz Count, and to pay homage to the young Plantagenet. Twelve thousand, the scouts said; then fifteen; then not far short of twenty. And all the while there were defections from the royalist ranks.

The king appealed to his brother to come and advise him. Yes, he was told, of course. Once I've met the Plantagenet.

Stephen was invited to the riverbank meeting, but declined. He would not make a move until he had spoken with his brother. If the corpulent bishop said fight, he would fight. If he said talk, he would do his best to shout across the river.

And if he said surrender?

The royalists were temporarily heartened by the death of the Plantagenet's great-uncle, King David of Scotland. But that had occurred in the north, and did not materially affect the situation at Wallingford.

Stephen appealed to God to visit a plague upon the Angevins, then asked to speak with his dead wife. He gave exaggerated assurances, promising to found monasteries and hospitals, but he heard no voices, and his scouts reported the rebels in good health. Each time the king arose from his knees he felt more lonely, more desperate.

His bishop-brother sent word that he was on his way, and that on no account was Stephen to move. Certain arrangements had been made, and the situation was well in hand.

It was a time when even Brien and Alyse felt some sympathy for the king, for they had attended the conference between the Henrys, Plantagenet and Winchester, and they knew what the arrangements were.

*

The rebel army moved two miles north of Wallingford, then drew up in battle formation, facing the river. The east bank was devoid of trees at this point, and it was here the royalists assembled, also in battle formation, glaring across at their enemies. A spur of land jutted out into the river, and Stephen walked along it, closely followed by his barons. The ground was spongy underfoot, and he glanced anxiously at the water that swirled around the promontory. He wanted to tell his companions to move back, lest they sink the spur, but he knew they would not forego a close look at Henry Plantagenet. Instead, he settled for a nervous, 'Far enough! Far enough! You'll have me in the Thames!' They stopped where they were, peering over shoulders and between helmeted heads.

Bishop Henry stood immediately behind his brother, intoning a prayer for peace. A few days earlier, he had ridden up

to Oxford to acquaint Stephen with the details of the conference. Or rather, with some of the details. Enough to get the
king to the riverbank.

They were kept waiting a while, and the mood of the armies
soured in the sun. The royalists could see the Earl of Leicester
and other latterday defectors, and roared their disgust. In reply,
the Angevins singled out those who were known to have acted
treasonably towards Empress Matilda, and treated them to a
barrage of invective. Then some of the more excitable archers
let fly across the river, and twenty thousand arrows were
notched into bow-strings.

Stephen yelled at his sergeants to control their men, while,
on the west bank, Brien Fitz Count thundered along the line,
vowing to hang the next archer who loosed a shaft. The
arrows went back into the quivers, and the insults were muted.

Then, accompanied by a phalanx of barons from Normandy,
Aquitaine and Anjou, the red-haired Angevin rode to the front
of his army. Brien came alongside, and Henry asked, 'Is that
him, out on the spur, that river-reed?'

Suddenly annoyed by the description, Brien said, 'Stephen
of England, yes. You recognise his brother?'

'A toad among the reeds. Very well, let's get on with it.
Who has the paper?' One of the barons passed him a sealed
scroll, and he dismounted – a boastful, balanced spring from
the saddle. He landed without faltering and strode down to the
river's edge. Still wearing the plate armour, he slid his elbows
back against his body, pushed the cloak away to expose the
moulded iron. The royalists stared at the chest shield, then at
the scarred, old-young face. Christ, they thought, who said
he was only twenty?

He reached the bank, felt it yield under his weight, and
stepped back on to firmer ground. Then he raised the scroll,
pointed it like a hollow finger at Stephen and boomed, 'Henry,
Duke of Normandy and Aquitaine, Count of Anjou, true son
of Count Geoffrey of Anjou and the Empress Matilda. I
address you, Stephen of Blois called King of England. I
welcome you to this meeting, and am pleased you could
finally find the courage to attend. Now, I have something to

propose. But first I shall accept your rejoinder, so we may all hear you speak.'

On the other side of the river the bishop murmured, 'Pitch your voice deep, brother. He's out to make you sound a fool.'

Stephen hesitated, then sucked air into his lungs, pushed his head down and shouted, 'I thank you for your welcome – kinsman. I do not dispute your foreign titles, but you are no more to me than my cousin's son. And I must correct you on a point of fact, once and for all. I am called king because I *am* king, make no mistake about it. If this meeting is to go forward, you will give me my title. If not, withdraw from the river. Courtesy, kinsman, or is that a foreign term in Anjou?'

Well, well, his brother grinned, he must have been practising in the corridors at Oxford.

Henry Plantagenet smothered his surprise. They told me he had a voice like a troubadour, all whine and whistle. Still, no matter. Plenty of time to make him shrill.

He raised the scroll again. 'We have not met here to trade courtesies. I have in my hand a proposal, prepared by myself and your own brother, Bishop of Winchester – '

Stephen glanced at the bishop, who said, 'Arrangements. I told you. Best pay attention,' then stared intently at the Plantagenet.

'I advise you, all of you, to listen carefully. This is my first and final proposal, and its rejection will turn this country to charcoal. My mother, the Empress Matilda, Countess of Anjou and only legitimate child of the revered King Henry of England, gave fifteen years of her life in pursuit of her claim. It was *she* who should have been monarch here, not you, Stephen-called-king. You rode a faster horse from Boulogne to Westminster, I'll admit, and I see you still have a smattering of supporters. But I have these men here, twenty thousand of them, and more arriving by the hour, and the whole might of Normandy and Anjou, and my new-won territory of Aquitaine, and I tell you in all honesty, you *cannot* win. You will never defeat me in battle, nor in the extent of your power. You are at an end, and I think you must know it.'

Again Stephen turned to his brother. 'I trust you didn't prepare *that* speech for him.'

'Don't be foolish. He's just sounding off. He – wait, let's hear the rest of it.'

'There is much I could do to you,' the Plantagenet continued, 'but I am influenced by Winchester. He, along with the loyal Fitz Count and others, seeks peace. They are tired of war, whatever its spurs. They have seen this country torn and ravaged for – yes, for almost the period of my life. Eighteen years, Stephen of Blois; that is how long you have maltreated your kingdom. Like you, it's time it came to an end. And this is how we propose it should be done.' He raised the scroll, then ripped the unnecessary seal from it and recited its contents across the fast-flowing river.

'You, Stephen of England, shall recognise Henry, Duke of Normandy, as your successor in this kingdom, and as your heir by the rights of heredity. You shall in time give and confirm to me and my heirs the Kingdom of England.

'I, Henry, Duke of Normandy, shall, in return for this gift, honour and confirmation pay homage to you, and give you my surety by oath. Furthermore, I do graciously concede that you, Stephen of England, shall hold this realm for all your life, and that none shall attempt to usurp you.

'Should I survive you on your death, the kingdom shall pass peaceably and without opposition to me, to hold as king. Should I precede you to the grave the kingdom shall, on your death, pass peaceably and without opposition to my heirs.

'Meantime, I shall be faithful to you and guard your life and honour with all my might, as you will guard mine.'

He read on, providing for an exchange of prisoners, the custodianship of certain castles, the autonomy of the Church. Stephen was asked to accept that on all state business he would seek and abide by the advice of Henry Plantagenet. He was asked to accept many things, each of which allowed him to live with the crown on his head, yet guaranteed that the young

Angevin would act as king. It was not so much a proposal as a deposition.

The reading of the scroll took more than an hour, and Henry's voice grew hoarse and guttural. When it was over, Stephen turned once more to his brother and asked, 'Was it primarily your work? It's a very pretty piece.'

'Well, now,' Henry beamed, 'I am relieved. I cannot claim all the credit, but yes, I suppose I am the prime mover. I imagine that, if the whole thing was balanced, phrase for phrase – '

Keeping his back to the Angevins, the weary king brought his hand up, as though to worry his moustache. Then, instead, he slapped his brother in the mouth. It was as forceful a blow as he could manage, and most sincerely meant.

The bile of defeat rising within him, he faced his enemies again and bowed across the river. *Yes, I accept . . . I accept all of it . . . Yes, yes . . .*

He shouldered aside the bleeding bishop and pushed his way through the group of iron-clad barons. They let him pass, not sure whether they should cheer him or tear him apart.

*

And so, for England and Normandy, Anjou and Aquitaine, it was over. The first great civil war and the longest in the history of England was at an end. There would be others, better known, but there would be none like this, built on the simple foundation of a thrice-given vow. The men who engaged in it were often deep and devious, and they clouded the issues and turned them to their own advantage. But the foundation remained. It had been a war of words, an affair of honour.

*

The Treaty of Wallingford, as it came to be known, was ratified at Winchester on 6th November, 1153.

One week later, Brien Fitz Count received a letter from Empress Matilda. In it she wrote:

'My sweet Greylock, I have heard of your injuries, and of

how you rallied my supporters to your side. My son writes glowingly of your loyalty, and it is because of this, and the love you still bear me, that I set out to persuade you and the enchanting Lady Alyse to remove yourselves from that unhappy country and settle in Anjou. I have reserved a fine castle for you, and purchased a large area of land, containing several profitable villages. You will be happy here, I am sure, and you will be able to live out your lives content in the knowledge that you have been more than compensated for your efforts.

'I shall ask nothing of you, other than this; when you are visited by friends, or approached by envious strangers, tell them you reside beneath the banner of Empress Matilda, mother of England's king. And, if you feel so disposed, tell them it was my gift to you. Dearest Greylock, I await your answer.'

He showed the letter to his wife, and then to Morcar and Edgiva, and to Ernard and Eadgyth, and then he nailed it to the inner face of the main gate, so that everyone in Wallingford could read it, or have it read to them. Then, when he had asked their opinion on the matter, he settled himself in the solar and penned a reply.

'We are grateful for your offer,' he wrote, 'but unhappily your letter was delayed twenty years. Would that it had come sooner.'

With no one there to see him, Brien Fitz Count moved away from the table and gazed at Varan's statue. Then he crossed the chamber and stared down into Ironglove's mirror. Eventually, looking from one to the other, he asked, 'Well, Constable? Well, my lord? Do you agree?'

Standing in that position, his shadow animated the painted wood and brought a positive reflection from the hammered silver. They said what Alyse had been saying for days, and he went back to the table to warm some sealing-wax.

AFTERMATH

In the following month, the Earl of Chester, Ranulf the Moustache, was invited to dine with one of his neighbours, an influential baron named William Peverel. Throughout the meal, William flooded his guests with wine – no hardship for Ranulf – though William himself bemoaned the fact that he dare not drink for fear of aggravating an ulcerated throat.

True to form, Ranulf said he would drink for both of them. He left the table after midnight, but was called back from his bed-chamber to minister to one of his companions. For some reason the man was writhing on the floor, and the left-over meats were brought out for inspection.

By the time the suspicion had taken hold in Ranulf's mind, his companion had been joined by the others who had ridden with him from Chester. While they screamed through clenched teeth and flailed the rush-strewn floor, the first man died in agony.

Stupefied with drink, Ranulf dragged his sword from its scabbard and accused William of having administered poison. 'In the wine, eh, Peverel? You'll deny it, but Christ, it's clear as day to me!'

'I deny nothing,' William retorted. 'You've guessed right, though it took you long enough. Yes, Ranulf, you've been poisoned. I knew you would out-last the others, and that pleases me. You're as strong as an ox, and it'll take you a long while to die. Do you feel any pains yet?'

'Not a thing. But *you* will. A bad throat? It will be beyond repair by the time I've fin – ' He doubled over, and his sword nicked the table. He heard William say, 'Another one's dead. One more to go, then you.'

With the last of his strength, Ranulf pushed himself away

from the table and hurled his sword at the dim outline of his
host. The weapon clattered into the fireplace, and William
said, 'You'd better find a seat, while you can. You are a vile
and hideous man, Ranulf of Chester, and I am doing tonight
what others should have done years ago. You have thrived
on the profits of pillage, and entertained yourself with acts of
rape and torture. You are an abomination, there is no better
word for it.'

'My business . . .' Ranulf gasped. 'What is it to you?'

'You don't know? Well, that would be ironic, if you died
without knowing why. You are thick with the Plantagenet, are
you not?'

'Friends . . .' He dragged himself to the nearest bench and
bowed forward over the table.

'Friends, yes,' William continued. 'And, as such, he intends
to give you my lands here.'

Even then, Ranulf managed a sneer. 'Don't want them . . .
Paltry fief . . .'

'I agree, they are not so extensive, and he'll give me something better. But I cannot let you have them. Not when you
will turn them into one great torture chamber. I would not let
these people suffer your presence.'

'So you kill me . . .'

'Hell,' William snapped, 'you're long overdue; don't complain.' With a last glance at the others, yes, the third was dead,
he collected Ranulf's sword from the grate and slid it back in
the scabbard. That would cause the Moustache the greatest
pain of all, knowing he would die with his weapon sheathed.

Ranulf asked for a priest, but his lips were no longer moving,
and the slam of a door told him there was no one to hear . . .

*

Throughout 1154 Stephen and the Plantagenet toured the
country. They were an ill-matched pair, though Henry's utter
lack of regard for the river-reed was soon replaced by a more
compassionate viewpoint. The rigours of monarchy were far
greater than he had anticipated, and he looked more and more
to Stephen for guidance. This was given reluctantly at first,

for Stephen was clearly intimidated by the booming Angevin. Gradually, however, he accepted the role that had always been denied him, that of advisor and counsellor. Henry was eager to learn, and Stephen was overjoyed to find that his advice was taken, his counsel respected.

He risked the occasional joke, and flinched in the face of Henry's resonant laugh. 'You must tell that when we get back to court! No, better still, let me tell it! You can rehearse me.' He reached over and cuffed Stephen on the shoulder. 'Very good. Let's see now, how does it go again?'

But the joke was destined to go unrepeated, for Stephen was suddenly stricken with internal bleeding, and died at Dover on 25th October. He was buried beside his wife in the Cluniac monastery at Faversham, and Henry went on alone to collect his crown.

This son of Blois had never shown the resolve that was required of a king, and he had often borne out the poet's insolent assessment of his character. But he was not a river-reed, not by a long way.

*

His brother mourned him, then set about arranging the new king's coronation. This was celebrated on 19th December, and shortly after the service King Henry II of England asked the bishop whom he would recommend to fill the post of chancellor. This other son of Blois suggested one of his protégés, an ambitious, middle-class clerk named Thomas Becket. The king agreed.

*

On the other side of the Channel, Empress Matilda moved between Anjou and Normandy, between good works and politics. She would not die for another thirteen years, but she never again made contact with Greylock of Wallingford. He had had his chance. If he chose to live like a pauper, he was free to do so. And it was that thought that haunted her – that he *was* free.

*

As for Brien and Alyse, they lived rather better than paupers. The king saw to that, though he did not think it worth mentioning to his mother.

When their son Alan was twelve years old, he was taken into the royal court and placed under the king's protection. This was what Ironglove had done for his bastard, Brien Fitz Count, and, if the disciplines of court life had taught Brien to honour his word, they might do as much for Alan. Such men were, after all, a rarity. Then as now.